Bon Appétit

"Ahh. I see, Majesty. I follow your serene drift, Serene Majesty. You require a man."

"Quite so," I told her. "A man. A man complete with candy cane."

"Do you have some particular man in mind, Majesty?"

"No. It doesn't matter who he is. Just as long as his candy cane is suitable to the experiment."

"With just the right candy cane." Yolande nodded.

"You will find me such a man," I told her. "That is my royal command." I got to my feet and tucked by breasts back into my bodice. "A man and a candy cane," I told her. "Report to me when you've found someone suitable— that is someone with a suitable candy cane," I amended.

"As you wish, Majesty." Yolande staggered to her feet and curtsied, her wide-spaced breasts tumbling free.

"Of course it will be as I wish." I giggled. "I'm a majesty!"

THE COURTESANS

The Erotic Memoirs of Marié Antoinette

by Hillary Auteur

PINNACLE BOOKS NEW YORK

The author of this work is a member of the National Writers Union.

This is a work of fiction. All the characters and events portrayed in this book are fictional, and any resemblance to real people or incidents is purely coincidental.

THE COURTESANS #1: THE EROTIC MEMOIRS OF MARIE ANTOINETTE

An original Pinnacle Books edition, published for the first time anywhere.

First printing, February 1984

ISBN: 0-523-42139-7

Can. ISBN: 0-523-43125-2

Cover illustration by Harry Burman

Printed in the United States of America

PINNACLE BOOKS, INC.
1430 Broadway
New York, New York 10018

9 8 7 6 5 4 3 2 1

This book is . . .
For Phillipe . . .
And for Nicole . . .
And for myself . . .
In Fond Memory of Our
Ménage à trois

The Erotic Memoirs of

MARIE ANTOINETTE

Chapter One

"It was the best of times, it was the worst of times. . . ."

In the front row of spectators, the Englishman scrawled with his quill pen and spoke the words aloud as he set them down. Beside him sat a crone with constantly clacking knitting needles who never seemed to stop snarling and muttering to herself. "Off with their heads!" she shrilled, punctuating her mutterings. "Off with their heads!"

The chief judge of the Revolutionary Tribunal pounded his gavel for order. "Citizeness Marie Antoinette!" He thundered out my name, deliberately omitting my title as Queen of France. "Death by the guillotine!" He pronounced sentence on me. The scribe's pen scratched; the hag cackled. "You may address the sentence?" the chief judge told me.

"I would rather make love than die, messieurs."

My *mot* was wasted. The Revolutionary Tribunal had not the wit to appreciate royal irony. These merciless French peasants were as immune to Hapsburg hauteur as they were ignorant of the carnal cunning exercised between silken palace sheets.

"Ecstasy is in the bloodline; one must be to the clitoris born." So whispered the Empresses of Austria, my maternal forebears. How right they were! The lower classes rot; aristocrats make love; royalty practices an erotic art of infinte possibilities. And I, Marie Antoinette, Queen of France, Archduchess of Austria, have attained— as is my birthright—the most exquisite pinnacles of sensual ecstasy.

Oui, *mes amis*, it is a royal sport, and I its most royal champion!

Now, removed from the courtroom to my confinement, trapped between the sentence and the execution, this was my solace. Only my libido could hold the shattering terror of the morrow at bay. I relied on it to assuage me through the long, cruel night.

Such royal sublimation had sustained a doomed Bourbon, so why not a Hapsburg? Only nine months ago my late husband Louis—"Citizen Capet" they called him in the dock, but he was King of France and met his fate with Bourbon dignity—actually managed one of his rare erections the night before he lost his head. I had used all my wiles to keep it tumescent and trapped and pleasured by my Hapsburg flesh before I squeezed it dry of passion and released it to the fatal sunrise. *Cher* Louis died a happier man than our royal marriage bed had left him in a long, long time.

Alas! Now I was alone. There was no one to provide the lascivious proddings for which my patrician pussy— quivering and honeyed with fear—was yearning. Even Louis' undersized member, with all the problems of malfunction it had brought to our marriage bed from the very beginning, would have been welcome this night.

And there were others—male and female—whose hot flesh melting into mine would have crafted a climax to blot out the one promised by Madame Guillotine.

But such a joining was not to be. I had only myself to fill the void between my thighs. And my situation was not conducive to relaxing into erotic fantasy.

The reality was that I was imprisoned in the Conciergerie, the very prison of the Tuileries Palace to which I had myself occasionally consigned those members of my court who had for one reason or another fallen out of favor with me. Such unfortunates had often been whipped here, or branded. A few had fallen victim to more esoteric tortures. Now, although neither tortured, nor branded, nor whipped, I had been for some two and half months incarcerated here myself.

Ah well, *mes amis*! Even royal chickens come home to roost.

My cell is called the "Little Pharmacy." I'm not sure why. It is eleven and a half feet square with five-inch-thick double doors of reinforced steel. Three enormous locks secure the doors. They are buttressed by stout bolts and iron bars.

The thick stone walls of the chamber have been papered in my honor. The design consists of revolutionary emblems and slogans. The phrases "Liberty! Equality! Fraternity!" and "Constitution!" and "Rights of Man!" scamper over the four walls in boring and meaningless repetition. I have long since grown used to the insult and no longer pay it any mind. Besides, the wallpaper is decomposing into tatters, the slogans washed away by the prison dampness, a fine joke on the Republic—*n'est-ce pas*?

A screen divides the cell, cutting down on the living area available to me. Two sets of eyeholes have been cut out of it. Through them, day and night, a pair of National Guardsmen keep a constant watch over me.

At the most intimate and private times, I think how I must appear to their voyeur gaze. These guards are frequently young, boys really, albeit peasant louts, and I can well imagine how the sight of a woman's body— the body of a queen in the sensual prime of her life— must arouse them. At such times, gazing into the full-length mirror I have been granted by my captors, I see myself through their hungry eyes.

In my thirties now, I am more buxom, more developed, perhaps not quite so slender as the fifteen-year-old Austrian Princess who took the royal court by storm when she arrived to wed the Dauphin and to share the throne of France. I was as tall then, but surely not quite so voluptuous as I am now. My breasts were likened to rosebuds by one courtier in those days; more recently the palms in which they have nestled have had to open to their widest, as if holding melons.

Some things have not changed. I have still the long, tapered, Hapsburg legs with the hint of Austrian baby flesh rounding the thighs. I have the high, plump, cushiony derriere of the Hapsburgs as well, and the arrogant, flaring hips. Along with my high-mounted *mons veneris*, I am truly endowed with the traditional Hapsburg "Empress's Saddle." Nor have I ever lost my appetite for the gallop.

My mirror tells me that my queenly visage is as lovely as ever. *La dolce vita*—ahh! the Italians!—has left my face as smooth as in girlhood. My complexion, alabaster flushed with the faintest pink of tea roses, is still delicate, still young. The features have always reflected a combination of blue blood and coquetry. I cannot allow modesty to deny the fascination of my noble visage—the soft oval shape, the high cheekbones, the aquiline nose, the blue eyes, deep and sparkling with sensuality.

Above all, mine is a Hapsburg face. The mouth is very small, as were the mouths of the Empresses who were my mother and grandmother. A slight expression of disdain has curled my lip since infancy. It is a Hapsburg lip, and if there is arrogance in its permanent pout, there is the promise of debauchery as well.

Ahh! Let me confess without shame that this moist and red-lipped mouth of mine has fulfilled this promise to the fullest. It has known the clinging kisses of other lustful mouths, the heat of other lips, the prick of sharp teeth, the passionate tangling of tongues. It has tasted the risen nipples on the flat, hard chests of men, and the quivering tips of the soft, round, panting breasts of other women. It has scattered kisses on the hairy, swollen undersides of men's scrotums, licked the raw, pink meat between the purple lips of ladies' quims, sucked the thick and pulsing shafts of manhood, nibbled at the oily, elusive clitties of squealing maidens, and quaffed thirstily of the creamy spendings of many a male lover.

Oui! This small, delicate mouth pursed in my mirror is the mouth of a queen, the daughter of an empress! It knows no higher authority. Desire alone has dictated its erotic meanderings. *Noblesse oblige!*

Considering this Hapsburg mouth in my mirror now, I made a moue. Behind my reflection there was the almost imperceptible movement of eyes glued to one of the peepholes of the screen. The young, oafish sentinels were at their posts. I decided that on this, my last afternoon, I should not disappoint them.

I removed the powered wig I had worn for my final appearance before the Tribunal. Raising my arms to reach behind me and stretching so that the plump upper half-moons of my breasts swelled above the decolletage of my low-cut afternoon frock, I pulled out the hairpins holding my long, naturally curly ash-blond tresses in place. Then I ran my fingers through the strands, shaking from side to side to fluff out the curls. My ivory bosom bobbled enticingly in the mirror.

Standing, I put one foot on a stool and bent to unlace the high shoe. In this position, my petticoats were swept aside to reveal my long, shapely legs in tight, white silk stockings. Visible also was the curve of one plump cheek of my derriere as it thrust against my tight, off-white satin bloomers. And, as I bent to the task, the upper half-moons of my milk-white melon breasts tumbled free almost to the nipples themselves.

I undid the laces slowly, considering what the reaction might be behind the screen. The uniform of the National Guardsmen is coarse wool of a butternut hue—scarcely a uniform at all. There is none of the panoply of my own favorite Swiss Guard and little attention to the tight fit which so deliciously displayed their crotch wares. Nevertheless, loose as my jailers' trousers might be, I had noticed on occasion the unmistakable betrayal of an erection tenting the material over their peasant groins. Thinking about this now, as I unlaced the second high shoe, I felt my swaying nipples grow warm and harden.

Beasts of the field have bigger cocks than human males, peasants larger and hairier pricks than aristocrats. As a young girl I had suspected this; as a woman I had indulged myself and proved it on more than one occasion. There was a woodchopper at Versailles, a sullen chap with dirty fingernails and a chest like a wine cask, who had serviced me with a pike ten inches long and so thick around that I could not sit a horse for a full two weeks after the event. To romp with him was to risk being split in two, but I could not resist going back again . . . and again . . . Ahh, the beastly peasants!

But that is another story, and not even the main one, for in truth it was the more subtle sensualities of aristocratic lovers which most frequently claimed my erotic attention. Now, however, it was the possibilities of just how aroused my base-born guards might become watching me which I was considering. Had their balls yet grown heavy in their homespun pants, their pricks semitumescent and tenting the crotches?

I panted with the strain of my exertions, and with the picture in my mind as well. Would they be touching themselves through the coarse wool? Would they be fantasizing the sensation of my soft Hapsburg flesh— Austrian, foreign, exotic—alive in their callused hands? I straightened up and reached behind me to massage the kink which had developed in the small of my back. I squirmed to get the knot out. My body strained sinuously against my gown. My pushed-up breasts panted shamefully. *Eat your hearts out, peasants! This is royal flesh! You may rule now, but still—still!—you can look, but you mustn't touch!*

Angling away from the mirror now and towards the screen, I put my foot back up on the stool and raised my skirts and petticoats. My fingers, the nails still long and impeccably manicured even here in my prison cell, located the ruffled lace garter high up in one shapely thigh. I removed first one garter, then the other, and then my stockings. My legs were white, but the insides of the thighs glowed pinkly. Unthinkingly, I had been rubbing them together while pondering the tumescence of my unseen guards. Now I examined them for the effects of the abrasiveness.

From behind the screen came the sound of a hoarse, deep gasp. It was followed by a faint groan in a different key. Were both guards peeking then? Were both cocks rising?

The thought made me touch myself fleetingly through my panties. . . .

"Every time I turn around, I find you with your hand between your legs, Your Highness!" Thus my nurse used to scold me when I was a very little girl at the court in Vienna. "It is not seemly, Your Highness!"

"It is my hand!" I had stamped my foot. "And it is my pee-pee!" Again I stamped. "And I am a royal princess of the House of Hapsburg, and if I wish to touch my royal pee-pee with my royal hand, I will most certainly do so!"

I have never since had any reason, *mes amis*, to doubt that royal prerogative! . . .

And so I now squeezed my soft, silken, curly ash-blond bush through the silk of my bloomers. They were sopping, a disgrace. But I would have fresh linen for the morrow. The morrow! I shuddered. I squeezed my hungry quim again. I concentrated on peasant cocks growing thick and hard as hidden peasant eyes spied on my disrobing.

I stood barefoot before the mirror now, bare-legged beneath my skirt as well. The polonaise afternoon gown I wore was slightly out of fashion (my movements had been restricted for some years by now and my couturier not made available to me), but nevertheless quite becoming and provocative. The square-cut bodice, as I have indicated, was scandalously low. It was laced with ribbons across the front, and the push-up stays were not part of a corset or any other separate garment, but rather incorporated into the dress itself. (Loosening these ribbons offered easy access to the untrammeled breasts nuzzling behind the flowered, delicate, dimity material.) The skirt was curved away from the front and caught up on either side behind the hips so that it fell in three large loops. This most provocatively revealed the intricately embroidered petticoat stretched over the modified hoops which were even now going out of style. Indeed, the effect of these modified hoops was more that of a bustle, so that while the dress was full behind, the petticoat was flat against the belly in front. Long-waisted, this design accentuated aristocratic treasures long deemed too intimate for notice.

Oui! For an afternoon frock, it was a most sexy gown! I admired it in my looking glass and then slowly began to undo the ribbons at my bodice. Soon I was sitting with my breasts semiexposed and my high cheeks flushed. I was breathing heavily. An echoing harsh respiration was audible from behind the screen.

The lowborn animals! The horror of my situation made my mood change irrationally. They were peeping! Of course they were! And lusting! Used to sows, the sight of a queen disrobing was raising them to stud. How disgusting!

Soon, however, their voyeur view would be dimmed. Daylight would fade. The blanket of night would fall.

Small consolation! The next light I saw—dawn—would be the herald of my death. With this thought, suddenly, the afternoon light became quite precious to me.

Was it really dying? It was hard to tell. There was one small window in my cell and it was set high up in the wall. It had been boarded over from the outside so that there were only two-inch-wide slits admitting light. These slits were my only access, and that only visual, to the world beyond my cell.

It was not much of a world. I discovered this the first time I climbed up on a table to the window and peered out through the slits at it. The view was that of a courtyard where the other women prisoners—but not I—were allowed to promenade from dawn to dusk.

The courtyard was surrounded on three sides by the stout stone masonry of the prison. On the fourth side there was a wrought-iron fence, high and sturdy and intricately designed. This design formed quite a few unexpected apertures--none so large as to threaten security, but none so small as to curtail other activities of a shocking (and frequently ingenious) nature.

On the other side of the fence was a narrow, open-air passage. Behind it was the men's section of the prison. From the windows of their cells, the men could look across the distance to the Place de la Revolution where the guillotine perched atop its scaffold. The men were permitted to stroll in the passage during the day.

Actually, they did not so much stroll as scramble for a position up against the fence which they might hold. There were occasional fights for such positions even among the aristocrat prisoners. Such struggles were likely to take place in the early morning, at noon, and—most likely of all—at dusk.

The reason for this, of course, was the women on the courtyard side of the fence. Many of these women were aristocrats, ladies of the Royal Court, wives of titled landowners awaiting trial by the Tribunal. Some of them had already been tried and, like myself, were waiting their turn 'neath the guillotine.

Some of the women, however, were not ladies at all. They were prostitutes and petty thieves, strumpets, the feminine dregs of the *ancien régime* and of the Revolution as well. Many were crones, hags, but there were a few, I must confess, who even in their rags seemed comely. The noble ladies, of course, even with the blade hanging over their heads, would have nothing to do with this rabble.

I should remark that this was not a matter of morality. In matters of the flesh, as we shall see, there was no distinction between the plebeian females and the patrician ladies. It was a question of breeding. One was either born a lady, or one was not. If one was highborn; then the only discourse possible with one who was not was the giving of orders. Since the lower-class women prisoners of the Conciergerie were not inclined to obey such commands, any discourse at all with them was unthinkable.

This did not necessarily apply to the gentlemen who were prisoners. Men have always been weaker than women when it comes to maintaining caste. Traditionally they have consorted with lowborn wenches. It is overlooked. They have their whores as I had my woodcutter at Versailles. The difference is that they not only fuck their whores, they actually talk to them!

Men!

Ah, well. They congregated, the men, along the wrought-iron fence quite early in the morning. There was a fountain with running water in the women's courtyard—a boon—and the ladies would appear with the sun to perform their ablutions. Some of these, of necessity, were quite revealing, quite titillating, and it was such moments which caused the men to battle for their places by the fence.

Peering through the apertures of the wrought iron, a condemned man might catch his last glimpse of a lovely breast being sponged, a lissome thigh as it was patted dry, even a plump derriere being powdered before the donning of fresh lingerie. These flashes of female flesh softly gleaming with morning dew from the fountain greatly excited the men. My guards, it seemed, were not the only dedicated voyeurs at the Conciergerie.

After washing, the women would drift back into their

cells to eat their sparse breakfasts. Reluctantly, the men too would disperse. They would reassemble at noon, scrambling again for their places at the fence, for it was then that the ladies would promenade to some purpose.

This time when they appeared, there was a certain strut to the ladies' gait. They brought with them a perfume which wafted over the prison yard to the men's side like a fragrant, aphrodisiac mist. As the men sniffed it, their nostrils twitched like bulls brought to the cow barn to couple.

It was evident that the ladies had paid careful attention to their toilette. Their cheeks were pink, their lips rouged, the shine powdered from their noses and from that portion of their bosoms escaping from their decolletage as well. Waists pinched in and breasts pushed up, hips swaying, they reminded me more of Spanish women than of French. Yes, Spanish women, eyes flashing behind their fans, bodies inviting under the lace of their mantillas, tongues darting an unmistakable invitation to such young and noble rakes as they found appealing.

The message was clear to the men on the other side of the wrought-iron fence. They responded with whispered suggestions whenever a lady they found attractive came within range of them. As often as not these whispers found murmured answers. Arrangements were made, assignations—bizarre under the circumstances—agreed upon.

As the sun heated the sky, the women drifted back inside to their quarters again. An afternoon nap was part of the routine of every wellborn young lady, and the tradition persisted even in prison. The regimen of evening soirées which had been their former life demanded that one rest to look one's best when the festivities began. It was necessary to claim and hold the attention of the members of the opposite sex. Now, in prison, the reasoning was the same. Only the soirées took place earlier, commencing at dusk. Also, with time cut short by the ever-present specter of the blade, the flirting process was speeded up and the road to assignation foreshortened considerably.

Indeed, Madame Guillotine had effectively dispelled inhibitions on both sides of the wrought-iron fence. With the end so manifestly in sight, a tacit decision had been reached by women as well as men to enjoy life to the fullest before the final moment. The urgency was fierce—a sort of unspoken hysteria—and the most modest of maidens performed under the eyes of her sisters (a necessity if one was to perform at all in this situation) in ways formerly reserved for only the most *intime fête de nuit* at the Petit Trianon.

Now, judging by the quality of the light trickling in through the slits between the boards covering the small, high window of my cell, that time was approaching when the women would reappear and the naughty frolics commence. My contempt for the guards hidden behind the partition of my small cell made me brazen. I took off my afternoon frock and petticoats and stood proud before my mirror in only my chemise and bloomers one step away from nudity. The red nipples of my breasts betrayed themselves against the silk of the undergarment. A trick of candlelight reflecting from the mirror revealed the shape of my legs and the curl of my ash-blond pubic hair.

Quickly, but aware of how even the briefest exposure of my large, round, high-mounted breasts must excite my peasant guards, I slipped off my chemise and donned a negligee over my bloomers. It was silken, clinging, scarlet—a royal color, a sensual hue; why not?—and pulled a small table over to the wall beneath the window. I mounted the table, rested my elbows on the rough stone of the windowsill, and peered out between the boards.

Pools of shadow were already dispelling the last of the dying sunlight, and events were developing rapidly. The men were at the wrought-iron fence, dressed in the soiled finery which marked them as aristocrats. Those who had not fought their way there had probably paid off the pickpockets and the cutpurses and the jackrollers to secure a place for them. As the women made haste to partake of the joys the fence afforded, the guards stationed around the perimeter of the prison yard lit discreetly placed torches at wide intervals.

These torches were in no way a mark of concern for the incarcerated aristocrats. Rather they were a deliberate infringement on their privacy. The guards could have forbidden these lewd twilight frolics. Instead they permitted them for their own amusement. Like the guillotine, it was part of the spectacle of the Revolution. And the torches were the footlights for the stage where the ribald drama was presented each day at dusk.

Like the guards, I too was part of the audience. It was the last performance I would see. Hopefully it would establish the erotic ambience I relied on to carry me through my last, long night.

Now the sunlight was completely gone. An early moon had risen. Along with the flickering torchlight, it illuminated a series of erotic tableaux worthy of Restif de la Bretonne's erotic masterpiece, *La Paysanne Pervertie*. The wrought-iron fence was a living human frieze of sexual possibilities.

A small-breasted comtesse had bared her pretty little banana-shaped breasts and forced them through two of the large holes in the fence so that a group of three or four men might fondle and suck on them. I recognized one of my former ladies-in-waiting raising her skirts to impale herself on a long finger hooking through the ironwork. Several ladies were engaged in tongue-kissing with several gentlemen, and the tongues were already discolored from the black iron. Two sweet young things simply stood with their backs pressed against the fence. Behind them a pair of roués had raised their skirts and were contriving to caress their bottom cheeks and play in their sensitive bungholes. One baroness I had known from the old days, a bit over the hill now, I fear, but determined to squeeze the last drops from life before the tumbril came to fetch her, had spread her legs double-jointedly and managed to mount a remarkably lifelike dildo proffered through the wrought iron. And another noblewoman, a stranger to me, had raised her skirts and lowered her bloomers and pressed her pussy to the fence to receive the straining lickings of some anonymous male tongue tip. These and other vignettes were repeated with many variations.

Sounds reached my ears to match these sights, although I must confess that I could not tell who was saying what to whom. Nevertheless, in their way, these sounds were as stimulating as the sights. There were heartfelt sighs and tender moans, harsh pantings and hungry groans, breathless, throaty giggles and wild whimpers and the snarling animal noises which accompany erotic climax. And there were words, anonymous words, floating up to my ears from the bizarre, lascivious torchlit scene below:

"Lick it, *cheri*! . . ."

"I feel so randy when you sink your teeth into my plump derriere like that, m'sieur! . . ."

"Harder! . . . Faster! . . . Harder! . . . Faster! . . ."

"Have you a carrot, m'sieur? . . . A stalk of celery? . . . Even asparagus? . . ."

"Higher with your nose! . . . Now suck! . . . Suck! . . ."

"*Mon Dieu!* I am impaled, stuck! But I don't care! I don't care! . . ."

"Faster! . . . Harder! . . . Faster! . . . Harder! . . ."

"Your breasts are like white doves with sharp little red noses, *madame*. . . ."

"That tickles! . . ."

"Your breath, *m'sieur!* However did you find cloves of garlic in such a place as this? . . ."

"Faster! . . . Faster! . . . Faster! . . . Faster! . . ."

"If you move this way, *madame*, and I move that way, perhaps then we can disengage. . . ."

"Use your fist! . . . Stretch me wide! . . . I want to see your wrist vanish up there, *cheri!* . . ."

"Suck, *ma petit!* . . . Suck! . . ."

"I did not know that it was possible to do it like this, *m'sieur!* . . ."

"Harder! . . . Harder! . . . Harder! . . . Harder! . . ."

"How red the inside of you quim is, *mam'selle!* . . ."

"Don't stop! . . ."

"It is from fucking so much. I love it. I shall fuck until I die! . . ."

"I'm coming! . . ."

"Faster! . . ."

"COMING! . . ."

"Harder!"

"NOW! NOW! NOW! . . ."

"Don't stop! . . . Go harder! Go faster! . . . Harder! . . . Faster! . . ."

"Has anyone seen my bloomers? I can't seem to find them anywhere?"

"Or perhaps a broccoli spear? . . ."

"DON'T STOP! . . ."

It was too much. I put my hands over my ears and closed my eyes for a moment. I cleared my senses of the overload. And when I took my hands from my ears and opened my eyes, it was to focus my attention on only one tableau, but one well worthy of such focus.

I recognized the man involved immediately. He was the English scribe I had overheard mumbling to himself just before the Revolutionary Tribunal pronounced sentence on me. I wondered at his presence in the men's prison of the Conciergerie. Whatever the reason, the outcome would probably not be too serious for him. At this point in the Revolution, those in power were making every effort not to bring down the wrath of royalist England on their heads. No matter his crime, they would never dare to bring an Englishman to the guillotine.

Perhaps he had committed no crime at all. Perhaps in his quest for background information for whatever he was writing, he had bribed a guard to admit him to the Conciergerie. Guards were easy to bribe. It was a common occurrence. Bribes were a fringe benefit of a job which frequently went unpaid by a financially unstable revolutionary government that had not as yet come to terms with the bankers of Europe. Yes, probably the Englishman had bribed his way in—either to do research, or to participate in the bizarre orgy of the condemned which took place nightly.

He was a slight young man, thirtyish, sensitive-looking. At the moment he had put his quill pen aside in favor of unsheathing another tool—one made of flesh. This tool was not very thick, but it was long, and sleek, and quite erect. Indeed, its arrogance seemed not in keeping with his soft brown eyes and high, intellectual brow. Had I seen this implement apart from its owner, experience might well have had me take it for French, or even Nordic, rather than (forgive the prejudice, but Biology truly is Destiny) British.

The Englishman had been fortunate in laying claim to one of the larger holes in the wrought-iron fence. The slenderness and length of his erect instrument worked well to his advantage, and all save perhaps an inch of it was able to invade the women's courtyard. The hole was so shaped as to allow his not very hairy testicles to rest on the lip of the grillwork. A lady on the women's side of the fence was already taking advantage of this circumstance.

She had stooped over in front of his erect cock. Her skirts raised, her bloomers down around her ankles, she had backed up against it quite accurately. Now her round buns enveloped it, and her bottom reared high to suck it deep into her pussy. Rising up and down, she sucked the long shaft in and out of her inflamed cunt. Her head hanging down and bobbing so that all I could see was the powdered wig atop it, she slammed back against the Englishman's cock, slid down its length, and then slammed back into it again. After a while, there was a subtle change in the rhythm of her movements.

At first I did not perceive this change of tempo. There were two reasons for my missing it. One was that the sight of that shiny English cock thrusting through the fence and into the honeyed, clutching quim on the other side had fired my own libido. Forgetting all about the guards watching me through the peepholes, I had pushed my scarlet negligee aside to fondle my burning nipples as I watched the scene in the courtyard below me. Soon one of my hands dropped further down, inside my bloomers, and my own syrupy pussy was puckering around my fingers as I continued watching. My behind was moving in hard, jerking circles against the tight-stretched material of the negligee—a sight to surely gratify the eyes of those hidden peasant voyeurs.

The second reason I missed the change in rhythm

momentarily cooled my passion. With the alteration, the woman bending over to the Englishman's thrustings suddenly raised her head and her upper body. The shock stopped my clitty-strumming fingers immediately. It was like looking into a mirror! Her form as well as her face came into sudden sharp focus and the figure as well as the features were mine own!

Her breasts were full, round melons, just like mine. She was tall and long-legged, and the slightest bit fleshy around the thighs, just as I was. Her high derriere was like a firm pillow—pure Hapsburg.

Hapsburg too her visage, the image of my own. Like me she had deep, sparkling blue eyes looking out over high cheekbones in an oval face. Her complexion was the pink white of Dresden china, as was mine. Even the way she curled her lip—the pouting, fellatio-styled Hapsburg lip—was a perfect mimicry of my expression during the act of making love.

Only one thing was different. On her naked, down-hanging left breast, perhaps an inch above the nipple, there was an angry purple mark. I knew that mark well, as would anyone in France. It was the mark of the convicted criminal, the fleur-de-lis, and it had been put there by a red-hot branding iron!

More disturbing than the uncanny resemblance to me was the fact that I knew this woman. Our resemblance had altered the course of my life, and the course of history as well. Indeed, that resemblance was the reason for the fleur de lis on her breast, and I the one responsible for its having been put there!

She was Mlle Jeanne de Valois, also know as the Comtesse de La Motte, alias Milady, and she had died two years ago! She was dead! She had been dead for two years! But if she was dead, what was she doing propelling her quivering bottom against the cock of an

Englishman with a quill pen sticking out of the breast pocket of his ruffled shirt?

I must be hallucinating! The prospect of the guillotine was already driving me mad! Milady had popped into my mind because she looked like me and I wanted to be the one cavorting with the Englishman. Since I was confined to the Little Pharmacy and could not join in the licentious frolickings of the courtyard, my mind, under this awful strain of impending death, had played a trick and resurrected Milady as a sort of surrogate with whom I could easily identify.

Shaking my head to clear it, I focused on the scene again. The woman had lowered her head, and her features and the upper part of her body were once again shielded from my view. She was clutching at her powdered wig to keep it from falling off, and this too helped restore her anonymity.

Nevertheless, as I now finally comprehended the change in rhythm and the reason for it, I identified with what she was feeling so fully that to my erotically frantic mind she once again was the mirror image of myself. The revised tempo was due to the fact that she was now impaling her bunghole on the Englishman's thrusting prick, as well as skewering her quim. She was alternating the target she offered him with each backward lunge. Half laughing and half crying loudly enough for the sounds to reach me, she was contriving to be stabbed to the testicled hilt in her honeyed cunt and her tight, sensitive anus by turn.

There was agony wrenched from her lips each time she engloved him with the forbidden passage. (Was she accustoming herself to small stabbings of pain, I wondered, in anticipation of the major, final slicing anguish of the guillotine? Or was it just that the cock tearing at her bottom brought that much more joy by comparison when it glutted her hot, clutching pussy?)

The Englishman's thrustings became more urgent with the writhings of the dual targets. My own hand went back inside my bloomers and found my pussy. Beyond subtlety, I rammed two of my fingers up inside myself with a movement that was both quick and hard. I frigged myself violently as I watched my double clawing at her perspiring, swaying breasts. Both she and the Englishman were grunting like animals in a barnyard. They were both obviously approaching the climax of their two-holed coupling.

The sight of my look-alike offering her hot cunt and her squirming ass with such abandon made me feel faint and a little dizzy as my hand slapped against my wet, open, spongy pussy. My mind raced ahead of my physical desire to be with them. My fingers strummed my clitty on a sort of plateau of ecstasy just short of orgasm.

Such was my state as I watched their mutual explosion gathering. And then it came! The Englishman lunged so hard that his scrotum became wedged in the iron scrollwork. My double bayed like a mare being pinned by a stallion and took—perhaps by choice—the erupting geyser of his jizzum deep in her bowels. Her orgasm seemed none the less powerful for the emptiness of her pussy.

Watching this, a frenzy seized me to catch up with them and reach my own climax. My fist pounded violently at my pussy. The little table on which I was standing to look out the window rocked dangerously.

The teetering motion threw me off my stroke. Beside myself, I clamored down from the table and flung myself into the chair. It never occurred to me that I was now facing the screen behind which the two guards were watching me. I was beyond giving them a second thought.

I pushed my bloomers down to my ankles so that they would be out of the way. I sprawled in the chair with my honey-drenched thighs wide apart. The scarlet negligee had fallen away from my breasts, and now I cupped them both and raised them. The nipples were distended brazenly, long and blood red, arrogant and twitching. Deliberately, wanting to prolong all of the delicious sensations, I stroked the tips to even more swollen rigidity. Then I stuck out my long, pointed tongue and licked down the top side of one breast to the quivering berry tip. An instant later one nipple was between my lips and my hand was trapped between my tight-clenched and squirming thighs.

I forced myself to relax my thigh muscles. I parted my legs. My white thigh flesh—the alabaster flesh of a born aristocrat, a Hapsburg—gleamed in the candlelight. I slid my hand back and forth over the swollen lips at the entrance to my wet, burning pussy.

Still sucking hard on one nipple, I stroked the quivering flesh gates until they opened to their widest. Then I made a fist and pushed my hand further down between my legs. I worked two knuckles in and out of my spread cunt, sending a thrill through my stiff clitty each time I bumped it.

My passion built very quickly. On impulse I pulled my bloomers back up and then held them away from my belly with one hand while I continued playing with myself with the others. Somehow this made what I was doing seem (I confess!) quite obscene. I stared inside my bloomers as my fist moved back and forth between my quim and my bunghole, forcing itself into both passages. Soon, I could tell, I would spend, and the bloomers would be too confining to accommodate that event comfortably.

Fingers clawing, I again pushed them down around my ankles. I slid down in my chair and raised my legs high, spreading them, the bloomers caught and stretched by my feet. My gaping pussy and red, abused bottom hole focused directly on the peepholes of the screen. In my frenzy, I was oblivious to the spying of my lowborn jailers.

I stared blindly at the screen. My breast was in my mouth. My fist was battering my pussy. And then my breast was released and my Hapsburg lip was curled back in an ecstatic snarl and the animal sounds from deep inside me were released through my open mouth and I came close to howling as my grinding fist carried me over the crest of my orgasm.

Writhing still with the last of it, my eyes refocused on the screen just as it toppled. The sight of my uninhibited spending had proven too much for my young voyeur guards. Indeed, it had impelled them to a response as urgent as my own. And they were so careless in their frenzy as to push over the screen and reveal themselves.

I regarded this happenstance with open mouth. In no way was I prepared for the sight which I beheld. However negative my expectations of the hoi polloi of the Republic, I had not anticipated this.

The fallen screen revealed that both National Guardsmen had dropped the trousers of their homespun uniforms. Both sets of plump, naked, pink boy-cheeks were blurs of jiggling motion. Each guardsman's arm was extended, and each guardsman's hand was formed into a loose fist. And each fist was jerking wildly at the stiff and swollen penis of the other guardsman. My two jailers had been inspired by their spying on me to jerk each other off!

Now, the toppling of the screen cost them the last of their control. Both their muskets of manhood fired, discharging without aim, a wild sort of scatter fire which spattered both of them. One took a powerful spurt directly in the eye and screamed that he was blinded. Return fire to the ear temporarily impaired the hearing of the other guardsman.

Thus their mutual loss of composure dulled their senses to the amused contempt with which I regarded them. *"Vive la République!"* I pronounced sarcastically. *"Vive fraternité!"*

Like my *mot* to the Tribunal, this one too went unappreciated.

Embarrassment, however, quickly replaced my initial reaction. I was not used to having the lowest of the lower classes observe me in moments of masturbatory intimacy. And so, while they were untangling themselves, I pulled my negligee around me, turned my back on them, climbed back up on the small table and once again looked out between the boards covering the window. It was the only place in the small cell where I could feel somewhat removed from my jailers.

The courtyard had the look of a particularly disreputable orgy. The scene which I had been watching, however, was over. My look-alike, Milady de Valois, alias Comtesse de la Motte—if indeed it was she, risen from the grave— was nowhere to be seen. But I did spy the Englishman. He was standing well back from the wrought-iron fence. One of the guards was standing silently beside him, and on his other side a churchman in the unmistakable robes of a cardinal was speaking to him in a manner that suggested the spelling out of instructions—or perhaps firm orders.

I caught my breath. This cardinal was no prisoner! By virtue of having made himself my implacable enemy, he was an ecclesiatical hero of the Revolution. He had been my lover, my nemesis, my salvation as a woman, and my bête noire. His name was Louis de Rohan and he was a prince of the realm, as well as of the church. Once he had been second only to the King in France, and in the eyes of the pious, superior to him. He had certainly been superior as far as I was concerned. I never knew a man I loved as much as Prince Louis de Rohan. I never knew a man I hated as much as he.

Now he nodded to the guard and both he and the Englishman were escorted from the passageway into the main building. Somehow I was sure that neither of them was going to spend the night inside the walls of the Conciergerie. I sighed, wondering. . . .

Idly, I allowed my eyes to wander. They came to rest on two *jeune filles* who had bypassed the sensual offerings of the wrought-iron fence in favor of each other's company. They were locked in an embrace just beneath my window.

Watching them, I was deeply touched. They were so young! Surely neither of them was more than sixteen years of age. And there was such innocence to their fumblings, such lack of calculation. Each sweet caress was a discovery.

Wonder lit their naive schoolgirl faces as they kissed, their lips clinging, their timid tongues touching and then becoming more bold with the thrill. Hugging each other, their breasts crushed together, they squirmed, found the squirming titillating, and soon were toying with each other's bosoms under their clothing. Then a budding breast was bared and stroked and kissed and then more lingeringly sucked. The favor was returned and the pantings of both maidens became harsh.

Both bosoms bare, it was natural that a hand should creep under a skirt. The lass whose pussy was touched moaned and this inspired her companion to raise her skirts and offer her own sparse-haired quim to be caressed. They played with each other hotly, experimenting, marveling at the honeyed wetness their toyings provoked, teasing with their fingertips, and then pushing in deeper and deeper as they frigged each other. And then, instinctively, they changed position, buried their sweet, moist lips in one another's virgin pussies, and began licking and sucking in the traditional *soixante-neuf* position.

The sight filled me with nostalgia. It took me back to the time when I had been just such a girl as they—young, innocent, naive, but with a fire in my blood. Ahh, *oui*! Tears in my eyes, I thought of that time when I, a royal virgin (my virginity quite carefully preserved for reasons of state), was introduced to the joys of woman love in my royal bath chamber at the palace in Vienna.

Vienna . . . Helga, my first very own lady's maid, little older than I was myself, but not being a princess royal, shielded far less from experience than I . . . Helga, the sweet stickiness of her blue-black bush . . . her clever fingers on my rosebud nipples, and then between my legs, careful (the royal hymen must be preserved), but knowing just where and how to touch me . . . and then her mouth, her lips, her tongue, and the excitement of clutching her shining face between the baby fat of my thighs and spending over it . . . Helga! . . . Vienna! . . .

Vienna . . .

Chapter Two

Vienna . . . When I was a girl, it was a city of dancing spires and gingerbread facades, with two exceptions. The exceptions were the two palaces, Hofburg and Schönbrun, which were the homes I shuttled between. Both were massive structures of cold stone, with long, drafty hallways and fireplaces far more picturesque than productive of heat.

(A "nose in the air" has always been a symbol of high caste. The more arrogant the tilt of the head and the wider the flair of the nostrils, the more aristocratic the rank. And nobody, not even the Bourbons, tilted their heads more arrogantly, nor flared their nostrils more widely than we Hapsburgs. Well, darlings, now it can be told. Royal blood did not decree this pose. It was those drafty halls and faulty fireplaces! We had the sniffles, one and all, were born to them, coped with them all through childhood and adulthood, and left for posterity a gallery of portraits showing us looking quite snooty indeed when in truth we were only trying to hold the pose without sneezing.)

Schönbrun Castle lay just outside Vienna on an estate of some five hundred acres, most of which had been landscaped into parks. Hofburg was in the center of the capital city and hovered over it more like the fortress it was frequently used as than a palace. Both were decorated in what came to be called "the Theresian Style," after my mother, Empress Maria Theresa. This was a combination of the massive baroque furnishings and tapestries which have always marked the domiciles of the Hapsburgs and a gay, sort of rococo melange of objets d'art which seemed to be poking fun at the more classical pieces. When it was decided to court the Bourbons with an eye towards an arranged marriage between myself and the Dauphin, Louis, a French neo-classical style began to intrude in the royal apartments and many a disapproving Austrian eyebrow was raised at the decadently curved gold-leaf legs of Louis XIV sofas and chairs.

Indeed, it was on just such a white satin sofa that my beloved Helga and I frequently sipped the nectar from each other's virgin goblets of joy. But I am getting ahead of my story. . . .

In spring and summer the royal family, myself included, usually resided in Schönbrun, with occasional side trips to our palace at Innsbruck and our Laxenburg shooting lodge near the Hungarian border. When the weather grew cold, however, in late autumn and winter, we repaired to the drafty old Hofburg. It was from here, at precisely fifteen minutes past five on the evening of Thursday, February 7, 1770, that a courier was dispatched at full gallop to Versailles with news for the Monarch of France, Louis XV, grandfather to the Dauphin who would be my bridegroom.

The royal courier rode day and night, pausing only to change mounts and—one presumes—to relieve himself.

He pressed one steed so brutally that the poor beast fell out from under him, frothing at the mouth, and died. The messenger himself was so exhausted by his arduous journey that he was scarce able to stand before the French King to deliver the news from the Austrian Empress.

The news, of course, concerned me. I had been the subject of delicate negotiations for many years now. My beauty, you see, was the carrot being held out to the Bourbons to prop up an alliance between Austria and France. Every quality of my character had international implications. Child that I was, nevertheless every rumor of indiscretion was pored over by royal ministers and advisers in Paris and at Versailles, as well as in Austria.

Was Maria Antonia Josefa Johanna, as I was called before my name was gallicized to Marie Antoinette when I married Louis, a headstrong girl? Was she willful? Was she obedient enough to deserve a Bourbon husband? Would her charms tempt him to those acts which would result in royal heirs? Was her pelvic structure conducive to producing them? (It was promising, of course, that Mama had successfully given birth to sixteen royal progeny; it boded well for her youngest daughter's loins.) And, most important of all, for there were pressing reasons of state to hurry the marriage plans along, were there signs that this child was entering puberty?

This last was a key question. I was already past my fourteenth year and it still hadn't been answered. I was a late bloomer, although history would certainly confirm my ripeness once it arrived. Diplomats frowned over this and my mother fretted over it. For some time now, I had been frustrating their plans. (As for myself, I could only wonder if those interludes with Helga on the Louis XIV couch might have had anything to do with continuing delay. To this day, I am not sure of the answer.)

Now, at long last—*voilà!*—the issue was resolved. The burnt-out messenger stood swaying in front of King Louis XV at Versailles and delivered the good news. The royal flag was up! The youngest Hapsburg Archduchess at long last had her first period! At exactly quarter past five as dusk was falling on February 7, 1770—a Thursday—I had stained my royal bloomers with Hapsburg menstrual blood.

The wedding, *mes amis*, could now proceed!

"Not tonight," I told Helga later that evening. "I've got the curse, darling."

Of course I was bragging. Helga, a couple of years older than I, had been menstruating since she was twelve. But like me she was a virgin, and some things were new to her. Now she raised an eyebrow as if to say that my condition might make things interesting. But it was not to be. My mother, as soon as she became aware of my condition, had a bed for me moved into her boudoir. Here, between menstruation and marriage, she gave me a crash course on the birds and the bees and how best to go about raising the royal French scepter.

Not that Mama knew so very much. After sixteen children and with a husband known for his many mistresses before his death from a stroke brought on by overexertion, the Greek chorus of her advice was that "passionate love soon disappears." Having already tasted lust with Helga, I wasn't so sure about that!

Helga had been assigned as my personal maid the previous autumn when we returned from Schönbrun to Hofburg. She was the first body servant I ever had who was exclusively my own. In the past I had always had to share a lady's maid with one of my sisters. Since they were all older, I always received the lesser part of such servants' attention spans. I was ecstatic to have my very own maid to order around.

This privilege was the latest in an ongoing program to groom me for marriage to the French Louis if the delicate plans bore fruit. The program included instruction in playing both the clavichord and the spinet by Christoph Willibald Gluck, Mama's court composer and conductor, who wrote music in the Schönbrun gardens with two open bottles of champagne perched on top of his clavichord to provide needed inspiration. I was taught French, first by a Parisian actor who told me titillating stories but did nothing to banish my Austrian accent, and later by the Abbé de Vermond, who thought me "lazy and frivolous," but nevertheless managed to drum Gallic grammar into my head. I also received instruction in all the latest dances from a French ballet master, as well as tutoring in the arts of sketching and painting miniatures. One course of training which came in quite handy later at Versailles taught me how to conduct gambling games and how to plan my wagers at racing events and gaming tables.

My body, as well as my mind, was groomed for the royal marriage. Mama summoned a famous hairdresser from Paris to style my coiffure. He touched up the natural ash-blond color with red lights to render the line of my brow more aristocratic in the French fashion and to complement the natural sparkle of my blue eyes. A French dentist was also imported to check my teeth to be sure they would be acceptable to the Dauphin. And finally, I was given my own maid, Helga, to accustom me to deal without self-consciousness with servants who might be providing the most intimate services to my person.

A word here about Mama vis-à-vis Helga. Mama, you see, was really quite puritanical. As empress she had outlawed illicit love affairs among her courtiers. (Later, as queen, I demanded them!) She had actually set up a "Chastity Commission" which became notorious throughout the royal courts of Europe. One of its investigations so embarrassed her head minister that he was forced to resign and retire to his country estates with his wife, two mistresses, and his apple-cheeked young page. I mention this to point out that when Mama provided me with a maidservant to perform intimate services, she had not the vaguest idea of just how *intime* those services might be!

Mama had personally chosen Helga to serve me because of her comeliness. Despite her old-fashioned morality, Mama was a Hapsburg with a Hapsburg eye for beauty. It pleased her to find among the blonds of Vienna a maiden with lustrous ebony hair and a darkish Magyar complexion to complement my own light skin and fair tresses. That her figure should be graceful was something that Mama would take for granted without even noting that it was curvaceous and voluptuous beyond Helga's tender years.

As I have remarked, she was but a couple of years older than I, really just a girl herself, and (Mama would allow no less among the unmarried palace staff) a virgin. Despite this, not being a princess royal, Helga was not quite as naive as I. A servant and the daughter of servants, she had grown up around the palace. Early breasts had assured her of many fondlings from the time she was twelve. She had played with the stableboys in the haystacks, pulled on their crops, and watched the boy cream fly. She had kissed with her tongue and sat astraddle a footman's knee, rubbing back and forth until her thighs were drenched and the ceiling spun. Indeed, only the strictness of Mama's household had kept Helga's virginity intact.

If she hadn't been assigned as my maid, she probably would have shucked it anyway. As it was, this circumstance directed Helga's libido in another direction. She thought my slender Hapsburg body and Hapsburg face most beautiful, and when her duties brought her into the most intimate contact with my royal flesh, her fingers trembled with new desire.

I felt the tremble in my bath one day. I was drowsing in the warm water, blowing bubbles and stirring froth, while Helga walked back and forth with fresh kettles of hot water to maintain the temperature. Her olive skin was quite flushed with her exertions and she was breathing very hard.

"You had best loosen your stays," I remarked innocently, "or you will faint from the heat."

She did as I suggested, and the next time she bent to pour the hot water I saw clearly inside her bodice. Her breasts were large for her age, and quite high and firm. The nipples were hard and purple. I caught my breath when I saw them, and without thinking my hand moved under the water to stroke soapsuds into my maiden's sparse bush.

"Do you want me to wash you, Your Highness?" Helga's eyes were very sharp. She had noticed my sudden squirmings and the location of my splashings.

"All right." My heart was beating very fast.

"If you'll sit up please, Your Highness."

I sat up. Helga sponged my back and scrubbed it gently and then rinsed it clean with hot water. Even at this innocent touch, my thigh muscles were clenching. Now she moved around in front of me. She knelt beside the tub and cupped one of my small rosebud breasts in her hand. I gasped, and it moved in her palm as if alive with a will of its own.

"If you don't mind my saying so, Your Highness,

your bosom is most charming." Helga's fingers tickled as they gently massaged the soap into the pink areola around the nipple.

"I'd rather have big woman's breasts like yours!" I blurted out. "They're really beautiful."

"You will have such breasts, Your Highness. In a year or two, perhaps less." Reaching for my other naked breast, her own bosom dipped into the tub. With her stays loosened, the wet material clearly displayed one long, purple-dark distended nipple.

"You're getting wet." I turned to Helga. I had a sudden fierce desire to kiss the nipple through the sopping material, to put my small Hapsburg mouth around it, to suck its magenta hardness.

"There are still some soapsuds on the back of your neck." Reaching behind me to get at them, she pressed my face into the plump, bare flesh rising from her bodice.

I felt dizzy. Once I had sneaked some champagne from a party at court, and now the perfume rising up from between Helga's breasts was affecting me the way that champagne had. I put my wet arms around her to steady myself.

She held me like that for a moment. When she released me, one of her high young breasts was exposed. My nuzzlings must have rendered it so. I licked my lips and unthinkingly sucked my tongue at the sight of her magnificently stiff nipple.

My reaction was not lost on Helga. "Shall I do your bottom now, Your Highness?" she asked softly. Her naked breast was rising and falling very quickly as she spoke the question.

"Yes!" I told her. "Do my bottom!" I spoke the order more harshly than I'd intended. My voice was hoarse with a lust I had not even identified.

"If you will crouch on your hands and knees in the water, Your Highness, I will be able to wash you more thoroughly."

"Very well." I did as Helga wanted. My small breasts looked fuller and rosier as they swayed in this downward position. My head, also hanging down, was peering between them. I widened the space between my thighs so that I could see between them as well and watch Helga as she soaped my thighs and my hips and my belly and my derriere and my other private parts.

She laughed when I squirmed as her hand moved between the plump cheeks of my bottom. "Does that tickle, Your Majesty?" she inquired.

"Yes." I was too choked up to say anything more.

As she reached around me to rub lather into my sparse, ash-blond bush, I felt the erect nipple of her naked breast press into the pinkened flesh of my bottom cheeks. This time my squirming bore fruit. I captured the hot breast tip in the cleft between them. Not being able to see what I was doing there somehow made it all right to do it. I squeezed her nipple and rolled it tightly and savored the sensations of its probing that delicate orifice.

"Ohh, Your Highness!" It was a moan. Helga's soapy hand squeezed my thigh flesh. "Do you want me to play with you?"

I wasn't actually sure what she meant. "Yes!" I agreed anyway.

An instant later she was stroking softly between the lips of my pussy. A loyal subject, she was being very careful not to do anything to endanger my royal chastity. At the same time, this activity, coupled with the squeezing of her already aroused nipple between my ass cheeks, was arousing her greatly.

Watching between my legs as I crouched, I saw Helga

move her free hand to her belly. Using her clutching fingers and the edge of the tub, seeming not to care how she was drenching her clothing, she managed to raise her skirt and petticoat. Then her clawing hand pushed her bloomers deep into the crevice between her legs and stirred in hard, violent little circles. Helga was not being as careful of her own hymen as she was of mine. But then she wasn't a Hapsburg princess.

"I want to touch you there as you are touching me!" I scrambled in the water, splashing both of us with soap-suds as I turned around. Then, kneeling, I pushed Helga's hand away from her pussy so that I could see it. "Take down your bloomers," I commanded. "They're sopping anyway."

"Yes, Your Highness." She pushed down her bloomers and stood back a little so that I might see.

Her thighs were beautiful, all golden tan and firm with servant muscle. Her belly was flat and tight and her navel deep with Magyar mystery. Her sporran was a lush blue-black triangle over her lower belly, tangled with honey at its lowest point.

I reached out and touched her there. "Now play with me again," I told her. "We'll play with each other at the same time." I reached up and touched her naked nipple. "It's so hard," I marveled. "So hot and hard."

"So are your nipples, Your Highness."

I looked down at my wet, still slightly soapy bosom. Helga was right. My berry nipples at the end of my girl breasts were sticking out a full half inch. They were bright red. A translucent soap bubble hung off the end of one of them.

"You may touch them," I decided. "You may fondle them." Then, as Helga complied, "Oh!" I gasped. "Oh, my!"

Helga's nipples tickled the palms of my hands as I

clutched at her breasts in response. Her naked pussy rubbed in small circles against the rounded edge of the marble bathtub. Her dark brown eyes were heavy-lidded with passion.

I clutched at her lush breasts like the greedy child I was, savoring their fullness and the heat of the long, hard, damson nipples. She, however, handled my small girl breasts more delicately and with more finesse. She closed just the fingertips of each of her hands around the sensitive pink button tips and manipulated them so adroitly that soon I was splashing up and down so violently in the water as to wet down the entire floor of the bathroom.

"Perhaps it might be best if you got out of the tub now, Your Highness," Helga suggested, her lovely cunt twitching on a level with my wide and staring blue eyes.

"Very well." I stood and stepped into the large, soft towel Helga held out to me.

Gently, she patted me dry. I rested my head on her naked breast as she did so, and closed my eyes. Her nipple, still hotly erect, tickled the inside of my ear. Her hands, patting my damp flesh through the towel, were buiding a new excitement in my blood.

When she was through, Helga stepped back and started to pull up her bloomers which were still down around her knees.

"No!" I reached out my hand and stopped her.

"Your Highness?" There was mischievous understanding in her eyes as she cocked her head saucily with the question.

"Play with me again," I commanded, remembering her phraseology from before.

"Like this, Your Highness?" Standing in front of me, she reached under the towel she had draped over my body and cupped the cheeks of my behind. She had already rubbed them pink with the towel, and now her fondlings made them truly burn.

"Yes." I squirmed under her teasing touch. "Do what you did before," I panted.

Helga's fingers tiptoed over the sensitive inner flesh of the cleft bisecting my squirming bottom. Then she stepped closer and parted the towel so that my own young girl pussy with its sparse covering of silky ash-blond curls was revealed. Still kneading my writhing bottom, she pressed her naked pussy against mine so that our contrasting bushes entwined and rubbed gently.

After a moment I felt her swollen pussy lips nipping at my own. Both our quims were quite syrupy and there was a titillating stickiness as they squirmed against each other. Helga's brown eyes staring into mine reflected the mounting excitement both of us were feeling.

"May I kiss you, Your Highness?"

"Under these circumstances, Helga, I don't believe you have to ask for royal permission," I told her. "Just do what instinct dictates, and if I should take royal offense, I will let you know."

"How wise Your Highness is for one so young." Helga kissed me.

Her lips were full and moist on mine. Her tongue seemed to fill my mouth, spreading ripples of excitement. Our pussies ground together as we stood there kissing and quivering. Her breasts crushed mine, nipple pushing against nipple.

"Oh! Oh! Oh!" Even as the lingering kiss ended, I kept on pushing back and forth with my hungry virgin pussy against Helga's high-mounted, squirming *mons veneris*.

"Your Highness." Helga sank to the ermine bath mat

on the Venetian tile floor. She tugged at my hand until I too was on my knees, facing her.

We kissed again. In this kneeling position, it was hard to rub our pussies together. But when our nipples dueled thrillingly with each other, the feeling of burning breast tip against burning breast tip, was so intense that our hands moved naturally between each other's legs. Again Helga stroked the honeyed inside of my quivering virgin pussy. This time I reciprocated and was filled with wonder at the way the mouth of Helga's quim closed around my fingertip and seemed to suck my finger up inside the tight, narrow passage until I could feel the thin flesh obstacle of her hymen.

Its presence in no way seemed to lessen Helga's enjoyment. She put her hand over mine and guided a second finger up her honeyed hole. Then she resumed playing with my pussy, stroking rhythmically and stirring until the hot spurtings of my honey were disgracing the ermine bath mat between us.

Finally Helga twisted her finger in my cunt until it was coated with this sweetness, and then removed it and held it up in front of her mouth. She stuck out her long, slightly thick tongue and licked the syrup from the finger slowly. Her brown eyes sparkled as she did this, her tight, clutching quim kept pumping up and down on my two fingers.

When she had licked her finger clean, Helga slid it up inside me and stirred again. This time when she took it out, her generous mouth was formed into a tight, pout-lipped O. She put her fingers into it and sucked my honey from them. There was a faint, audible pop when she removed them.

The sound made me laugh. It also excited me. I had heard tales from my sisters of women putting men's pikes in their mouth and sucking the lotion from them

in just such a fashion. I wondered if the female taste
was as satisfying. I asked Helga, "Does it taste good?"

"Delicious, Your Highness."

"I want to try it," I decided. I squeezed Helga's
pussy with my fingers to make sure that she drenched
them, and then I put them in my mouth. They were
sticky and the taste mildly sweet. It was the aroma,
however, which was the real aphrodisiac. I had never in
my life smelled anything so deliciously stimulating. "Sit
back and spread your legs," I told Helga. "I want to sip
directly from the cup."

"Your Highness! Perhaps we are going to far!" Helga
was worried.

"Silence!" I thundered. "That is for me to decide." I
was a princess who was used to getting her own way,
and I was not accustomed to having my wishes challenged by servants. "Now take off your clothes and do
as I say."

"Yes, Your Highness." Helga quickly stripped naked
and lay down on the ermine mat with her legs spread.
Her tawny golden body was athletic as well as voluptuous.

I threw aside the bath towel and straddled her, as
naked as she was. I was facing her feet, and now I put
my hands on her bent knees to widen her legs even
more. I bent my head and my ash-blond tresses trailed
over her glistening ebony muff. I kissed the inside of
her thighs, wiggling my tongue in a way that made the
muscles there tense and strain even more than they had
been.

"Oh, Your Highness!" Helga moaned. "Lick it!"

I moved my tongue up to the pulsing entrance of her
pussy and licked the purple lips. When Helga moaned
again, I stuck my tongue inside and probed. My stirrings must have grazed a particularly sensitive area, for

then she squealed. I pressed my lips to the lips of her pussy and began sucking gently as I continued licking inside her with my tongue. Helga rose up to envelop my mouth with her pussy and began to rock from side to side.

Suddenly she closed her thighs fiercely around my head. Her grip was so tight that it brought on a ringing in my ears. It was so tight that it prevented the royal protest I would have made if I could. And then, suddenly, I didn't care. . . .

Helga had clasped her hands over my hips and pulled me backwards and then raised and lowered me so that my own quivering pussy was spread over her mouth. Now, as the spasms of her lower body twisted my head back and forth, she began sucking deeply at my cunt.

I almost fainted. With my face buried in Helga's cunt as she started to spend, not much air was reaching my lungs. And then the sensations brought on by her sucking had me spending as well, and we came off together so violently that I truly thought I should die.

"How marvelous!" I said when it was over. "Have you ever done this before with anybody else, Helga?"

"No, Your Highness. I have played with myself of course, and made myself feel good, but I have never before done it with another girl as we have just done."

"Well, it feels quite delightful. We shall have to do it again," I decided. "We shall have to do it very often."

"As you wish, Your Highness." Helga sponged the glistening honey from both our faces and put on her clothes. Then she washed me off once again, dried me with the towel, and led me into the adjoining bed-chamber.

A few moments later, Mama joined us there. Helga curtsied deeply. Still wrapped in the towel, my own homage to the Empress, my mother, was more per-functory.

"How clean you look, Toinette," she remarked, using the pet name she reserved for those occasions when she was not displeased with what she harped on as my "frivolous, thoughtless, headstrong" ways. "Your complexion is positively glowing. We must have Helga guide your ablutions more often."

"As often as you like, Mama." I shot Helga a wicked wink over my mother's powdered shoulder.

"Why, Toinette, I do believe you are really growing up. You never used to want to bathe at all. You always stamped your foot and caused a scene at the very suggestion. If you are responsible for this change in attitude, Helga, you are to be commended."

"Thank you, Your Majesty." Helga curtsied deeply again and lowered her eyes. "I do believe that Her Highness found her bath enjoyable."

After that first time, of course, Helga and I did not only indulge our passion in the bath. In love, hot with a lust that seemed to mount with each meeting, we contrived to meet frequently and in all sorts of places. I have already remarked on our cavortings on the Louis XIV satin couch in my sitting room. We also pleasured one another on a picnic blanket beside a riverbank, in a hallway closet, giggling with the danger of being caught, inside a coach carrying me to a ball, and in the hay behind the stables where a carelessly flung pitchfork came within an inch of skewering my royal derriere before ever it might grace the throne of France.

Now after some months of such deliciously satisfying escapades, the menstruation signifying my womanhood had brought that throne within reach. It marked the beginnning of a new era, the end of an old age. For a hundred years or more, France had been a thorn in the side of the Hapsburgs. She made war every time our empire expanded. Indeed, in this century alone, our two countries had fought over Poland and Italy and the boundaries of the Rhine.

While this had not stopped our expansion (dear Papa, before his death, had been Holy Roman Emperor of a German nation which included Austria, Hungary, Czechoslovakia, half of Romania, a third of Yugoslavia, and Lombardy and Tuscany), the constant battling had drained the wealth of both empires. Indeed, history has known no more costly feud than the one between my family, the Hapsburgs, and the family of the man who would be my husband, the Bourbons. Despite this, my mother the Empress believed firmly in the motto by which Hapsburg power had always been most successfully spread: "Others make war, but thou, O happy Austria, makest marriages." I was the instrument of that policy, the Viennese cream puff offered to a French king with a sweet tooth in exchange for peace.

The King was Louis XV, grandfather of the Dauphin I was to marry. He was as wily at diplomacy and shifting alliances as he was malleable in the boudoir. (Louis XV ruled France, but his mistresses—first Madame Pompadour, now Madame Du Barry—it was said with justification, ruled Louis XV.)

One year after I was born, Louis XV was callously abandoned by his longtime ally, the King of Prussia. Unexpectedly, a brilliant stroke, Louis established an alliance with France's traditional enemy, Austria. The prospect of no longer having France nipping at their heels made the Hapsburgs eager to accept this alliance. And so, for fourteen years the Austrians and French fought on the same side. And for fourteen years these allies were losers.

Both Frenchmen and Austrians were disgusted. If they couldn't beat these new enemies, then they wanted to go back to killing each other. Tradition! However, their rulers knew that the two nations were dependent on each other for military support. Alone, each of them would have been too vulnerable to enemies. And so, from the time of my father's death when I was a little girl of nine years and the Dauphin was a young boy, a delicate diplomacy had flowed between the two countries.

The object of this diplomacy, *mes amis*? Why, Mama's motto, of course. The object was matrimony!

Towards this end, now that I had entered puberty, Mama's advice giving in the privacy of the boudoir we now shared, became even more urgent. "Nature seems to have denied everything to Mousieur le Dauphin," she told me in describing what her emissaries at Versailles had learned about my future husband. "He has, I fear, only a limited amount of common sense."

I confess that I shrugged off this particular warning. After all, Mama had always regarded me as a flibberti-gibbet not given to serious thought. Why then should I worry about Louis' intelligence? Somehow Mama did not manage to get across to me that it might have something to do with his ability to rule France when the time came. If she had, I might have been better pre-pared for our fate, Louis' and mine.

Some of Mama's advice gave me a start. One night, pacing back and forth in the vast boudoir with its mas-sive gold and white pieces of sculpture, she spoke to me as follows: "Don't show curiosity; this is a point on which you give me great anxiety."

It was as if she had been watching when, only an hour before, I had made Helga stretch her pussy wide with the fingers of both hands so that I might examine just how it looked inside following the orgasm my lips had drawn forth from it!

On another occasion, Mama had tried to drive home another point by pounding her fist on a marble dressing table with ormolu trim. "You must learn how to refuse!" she told me, spacing out the words to make her point.

Again I was startled. That very day I had given in to Helga's caresses and missed my elocution lessons. Alas! Mama was right, but I never did learn to say no when my body was urging me to say *oui*.

One piece of advice that Mama gave me, however, I did follow. I followed it even when I became Queen of France. I followed it, I fear, to the guillotine. The advice was this: "Remain a good German!"

Ahh, Mama! You chose to ignore that I had been born and raised in Vienna. To a Viennese such advice means only that one should enlarge one's libidinous horizons to include shackles and whips now and then.

As a girl in Vienna, of course, I knew as little of such matters as did Mama herself. When I wasn't engaged with Helga, or mooning over her, I frequently caught myself daydreaming over my husband-to-be. I knew very little about him except that he was a year older than I was.

Mama knew little more than I did, and what she did know was hardly reassuring. "He evidently indulges a queer taste for lock making," she told me. "And the King has been overheard remarking that his grandson is 'not a normal boy.'"

Lock making? Not normal? I repeated this to Helga who thought it made the Dauphin sound intriguing and that it boded well for an interesting wedding night.

The only picture I had of the Dauphin was not a

picture at all but a symbolic representation. It showed a shining black dolphin leaping into the air and discharging fire into the sky from its nostrils. The background looked vaguely like Laxenburg, where we Hapsburgs had our shooting lodge. Some obscure attempt at détente had doubtless dictated the French dolphin spewing his fire over an Austrian landscape. However, it is only in retrospect that I perceive this.

At the time I thought the picture silly. When Helga tried to translate it into phallic terms for me, I commanded her to stop her teasing. Hungry as my royal pussy was to learn at first hand the mysteries of lovemaking with a man, I was put off rather than aroused by the idea of some eellike fish inserting its cold nose there and blowing hot fire to burn away my chastity.

Finally, after repeated requests, three portraits of the Dauphin, realistic engravings, were received from Paris. They showed a hulk of a boy, fat and dull-eyed, plowing in the fields. The informality of these poses made Mama furious. She fumed over the lack of gallantry. And as for me, my heart sank at the peasant appearance of my future husband. Even Helga's consolations that he looked quite the animal and so would doubtless be a fierce lover could not lift my spirits.

These feelings were only assuaged when two formal portraits were subsequently sent. These showed Louis-Auguste (as the Dauphin was sometimes called to distinguish him from his grandfather the King) in full ceremonial dress, wigged and powdered. The artist had been kinder, and a monocle disguised the dullness of at least one of his eyes. The royal scarlet made him look portly, but he also looked imposing, and by squinting, I could even convince myself that he looked quite kingly.

Mama's ire was also soothed. "Now here is a prince

more deserving of the hand of a daughter of the Caesars," she said. It was the same description of me—a family boast—which she had been using all along to promote the marriage to the French.

At long last the marriage itself did take place—albeit by proxy. It was preceded by a ceremony in which I signed a paper renouncing my claim of succession to the Austrian throne. (Mama was taking no chances that the Bourbons might ever use the marriage as an excuse to move in on the realm of the Hapsburgs.)

Following this ceremony, I was guest of honor at a supper hosted by my brother in the Belvedere for fifteen hundred guests. This was followed by a ball attended by six thousand aristocrats wearing masks and white dominos. The ballroom, lit by some 3,500 candles, was lavishly decorated with carved wall sconces bearing flaming "torches of love," sculpted dolphins in tribute to my absent bridegroom, priceless painted Greek vases flowing with Rhine wine and borne by children dressed as seraphim, papier-mâché hearts and garlands and flowers. There were eight hundred firemen present, moving through the guests with damp sponges to extinguish such sparks as fell from the chandeliers. There was a corps of dentists on hand to assist guests suffering from toothaches brought on by the rich viands, even equipped to extract their teeth if necessary. Indeed, it was the most elaborate royal affair which Vienna had seen in some time.

And how did I disport myself during these festivities? I drank wine (Mama allowed it since soon I would be a married lady). I circulated among the guests and conversed with them. I danced with the most important nobles and members of the court, the older ones, and even one or two of the younger men as well. I performed the role of a queen-to-be to perfection. And when the time was auspicious, I slipped from the scene to the quarters of my maidservant, Helga, doffed my elaborate ball gown, slid between the sheets of her bed, and licked her delicious pussy while she in turn sucked at mine.

The next day there was another fête given by the French ambassador in my honor. And the day after that, at six in the evening, I was escorted in great pomp—fireworks and trumpets and kettledrums—from the palace to the Church of the Augustines for the proxy marriage ceremony. Here my brother, the Archduke Ferdinand, only a year and a half older than I, stood in for Louis-Auguste and exchanged the nuptial vows with me. The Papal nuncio, Monsignor Visconti, performed the royal ceremony. And all the time he was intoning over us in Latin, that toad Ferdinand, the brother of mine whom I liked least, had his hand up under the train of my dress where I was kneeling and was pinching my bottom.

"The frogs will eat you!" he whispered nastily under cover of the ritual kiss we exchanged. And he contrived to twist my breast cruelly.

It did not seem an auspicious beginning to my marriage!

Helga helped me laugh my qualms away. "If the frogs eat you," she pointed out, "perhaps you will like it. I have heard that the French are most adept in such matters."

"As adept as you, my dove?" I asked.

"I learned from you, and you from me, and now you will learn from them and perhaps they from you, Your Highness."

Ahh, Helga! Always so practical. How I would miss

her in France. I had wanted to take her with me, but Mama had explained the strict French protocol which forbade me to bring anybody or anything Austrian with me when I crossed the border. It was symbolic of my wholeheartedly adopting French nationality, and necessary if I was one day to be proclaimed Queen of France.

Two days after the ceremony, I left Vienna forever. My entourage included 132 guardsmen, fifty carriages, each drawn by six white Lipizzaner steeds changed four times a day, and an elite group of ladies-in-waiting and maidservants—Helga among them—who would see to my needs until we reached French soil.

The journey took a week. At the end of that time the royal procession arrived on the banks of the River Rhine near Kehl. Across the river was France. On this side was Austria. In the middle of the river was a small island, unoccupied, and therefore owing allegiance to neither country. It was on this island that the transformation of my person from Austrian to French was to be accomplished.

To expedite this, a lavish domicile had been built on the island. It had two entrances—one Austrian, one French—two antechambers, and four small rooms. There was also a large hall. It was here that the transformation ceremony was to take place.

Before that, however, a less public but equally symbolic rite was dictated. A select quartet of Austrian ladies-in-waiting was to strip me naked and deliver me in this condition to an equally select quartet of French noblewomen who would dress me in French regalia for the diplomatic ceremony.

The first thing I noted when I arrived on the island was the difference between these two foursomes. My Austrian ladies were young and gay and perhaps a bit frivolous. The Frenchwomen were all middle-aged and circumspect and obviously took their duties towards me very seriously. As soon as I saw them, I was glad that I had brought Helga along as the maid to perform the actual undressing of my body.

When she had done this and I was completely nude, I asked my Austrian ladies to wait outside the room. When I was ready, I told them, I would emerge and they could then conduct me to the French chambers and deliver me to the French noblewomen waiting there. But first, I told them, I wanted to be alone, to pray. Not one of them, of course, dared to question why Helga remained behind with me whilst I said my prayers.

By the time I emerged from the room, having bid Helga good-bye for the very last time, my Austrian ladies were growing impatient. The expressions on their faces said that they were wondering why I had been so long at my prayers. I ignored this, however, stood before them proud and tall and naked, with the nipples of my budding breasts still quite stiff, and announced that I was ready to be delivered to France.

This they did, some of them weeping as they handed my nude person over to the French. The Frenchwomen, for their part, received me with cold formality. It was not hard to guess that they disapproved of an Austrian princess marrying into the line which would rule over them.

Their eyes pored over my naked figure. They studied every detail. Grudgingly, they satisfied themselves that I had brought nothing Austrian to sully French soil save my person. Only then did they begin to dress me in French finery for the ceremony.

Ahh! Even then, young as I was, I had contrived to outwit those bourgeois French noblewomen. They thought my nakedness proof that nothing Austrian save my flesh had invaded their country. Well, *mes amis*, they were mistaken!

On my unwashed lips, even as they laid hands on me, was the sweetest of Austrian cunnilingual honey!

Chapter Three

No matter the Viennese syrup on my tongue, when I entered France I was a virgin, trained to modesty, accustomed to lowering my eyes in the presence of noblemen. I had been trained to do this; first a fluttering of dark gold lashes, and then a casting down of my brilliant blue eyes until their golden spiderwebbed gaze fell to that level deemed most indicative of shyness. What a farce, *mes amis*! Despite Mama's warning, it was my curiosity which focused that downcast glance. And what it focused on was the tight crotches of the gentlemen's britches as they made their sweeping bows to me!

"What can it be like to have a stick of flesh hanging between one's legs?" I had voiced my curiosity to Helga more than once back in Vienna as we lay panting in each other's arms after spending. "Do men ever sit on it inadvertently? How do they decide which trouser leg it should hang down?"

"And what about that little bag with the two marbles?" she had replied on one such occasion. "If ladies must ride sidesaddle to protect their chastity, how is it that men riding astraddle do not destroy their virility with each crunch of the scrotum?"

"*Oui*! Truly such genitalia are fraught with danger," I had decided. "I have heard that they swell to twice their size upon the slightest provocation. And they grow so stiff that surely within the confinement of men's britches they are in danger of snapping and breaking off!"

"It is surely less perilous to be a woman, Your Highness." Helga's brown eyes had twinkled. "It may be better to give than to receive, but it is surely safer to receive!"

"But Helga—" My own eyes grew very big and round. "What if when it is all swollen and hard and the man puts it up inside a girl's delicate pussy, what if it should snap and break off then?"

"Ahh, Your Highness, that could be both good news and bad news for the lady involved."

"What do you mean, Helga? Explain yourself."

"Well, Your Highness, how often in my virgin dreams I have wished for a man's thing inside me, and so might it not be good news to have one wedged there permanently? On the other hand, it would be the same one always, and would prevent the insertion of another which might be more desirable, thicker, or longer, or more innovative, and would that circumstance not be bad news?"

"Indeed it would!" I agreed with her second scenario. "And speaking for myself, Helga, I should hasten to have such a snapped-off blade extricated. After all, variety in such insertions is surely intended to be the spice of any queen's life!"

How advanced were our Vienna wonderings, considering how little actual experience we had of masculine appurtenances. Helga, having fondled a few cocks in their breeches to the point of discharge, knew more than I, but truly not so very much more as to have the anatomy down quite right. In truth, when I left Vienna, men's groins were far less a matter of knowledge than of speculation to me. However, with my modestly downcast, crotch-directed gaze, I was prepared to speculate quite intensely upon crossing into France!

As it happened, the very first object of this speculation was a succulently bulging crotch which one day would affect my life more than I could have dreamed at the time. The *epée* ensconced there, more than any other in France, would be responsible for bringing down the *ancien régime* and for the bloodbath which followed. In truth, it may be said that this *epée extraordinaire* altered the course of history.

This bulge which drew my eyes was caused by the noble pike of Prince-Bishop Louis de Rohan, nephew to the venerable Bishop-Cardinal Prince de Rohan. Louis De Rohan was already designated to succeed his uncle as Bishop of Strasbourg. He would one day be Cardinal of France.

Prince de Rohan was the official greeter for the church at Strasbourg, my first destination in France proper. My new French ladies-in-waiting escorted me there. We were preceded by an honor guard in full regalia, which had been provided by King Louis XV to replace the Austrian entourage I had left behind me. Prince-Bishop de Rohan did not actually pronounce his benediction until the morning after my arrival.

My arrival itself was greeted by a spectacle I shall never forget. Cheering French throngs lined the road into the city. Buxom young farm girls risked the high-kicking hooves of our horses to strew the road with flowers. Little boys and little girls dressed in shepherd costumes deluged me with bouquets. A miniature regiment composed of small boys in the uniform of Swiss Guards flanked the procession. We were forced to make many stops over the last few miles as local aristocrats with their liveried servants rode up on horseback to present their compliments and to ply me with their prize champagne served in golden goblets.

After entering the city I was presented to the aged Cardinal de Rohan and to the flatulent curmudgeons who comprised the Council of the Cathedral. I also received thirty-six noble Alsatian dowagers, each with a visage more forbidding than the other. Then the afternoon trailed into evening with presentations of gifts from the various craft guilds in the area. (These guildsmen, at least, were neither female, nor pious, nor over seventy, and some of them indeed appeared quite interestingly firm of flesh.)

More to a young princess's liking was the entertainment in my honor that evening. A feast of Bacchus had been arranged, and, fittingly, the champagne flowed like water. The highlight of the dinner entertainment was a wild dance performed by savagely gyrating coopers twirling and leaping in and out of the hoops of the barrels they made.

After dinner I was escorted to the theater to view my first French play, *La servante-maîtresse*. Strasbourg was lit up in my honor as if for a Festival of the Sacred Virgin. On the way back from the theater I was shown the barges draped with garlands on the River Ill and the decorations draping the trees of the park across the river.

Later, from the terrace of the Bishop's palace where I was staying, I watched fireworks explode from the barges and light up the sky. Jets of water rose into the air from both shores of the river. At the finale, the fireworks spelled out the initials of Louis-Auguste Bourbon and

Maria Antonia Hapsburg in the night sky while nearby a choir of several hundred voices sang a lusty rendition of "Long Live the King."

The next morning I was conducted to the cathedral to receive the blessing of the church from the handsome Prince-Bishop Louis de Rohan, Bishop Coadjutor of Strasbourg. He received me on the front steps of the edifice. Behind him the huge doors had been thrown open and the music from the mighty organs was drowning out the shouts of acclamation from the throng gathered behind me. Even as I mounted the steps to approach him, I was struck by the sensual charisma of this tall, handsome churchman.

At this time, when first I met him, Prince de Rohan was in his early thirties, at the peak of his physical attractiveness to women. His deep-set eyes were as blue as my own, and his dark, straight hair blended into an intriguingly premature gray at the temples. His features with their high cheekbones, square, cleft chin, and Grecian nose identified his profile immediately as that of an aristocrat. (Indeed, his visage seemed almost a symbol of his noble family's motto: "If I cannot be a king, I disdain to be a prince; the name of Rohan shall suffice!" This motto appeared over the gates of all the Rohans' Strasbourg palaces.) Standing before me now on the steps in the full-length, ermine-trimmed silken scarlet robes of his office, the heavily gold-encrusted and bejeweled miter of the church circling his noble brow, Prince de Rohan was so sensually charismatic that my knees trembled and I felt a familiar warm liquidity well up deep inside me.

His words, summoning up the disapproving visage of my mother as they did, brought me back to my senses. "You will be for us the living symbol of the beloved Empress whom Europe has so long admired and whom posterity will continue to venerate. The spirit of Maria Theresa and the Hapsburgs of Austria is about to be united through you with the spirit of the Bourbons."

I knelt briefly there on the steps of the cathedral, kissed his ring, and then rose and followed him inside. He led me to the altar, and there, under the high Gothic arches, he delivered a tribute to my marriage to the Dauphin: "The golden age will be born from such a union and under the happy rule of Marie Antoinette and Louis-Auguste, we will see the continuation of the happiness we enjoy under the reign of Louis the Beloved."

Flowery words, but I thought I detected just the slightest hint of amusement in the tone of the voice which delivered them. I had no time to dwell on this. It was time for the benediction.

Again I knelt, this time on the thick red velvet arranged at the base of the altar. The tall, slender, magnificently robed figure of Prince-Bishop de Rohan towered over me. As he raised the monstrance, the heartbreaking notes of a harp sounded from high up in the choir loft. After a moment his hand descended and I kissed the jeweled bishop's ring he wore. Then I bowed my head and he clasped his long, slender, aristocratic hands on top of it for a moment of silent prayer.

And that's when it happened!

There was an almost inaudible rustling inside his long robe, and then he contrived to kick its folds to one side. I—and I alone—was in position to see what this maneuver revealed. The way his hands were holding my head, you see, my eyes were on a level with the crotch of the prelate's satin britches. Inexperienced as I was, there was no mistaking the throbbing evidence in front of my eyes.

Prince-Bishop Louis de Rohan had a full-blown erection!

After a moment, his hands eased on the top of my head. Then they pressed gently towards the back so that my face turned upwards towards him. There was open and laughing lechery in the eyes which looked down at me.

I was a Hapsburg princess, "a daughter of the Caesars"! No man—certainly no Frenchman—had the right to mock me in this fashion. Without even stopping to think about it, I stuck my tongue out at the Prince-Bishop.

He misconstrued my impertinence. He raised his head towards the high Gothic arches of the cathedral. There was a look of exaltation on his face. At the same time his hands tightened at the back of my head and pressed my face into voluminous folds of his scarlet robes. A sigh swept over the aristocratic onlookers at this reverent interlude of silent communion between us. They could not of course see that under the cover of his robes the Prince-Bishop had contrived to press my pouting Hapsburg lips to the bulge of his crotch.

Instinctively, I caught my breath as I felt his shaft pulsing against my lips through the satin. The sudden strong inhalation caught him offguard. His cock bucked violently against my teeth. A slippery wetness spurted through his trousers and smeared my pouting lips.

It was there still when he rearranged his robes and lifted me to my feet. I washed it away with the sacrament of the wine and resisted the impulse to suck at his long, penislike fingers, when he placed the wafer on my tongue. He blessed me again, his blue eyes more tender than mocking now, and the meaning of his gaze was unmistakable. It said that young as I was, I was a most desirable woman, that this was only the beginning for us, that he wanted me completely, and that he was arrogantly sure that I wanted him as well.

The rest of the ceremonies went by in a blur for me.

That afternoon I embarked with my entourage on the seven-day journey across France to my Bridegroom. In the privacy of my carriage, I listened with interest as the grim-faced middle-aged ladies assigned to me let down their hair enough to gossip—albeit disapprovingly—about the handsome and magnetic Prince-Bishop Louis de Rohan of Strasbourg.

Even these ladies were not so naive as to think that just because he was a man of the church, de Rohan would deny himself the pleasures of the world. It had become commonplace to wink at the escapades of hard-drinking and hot-blooded churchmen. But de Rohan, they sniffed, went too far!

For one thing, he was a sadistic and insatiable quail hunter. He held the world's record for the number of shots fired in one day—1,328—which meant that he had gotten off two a minute for more than ten straight hours despite the necessity of reloading after each discharge of his musket. For another, the hunt parties he hosted at his Saverne château were renowned for their drunkenness. His licentiousness with free-spirited ladies of the local aristocracy was the scandal of the province. And he had left a trail of cuckolded noblemen in Paris so long that Louis XV—himself no stranger to forbidden beds—had suggested he absent himself from the city until husbandly tempers cooled down.

Currently, de Rohan was involved in a scandalous relationship with the petite and beautiful Marquise de Marigny. De Rohan had dressed his Marquise as a choirboy so that she might travel with him in his ecclesiatical carriage. Once he had been observed pleasuring her in the coach, and at first it was thought that the prelate was sodomizing some young soprano castrati. But then the Marquise de Marigny turned over and her naked pear-shaped breasts attested that while de

Rohan might be an incorrigible libertine, one even given to buggery on occasion, for him the buttocks of preference were undeniably female.

Such gossip fired my imagination. That hard, spurting shaft against my lips was an omen to be treasured. Were the groins of all Frenchmen given to such impetuous tributes? Or was it only French churchmen who consecrated in this manner? Was royalty also given to such gestures? Would my Dauphin, Louis, lay on his nuptial blessing with such a bold and sizable royal scepter? Inexperienced as I was, I could only hope.

Ahh, the optimism of youth, particularly of young, virgin princesses. I clung to mine even after my first meeting with Louis. The meeting took place at a crossroads in a forest near Compiègne.

The Dauphin was waiting there with his grandfather, King Louis XV of France, surely the most ungrandfatherly looking monarch one might imagine. Nor was the King's attitude towards me grandfatherly. When reading the sparkle in his eyes aright, I presented my cheek for his welcoming kiss, King Louis contrived to turn me away from the rest of those gathered to greet me and to squeeze each of my breasts in turn before releasing me.

(First the Bishop, now the King! What promise France showed!)

Of mature years, King Louis was nevertheless quite attractive. He was a *man*, not a boy, and what he had learned from his famous amours was writ intriguingly in the laugh lines of his craggy visage. He was tall and his complexion was florid (he was a connoisseur of wine as well as women, a taste which permanently pinkened his countenance). He had an outdoorsman's body, sat a horse with aristocratic ease, and turned a fine, silk-stockinged leg. Irresistible to women, occasionally irascible, he nevertheless conveyed a truly kingly manner in which dignity was leavened by humor.

When he and the Dauphin joined me in my carriage to continue the journey, replacing the elder two of my three French ladies-in-waiting, the King claimed the seat next to me and put his hand immediately on my knee. "Marie Antoinette." He addressed me by the French name which was now mine. "I am relieved to meet you in person." He squeezed my thigh, ignoring his grandson, my husband-to-be.

"Relieved, sire?" I cocked my head prettily, flattered by the obvious approval of this mature monarch.

"Yes, my dear. You see, our emissary in Vienna was an idiot. I asked him upon his return what he thought of you. In particular, I inquired if you had developed any breasts."

"Oh, sire!" I blushed prettily and lowered my eyes. King Louis' velvet crotch was quite interestingly distended. I think it was at that moment that I began to get some idea of the power I might have over the mightiest of Frenchmen.

"The idiot told me that you had a lovely face and charming blue eyes!"

"And have I disappointed you, sire?" I flirted with the King.

"No, my dear. You most certainly have not. But you see, that was not the question I had asked the gentleman. I had inquired as to your bosom."

"Well, perhaps he was being gallant, Your Majesty. I am still quite young and my breasts are small, but they are developing quite nicely, I think."

"Quite nicely indeed, my child." He stroked the creamy naked mounds rising from the bodice of my gown. "And he was indeed being gallant. He told me that he had not taken the liberty of studying your budding breasts with his eyes. And do you know what I told him, my dear?"

"No, Your Majesty. What?"

"I told him that he was a fool! I told him that it was the first thing one should look at in a woman!"

"Then you are not displeased, Your Majesty?"

"Not at all." He leaned close and whispered in my ear. "I find you quite delicious," he murmured. "*Oui*, a succulent Viennese pastry quite to the taste of an old lovemaking machine such as myself." He leaned back and winked and for the first time turned his attention to his grandson, the Dauphin. "How I envy you the deflowering of such a treasure, my boy," he told him.

Blushing even more deeply, I looked at the Dauphin from beneath my lowered lashes. His only response to his grandfather's remark was a noncommittal grunt. I smiled at him, tremulously, but with warmth. The younger Louis did not smile back.

"It was good of you to take such trouble to meet me." I addressed the Dauphin directly.

"Grandpapa made me." His tone was sullen.

"Oh." I continued to study from him from my lowered eyes, trying not to be obvious about it. After all, he was to be my husband.

The Dauphin Louis was even then quite large—which is to say both tall and stout and of a somewhat lumbering appearance as well. He was almost sixteen years old, but he had not as yet developed any poise (nor would he). Climbing into the coach, his movements had been quite clumsy and uncoordinated. His eyes, without sparkle, were like those of an owl, large and round, and they bulged in a singularly unattractive fashion. There was—alas!—no corresponding bulge at the juncture of his britches. Indeed, his manner of dress was so slovenly and loose as to reveal nothing at all of his manly potential.

"I have been told that you are interested in lock making," I remembered, trying to draw him out.

He grunted and nodded. His grandfather sighed and squeezed my thigh again as if to reassure me that regardless of what the future might hold with this dolt of a boy, he would be there to console me. In truth, as I regarded my husband-to-be, I was not ungrateful for such consolation.

"Would you like to tell me about your other interests," I suggested to young Louis.

"Horses," he muttered.

"You like to ride? Oh, good!" I clapped my hands. "So do I! We can go for a ride together every morning after we are married."

"It is the late-night gallops that make the marriage." The King winked at me.

"I don't like to ride, "Louis grunted. "I always fall off the horse."

"But I thought you said? . . ."

"Horses is what I said. It's one of my other interests."

"Oh. Breeding them?" I guessed again.

"Breeding women is a lot more fun, my boy!" The King smiled cynically.

"Not breeding them," the Dauphine explained. "Shoeing them."

"I beg your pardon?" I was confused.

"Blacksmithing. It's a hobby of mine, like lock making."

"I see." It explained Louis' bouquet. He smelled of the stables. This aroma would follow him throughout our marriage. Alas, it was not so much the aroma of horses, which I like and even have on occasion found to be virile and interesting when it attaches itself to a man, as it was the odious odor of their leavings.

"Also, I lay bricks," Louis added.

"Oo-la-la!" The lady-in-waiting who was riding with us had misheard.

"An odd euphemism." The King also misunderstood. "But I think you're getting the general idea, my boy."

Now it was I who sighed. Somehow I did not at all think that Louis was getting the idea. My optimism had survived his dry-lipped and uninterested kiss of greeting back at the crossroads, but now his total lack of response to my usually infallible Viennese coquetry was cooling my anticipation of the wedding night.

That unmemorable event—my wedding night—took place two days later. It was preceded by the wedding itself, and by other ceremonies as well. I think that of all the gala events of that day, my bridegroom enjoyed the banquet between wedding and wedding night the most.

The wedding took place in the Chapel Royal of the palace at Versailles. I wore a white brocade gown sewn with diamonds. I had brought some of these stones with me from Vienna. King Louis XV presented me with other jewels to be sewn on my wedding gown. He was very specific as to where they should go and spent an interesting prenuptial half hour pressing these gems against different parts of my bodice to judge their effect. (The effect on me was to harden my nipples; the effect on King Louis was to harden his priapus; the effect on the bridal gown? *Très chic!*)

My bridegroom wore a golden suit which was also trimmed with diamonds. Perspiring profusely, he looked like a rhinoceros which had just stepped out of its waterhole and into the glow of a rainbow. His nervousness caused him to jolt my arm at the end of the ceremony as I was signing the marriage register. The blot this caused, I suppose, was a sign of marital things to come.

Over five thousand guests, aristocrats all, attended the wedding. They not only filled the chapel, but the Hall of Mirrors as well. All were dressed formally, and in the height of fashion. To my Austrian eyes, this French display of opulence seemed not unlike a convocation of peacocks.

Following the ceremony, I received those members of my personal household who wished to tender their oaths of allegiance to me. Among them was my wig maker, my bath attendant, my perfumer, my manicurist, my poodle walker, and my food taster. I received them graciously, as I had been taught, and accepted their good wishes for my wedding night without any undue display of embarrassment.

This over with, I joined the King and my bridegroom in the Hall of Mirrors for a game of whist. Some six thousand people, admitted by invitation only, paraded through the hall to observe us as we played our cards. Nervous as I was at being so observed, my Viennese training in the arts of gaming held firm and I won three games from King Louis and my bridegroom. Only after I got to know him much better did I realize that the King had let me win for the pleasure of watching my breasts bounce up and down as I flung down the final cards in triumph. The Dauphin, on the other hand, was an execrable whist player.

He was also, I learned later that evening, an impossible dancer. When, by tradition, as bride and groom we led off the first cotillion, poor Louis not only tripped all over his own feet but mangled mine as well. When the King took pity on me and replaced him as my partner, I was quite grateful. So grateful, indeed, that I made not the slightest protests at his rather public pawings of my person.

Once the ball was underway, we were free to sit down to our wedding dinner. The King sat at the head of the royal table with myself on one side of him and the bridegroom on the other. I noticed that at the far end of the table was seated a strikingly beautiful woman whose powdered wig could not hide her curly black hair. She had a complexion like peach blossoms and the large breasts rising from her low-cut gown were truly magnetic to the eye. From my very first sight of them, I was jealous of those breasts.

"Who is she?" I inquired of the woman seated on my other side, one Mme. de Noailles.

"Madame Du Barry," was the answer.

"And what is her function?" I asked.

"To give the King pleasure!" King Louis himself had overheard our conversation and now it was he who forthrightly answered my question.

"In that case, sire," I answered just as boldly, "I am going to be her rival."

King Louis threw back his head and laughed. All heads turned to observe the monarch's merriment. But at the far end of the table, Du Barry was not looking at him. She was looking at me. The expression on her lovely face told me that I had made an enemy. The sensual heaving of her bosom told me that she could be a very dangerous one.

All of this passed right by the Dauphin without his noticing. For the first time on this our wedding day, my husband was engaging in an activity he enjoyed. He was shoveling food into his mouth with great gusto, pausing only for an occasional burp. "Fat Louis," as he was called behind his back, was doing what he did best: overeating.

The King regarded his grandson's gustatory gusto with dismay. He stayed the hand wielding the fork with his own and tried to advise him. "It is not a good idea to overload your stomach tonight," he told him, his wily eyes sliding meaningfully towards me and back.

"Why not?" Young Louis was oblivious. "I always sleep better after I've eaten well."

The King looked at me directly and shrugged sadly. I managed a tremulous smile, although it did not reflect the way I was feeling. The King found my hand under the table and carried it to his lap. The throbbing lump there belied his age.

"No matter," he said aloud. "Hot Bourbon blood will wash away the indiscretion of youthful gluttony. Particularly," he added, "with the inspiration of such delectable Hapsburg flesh."

And if not, the throbbing under my fingertips was saying, foxy Grandpapa will be around to provide solace!

Faced with my bridegroom smacking wet lips over his food and belching, such reassurance, despite its lecherous nature, was indeed comforting. This time I meant the smile I bestowed upon the King. At the far end of the table Madame Du Barry's cannonball breasts rose and fell angrily. I half expected to see fire spewing from her quivering nostrils.

After the wedding dinner, as befit a royal couple, young Louis and I were put to bed. A throng of aristocrats pressed into the bridal chamber to watch as the Archbishop of Rheims sprinkled the bed with holy water and prayed that our union would be fertile. Still blushing from all the attention, I retired to an antechamber where the youngest of my ladies-in-waiting, Mme. de Chartres, helped me into the clinging satin nightgown Mama had calculatingly selected for the occasion.

Her hands were kind, but the prospect of Louis made me long for the more intimate attentions of dear Helga.

Meanwhile, the King himself was helping his grandson into his nightshirt. Doubtless he was attempting some last-minute instruction. Doubtless the bridegroom had no idea what his grandfather was trying to say.

Finally the King came into the antechamber and requested a moment alone with me before I should join my bridegroom. Mme. de Chartres glanced at my revealing nightgown and raised an eyebrow. Impatiently, the King waved her away and she left the room.

"I wanted to take this last opportunity to convey my royal blessing." He embraced me. Both his hands slid appreciatively over the slippery satin stretched across my high, firm, well-rounded bottom.

"Thank you, sire." I could not courtesy. His grasp was too firm.

"Marriages are never happy," he counseled me. "Occasionally, however, they are pleasant." He squeezed my buttocks appreciatively, the gesture of a connoisseur. "Let us hope that this marriage will be pleasant."

"I too hope so, Your Majesty." I stepped back as he reluctantly released me. And then, on sudden impulse, I asked an impertinent question. "Will you go to Madame Du Barry tonight?" I blurted out.

The King threw back his head and laughed so loudly that all those waiting in the next room, my bridal chamber, could not help hearing. "Of course, dear child. I must. It is an absolute necessity." His jaded eyes riveted themselves to the nightgown from my body and intimately caressed my trembling, naked flesh. "But I will be thinking of you, Marie. Rest assured of that. I will be thinking of you!"

I accepted his arm and he escorted me into the bridal chamber. Here the King formally turned me over to his grandson, the Dauphin. Then the King superintended the ritual of our getting into the four-poster bed together. He personally drew the silken monogrammed sheets over our thin-clad bodies. He bestowed his royal blessing once again and then turned on his heel and led the exodus from the bridal chamber. The two attendants who were the last to leave drew the side curtains of the royal four-poster bed. Their footsteps faded away and there was the sound of the door closing behind them. At last my bridegroom and I were alone.

Louis burped loudly.

"Do you feel well?" I inquired.

"*Oui,*" he grunted.

I waited for him to make some movement, some comment befitting a bridegroom.

He made none.

He's just a boy, I reminded myself, *with less experience even than you. He needs encouragement.* Some of Mama's birds-and-bees advice came back to me. I took his hand in mine and pressed it against my breast. "Feel how soft my bosom is," I murmured.

"I don't like soft," he responded. "I like hard. That's why I like to lay bricks. Because they're so hard."

"I like hard too," I assured him. "Hard is so manly." I slid my hand down to the base of his belly and squeezed. Alas! No hardness there. Through the material of Louis' nightshirt, my fist had closed around a sleeping worm.

"I like horses too," Louis reminded me.

"And women?" I inquired. "Don't you like women?"

"You can shoe horses. That's fun."

"You can shoe me if you like." I wasn't quite sure what that might involve, but I was becoming desperate enough to try any innovation.

"Can I hammer the shoes onto the bottoms of your feet?" For the first time Louis sounded a bit interested.

"That sounds quite painful," I told him. "Perhaps we'd better think of something else." Still a girl, I had no knowledge of the interesting combinations of pain and pleasure which aroused some men.

"Plowing?" Louis stifled a yawn.

I giggled.

"What's funny?"

"I had a maid back in Vienna who told me that plowing is what peasants call it when they—when they—well, you know, what we're supposed to be doing."

"They call that plowing?" Again Louis' attention was stirred. "But how?"

I was no expert, but I was more than willing to improvise. "Think of me as the field," I suggested. "Now you are the plow and this is your plow blade." I squeezed his member through his nightshirt again. It was more the consistency of a sponge than of a plow blade. "And this"—I ran my fingers down over the satin nightgown from my belly to my thighs, fingering the satin to display the cleft of my high-mounted mons veneris—"is the furrow which you shall plow."

"That sounds silly," Louis decided. "And besides, I don't think I can remember all that."

"It's a game," I cajoled. "Please play it. To please me."

"Why should I care about pleasing you?"

These were not the words I had anticipated hearing on my wedding night. Gritting my teeth, I nevertheless persisted. "You're going to like this game," I insisted. "It's going to make you feel good. Now get on top of me."

"Oh, all right." Ponderously, he moved until his weight was squashing me into the mattress.

"Could you lean on your elbows?" I gasped. "So I can breathe."

Grudgingly, he shifted so that his weight was not so oppressive. "What now?" he inquired.

"Perhaps you should lift up your nightshirt," I suggested.

"Why?"

"It's how you play the game, Louis," I told him a bit wearily.

"Oh, all right." He lifted his nightshirt, holding it up and out and away from his substantial belly.

I reached between his legs. . . .

"That tickles!"

"Doesn't it feel good?" I cooed.

"No. It just tickles."

"You can play with me too." I ignored his disappointing response and pulled my nightgown above my belly. Still tickling underneath his balls delicately with the fingers of one hand, I grasped his hand with my other hand and pressed it to the entrance of my pussy. Holding it there firmly, I squirmed against it.

A few moments of this, and suddenly Louis jerked his hand away. "Hold on!" he said. "You've wet the bed!"

"I've done no such thing!" I was indignant.

"It's all right," he assured me. "I do it all the time. Sometimes I even—"

Oh, God! Why had I ever left Vienna?

"That's not from . . . that's the way I . . . it's what happens to a girl when a man excites her." Finally I managed to phrase it.

"You didn't make pee-pee?"

"No!"

"Oh." Louis sounded disappointed. He pulled down his nightshirt and stretched out on the bed as far away from me as he could get. "I knew I wasn't going to like this game! It's nothing like real plowing at all!" And with that observation, he turned over on his side facing away from me and closed his eyes. A few moments later he was snoring.

I lay there with my nightie up. I kicked off the sheet. The night air tickled the tendrils of blond hair over my mound of Venus. I thought longingly of Helga and sighed. I thought of Prince-Bishop de Rohan blessing my lips through his britches at the Cathedral of Strasbourg and pursed my mouth. I thought of King Louis, that old lovemaking machine, and the expertness of his hands on my breasts and buttocks, and I squirmed. I slid one of my hands down the bodice of my nightgown and found the stiffening nipple of my girl breast. I curled my other hand between my legs. I closed my eyes. . . .

Helga's tongue—warm, wet, velvety—licked my straining nipples in that tantalizing way that only Helga's tongue could. . . . The Prince-Bishop's hard, thick, naked pike stuck out of his britches behind the parted folds of his ecclesiatical robes and forced its way between my hot, moist lips, sliding all the way into my mouth, down my throat, brutal, pumping. . . . The King's royal scepter rubbed against my naked bottom as I sat on his lap, my pussy bouncing and clutching, laughing because the beautiful Du Barry was watching, snarling, her fabulous breasts panting with fury. . . .

Du Barry, bare breasts free of the bodice of her gown, raven tresses flying wildly with her violent motions, snapped a whip over the bare haunches of the King, leaving streaks of blood behind while at the same time impelling His Majesty to ram his gnarled and randy prick—tough as a mutton bone—all the way up Helga's sopping, twisting quim. . . . Prince-Bishop de Rohan came up behind Du Barry and lifted her skirts and pulled down her bloomers and plunged his thick pike deep between her buttocks just as he was rumored to have done to his petite mistress in his coach. . . . I watched the writhing four-some as they whipped and buggered and fucked each other and I pushed a fist up between my legs, not caring about my virginity, and pounded my pussy until I couldn't stand it, and then I flung myself into their whipping, moaning, flesh-joined midst. . . .

I licked Helga's lovely plump white bottom down the cleft to where her slavering cunt was engorged with the King's prick and there I sucked gently—her honey-drenched cunt, his hairy balls, the tough, thrusting red shaft of his prick. . . . Du Barry spanked my bare behind as I did this, her hands lingering, her fingers dipping into both vulnerable orifices, her nails sharp and cruel, the laughter trilling with equal cruelty from her lips as my bottom pinkened and writhed. . . . The Prince-Bishop fell atop me and buried his rampaging cock between my budding breasts, rubbing up and down there, his swollen balls bouncing over my nipples, the heart-shaped tip of his prick tickling the underside of my chin, his muscular buttocks rip-pling enticingly with each thrust. . . .

The four of them spread-eagled me then, Du Barry riding one of my feet with the toes crammed up her juicy quim, Helga sucking on one of my naked breasts and playing with herself, the King holding one of my legs high and playing with my bottom, squeezing the spanked pink flesh, pinching it, running his fingers up and down the sensitive cleft separating my buttocks, pushing his finger up my anus to supply an intense sensation that caused me to laugh and cry at the same time that I stared at de Rohan, his fingers twining mine around his fierce, quivering prick. . . . A shifting and a merging and my mouth is stretched impossibly wide by two cocks at the same time, the King's craggy and stabbing, the Prince-Bishop's thick and corkscrewing in rhythm with Helga's tongue stabbing between his muscular buttocks as her scampering fingers teased my yawning pussy and Du Barry's midnight hair fanned out over her lap to screen the pink tongue lapping up the juices between Helga's quivering thighs. . . . Again a changing of positions and the King licks Du Barry's lush bush while his prick stabs in and out of my anus and his mistress sucks my breast, squeezing both of Helga's breasts as she sits on my face, her pink, widespread, juicy pussy spreading succulently over my mouth and squirming and squeezing and squirming some more as I swallow her honey, my legs thrashing in the air, my wide-open, pulsing pussy yearning for the giant, hard cock of de Rohan approaching, the giant prick throbbing and spurred on by my moans—"Fuck me!"—my sobs—"Fuck me! Fuck me!". . . .

De Rohan spreads my legs wide, puts his feet on my shoulders, and then plunges his thick, hard battering ram into my tight, honeyed, writhing pussy. . . . I scream at the sharp, knifelike pain tearing away the flesh barrier of my virginity, and then I whimper as the smarting pain melts into the pleasure of his cock pushing all the way up, rubbing against my swollen clitoris, moving out and in and out and in again. . . . "Fuck me! Fuck me!". . . . And I am delirious with the hard cock in my cunt, the hard cock up my ass, moving together, seeming almost to rub against each other deep inside me, fucking my cunt, fucking my ass, fucking, fucking. . . . My body thrashing, I suck Helga's juicy cunt, I push my breast in and out of Du Barry's mouth, I rotate my burning ass over the impalement of the King's cock, and I slap my sopping cunt against de Rohan's pelvis as he pumps tirelessly deep inside it. . . . "I'm coming! I'm coming!" It is Helga screaming as her pussy grinds into my lips, my tongue, my mouth. . . . "I too!" Du Barry is clawing at her pussy with both hands. . . . "Oui! Oui!" The King's balls are swallowed up between the cheeks of my bottom as he clutches my hips and plunges his cock all the way up my anus and begins to come with long, drawn-out, hot spurts. . . . "Now, Marie! Now!" De Rohan's cock, deep inside my pussy, filled with man cream, on the verge of exploding . . . "Now!" I echo, shouting the word up Helga's squirming, climaxing pussy. "Now!" *I claw at Du Barry's raven tresses, pushing her mouth around my straining breast.* "Now!" *I push back with my ass to feel the King spending to my very bowels.* "Now! Now!" *And a scream tears from my lips and I am coming even as de Rohan fires hot spurts of love all the way up my twisting, climaxing pussy. . . .*

"The vapors?" Louis mumbled the question in his sleep.

"No!" I gasped. "I'm all right."

"You groaned as if you had a bellyache."

"It's fine now," I told him, aware that I had drenched the sheet with my honey, concerned that Louis might accuse me of wetting the bed again. "Go back to sleep."

He went back to sleep. After a while, I went to sleep myself. That was our wedding night, one of the most elaborately celebrated in all Christendom. The next morning, writing in his diary, Louis summed it up in one word.

"Nothing!" he wrote.

And that, *mes amis*, said all there was to say about our wedding night!

Chapter Four

Marital relations did not improve over the days, and then the weeks, and then the months which followed. The Hapsburg mustard, it seemed, was simply not within Louis' power to cut. Nor was there any way that this failure could be kept secret from the rest of the nobles in residence at Versailles.

Like it or not, our sex life—or lack of it—was a matter of intense interest to every French nobleman with the slightest claim to the throne, and to every ambassador from the other countries of Europe as well. More interested than most, of course, was the Viennese ambassador who reported daily to my mother. If I could not seduce Louis into performing, all the years of her diplomacy aimed at tying the Hapsburg fortunes to the Bourbons would have been for naught. Letters from Vienna began arriving with the regularity of daybreak.

"Caresses and cajoleries" was Mama's advice. "Do not be in too great a hurry. To do so will only increase the Dauphin's timidity and thus make matters worse. And above all, 'Toinette, keep a check on your wicked temper!"

That last, concerning my temper, was perhaps the hardest of Mama's advice to follow. Again and again I was given reason to bypass it. You see, it was not just Louis' manhood but my sexual desirability as well which was laid open to derision.

I would have had to be blind and deaf to be unaware of the crude jingles and caricatures and cruel jokes circulating at Versailles. Where sex was concerned, the French Court knew none of the restraints which Mama had imposed on its Viennese counterpart. And of course Du Barry with her sneers at "that impotent fat boy" and "his milksop frau" made sure that the cruelest jibes did not escape my attention. It was she who originated a popular new guessing game which swept Versailles. The question the game asked was "Who will take the place of the Dauphin in the bed of Marie Antoinette?"

Perhaps the question stung the more for my having asked it of myself. Many girls my age were already married, and those who were not were most certainly enjoying stolen kisses and hot caresses in hidden corners. Quite simply, I burned with frustration and longed for a man to put out the fire.

It has been said that lust can drive one mad. I do not think that is the case. What drives one mad is not lust itself but the frustrating of it. *Oui!* While passion fills beds, its disappointment fills asylums.

Night after night I renewed my efforts to render the Dauphin tumescent. I flung off my bedclothes and stood before him naked. I cupped my growing breasts in my hands and held them out to him. I teased the nipples to hardness. I licked them lasciviously with a long, red, obscenely stiff tongue. I wriggled my naked derriere and presented it to his mouth for a kiss—a bite—anything. I turned and stroked my hot, squirming pussy under his eyes. I opened the swollen lips delicately with my fingers and showed him how pink and moist and sweet it was inside. Finally I sat before him with my quivering, fleshy thighs flung wide and played with myself. I strumnmed my aroused clitty until I came under my husband's very nose!

And Louis? What did he do?

Nothing!

And what did he say?

"You should try lock making, Marie. That's fun too."

Oui! It truly is frustration which fills the madhouses!

One evening I witnessed an incident which led me to wonder if perhaps it is not in the nature of the marriage relationship itself that husbands should be unsatisfactory as lovers, thereby making lovers as necessary to wives as pollen to the bumblebee. This incident occurred at a ball which, theoretically, my husband the Dauphin and I were hosting. In actuality, Louis danced the first minuet with me—as was customary, we had the entire floor of the ballroom to ourselves—tripped all over his own feet and stepped all over mine, and then retired to play with his locks and bricks. Happily, after his departure, I danced a quadrille with the Duc de Chartres, the finest dancer at Court. This was followed by six more minuets. I danced them all with different partners, for dancing was my way of releasing all the energy I was not expending in the boudoir.

With the announcement of the seventh minuet, I retired to the sidelines, sat on one of the couches, fanned myself and watched the dancers taking their positions. One of my more gossipy ladies-in-waiting sat attendance with me. When my eye was taken by one of the dancers, I turned to her. "Who is that?" I inquired.

The young woman I indicated was striking. She looked

not much older than myself (there was six years between us, I would later learn), and displayed none of the public stiffness which was customary at formal balls. Voluptuously uncorseted, her body moved with the ease of a country girl used to a lack of confinement in her clothing. Her complexion, however, was not that of a provincial. Her skin was very white in contrast to rippling chestnut hair (she wore no wig) and dark, flirtatiously long eyelashes. Of medium height, perhaps two inches shorter than I, her bosom was more developed at this time than my own. It was round and full and moved independently under her clothing as she danced. The low bodice of her gown shoed it to full advantage. Her visage was feline, piquant, as exciting in its way as her well-rounded figure. Her small, white teeth sparkled as she laughed at her partner and tossed her curls at him as they danced. She was vivacious; more, she was provocative.

"That is Madame Yolande de Polignac," my lady-in-waiting replied to my question, whispering. "She is dancing with her lover, the Comte de Vaudreuil. That is her husband over there by the champagne bowl, Your Highness."

"A ménage à trois?" I inquired, showing off my newly acquired French sophistication.

"Oh no, Your Highness. Everyone at Court knows of the affair, but not her husband. It is not in the nature of husbands to know such things."

"What would he do if he found out?" I wondered.

"He would surely call him out, Your Highness. M'sieur de Polignac is well known to be extremely jealous of his wife. And he is an expert swordsman as well."

"But not so expert as her lover. At least not in the boudoir, where it counts."

My lady-in-waiting gasped at my *mot*. It was one

thing for a lady of her station to gossip to the Royal Princess who would one day be her Queen. It was quite another thing—shocking, really!—for her royal mistress to reply in such bawdy fashion.

I ignored her reaction. My words, after all, were merely one more expression of my ever-present frustration. I watched Yolande de Polignac, envying her the illicit passion she shared with her lover. From the way the Comte de Vaudreuil looked at her as they danced, he was obviously mad about her.

When the dance was over, they separated. She went to her husband, spoke a few words to him, and then drifted away. She watched him from across the room until he was deep in conversation with another gentleman of the court. Then Mme. de Polignac slipped out the French doors of the ballroom to the darkened terrace beyond. A moment later, the Comte de Vaudreuil followed in her wake.

Moments tripped by and they did not return. At last my curiosity became too much for me. I was still, after all, a very young girl, very romantic, and very curious about what lovers did during their stolen moments. Casually, I crossed the ballroom and exited by the terrace doors.

The moon was very bright, and the sky was filled with stars. The darkest corner of the terrace was not really very dark at all. It was here that the lovers, oblivious to all else, were locked in an embrace. My heart beating quite fast, I concealed myself behind a tall potted form and observed them.

They were kissing fiercely, their mouths hungry, sucking, moving. Every so often their clinging lips would part and their tongues, red and swollen with passion, would duel in the moonlight. Seated side by side on a white wrought-iron garden bench, turned towards each other, their hands were every bit as busy as their mouths.

The Comte had extricated one of Yolande de Polignac's breasts from her bodice and was fondling it. The nipple was cherry red and unusually long and stiff and pointy. She was breathing with slow, long, shallow breaths and her breast swelled under his teasing hand to a rippling fullness. Her breasts were spaced wide apart and they angled away from each other, sharp-nippled, with an independence that was somehow erotic.

On the spot, I fell in love with them. Yolande de Polignac's breasts reminded me of all those passionate interludes with Helga, but it was also something more than that. Where Helga's breasts had been well developed, they had nevertheless been the breasts of a girl. Yolande de Polignac's breasts at this moment were those of a woman whose womanly lust was peaking.

My infatuation was confirmed when she pulled slightly away from her lover and I saw her face in the moonlight. There was something savage, almost harsh, writ across her feline features. Her lip was curled; she looked like a tigress; it seemed quite possible that she might tear out her lover's heart as impulsively as make love to him.

"Is your cock hard?" she snarled.

"*Oui.*" He bent and licked one of the small, quivering, red daggers tipping her breasts.

"Are your balls heavy and aching?"

"*Oui.*" He pursed his mouth and kissed the nipple, rolling it between his lips and tonguing it at the same time.

"Is the shaft pulsing with nectar?"

"*Oui.*" He opened his mouth very wide and drew her large, up-curved, out-pointing breast deep into it.

"I want it!" she snarled again. "I want your big, hard cock right now!"

He licked his way up from her breast to her neck, her ear, her mouth. He kissed her, sucking her tongue, biting it. "Does your cunt want my hard prick?" he asked.

"*Oui!*"

"Is it hot and wet and ready for it?"

"*Oui!*"

"Is your clitty all stiff and randy?"

"*Oui!*"

"Is your pussy wide open for my big hard cock?"

"*Oui! Oui!* Stop teasing me!" Her hand clawed at his satin britches until she had them opened. She took out his penis. It shone long and stiff and slender in the moonlight.

My response to the sight of it was hot and wet. My nipples stiffened so quickly inside my bodice that it hurt. Without thinking, my hand pressed my gown between my legs.

Mme. de Polignac slid her small hand up and down the slender shaft. Her violet cat eyes sparkled as she stared at the swollen ruby she revealed when she pulled back the foreskin. She stroked the heavy balls and licked her lips.

Her lover spread his legs widely and watched her as she pulled on his prick and fondled his balls. He closed his eyes and sighed when she bent over and rubbed the length of her distended nipple over the swollen tip of his cock. When she removed the red nipple, a drop of premature man cream clung to it. Yolande de Polignac slipped to her knees and made an O of her pretty mouth. . . .

It was at this precise moment that her husband stepped out onto the terrace. The moonlight made him squint at first, and so he didn't see his wife and her lover. Before he could adjust his vision, I stepped out in front of him, blocking his view.

"Your Highness." He made a sweeping bow to me. "I was looking for my wife."

"I saw her on her way to the powder room just a moment ago," I told him, holding my skirts wide to be sure that he should not see the scene which I had been watching.

"Really, Your Highness? One of your ladies-in-waiting told me she saw her step out here for a breath of air."

"She was mistaken. As you can see, she is not here. There is only myself, enjoying the solitude," I told him pointedly.

"In that case, Your Highness, forgive the intrusion." M. de Polignac made another sweeping bow and withdrew through the French doors into the ballroom.

I turned and faced the couple on the bench. Terror of discovery had immobolized them. Mme. de Polignac was still crouched in front of her lover with her fear-clenched fist around his stiff, cream-filled shaft. Her mouth was still formed in an O, but it had not reached its target. Her tigress eyes were staring at me with surprise and gratitude and (even under these bizarre circumstances) interest. The smile I now bestowed on her was meant to be reassuring, but I'm afraid that in actuality my interest in the picture before me rendered it quite lascivious.

No one of the three of us said anything. I could think of nothing to say. And I think that they felt that under the circumstances, if any conversation was to be inaugurated, it must be by royal prerogative.

Comte de Vaudreuil was staring. He was breathing deeply and heavily, caught between lust and apprehensiveness. Only the throbbing of his cock in the fist of his mistress disturbed the stillness of the tableau vivant the three of us presented. And then Yolande de Polignac loosened her grip and the tableau was shattered completely as a jet of thick silver liquid fired from the tip of her lover's prick and arced towards the moonlit sky.

A few warm droplets spattered my cheek. The Comte moaned at the shame of so sullying one who would one day be Queen of France. Yolande de Polignac rushed to remove the silver drops with her lace handkerchief. In her hurry, she forgot to reclothe her naked breast. And now it was I who moaned as that long, burning, distended nipple dug into my bare flesh while she patted at my face.

"Your Highness?" It was the first word either of us addressed to the other.

"It's all right." It was all I could bring myself to say. I turned on my heel and left them. If I had remained, I could not have kept control of myself. I surely would have engulfed her beautiful breast with my mouth. I dared not even think what I might have done if her lover had come in reach of me with his naked, still-hard, still-spurting prick!

You see, *mes amis*, this was really the first time I had seen a man's *épée* unsheathed. (Louis' curled caterpillar—alas!—did not count.) *Oui!* This was the first time ever that I saw a real man's prick not only naked, but hard. And then to see it geysering as well! Truly, it was too much for me! The picture would stay in my mind for a long, long time. And always it would emerge with the pouting face of Mme. Yolande de Polignac. And always the combination would add up to a fierce desire clutching at my bosom.

At the same time, it was all too intense for one as young and hungry for love and frustrated as I was. My poor pussy was both yearning and burning as I made my way through the ballroom. It was my intention to retire to the privacy of my boudoir where my frigging fingers might temporarily put out the fires, but the King stopped me from making my departure from the ball.

"Marie! Sweet child. Where have you been hiding?" He had obviously consumed quite a lot of wine. Indeed, if he had not been King Louis XV of France, one might have said that he was very drunk. He was seated on a divan with Mme. Du Barry and now, as I passed them, he reached out his hand, caught my wrist, and drew me to him. "A kiss for Grandpapa." He pulled me to his knee, ignoring Du Barry's glowering fury.

I too ignored Du Barry. This was in keeping with my mother's advice. "She is his mistress," she had written me. "She has no legitimacy unless you choose to give it to her. She will of course expect you to speak to her. Do not do so. That way when the King dies and you become queen, there will be no question of Du Barry's influence at Court. You will have labeled her the whore she is from the beginning."

Du Barry well understood this game. She knew exactly what I was doing to her. She was fighting back with all the influence she had acquired before I came on the scene, and this was considerable. She was an astute and subtle woman and she had long manipulated the King to her best interest. Nevertheless, she could not hide her anger and her jealousy when he was openly affectionate towards me.

At such moments the King contrived to be both brazen and underhanded at the same time. He would flaunt his kisses as a perfectly permissible expression of his paternal affection towards the Dauphin and myself, but he would be quite sneaky in the way he slid his tongue into my mouth and raised his knee to wedge it between my thighs. He did this now, as he held me on his lap, kissing me and bouncing me as one might a child, and all the time toying with me secretly as if I were some bawd whose buttocks and breasts existed for the sole purpose of being fondled.

Suspicious and sharp of eye, Du Barry saw more perhaps than the other members of the Court gathered around the Kind and I. Or perhaps it was just that they did not dare take notice of his hands scampering over my bodice and the sensual rhythm of his leg as he bounced me up and down. And surely not even Du Barry could have guessed how hard the royal scepter was, nor how firmly nested in the folds of my gown between the cheeks of my derriere.

Squirming over this disguised impalement and re-membering the all-too-recent spurting of the cock on the terrace as well as the lascivious hunger writ across the visage of Yolande de Polignac, I could not help but respond to His Royal Majesty's bouncings and thrust-ings and hotly impertinent kisses. I abandoned all con-cern for what those present might see, or might think. In particular, I banished Mme. Du Barry's smoldering fury from my mind.

In reply to his "grandfatherly" kisses, I thrust my own twisting tongue into the King's mouth, taking him by surprise. My heart thumping wildly, I tickled his ears and the nape of his neck as we kissed. Only dimly did I hear the spattering of handclaps and approving comments at this display of filial affection. I was too busy shifting position so that my rubbing pussy could press hard enough on his bouncing knee for my poor tormented clitty to feel. And then, overstimulated by the evening as a whole, I bit down savagely on my monarch's lip and began a long, drawn-out climax over his pumping knee and thrusting erection.

King Louis pulled away from me and looked into my

eyes. They were unfocused. Things had gone farther than he'd intended. Much farther. Drunk as he was, he could not allow my orgasm to continue in public. Not with Du Barry at the end of her fuse and about to explode!

"My kisses have made the poor child swoon," he announced. "Doubtless," he added with tipsy sarcasm, "her spouse has not accustomed her enough to such affection. In any case, some of you ladies had best see poor Marie to her room."

They had no easy task. I did not willingly release the King's knee from the clutch of my writhing, climaxing pussy. Nor did the cheeks of my derriere part willingly to free the royal scepter from the folds of my gown and the pocket its thrustings had made of my bloomers.

"How fond the child is of you, sire!" observed one of the ladies tugging at me.

"She is no child!" Du Barry snarled.

For once she was right. The uncontrollable spasms shaking me even as I was led away were the full-blown wrenchings of a hot-blooded Hapsburg woman. Dizzy as I was, one thing stood out clearly in my mind. I had to have a man between my legs!

In this state, I was conducted to the boudoir where my husband, playing with his bricks and locks, awaited me!

The end of my orgasm in no way banished my determination to have done with my unwanted chastity. Young Louis wasn't much, but he was male. Fired with a will to put an end to the farce of our unconsummated marriage, I once again flung off my clothes and presented myself naked to my husband.

"Kiss me, Louis." Without a stitch on, I slid onto his lap before he could protest and offered him my mouth.

Obediently, he kissed me. The sensation was not

unlike being nuzzled by a large St. Bernard. I wriggled over his lap throughout the kiss. He was wearing only a nightshirt, but I could feel nothing stirring between his rather stout legs.

I put his hand on my breast. "Squeeze it!" I directed. I kissed his ear, licking the bristly follicles of hair inside.

Again Louis was obedient. He squeezed my breast. My hard nipple bumped over his clenching fingers.

"Harder!" I panted.

"It's too delicate," he protested. "I'm afraid I'll hurt you."

"You won't hurt me! Be aggressive!" I sank my teeth into his shoulder through his nightshirt.

"That's just what I was thinking about when you came in, Marie." Louis clasped his hands and cocked his head thoughtfully.

"What did you say, darling?" That was the longest sentence Louis had spoken since our marriage. It took me by surprise.

"Aggression." Louis warmed to his subject, if not to my naked body squirming on his lap. "Aggression and defense. I was thinking about it. You see, Marie, one day I will be king. France will be my responsibility and I will be in charge of her wars. How to be aggressive and how to defend will be decisions I shall have to make."

Patience, Mama had cautioned in her letters. Understanding. Gain his confidence and he will be a husband to you.

"Of course, Louis." I hugged him, stabbing at his flabby chest through his nightshirt with my aroused berry nipples. "How clever of you to see that. France will need weapons. France will need guns. France will have to fire those guns." I dropped my hand casually to his lap. Nothing!

"We already have guns, Marie. And so does England. Of course we should make more guns so that we will have more guns than they do. Then, of course, they will build more guns so that they have more guns than we do. And then we will build more guns so—"

"Louis, darling," I interrupted. "Perhaps it is not so much how many guns there are as how they are positioned that counts." I reached deep under his legs and tried to push his artillery upwards.

"Our guns are on the coast. Their guns are on their warships. Our guns are on our warships. Their guns are on their coastline." Louis delivered this little speech in cadence, like a schoolboy reciting his lessons.

"But are they loaded, *cheri*?" I moaned. "Is your cannon loaded?" I stroked the unimpressive and flaccid shaft of his masculinity.

"Cannon?" Louis pouted. "I don't have a cannon. All I'm allowed to have until I actually become king is a musket. Only Grandpapa can have a cannon. And," he added, "my musket's not loaded. But of course that's not the problem. Defensive weaponry is the problem."

"We could load it, and then maybe we could fire it," I told him dreamily, thinking of the erupting cock of Yolande de Polignac's lover.

"Defensive weaponry," Louis continued single-mindedly, still oblivious to the yearning heat of my naked body. "What we need is a shield to cover our whole country, a shield that will deflect their cannonballs and musket shot and any other missiles the godless British may hurl at us."

"A shield?" I forced myself to pay attention to what he was saying. "But what could a shield impenetrable to musket shots and cannonballs possibly be made of?" I wondered.

"I'm sure I don't know, Marie. I'm a Bourbon, not a

scientist. It could be fashioned of bricks and locks and possibly horseshoes, I would venture. But that is a mere detail. The scientists will work it out. After all, they did invent the musket."

"Even if they could make a shield like that, Louis, I don't see how you could guard all of the coastline of France with it. And even if you could do that, what would prevent the British from aiming their cannons higher and just firing over the shield?"

"They couldn't fire over it, Marie. It would be too high."

"Too high? But what would hold it up?"

"Nothing!" Louis stamped his foot. "Nothing would hold it up!" He lay down on the floor and kicked his heels. "It would not be held up. It would extend down!"

"Darling, don't upset yourself." I reached for his penis, but it had vanished between his legs.

"It would hang from the clouds!" he screeched, throwing a full-fledged tantrum. "They're up there in the sky and the shield would simply hang down from them and cover the French coastline and prevent those godless British missiles from raining devastation on our people."

"How clever of you, Louis." I tried to soothe him. "And of course the scientists will figure out how to hang the shield from the clouds."

"Of course. They'll find a way. That's what we pay them for."

"So it is, Louis." I gave up. I slid between the sheets and turned over to go to sleep.

"You know, Marie," Louis mused to my back. "One thing worries me. We're not at war with the British, and my advisers may not agree to build this shield. It may interfere with their negotiations with the British."

"Don't ask them, Louis," I yawned. "Just go ahead and do it as soon as you become king. Build your defensive weapon system. The war will follow like the rain the thunder." And on that note, I drifted off to sleep. . . .

The next day, as I was walking down one of the long hallways of the Versailles palace, King Louis suddenly materialized, grabbed me, and pulled me behind a long, red velvet drapery. There was hangover written all over his reprobate face, but that didn't stop him from dipping into my bodice to fondle my breasts.

"Please, sire!" I struggled to squirm free. I had had quite enough of Bourbons for a while, thank you very much.

"Indulge me, Marie my dear. It is the very least you can do. You have no idea of the trouble you've caused me."

"Trouble, Your Majesty? But what have I done?"

"For one thing, it is what you have not done." The King fumbled at my nipples. "You have not as yet addressed one word directly to Madame Du Barry."

"Of course not, sire." I was haughty. "I am a Hapsburg. I will one day be Queen of France. I do not deign to speak with castle strumpets."

"In addition to that, she was most upset by the affection which passed between us last evening." The King fondled my derriere.

"But it was you who instigated that, sire. Perhaps you had a drop too much wine. In any case, it was all most innocent."

"Madame Du Barry doesn't think so. She is quite beside herself with rage at your response." The King's hand, up under my skirts, caressed the bare flesh of my inner thighs above my stocking tops. "She has called in the Germans, Bohmer and Bassenge."

"The jewelers? Oo-la-la!" I reacted in the French

fashion and at the same time managed to squirm free of his grasp.

The King had good reason to be upset. In the last sixteen months alone the national treasury had paid out two and a half million francs for diamonds for Du Barry! The King had been forced to raise taxes, drawing loud grumbles from peasants and bourgeoisie alike. And now, because of me, Du Barry was contemplating yet another diamond extravagance. To pay for this one, the tax collectors would have to go armed and travel in pairs.

She had summoned the jewelers, Bohmer and Bassenge, from the Imperial Court of St. Petersburg to consult with her on a necklace. They had been sent to St. Petersburg by the King of Poland whom they served as Court jewelers. They had intended to proceed from St. Petersburg to London where they maintained offices. Instead, the two foremost jewelers in all Europe were on their way to Versailles, where they would embark upon an ongoing dialogue with Du Barry regarding a diamond necklace to be made up of uncut stones totaling 2,800 carats and valued at several million francs. The necklace itself, still only in the talking stage, would be worth three or four times the amount of the uncut gems when it was finished.

This was the first time I ever heard of "The Necklace of the Slave"—so-called because of a conceit of Du Berry's which defined her role as both "Slave of Love" and "Queen of Diamonds." It would not be the last time. "The Queen's Necklace," as it would later come to be called because of its relationship to me, would result in the scandal which toppled the French throne, provoked the Revolution, and carried me to the threshold of the guillotine.

"Why do you not simply put your foot down,

Majesty?" I inquired of the King. "Tell her that the nation cannot afford such an extravagance as this diamond necklace for its King's wench."

"Ahh, Marie. It is obvious that you have never been in love."

It was true. I had yearned. But as yet I had not ever really been in love. That circumstance, however, was soon to be altered. The King's words now, as he changed the subject, were prophetic of that.

"You will dine with us tonight, Marie." It was an order. "We are welcoming a slightly blackened sheep back to the fold."

"And who might that be, sire?"

"Prince-Bishop Louis de Rohan of Strasbourg. Ahh, but I forgot. You have met him of course. He blessed you in the Strasbourg Cathedral on the occasion of your arrival on French soil."

"*Oui.*" I remembered. "He blessed me." And I blushed at the recollection of the phallic baptism by which this blessing had been accomplished.

Leaving the King, my heart was beating faster with the prospect of once again seeing this tall, handsome, charismatic prelate with his excitingly scandalous roué reputation. My lips quivered with the memory of the explosion he had brought to them. My pussy puckered with the possibilities of his presence at Versailles.

"Who will take the place of the Dauphin in the bed of Marie Antoinette?" asked the popular guessing game at Court.

Did this pucker of my pussy foretell the answer?

Chapter Five

Family dinners are always difficult. An honored guest does not necessarily make them less so. The small dinner that night—*intime*, really, by palace standards—with only the King and Du Barry, the Dauphin and myself, and Prince-Bishop Louis De Rohan and the Marquise de Marigny (not, however, dressed as a choirboy for the occasion) present, was no exception.

I, of course, did not address Du Barry at all. She, for her part, divided her attention among the three men, flirting with de Rohan, reassuring the King, and making sarcastic remarks to Louis-Auguste about the way he slurped his soup. The King grumbled about the extravagance of women, the outrageous price of diamonds, and the increasing difficulties of tax collection. Prince-Bishop de Rohan, even more attractive in this setting than I remembered, appraised me with humorous blue eyes while explaining to the King that church levies were sacrosanct and therefore not available to help alleviate the financial burdens of the state. The Marquise sulked at his attentions to me and seemed quite uncomfortable to find herself at table with the infamous Du Barry. My Louis talked about more bricks for defense against the British with his mouth full.

"Grow up first, my boy!" The King's attitude was scathing towards his grandson. "And learn to chew your food!"

"But Grandpapa, everybody knows that the British are stockpiling bricks! If we don't—"

"Forget international relations, Louis. Concentrate on marital relations," the King told him pointedly.

"Perhaps he needs new inspiration." Du Barry giggled nastily.

"Surely not." Prince-Bishop de Rohan was gallant. "The inspiration is magnificent." He bowed his handsome silver-templed head in tribute to me.

"Could we talk about something else, please?" Flattered as I was, I could not keep a slight whine out of my voice. My ongoing inability to seduce Louis into performing was wearing me to a frazzle.

"Have you heard from your mother, the Empress, lately?" the King inquired.

His Majesty may have thought that was changing the subject, but I did not. "Be prodigal with your caresses," Mama had written to me that very day. She added— thinking herself expert, although really quite naive—that this would surely change my huband's "strange behavior." She was also making inquiries of her court physicians in Vienna about the proper treatment for "sluggish glands" and "retarded blood."

"Mama is well." I answered the King noncommittally.

"Can't you do something about that?" Du Barry hissed to the King, her thumb indicating Louis-Auguste.

My husband was chomping away at a leg of mutton and the juices were dribbling down his chin.

"The doctors say that he must eat a lot of red meat," the King told her. "It will improve his—ahh—condition."

"It's ruining my digestion," Du Barry complained. "He is absolutely disgusting!"

"He is my husband!" Louis-Auguste was disgusting, but I could not allow him to be discussed in such fashion in my presence. And certainly not by that creature of the King's lusts! Of course I did not direct my words to Du Barry directly, but they were meant to silence her nevertheless.

They succeeded in doing so. Again King Louis changed the subject. "We have been following you in your travels through the provinces with much interest," he told Prince-Bishop de Rohan.

"Holy Mother Church is concerned with the least of her parishes. I was happy to tour in Her interest."

"And we have heard that you brought these poor peasants music." The King was teasing. "Your own choir."

De Rohan gleaned his meaning immediately and treated it blandly. "Not quite a choir, sire."

"Ahh. *Oui*. Only one choirboy. Still, Bishop, it was thoughtful of you."

The Marquise de Marigny blushed to the roots of her hair.

There was silence then. Nobody seemed to be able to think of anything noncontroversial to say. The only sound was of Louis' enthusiastic chewing. He was flourishing under this new diet of red meat and potatoes, prescribed by his physicians to fire his ardor. He grew fatter and flabbier with every meal.

"I do love family dinners." At last the King broke the silence. "They are always so warm and cozy."

As if in confirmation of this irony, Prince-Bishop de

Rohan's knee pressed mine—warmly and cozily—under the dinner table. . . .

I awoke early the next morning, after my usual chaste night, and decided that the only way to get the taste of that dinner out of my mouth was to take a brisk canter through the woods of Versailles. I quickly put on my riding clothes, went to the stables, and selected a mount. It was a large black stallion, not a gelding. I had had quite enough of nonperforming studs.

The morning was a delight. Sunlight was patterning through the branches of the trees with rainbow cunning. Dew sparkled on the bright green leaves. A light breeze rode the dawn, intoxicating the air and flattening my steed's ears against his head, although his gait was the mildest of canters.

After twenty minutes of riding, I dismounted and sat down with my back against a yew tree. I stretched out my legs, took off my riding jacket, and opened my blouse to the cooling air. I closed my eyes and day-dreamed of Prince-Bishop de Rohan. When I opened them, he was there, on the bridal path, right in front of me.

What a vision he was, atop his magnificent, pure-white steed. He looked much more virile in his riding outfit than in his ecclesiastical robes. His legs were thick with muscles as they curved around his mount. His face was heartbreakingly handsome—and yet just a bit cruel—in the early morning light. His eyes laughed down at me.

"Your Highness." He bowed without dismounting, an incredibly graceful maneuver.

"Your Grace." I started to rise to curtsey.

"Don't bother." The way he moved his riding crop as he spoke made it an order. Only when he was sure that

I had relaxed back into my position against the tree did he leap agilely from his horse and tether it beside mine. "I see that you too enjoy a solitary canter early in the morning," he said.

"*Oui*. It relaxes me for the travails of the day."

"And you have so many travails, Your Highness." He was amused. "I should have thought that at your tender age—and already to be a queen, I might add— you should not be so troubled."

"A throne—even the prospect of one, Your Grace— brings responsibilities as well as satisfactions."

"Ahh!" (Was he mocking me?) "How wise you are." (*Oui*. His blue eyes were laughing.) "Do you mind if I sit with you a moment, Your Highness? Only while I rest my horse. Then I will intrude on your solitude no further."

"You're not intruding," I told him bluntly. "I was not so happy in my solitude. I am glad of company."

"Even of company so unromantic as that of a churchman?" (Again his laughing eyes!)

"If churchmen are unromantic, rumor has it, Your Grace, that you are the least so among them." Boldly, I teased him back.

"I see that my reputation had preceded me." His tone was one of mock rue.

"And accompanied you as well," I reminded him.

"The Marquise de Marigny." He shrugged. "She was troubled in her soul and so traveled with me that I might bring her solace. I have done so, and she is healed. She will be leaving Versailles for her home in the very near future."

"How cavalier you are sir!" I chided him.

"Not really. It is just that your beauty, Your Highness, makes it difficult to concern oneself with other women."

"And how fickle too!" I laughed, the Hapsburg tremolo, not unlike the call of a nightingale in heat.

"Is it fidelity you seek in a man, Highness?"

"I don't remember saying I was seeking anything in a man."

"Or is it performance?" He ignored my comment and drew the truth from me with the intensity of his gaze.

Fidelity, or performance? My husband was faithful, but inactive. I was perishing of unsatisfied desire. Fidelity, or performance? Could there be a choice?

"I see." Prince de Rohan took both my hands in his and drew me to my feet. Holding me against the yew tree, he put his arms around me and kissed me.

I made no protest. He had known that I would not. I closed my eyes and surrendered to the experience gladly. I welcomed it the way the desert traveler welcomes the cool waters of the oasis. I drank deeply of his lips and quenched my thirst.

My lips clung to his as the kiss ended. He looked down at me with full comprehension when I opened my eyes. "*Oui*, performance," he muttered. "Has it been that difficult for you then, Your Highness?"

"I don't know what you mean."

"I think that you do." Almost a head taller than I, he seemed restored to his role as prince of the church and regarded me from his height with the clear gaze of a prelate to whom all human passions are familiar—which is to say sinful and forgivable.

"*Oui*." I laid my cheek against his shoulder. "It is very hard to be—to remain—"

"—chaste." He supplied the word for me. "It is indeed." Humor flitted across his aristocratic, hawklike visage. "I know."

"But you do not keep your vows of celibacy," I blurted out.

"Man is conceived in sin and lives in sin." His tone was cynical.

"And woman?"

He did not answer me with words. Instead, he enfolded me in his arms and kissed me again. My breasts were crushed against his hard chest. My tongue leaped from my lips to meet his and to entwine with it. I grew dizzy in his embrace and began to pant. His hands closed over my bodice and squeezed my breasts firmly through my riding blouse.

We stayed thus for a very long time. Behind us one of the horses whinnied as if with erotic empathy. A bold beam of sunshine penetrated the bough overhead and warmed the flesh of the hands on my bosom. The long green grass crept under my riding skirt and tickled my legs atop my boots as I swayed against the manly chest of the Prince-Bishop. A perfume from spring flowers opening to the early morning filled my nostrils, mingling with his man smell. And there was the faint thump of our hearts beating in sympathetic harmony.

"I want you, Your Highness," he murmured when this second kiss was over.

"I cannot!" I gasped, although I wanted him too, wanted him more than I had ever wanted anything in my life. "Austria . . . France . . . There is more involved than our needs, our desires. Too much depends on my chastity to risk surrendering it."

"I am the Prince-Bishop of Strasbourg," he reminded me. "I serve the crown as well as the church. Do you think that I am unaware of such considerations?" There was a cutting edge to his voice.

It filled me with concern that I might drive him away with a naiveté that had caused me to state the obvious. His tone made me feel suddenly quite childlike. Although he was youthful in every way, the stern set of his features now accentuated the gray at his temples and reproached me for pulling back from the carnal delights being offered.

"I'm sorry." The words tumbled from my lips pleadingly. "It's just that I don't see how—"

"The skinning of cats, Your Highness." His severity relaxed. "There are many, many ways to unpelt a feline without breaching the derma of its virtue."

"I don't think that I understand." I felt very young and inexperienced and stupid.

"You will, Your Highness. You will." This time when Prince-Bishop Louis de Rohan kissed me, his hands were more cunning. They drew up my riding skirt in back and bunched it above my waist. Then they cupped the high globes of my buttocks (well warmed from posting during my canter) and kneaded the firm flesh through my bloomers.

This so excited me that I rubbed the length of my body against him most enthusiastically and without even thinking what I was doing. My risen nipples fought the material between their burning tips and his hard chest. My thighs parted to clasp around the outsides of his thighs. My mound of Venus rode up and down the hard shaft I could feel ridging the belly of his riding britches. My tongue pumped in and out of his mouth every bit as insinuatingly as his tongue pumped in and out of mine.

"Do you feel randy, Your Highness?" he asked me teasingly when this, our third kiss was over.

I had never heard the word before, but instinctively I knew what it meant. *"Oui!"* I panted. "Most randy."

"Come sit with me." He sank to the grass against the tree and drew me down beside him. He opened my riding blouse to the waist and bared my breasts. He extended his incredibly long tongue and licked one of the nipples.

"*Mon Dieu!*" An ecstatic shiver ran the length of my body. My hands tangled in his straight black hair as I clutched him to me. "Kiss it!" I pleaded, and he did so, rolling the nipple around between his expert lips until my body was shaking as if with a fever. "Suck it!" And he opened his mouth wider and took a goodly portion of my breast in it and sucked so hard and so thrillingly that I feared I might spend from this alone.

As if sensing this, de Rohan stopped sucking. He sat back and played with my naked breasts with his hands, giving us a respite—albeit still a somewhat titillating one. A robin on a nearby branch swelled out its chest and chirped at us disapprovingly. A soft morning breeze cooled my swollen berry-nipples. An aroma of jasmine from the formal palace gardens in the distance mingled with the musk of our passion. De Rohan took my hand, opened it flat, and laid it across his lap.

Slowly, savoring the feel of it, I traced the hardness of his penis through the reinforced velvet of his riding britches. Then, growing bolder, I closed my hand and rubbed it up and down over the rigid shaft of flesh. Finally I bent and pressed my cheek against it.

"My prick is to your liking, Highness?" de Rohan asked.

"*Oui,*" I crooned, bestowing a quick kiss through the material.

"Then say so," he suggested.

"I like your prick." I kissed again, a bit more lingeringly. "I love your prick."

"Your Austrian mouth does wonderful things when it says 'prick.' " He laughed.

"My Austrian mouth is very talented." I nibbled at the tip of his prick through his britches. "Remember?"

"Indeed I do." He laughed. "The day I blessed you at Strasbourg." He laughed again. "I have not been taken so by surprise and reacted so impetuously since I was a boy just verging on manhood."

"The taste was good." I sucked at the crest through the layered velvet.

"Your other mouths, Highness, will find it even tastier." His hands slid up under my riding skirt and tugged at my bloomers.

"I dare not." Panting, a welter of yearning emotions, I nevertheless pulled away.

"Fear not, Highness." Stronger than I, he regained his advantage and held it firmly. "Your chastity is safe with me. Trust me." This time he succeeded in pulling my bloomers down over my boots.

"Why should I trust you?" My struggles were only making me more eager.

"I am a man of the cloth."

"Well you certainly aren't behaving like one." I laughed wildly. And then, as I felt his bare hand caressing my naked bottom, my passion grew to such a frenzy as to banish any further considerations of the need to protect royal chastity from my mind.

"I am also a patriotic Frenchman," he added in a voice grown thick with lust. "I will treat the virgin treasure of my Queen-to-be with the caution it deserves." "His fingertips crept between my legs to stroke my moist and silken bush.

"Frankly, *cheri*," I told him, panting, "I don't give a damn!"

Despite my disclaimer, he remained considerate of my virtue. This is not to say that he in any other way neglected to goad me to the heights of rapture. Holding me in a seated position across his lap, the Prince-Bishop caressed my naked underside with an expertise that soon had me wriggling in a hungry passion.

"Oh, sir! What are you doing?" I gasped. And then, "No! Don't stop! Please don't stop!"

One of his hands was between my thighs, spreading the honey over the lips of my pussy and dipping between them just enough to tease my clitty to swollen hardness without compromising me. His other hand was lightly spanking my squirming, naked bottom cheeks and playing in the cleft between them in a manner which had me quite beside myself. At the same time his long tongue was assaulting the nipples of my naked breasts, each in turn.

Cooperating in these endeavors, I had stretched my quivering thighs wide apart. In some perverse fashion, his velvet-sheathed erection had contrived to press itself against one of them as he played with me. Feeling it throb against the honey-slick flesh, my movements became even more abandoned.

Finally de Rohan lifted me from his lap and positioned me in front of him. I stood there holding my skirts up shamelessly. My sopping pussy and pink derriere flashed nakedly at the watching robin.

I too was watching. My eyes were fastened on de Rohan as he removed his riding boots and then his velvet jodhpurs. Standing to do so, his silken shirttails flapped around his hard, angry, naked bobbing prick.

"Lovely!" Reaching for it with both hands, I sank to my knees without thinking. I carried it to my budding girl breasts and folded their softness around its throbbing tumescence. "Lovely!" I could feel it pulsing against my heart!

De Rohan allowed me to fondle it in this manner for a few lovely moments. I was entranced by it. In every way it was the prick of a man who used it frequently and vigorously. It was a trifle purplish, and quite thick as well as long. The wedge-shaped tip was a deep red color, swollen and blood-filled with a hole in the center that made me think of the spout of a watering vessel used in gardening. There was a swirl of smooth black hairs around his balls; it tickled my nipples as I manipulated the prick between my breasts. The balls themselves seemed very large and the sac which held them was stretched tight. On impulse I kissed each of them, sucking them gently between my warm, moist lips. Remembering the cathedral, I thought that perhaps the Prince-Bishop meant for me to suck his prick again, but he had other ideas.

"Bend over and put your arms around the yew tree, Your Highness," he told me.

When I did as he said, he tucked up my riding skirt so that it was out of his way, making sure also that it did not interfere with his access to my naked down-hanging breasts. I peered over my shoulder at him and saw the reflection of how I must appear in his eyes. My naked bottom jutted out from under my raised skirts with my slavering pussy framed between the trembling, pink cheeks. My thighs, braced wide apart, were straining above my riding boots. And the nipples of my girl breasts pointed like bright red arrows towards the ground. I was truly—to use his word—a randy sight!

So too was he. Shirttails flapping, balls and erect prick bobbing, the large gold cross of his office hanging in front of his bright red riding jacket, he came up behind me determinedly and grasped my naked hips firmly. He altered my position a bit until it suited him. He pressed the length of his penis in the long, sensitive crack of my ass. As he did so, his hot balls bounced against the swollen lips of my pussy. Then he reached around in front of me with one of his hands and began playing with my wet quim as he moved up and down with his hot prick.

"Ahh!" I squirmed and moaned. "That feels nice. So-o-o nice!"

"You like my prick, Marie?"

"I love your prick."

"You like the way I play with your cunt?"

"I love it when you play with my cunt!"

"And your ass?"

"My ass too! I love the way your prick feels there!"

"Shall I put my prick inside your ass?"

"You will hurt me!" The suggestion excited me, but it also filled me with alarm.

"No I won't, Marie. I will be very gentle. It will feel good. Very good."

Slowly, changing the angle of his assault, he inserted his stiff prick in the entrance to my anus and began sliding it up. When I winced, he stopped, held it in place, and played with my down-hanging nipples, or my trembling, hungry pussy. Then, after a moment, he would resume, inching his long, hard prick further and further up my ass.

"No!" At one point I screamed. "You will split me in two!"

"Not at all, Marie." He kissed the back of my neck. "You will take it all, and it will feel marvelous. It will make you feel as you have never felt before. Just relax."

I relaxed. And, as he moved again, deep inside me the muscle of my sphincter relaxed as well. And then he was all the way inside me, his balls wedged in the cleft of my ass, his hard prick pumping in and out, his naked thighs pounding against the hot, pink, abraded cheeks of my ass.

"*Oui!*" I gasped. "Do it! . . . *Oui!* . . . Oh, that feels so good! . . . *Oui!* . . . *Oui! Oui!* WHEE-EE!"

As I started to come, I pushed back with my ass as hard as I could. My pussy locked around his fingertips. And deep inside my violently clenching ass, his prick released a hard-driving torrent that tickled my very bowels and then spilled out to drench my bottom and his balls as well.

It lasted for a long and delirious eternity, but finally his prick, no longer quite so hard, withdrew from my bottom and flopped between his legs. I released the trunk of the yew tree, straightened up, and turned towards him. As I moved, the pain of the impalement, which I had not felt while it was happening, communicated itself to me. "Oh!" I gasped. "I will surely not be able to ride my horse back to the stable."

"Poor Princess Marie." Prince-Bishop de Rohan was amused. "Are you sore?" He was already pulling up his britches and reaching for his boots.

Men!

"Yes, I am!" The pain brought tears to my eyes. "And since you have more experience in such matters than I, Prince-Bishop, you should have warned me of the result."

"It will wear off in time." He set his boots down and embraced me. His kiss was reassuring. "Trust me. It really will. And listen, Marie, if we are to be lovers, don't you think we might dispense with titles. I'll call you Marie and you call me Louis."

"Louis is my husband's name," I reminded him.

"All to the good. You needn't worry about betraying yourself by murmuring your lover's name in your sleep."

"He wouldn't care." A sudden thought made me giggle. "It is also the King's name."

"The King, the Dauphin, and the Prince-Bishop all named Louis." De Rohan smiled. "Why, Marie, you will never have to worry again." His expression said he had guessed at the King's frequent fondlings.

"But I do worry. Louis might not care about us having an affair, but the King would be furious."

"Ahh, but you don't understand kings, my dear. If he should hear you murmuring 'Louis' during a nap, he would assume that it was he your dreams desired. To the King there is only one Louis, and that is himself, the King." De Rohan pulled on his boots.

"Then I suppose that you are right. It is fortunate that all three of you are named Louis. But suppose—" I caught myself and didn't say it.

"Suppose?" When I made no reply, Louis de Rohan said it for me. "Suppose you should take another lover whose name is not Louis?" He laughed cynically. "And suppose you should inadvertently speak his name in your sleep. Even worse, suppose that you should speak it in the throes of passion. And if this name was not Louis, what then?"

"What then?" I repeated.

"That would depend on the one who heard. If it were your husband, despite the way things are between you, it would be incumbent on him to challenge this lover to a duel. If it were the King, I suppose he might settle for banishing him from the realm."

"And if it were you?" I wanted to know.

"If it were me?" He laughed. "Why, if it were me, Marie, I should have no choice but to inflict the sternest punishment on one who cuckolded the heir to the throne of France."

"And what would that 'sternest punishment' be?" I wondered.

"Why I would excommunicate him, my dear! After all, I would be acting in the name of the church, and Holy Mother Church does not take half measures."

Laughing, he took my elbow with one hand and the reins of our two horses with the other, and led me back towards the palace.

When we reached there, we separated. Prince-Bishop Louis de Rohan, my lover now, I suppose, although my virginity was still technically intact, took the horses back to the stables. I went to my chambers and summoned my maid, the French one who had taken Helga's place.

"I need a bath," I told her, wincing at the fiery smarting between my buttocks.

"I will have the water boiled immediately, Your Highness."

"*Oui* . . . Wait. No!" I was struck with a sudden idea of how this painful inner abrasion might better be assuaged—perhaps even to the extent where I might be able to sit down later to my breakfast. "Warm goat's milk," I told her. "And fill the tub with it."

"You wish to bathe in goat's milk, Your Highness? But why?" The girl was bewildered.

"Because I am royalty, you fool," I told her. "I am a Hapsburg! We Hapsburg princesses always bathe in goat's milk! Now stop asking questions, you foolish wench, and go fetch warm goat's milk for my bath!"

Thus, *mes amis*, from the banal result of my first anal reaming, was the tradition born!

Chapter Six

Ours was truly a "back-door affair." Both the necessity for discretion and the obligation to retain my royal virginity until my husband became competent to wrest it from me dictated this. Nevertheless, in my girlish innocence, I was convinced that I was in love with Prince-Bishop Louis de Rohan. The devilishly handsome, anal-intensive prelate aroused my libido as I had never dreamed it could be aroused.

"I love you!" I told him how I felt one day as we lay side by side resting after having made love.

Alas! My words seemed only to amuse him. "Love is for moonstruck milkmaids," he replied cynically. "It's a sloppy emotion, and not for those of us born to the purple, Your Highness. Indulge yourself by all means, but do not deceive yourself, my dear Marie. Experiment. Innovate. Enjoy. But leave love to the peasants. Love is their laudanum. We who rule cannot afford it."

"But I do love you!" I dug my long, sharp fingernails into the sleek black fur of his groin.

"This is what you love!" He shook his semitumescent prick under my nose.

My nostrils flared and I shrank back. The aroma was very much my own. It served to remind me of just where this instrument had so recently been buried.

My reaction amused my lover. "How fastidious you are, Marie. *Très* prudish. *Très* Austrian. *Très, très* Hapsburg!"

Stung, I took his *épée* in my hand and rubbed it back and forth over my naked breasts. I drew back the foreskin and rubbed the ruby tip against each of my erect berry-nipples in turn. Then I moved the shaft up and down in the cleavage between my budding girl breasts. "Do you still think I'm prudish?" I inquired.

"*Oui.*" Prince-Bishop Louis was laughing at me.

He recognized that I had removed his besmirched organ from the vicinity of my flared Hapsburg nostrils and my squeamishness continued to amuse him. His attitude infuriated me. I'd show him! I bent my head, pursed my warm, wet lips around the heart-shaped head of his cock and looked up at him.

I had the satisfaction of seeing that my gesture took him by surprise. He caught his breath and then shifted position so that he was kneeling with his muscular thighs wide apart and his stiffening prick rising like an arrow to the bulls-eye O of my mouth. I was forced to crouch over very low to keep the tip of his cock from escaping my lips.

The aroma did not bother me now as it had at first. On the contrary, associated as it was with my own forbidden orifice, I found the scent—in combination with the velvety cock tip in my mouth—most stimulating. My thighs clenched with excitement and I sucked the shaft of my lover's cock deeper into my craw.

Prince-Bishop Louis' hands clasped over the top of

my head. His graceful fingers tangled in my long, disheveled, ash-blond hair. His large bishop's ring, the one I had kissed when he blessed me upon my arrival in France, pressed down upon my scalp.

I circled the head of his cock with the tip of my tongue. I probed the little hole. I snaked my tongue around the shaft, first in one direction, then the other.

The cock swelled remarkably and hardened in my mouth. De Rohan snarled and, heedless of my small, sharp teeth, forced his prick further in. He began moving it in and out with short, sharp, slightly rotating movements. His balls, also swollen inside their tight-stretched sac, felt very hot as they bounced against my rounded chin.

On impulse, I reached under him as he squatted and dug my nails into his naked bottom. The violence of his reaction took me by surprise. He slammed his cock so deeply into my mouth that it seemed to slide down my throat and cut off my ability to breathe. Immediately, I began to sputter and choke.

"Ahh, Marie!" He pulled his prick far enough out so I could breathe again. "You must learn to relax so that you will not gag."

His cock was still in my mouth, so I could not answer him with words. Instead, I raised my blue eyes pleadingly. I wanted to try again.

"Very well." He once again pushed his cock all the way into my mouth.

He was more gentle this time, but as his ardor increased he again began to move violently. Again his rampaging prick slid down my windpipe. Again I choked.

"Ahh, Marie. There is a knack. You will learn it. But I have not the time now, my dear. I must get back to the affairs of the church." He pulled his prick completely out of my mouth and stood up. It bobbed in front of my face like a thick purple club.

"But I'm so randy!" I moaned, using the word he had taught me the first time I had raised my skirts to his scepter.

"And I, my dear! And I!" His buccaneer expression was truly wicked. "Assume the position!" It was a command.

How dared he give me orders like that? I was a princess of the House of Hapsburg! I was a daughter of the Caesars! I was the wife of the heir apparent to the throne of France! One day I would be Queen of France!

But my pussy was throbbing like that of any serving wench in heat, and so I assumed the position. I stood up and spaced my feet wide apart. I bent over and reached behind me with both hands. I grasped my bottom cheeks and pulled them wide apart and waited. . . .

Well, *mes amis*, you must surely appreciate that such liaisons were a far cry from the lack of activity in my boudoir every night. My husband, Louis-Auguste, could not but suffer by comparison with my lover, Louis de Rohan. Indeed, there could be no comparison, for the Dauphin had yet to achieve tumescence.

Oui, I was indeed a wife in name only. Or, as I put it in a sealed letter to Helga in Vienna (a missive that I cautioned her to burn as soon as she had read it): "I am the Dauphine of France, one day to be the Queen, but at present my title is the Great Unfucked!"

Such language would surely have given Mama the vapors. Nevertheless, she was almost as distressed at the state of my marriage as I was. Her letters of advice— based as they were on the total lack of distinction in her mind between childbearing and sex-as-fun—were more revealing of her inhibitions than helpful.

"Do not be forward!" she cautioned again and again. "Touch only your husband's hand and no other part of his person. Speak softly and soothingly, but without suggestiveness. Behave chastely with him, and with others as well, lest you arouse a jealousy that may further alienate him from his manliness."

I did not follow this last piece of advice. It was Mama's theory that womanly gentleness would bring Louis-Auguste around, but even with my limited experience with men, I knew that it takes more than patience to raise a reluctant cock. Besides, the nights I lay awake and burning with exotic hunger beside my snoring husband were taking their toll on me.

They sent me flying to the arms of my lover. But the Prince-Bishop, with duties to perform for church and state, was not always available. At such times, I might willingly wander into the presence of the King, swinging my hips a trifle perhaps, or dropping a lace handkerchief so that by the act of retrieving it I might call his attention to the sweet swelling of the child breasts escaping my decolletage.

On such occasions, keeping a weather eye out for his fiercely jealous mistress, Du Barry, the King might stimulate me with roguish caresses under the guise of grandfatherly affection. He may have been getting a bit on in years, but his randiness never waned. He sucked at my cherry lips with a tongue always full drawn from its scabbard. He loved to dandle me on his lap and bounce me up and down as if I were still a child while all the while toying with my hot, swollen nipples inside my bodice. On my part, frustrated, I frequently abandoned myself to these caresses without regard to the difference in our ages. Bouncing in such a way as to make myself spend had become habitual with me when the King positioned me over the bulge in his royal lap.

Sometimes neither the King nor the Prince-Bishop were available. On these occasions, I did not hesitate to seek attention elsewhere. There were many young rakes at the Court of Versailles, and among them more than a few willing to help their future Queen wile away a lonely hour or two.

For the most part, these flirtations consisted of no more than a few hot and teasing kisses and intimate caresses. None of these gentlemen dared risk the broaching of the future Queen's virginity, and even if they had, I would not have allowed it. Neither had any of them the erotic finesse to approach me as Prince-Bishop Louis de Rohan did.

So I played with them and they with me as children do. I fondled their penises through their britches, and sometimes took them out. Such variety! Who would have thought it? Not just long and short and thick and thin, but in color and hairiness as well. In aroma, and in the manners in which they swelled up when I touched them, or—rarely and briefly—when I quickly licked or kissed them. (I would not suck any of them. I was waiting still for further instruction from the Prince-Bishop.)

Also, they played with me. Sometimes I let them squeeze my breasts, and if I was with a particular favorite or if I was feeling particularly randy, I might let one of them suck my naked nipples. One or two I permitted access beneath my petticoats. Again, it was my randiness which usually led to the granting of such favors.

At such times the lucky gentleman would play with my pussy with trembling fingers, fearful of doing damage to the royal cherry. On one or two occasions I became so impatient with such craven fumblings that I grasped the wrist and bore down on the nervous hand until I spent. But such incidents were rare, and while these interludes were titillating, they were on the whole quite innocent.

De Rohan's attitude infuriated me. Particularly so because it was true. None of the young bucks with whom I dallied stirred my juices as did the bottom-battering Bishop of Strasbourg.

But if my lover was not concerned with my flirtations, others were. The King, doubtless goaded by the malicious Du Barry, spoke to me quite sternly about my behavior. "It is not seemly for one who will one day be Queen of France," he chided me, taking one of my hands in one of his and pressing it against the erection ridging the front of his velvet pants while he wagged a finger of his other hand under my nose. "You have a royal husband, Marie, and you owe him fidelity."

"And you have that woman," I reminded him, stroking his sheathed *épée* fondly.

"Madame Du Barry." The King squirmed. "Will you not speak her name, Marie?"

"I do not speak the name of strumpets."

"Peace!" The King closed his hand over mine and rubbed, moving slowly up and down on his toes. "Why can my royal household not have peace?"

"Perhaps you should ask your wench the reason for that, Your Highness."

"I dare not!" the King panted. "Her tongue is sharper than a merciless headsman's ax."

"Now there's a solution to your problems, Majesty." I squeezed the throbbing velvet lump.

"It would certainly ease the strain on the royal exchequer." He laughed breathlessly and redoubled his efforts.

"I have heard that the cost of the Necklace of the Slave is mounting, sire. It is said that the jeweler Bohmer has found a flawless fifteen-carat button stone for the cluster center and that he has personally taken this diamond to the best cutters in Amsterdam. All agree that this will be the most extravagant diamond necklace ever created and that its cost will be astronomical." Through the velvet I felt the juices swelling his stiff prick. "Can France afford this, sire? For a backstairs palace wench whose bosom will soon begin to sag?"

"You go too far, Marie!" He rose high on the tips of his toes, leaned into my hand, and remained motionless for a moment, climaxing. "Madame Du Barry's breasts are firm as ripe melons and grown to womanliness, my girl, which yours as yet have not!"

"They will." I wrung him dry.

"Enough!" The King brought the conversation to a close. "It's time for me to go and change."

I curtsied deeply as he swept past me. My bowed head hid my knowing smile. The King had to hurry to change his britches lest Du Barry discern the evidence of our dalliance.

"I meant what I said about your flirtations, Marie," he called back over his shoulder. "They are beginning to cause talk. Be more circumspect, my girl."

Rumors of my careless coquetries were indeed spreading. Mama, of course, had her spies at the French Court and quite soon I received one of her blisteringly moralistic letters regarding my "disgraceful behavior." It was a missive quite typical of Mama's puritanical outlook.

"Word has reached me of your antics with gentlemen of the Versailles Court," she wrote. "My worst fears are confirmed. French frivolity has overwhelmed you. I blame myself. You are a headstrong and willful girl and I am responsible for placing you in the Gallic environment most corruptive to one of your temperament.

"If only the diplomatic situation had been different! I

would have kept you here with me, safe and virtuous. Our Vienna Court is devoted to ruling the empire. There is none of the illicit pairing indulged in by the French. The gentlemen of my court do not betray their wives. The ladies do not cuckold their husbands. Lovers and mistresses are strictly forbidden. And who defy my will in such matters suffer in my wrath to the fullest.

"Court is a place to exercise the responsibilities of noble birth. If your surroundings do not reflect this, my dear, then you must learn to ignore them. You must behave just as you would if you were still here in Vienna where marriage vows are meant to keep and responsibility, not romantic folly, is the order of the day."

I showed this letter to my lover. He folded his hands and raised his eyes heavenward. "May Our Blessed Savior spare me from ever coming under your mother's rule," he intoned with mock piety.

"I too prefer Versailles to Vienna," I told him, bringing his naked cock to my exposed bush and rubbing it back and forth over the silken, ash-blond hairs.

"I wonder why." He laughed.

"You really would go mad there," I assured him, turning over on my belly and raising my bottom to his fully aroused prick. "Absolutely mad!"

"Then I shall stay right where I am." He thrust home. "And give Vienna a wide berth."

Not long after this conversation, I went with a party of young dandies and court ladies from Versailles to Paris by coach. It was Carnival time and the city was alive with gaiety and excitement. The streets were filled with the lower classes in their tattered, pathetic finery. Cheap wine flowed freely and the songs were loud and bawdy. The priests of Paris had their hands full trying to safeguard their flocks against sin. Passing through these streets, I momentarily envied these commoners their uninhibited freedom from the conventions which dictated appearances (but not behavior) to royalty even in such a loose country as France.

The need to keep up these appearances made it impossible for me to follow the impulse to abandon myself to the streets. The next best thing was to indulge myself in relative anonymity at one or another of the aristocratic mansions where Carnival was being celebrated. From the outside these palaces were ablaze with candlelight and sparkling decorations. Inside, this glitter prevailed through a series of rooms where foods running the gamut from caviar and pâté de foie gras to sides of mutton and Viennese tortes were served. The wine was vintage champagne, but it flowed just as freely as the vin ordinaire in the streets outside.

Beyond these chambers there was usually a ballroom for dancing and a garden hung with the Chinese paper lanterns which were all the rage in Paris this season. The orchestras would be concealed behind screens in the ballroom and the dancing would take place in the atmosphere that was dimly lit and most intimate. Both ballroom and garden were usually quite in keeping with the naughty and uninhibited spirit of Carnival.

I did not know the particular nobles who were to be my host and hostess. There was nothing unusual in that. The very idea of the bal masque at Carnival time was anonymity.

Towards this end, aristocrats—unlike the hoi polloi in the streets who favored wearing their most outlandish clothing—all dressed somewhat alike. This applied to noblemen as well as ladies. The traditional Carnival garb was the domino and mask.

The domino was a loose cloth with a full cowl like a

monk's hood and wide, concealing sleeves. The mask was full-face and pinned to one's wig to hold it securely in place. The dominos were of a solid color, but the hues varied. This particular season deep scarlet and royal blue were in fashion. The masks were always jet black. Such dominos and masks were worn by ladies and gentlemen alike.

Perversely (we Hapsburgs have always set fashion, not followed it), my hooded cloak was of the same ebony shade as my velvet mask. In this disguise, I was as unrecognizable as any wellborn young maiden of Paris out to have a good time. The mask and domino freed me from all restraint.

We entered the party in a playful, laughing group. One of us identified himself to our hostess and we were all heartily welcomed. Determined on adventure and not wanting to be hampered by anyone who knew my true identity, I separated myself from the others at the first opportunity. While they were still pouring themselves one glass of champagne after another, I slipped from the brightly lit antechamber into the ballroom itself.

It was so dim that I had to grope my way to a sideline banquette. From here I observed the shadowy, deliciously naughty cavortings of the dancers. With men as well as women concealed by their cloaks and masks, it was difficult to tell who was doing what to whom as they moved through the steps of a quadrille in a manner that was more haphazard than traditional. It was also difficult to tell just what—if anything—the members of either sex were wearing underneath their full cloaks.

I, myself, had been quite daring when I prepared for the bal masque. Dismissing my maids, I had attended to dressing all by myself. Unused as I was to doing this, it was really not difficult at all. Eschewing corsets and petticoats and lacings, under my domino I had worn the simplest of evening frocks—sheer black organdy with a daring decolletage worthy of the brazen Du Barry herself. And under the frock, I had worn nothing at all!

"May I have the honor of this dance, mademoiselle?"

It was impossible to tell anything about the person looming over me except that he was tall and that his deep voice identified him as a man. It was a little disconcerting not to know if he was thin or fat, handsome or ugly. I was used to deciding if I found a man attractive or not upon first meeting.

Nevertheless, I accepted his invitation. *"Merci, M'sieur."* I rose and curtsied in answer to his introductory bow.

He led me onto the crowded, dark dance floor. Close up, the shuffling about to the sounds of the hidden violins had even less to do with the intricate patterns of the quadrille. The movements were erotic, not stately. Hands wandered freely.

With the very first pirouette, my partner's hand slid smoothly inside the folds of my cloak and moved over my breasts. When he realized how relatively unfettered they were, he immediately became bolder. Dancing me into a particularly dark corner, he stroked the flesh of the naked half-moons above my bodice.

Flushed with champagne and exhilarated by my anonymity, I made no objection to these impertinent advances from a total stranger. Nor did I object when his tongue slid out of the mouth slit of his mask and dipped into my bodice to lick at my nipples. This had its effect. My heart hammered with excitement and I became slightly dizzy. The dizziness, of course, may just have been the champagne.

"Shall we go into the garden, *mademoiselle*?" he suggested.

"Very well." How I wished that I might see his face!

The garden was lit by the ubiquitous Chinese lanterns. They seemed to have been strung more for effect than to provide illumination. There were many dark nooks and crannies which the light didn't seem to reach at all. Squeals, giggles, and the sounds of heavy breathing marked the locations.

Moving further from the patio, we entered what I quickly realized was a hedge maze. Here the light from the lanterns was barely strong enough to follow the deliberately puzzling path. The degree of clarity with which I could make out the various couples embracing in one or another of the maze's cul-de-sacs varied from one place to another.

Finally my partner brought us to a halt at one of the unoccupied dead ends of the hedge maze. He reached for my mask with eager hands, obviously intending to remove it.

"No!" I pulled away. It was unthinkable to risk revealing my true identity to this stranger.

"But I want to kiss you," he protested.

"No! You may not see my face."

"Are you so ugly then?" He really did sound worried.

"If that's what you want to think," I teased him, "then by all means think it."

"Well, if your face is ugly, the same cannot be said of your body," he granted. He withdrew my breasts from my bodice and began toying with them.

Soon I was panting again. My nipples were hard and sweetly aching. When he sucked them through the mouth slit of his mask, I held his head in both my hands and pressed my breast more deeply between his hidden lips.

"You like that!" His voice was hoarse. "It's made you quite randy. I can tell."

"*Oui!*" I could not deny the obvious.

"Then you'll like this too." He took my hand and pressed it between his legs.

The contact provided me with some good news and some bad news. The good news was that he was quite hard. The bad news was that his penis was disappointingly small.

Nevertheless, as I squeezed it through his britches I was titillated. After a moment, I parted the folds of my cloak and rubbed up against it through the single garment I was wearing. Small as it was, there was excitement in its hardness moving against my pussy.

My enjoyment was communicated. "Take it out," my anonymous partner suggested.

"All right." I unbuttoned his britches and bared his erection. It was small, but not quite as small as it had felt before. I laid it in the palm of my left hand and stroked it with the fingers of my right hand. Playfully, I tickled his balls.

"Kiss it," he requested.

I obliged, widening the mouth hole of my mask with my fingers in order to give my lips access. His cock's aroma was musky. It bucked against my lips in a most interesting fashion when I bestowed the kiss.

"Lick it!"

I licked it from just under his balls, all the way up the shaft to the tip. It seemed to thicken and even to grow a little longer. I pressed it between my naked breasts.

"Let's fuck!" Abruptly, his hands were on my shoulders and he was trying to push me over on my back.

"No!" I struggled free. I certainly wasn't going to sacrifice my royal chastity on such an altar as this one.

"Do you have the curse, *mademoiselle*?" My reaction puzzled him.

I made no answer. Let him think what he wanted.

"I don't mind if you do."

Again I didn't answer him.

"Very well then." He guided me to my knees in front of him again. "Suck it."

I kissed his throbbing prick.

"I said suck it!" His tone was urgent.

I licked it.

"I said suck!" He grew angry at my teasing.

"No!" I refused. I was afraid that I would choke as I had with my lover, de Rohan.

"*Oui!*" One of his hands pushed back my cowl and tangled painfully in my ash-blond tresses.

"No!"

"I said *oui!*" He slapped me lightly across the face and then forced the swollen head of his small, erect cock into the mouth slit of my mask.

Any further protest I might have made was effectively cut off by the stiff prick in my mouth. I had gotten myself into a situation where my rank could not protect me. Either I must suck this stranger's cock until he came in my mouth, or he would brutalize me—perhaps do me real harm, perhaps even kill me! I sucked his cock.

It was much smaller than the Prince-Bishop's, so perhaps I would not choke on it after all. The thought flitted through my mind as I tongued his balls and sucked at the base of the shaft at the same time. But then the man became excited and he pushed my head against his crotch in such a way that his cock pushed quite deeply into my mouth until I finally felt it sliding down my throat.

I gagged and tried to spit it out. He slapped me again—not hard, but more as if to warn me what to expect if I defied his will. I tried to suck it again. It was all right at first, but then again I felt myself starting to choke and tried to eject it.

This time when he slapped me, I was expecting it. He, however, was not expecting my reaction. I bit down hard on the small prick in my mouth. As soon as I did that, he proved most cooperative in allowing me to expel it.

"*Merde!*" He clutched at his injured member with both his hands and howled at the moon in the sky above.

I thought it wisest not to linger. I sensed that any sympathy I might offer would not be appreciated. Indeed, I suspected that in spite of it, just as soon as his agony abated even slightly, the gentleman would seek revenge with both hands and perhaps his feet as well. And so I quickly took my departure.

Immediately, the hedge maze swallowed me up. Behind me the groans faded from my hearing. Replacing them were sighs and moans and liquid sounds of lovemaking. It seemed that quite a few couples were celebrating Carnival in the secret hiding places provided by the trickily twisting hedges.

My intention was to exit the maze and rejoin my companions from Versailles. Two things interfered with this intention. Firstly, I seemed to be going around in circles and unable to find the exit from the maze. Secondly, I kept being distracted by all the carnal activity around me. I would stumble on one lascivious scene after another, dawdle to observe for a while, and then find that I had lost track of my plan for extricating myself from the hedges.

Oo-la-la! The scenes I witnessed! . . .

A plump young woman with wildly disheveled black hair and extraordinarily large breasts and powerful thigh muscles sprawled on her back with her legs flung wide apart and her naked pussy raised brazenly to the attack of a very long and very slender prick. The prick moved all the way out and all the way into her pussy with slow, lingering strokes. She beat the chest of its owner with her fists, but he would not be hurried. She could not urge him on with words because there was a second prick buried in her wide-stretched mouth. . . .

The naked bottom of a very young man glowed like some golden Grecian sculpture in the moonlight as he stood upright and locked in the act of love with a petite maiden whose mask had slipped from her face to reveal her radiant enthusiasm for his attentions to her. Her legs, not long, but quite shapely, were locked around his waist and her hands clasped behind his neck so that she would not fall under his vigorous onslaught. Her cunt moved faster and faster, slapping wetly against his pelvis with each plunge of his cock. "Quickly!" she urged. "Come inside me quickly! I must return before my husband misses me!"

A figure stood alone, cowl turned upwards toward the moon. I could not tell if it was a man or a woman, but finally I decided that it must be a woman because of the way the belly of the domino swelled out. Indeed, I thought that it must be a pregnant woman. Then there was a shifting and I realized I was mistaken. It wasn't a pregnant woman. There was someone underneath the cloak. That someone, judging by the squirmings and the sobbing breaths being drawn, was either eating a pussy, or licking a cock. Even the onrush of orgasm did not define the gender. Many men's voices go up the scale under such circumstances. . . .

Two young women lay naked atop the cloaks they had discarded. Their faces were uncovered, their masks nesting beside them. They were moving in a blur of uncoordinated motion, caressing and kissing each other's breasts and buttocks and thighs and quims. They were most athletic and their lips and tongues displayed both experience and talent. "Bite my nipples! . . ." "Use your fist! . . ." "Spread the cheeks and get your tongue all the way up. . . ." Their frantic words reached my ears. And then they were scrambling into the *soixante-neuf* position and they were eating at each others' bottom holes and pussies with the rapacity of the truly sexually starved. . . .

I move along. The next tableau on which I stumble seems very familiar to me. It takes me a moment to realize why, but when I do, I cannot but smile to myself. The masked and hooded couple are in that position most frequently assumed by Prince Bishop Louis de Rohan and myself. Furthermore, the prick pumping in the light from the Chinese lanterns is steadfastly staying with the back-door target between the plump cheeks and not straying to the prettily pouting pussy below them.

A thrill courses through me as I identify with the figure bending over, hands clasping ankles. How well I know what she must be feeling! How delicious to have one's bunghole filled with rampaging cock! I am filled with a sudden yearning for Prince-Bishop de Rohan's cock battering up my anus.

As I start to continue on my way, my eyes linger on the prick sliding in and out of the writhing asshole. It looks strangely familiar. At first I think that must be because of the familiarity of the situation. Then, pausing, I realize that there is more to it than that.

I knew that prick!

I had fondled many, but there was only one like it. Only one prick had that look of frequent and vigorous use. Only one hard-on turned that particular shade of purple, featured that particularly extreme thickness, reached that wondrous length. *Oui*, I would recognize that wedge-shaped tip with its deep red color anywhere!

Only one cock head had that particular kind of hole like the spout of a garden watering can. There could be no mistaking it!

It was the prick of Prince-Bishop Louis de Rohan, my lover!

Jealousy ripped his name from my lips with a snarl.

Hearing it startled him. A less cool man might have lost his perch. The Prince-Bishop, however, was practiced at handling himself in such tricky situations. He barely missed a stroke.

"You are mistaken, *mademoiselle*." As anonymous in the recesses of his hooded cowl as I was in mine, he denied his identity.

"Mistaken?" Outraged beyond modesty, I bent over, tossed my cloak and skirt up over my hips, and thrust my naked derriere out at him. " 'Assume the position!' Are those words familiar to you, *m'sieur*? Does this rump not know your *épée* all too well?"

"Marie?" He withdrew, but not all the way. His shaft glistened with juices in the dim light. "But how can it be you?"

"Why not? I too celebrate Carnival," I told him sarcastically. "Although not so actively as you, Your Grace."

"But I thought—" He started to explain in a reasonable tone of voice.

"That you would give this sweet young thing communion?" I guessed sweetly—nastily.

"I thought that she was—"

"In need of a priest. And so you were hearing her confession. Doubtless that is why her back is turned to you."

"I was under the impression that she was—"

"Or perhaps you were demonstrating the nature of

sin so that this poor creature might recognize it if the devil placed temptation in her path."

"He was only—" The young woman spoke for the first time.

"Don't tell me, *mam'selle*, let me guess. He was showing you how to preserve your virginity by the administering of an ecclesiastical suppository. He's quite good at that as I can well testify."

"Surely, *mademoiselle*, you are not claiming to be a virgin." She was amused.

That, however, did not infuriate me as much as the fact that she was still bending over with my lover's prick embedded between the plump cheeks of her bottom. "I will tell you what I am, *mam'selle*, and who as well." I removed my mask and pushed the hood of my cloak to my shoulders. "I am Marie Antoinette, wife of the Dauphin of France, and one day to be your Queen!"

"Surely she is jesting." The young woman straightened up without quite ejecting de Rohan and looked over her shoulder at him. The cowl fell back to her shoulders, but her mask was still in place. Her long tresses, ash-blond and similar to mine in both hue and texture, shimmered in the lantern light.

"I fear not." Finally, reluctantly, de Rohan withdrew his prick all the way and tucked it back inside his domino. "She is indeed Marie Antoinette and one day to be your sovereign Queen."

"Your Highness!" Flustered, the girl let her cloak fall over her bare derriere and curtsied deeply.

"And just who is this wench?" I demanded of de Rohan.

"I have no idea." He shrugged. "You see, I thought she was you."

"My name is Jeanne de Valois, Highness. I am no one. Only a poor seamstress."

"Do you expect me to believe that you mistook a seamstress for me?" I ignored her and turned on de Rohan. "And what is a seamstress doing here anyway? It is understood that only aristocrats—"

"Oh, but I really am of noble birth, Highness. Indeed, blood royal flows in my veins. I am a direct descendant of King Henry the Second of the House of Valois. An illegitimate descendant it is true, but still—"

"SILENCE!" the Prince-Bishop thundered. "King Henry fathered enough bastards to populate all of Normandy. His sons sired enough bastards to fill France. And the bastards from the loins of their sons overrun Europe. So spare us your pretensions, mam'selle. We are not interested."

"Oh, but I am fascinated," I contradicted him. "I want to know all about this bastard seamstress you took for a Hapsburg. Tell me, Your Grace, just how did you come to make such a mistake?"

"She flirted with me and—" he started to explain.

"And naturally you assumed she must be a princess. After all, who else would flirt with such an exalted personage as yourself?"

"Oh, but I didn't know who he was," Mlle. de Valois interjected.

"I rather think she did," de Rohan told me. "She went to a great deal of trouble to separate me out of the crowd. Including dropping and raising her mask so that I might glimpse her face."

"You saw her face, and still you thought—" What sort of a fool did he take me for?

"Take off your mask!" he ordered the girl. "Show your face to Her Highness."

Jeanne de Valois removed her mask.

I gasped. Words failed me. The face I looked into was twin to my own in every respect.

"Now do you see, Highness?" The Prince-Bishop's tone was bland, his manner urbane. "I really did think that it was you."

"But—but—" I floundered. "Her body—"

"Like yours in every respect," he assured me. "Show Her Highness," he commanded the young woman.

She opened her cloak. The single garment she wore beneath it was pulled above her breasts. Her bosom, like mine, was not yet fully developed. The budding breasts were of the same size, the bright red berry-nipples identical with mine. She was my height—tall—and her legs were long and tapered just as mine were. Her thighs jiggled with just a bit of baby fat which neither of us would ever lose, and her pussy yawned pinkly beneath her ash-blond sporran just as mine did when I was aroused.

Amazing! We might have been identical twins! Her body and her face were as Hapsburg as my own. I wondered just how far afield the lustful King Henry II had actually wandered. Had he ever visited Vienna? It was the first time in my life that it ever occurred to me to question the legitimacy of my Hapsburg lineage.

"Now cover yourself and leave us," the Prince-Bishop told the girl.

She quickly complied. Watching her depart, I had no reason to think I would ever set eyes on my double again. Little did I guess what effect this seamstress, this daughter of bastards, was going to have on my life, on the monarchy, on France itself, and ultimately on my fate. How could I have guessed on that Carnival night that someday the resemblance between us would be a key factor in bringing about the revolution that would change the face of Europe forever?

"Well, Marie?" My lover was even more smug than

usual. "Now do you believe me? You are as like as two peas in a pod. How could I have known?"

"But didn't it feel differently?" I asked a bit wanly.

"You interrupted us too soon for me to be able to answer that question," he told me blithely.

"Poor Louis." I reached inside his cloak. In truth the sight of him pounding away at that derriere so like my own had made me randy even as it angered me. "Oh, my!" His cock was full risen and throbbing in my two hands. "You really have been left unsatisfied."

"One usually is in cases of coitus interruptus," he replied. His hands slipped inside my cloak and moved over my body. "But the situation is not beyond remedy," he told me. He raised my dress and cloak. "Assume the position, Marie!"

My sphincter pulsing with anticipation, I assumed the position. It seemed the very least I could do to relieve his tumescent condition. . . .

Some time later we emerged from the maze and parted company. Even in our anonymous dominos and masks, it seemed wiser not to be seen in each other's company. Louis, after all, was the Prince-Bishop of Strasbourg, one day to be Cardinal of France. And I was a princess royal who would be Queen.

I wandered through the garden seeking members of the group with which I had come. A sudden turn in the path I had chosen brought me unexpectedly to a gazebo. It was really a charming little edifice and I decided to have a closer look at it. Only when I leaned over the low railing to peer inside did I realize that it was occupied.

A hooded figure stood with its back to the railing opposite me. Its hands were reaching behind to clench the railing tightly, the knuckles white in the starlight. A naked and erect penis stuck out from the folds of its cloak, identifying the figure as a man.

A woman in a domino was on her knees in front of the stiff cock. She had pushed back her cowl and removed her mask in order to suck it more thoroughly. I recognized her immediately; I remembered her well.

It was Mme. Yolande de Polignac, the chestnut-haired beauty with alabaster skin who had attracted my attention at one of the early balls I had attended at Versailles. I had thought her most attractive then when she had drifted away from her husband to the passionate embrace of her lover on the terrace. I still found her so now as her cheeks hollowed out under her high cheekbones to suck the cock in her mouth with a gusto that could not have been feigned. The expression on her face was ecstatic. I thought to myself that I must make the Prince-Bishop teach me how to do this without choking very soon. I too wanted to sample this ecstasy.

The man's eyes were glazed with his heightening excitement and wide open. Now, before I could step back into the shadows, they fell on me! *"Alors!"* The sight of me watching rattled him. He reacted by releasing the railing and pushing against his partner's shoulders.

She sprawled over backwards, releasing his *épée* from her moist and ruby lips. It sprang upwards towards his belly at the very moment that he lost control. His nectar sprayed across the gazebo and soiled my mask, clouding the eyeholes.

Blinded, I removed the mask to wipe away the man cream. Yolande de Polignac recognized me immediately. "Your High—" Even as she started to speak she was scrambling to her feet to make a curtsey. Quickly, I raised a finger to my lips to silence her. When I was sure she understood, I winked at her broadly to tell her that the secret of her adulteries was safe with me. Then I retired from the scene so as not to cause any of us further embarrassment.

Would I ever see Yolande de Polignac again? My heart beat faster with the hope that I would. I was greatly attracted to her. I wanted her to introduce me to her uninhibited way of life and to all of the arts of love which I imagined her to have mastered.

A few weeks after that Carnival night, however, something happened that drove all dreams of Yolande de Polignac from my mind. The King banished Prince-Bishop Louis de Rohan from Versailles!

"You can't do that, Majesty!" Extremely upset, I confronted him.

"It is done, *chere* Marie." My breasts in his hands did not sway His Majesty. "The pleas of Madame Du Barry herself have not been able to alter my decision."

Du Barry again!

"But why?" I demanded. "Why are you taking such harsh action?"

"I am banishing Prince-Bishop Louis de Rohan from Versailles because he has once again broken his promise to me to behave circumspectly while he is at Court. He is a churchman and should set an example!" The King bounced me on his lap and squirmed against my bottom. "Instead, he uses his position in the church to behave like the worst of roués. No woman at Versailles, married or single, is safe from him. If a bishop can run amok among the wives of the aristocracy, then soon the stable grooms will be thinking that they can do the same!" The King's hand squeezed my pussy through my clothing. "Truly, Marie, I do believe de Rohan to be such a rascal as to press his seductions at the highest level. Why, the scoundrel might even direct his attentions towards you, Marie."

"Perish the thought," I murmured, rolling my buttocks back and forth over the King's erect cock.

"Ahh, Marie, you are too innocent to perceive what

goes on at Versailles. The fact is that the wench I discovered de Rohan with looks enough like you to be you yourself."

"You discovered him with a woman who looks like me?" I clutched the King's cock with sudden fury. "What were they doing?"

"They were in the stables and she was mouthing his member."

"Mouthing his member!" I squeezed harder, enraged with jealousy.

"Easy, my girl! Not so rough." He unclenched my fingers with his own and introduced them to a pattern of rhythmic rubbing. "*Oui*, mouthing his member, and he most certainly was enjoying it."

Enjoying it! Furious, I jerked savagely. The King, however, was now too far along to protest. "And where is he banished to, sire?" I asked.

"An ambassadorship." The forces gathered in the shaft under my hand. "I have named him French ambassador to your mother's court." The cock jerked under my hand. "He is banished to Austria." The stain spread over the velvet. "Vienna."

"Good!" I exclaimed, wiping my hand on the King's coattails. De Rohan's seemingly perpetual erection would wither away under the straitlaced rule of my mother. She would not countenance his having liaisons with seamstresses no matter how much they might resemble me.

Vienna would serve my faithless lover right!

Chapter Seven

Malicious mischief is a time-honored dispeller of ennui for those of us born to the purple. I confess that I have never been an exception to this. I am as addicted to the practice as to masturbation and marzipan.

Jealousy and envy, of course, are a great goad to malicious mischief. What, after all, is as satisfying as an additional turn of the screw added to an unfaithful lover's punishment? It was in this spirit that I wrote to warn Mama of Prince-Bishop de Rohan's reputation.

"The Bishop Coadjutor of Strasbourg . . . named to the ambassadorial post in Vienna . . . comes from a mighty house to be sure, but the life he leads more closely resembles that of a roistering military man than an ecclesiastic. . . ."

Mama's ear was subtle. Others might find the words of my letter mild, but she would hear in them a warning of loose French morals about to invade Vienna. To her they would be a bugle sounding the call to man the barricades against the imminent invasion of Gallic depravity.

Indeed, upon his arrival, Mama wrote to me immediately that my warning to her had been more than justified. She was opposed on principle, she said, to ecclesiastics embracing the pomp and pageantry reserved by God to royalty. But never had she seen this principle so brazenly ignored as upon the occasion of the entrance into Vienna of the new French ambassador, Prince-Bishop Louis de Rohan.

His arrival (I could picture her sniffing with distaste as she scratched the words with her quill pen) had been worthy of some Oriental sultan. An advance guard in comic-opera uniforms had preceded him. He himself had arrived with his entourage in two ostentatious carriages, both gilded and lacquered, which must have cost at least forty thousand francs each. A cacophony of martial music had rent the air, the product of the vulgar, scarlet-clad band which had accompanied him from Paris. It had taken the Viennese street cleaners a full day to clean up after the stable of fifty horses he had brought, and in the interim an undeniably French stench filled the nostrils of all Vienna. And the final insult (Mama took it as a reflection upon what she considered to be the most civilized and circumspect and certainly the safest court in Europe) was Prince-Bishop de Rohan's two personal bodyguards, Heyduc Guards, professional killers, Hungarian giants with high-plumed military bonnets and vicious, double-edged scimitars.

"Frankly, I am nervous about my Vienna ladies," her letter concluded. "Young and old, pretty, ugly, all alike are bewitched by the man."

Rogue that he was, I nevertheless missed the Prince-Bishop. There was no denying it. I sat more easily now, less painfully, but there was no one—not the King, not the young rakes at Court—to fill the libidinous void my lover left behind him.

Certainly my husband, Louis-Auguste, was not capable of filling it. It was common knowledge at Versailles that the Dauphin, after more than two years of marriage, still had not plucked my Austrian cherry. Which is not to say that he did not from time to time give it the old Sorbonne try.

Poor Lous! There was something touching, something almost valiant in the way he faced up to his marital responsibility, gritted his teeth and attacked the problem of fulfilling it. And if he approached it as he might a problem of lock making—well, that was the way his mind worked, poor dear.

"The court physician has given me a book which explains it all very simply," he informed me one night when we were in our canopied four-poster together. He looked very serious, sitting up in his frilled, monogrammed nightshirt with the tassel of his nightcap pointing down at his three chins. "Look. There are even diagrams."

I looked. There were indeed diagrams. Stick figures. I had been hoping for something a bit more realistic. "How interesting." I made an effort to sound enthusiastic. I also deliberately let the nightgown slip from my bare shoulder.

"It says that the female ear is an erogenous zone," he told me. "It says that blowing in it will stimulate the female. Shall I try it, Marie?"

"By all means, dear."

Louis leaned over and exhaled in my ear. "Did that excite you?" he inquired.

"What?" I was temporarily deafened.

"I said did that excite you?" Louis repeated loudly and distinctly.

"Oh. *Oui*."

"Oh, dear!" He was looking at the manual again and now he frowned and bit his lip.

"What's the matter?"

"I blew into the wrong ear. It says here that I should blow into the right ear while at the same time stroking the left breast."

"Don't blow quite so hard this time," I gasped. The reason I was gasping was that Louis was leaning across me to get to my other ear and his weight was on me, squeezing the air from my body. I felt like a sea urchin sat upon by a whale.

"As you say, Marie." He wheezed more considerately into my right ear. At the same time he stroked my left breast with the middle finger of his hand in much the same way as one might stroke back the whiskers of a particularly delicate Siamese cat. "Does that arouse you, Marie?" he inquired.

What it did was tickle me, but I squelched the impulse to laugh. Louis would have been shattered. "*Oui*." I managed a little heavy breathing. "It certainly does."

" 'Once aroused,' " Louis read, " 'the male may caress and fondle the breasts as freely as the female permits. However, should she shrink from his touch, he should not insist. The breasts of some young girls are extremely sensitive and the reaction to their being touched may be negative. Care should be taken not to prematurely shock the young bride. . . .' "

"I'm not a bride anymore, Louis. We've been married two years."

" 'He may even kiss the breasts. The nipples are particularly responsive, but also sensitive. If the bride does not object, he may place one between his lips and even touch it with the tip of his tongue.' "

"The bride does not object," I murmured.

" 'Sucking the bride's nipples may arouse the groom as well as the bride.' " Louis sucked my nipples, first one and then the other.

It was not unpleasant. It never is. His lips were a little dry with nervousness, but his tongue was satisfactorily velvety and sent shivers running through me. I held his hand to my breast and released it only after I spoke. "Has sucking the bride's nipples aroused the groom?" I inquired in a husky voice.

"*Oui*, Marie." He hiccuped. "*Oui*."

I looked at him with dismay. This was not the first time Louis had suffered an attack of hiccups when we tried to make love. I reached between his legs to see if he was aroused as he had said he was. Just as I suspected, he was soft as butter left out in the sun. Most men, when they're excited, get erections. My husband got hiccups. The luck of the Hapsburgs!

" 'At this point,' " Louis read, " 'the groom must determine if the bride's arousal has resulted in the lubrication necessary for coitus to proceed. He should reach under her nightgown and rest his hand lightly on the lips of her vulva and . . .' " As he was reading, Louis was attempting to balance the book with one hand and follow the directions with the other. Touching my pussy, he hiccuped violently again.

I felt like the royal coach having its axles checked. "There's something else necessary for coitus to proceed," I murmured.

"What did you say, *cheri?*" Another hiccup.

"Nothing, dearest." I wriggled. Clumsy as Louis was, the proximity of his hand to my hungry pussy was indeed having an effect.

"It says that 'if the groom finds the moistness satisfactory, he may attempt to gently part the lips of the vagina . . .' But Marie—?" He hiccuped.

"*Oui?*" I writhed over his fumbling hand, swallowing it up with my sopping pussy.

"The lips already are parted and you're not just moist, you're—" A spasmodic series of hiccups cut Louis short.

"Ready!" I panted. "That's what I am. Ready!"

" 'But first a word of caution—' " Louis read, continuing to hiccup.

"Put down the book, darling," I pleaded.

" 'In this era of the Enlightenment, it is no longer the woman's responsibility, but rather the man's, to be sure that precautions are observed to prevent unwanted conceptions.' " A barrage of hiccups left Louis gasping.

"Don't worry about that, darling," I moaned. "That's what we're supposed to be doing, making an heir to the throne. You can forget the book now and—"

"No, Marie!" For Louis, he was really quite firm. "I am determined to follow this marriage manual. And I am quite prepared to do so in all respects." Hiccuping, but proud of himself, he opened the night-table drawer and withdrew an object that looked like nothing so much as a rolled up balloon of the kind the peasants used for decorations at Carnival time.

I had never seen anything like it. I watched, fascinated, as Louis unrolled it and then once again referred to the book. "What are you going to do with that?" I asked as he struggled, hiccuping, to find his place.

"Put it on my—you know." He turned red and hiccuped more violently.

"But it isn't stiff, Louis. Aren't you supposed to wait until it's stiff?"

"It doesn't say anything about that. Now please don't go on distracting me, Marie. I'm trying to read the instructions here." He hiccuped some more as he read.

"But Louis—"

"Shh, Marie!" He hiccuped. Then he read aloud once again to insure my silence. " '. . . Since the tiniest aperture may prove disastrous (hic!) and since the naked eye (hic!) may not detect it (hic!) certain precautions must be (hic!) observed. The open end (hic!) of the device should be inflated to be sure it is airtight (hic!). Place it on your lips with the rim inside your (hic!) mouth, and then blow into it (hic!) to be sure . . ." Louis put down the manual and started to follow the instructions.

"Louis!" Suddenly I had had enough. Lust overwhelmed me. I threw off my nightgown and flung myself on him naked. "This is no time to be blowing up balloons!" I declared. "Make love to me!" I demanded. "Now!"

Louis' eyes bulged out even more than they ordinarily did. His little penis actually stirred between his legs. He reached for me, the balloonlike device still between his lips. And then. . . .

"HIC!"

It was the most powerful hiccup yet. The half-inflated device in his mouth suddenly deflated and vanished entirely. Louis turned a bright purple. His eyes now looked like they were about to escape their sockets altogether. He was choking!

"Louis?" I was alarmed.

His arms waved like a windmill.

"Louis!" I pounded him on the back.

He began to thrash about helplessly, still choking.

I leaped from the bed and rang for the servants. I dispatched them for the court physician. Several other nobles came running to investigate the disturbance. Finally the doctor arrived. Other doctors followed in his wake. They lifted Louis by his ankles (it took six strong men to do it) and held him upside down and struck him on the back. At last the device flew out of his mouth and he stopped choking.

By then it was assured that everyone at Versailles was privy to the latest disaster of the royal boudoir!

*   *   *

The King was particularly upset. He simply could not understand the sexual ineptitude of his grandson. He took the first opportunity to discuss the debacle with me privately. The occasion was a royal journey to Paris to preside over the opening of a new state theater.

Protocol required not only the King, but the Dauphin and I as well, to attend the function. Moreover, the King had insisted that his bawd, Du Barry, also attend. Since I had made it a rule never to share a coach with the King's whore, this necessitated our party traveling by two coaches.

"You ride with *madame*," the King instructed Louis. "I have matters to discuss with Marie."

"But Grandpapa—!" Louis started to protest. He knew that Du Barry had nothing but contempt for him and dreaded being in her company. She would devil him with sarcasm all the way to Paris. Nevertheless, a stern glance from the King stilled his tongue and he climbed into the coach containing Du Barry.

"The wench will be furious with you," I remarked to the King when he joined me in the first of the two coaches.

"Respect, Marie," he cautioned me.

"For the King's harlot?"

"Enough! I want to talk to you about your husband." As our carriage rolled smoothly down the road from Versailles behind six royal white horses, the King raised the hem of my traveling dress and put his hand atop my stockinged knee.

"Louis?" I patted the King's hand. "What about him?"

"I refer to the fiasco of the other night." His fingers crept up, savoring the fleshiness of my thighs above the garters holding up my stockings. "Things cannot go on between my grandson and you in this fashion. After all, one day you will be King and Queen of France."

"What do you suggest?" I shifted in the seat beside him, parting my thighs a trifle more and sighing.

"I have had a letter from your mother," was his unexpected answer. "She has been consulting with Viennese physicians who specialize in problems such as these." He stroked my bush through the tickling silk of my bloomers.

"Mama is really not very sophisticated when it comes to sex," I confided.

"I gathered that from her letters. Nonetheless, the recommendations of her Viennese specialists make sense." His Majesty continued the intimate strokings.

"And what were these recommendations?" The warm wetness of my reaction was making the silk slippery to his caresses now. "I cannot imagine that they suggest any approach that I have not already tried with Louis." I sighed, wriggled, and slid down a little in my seat.

"This plan does not involve you." Using his finger like a saw, the King followed the crotch of my bloomers as the lips of my pussy drew in the silk. "It is their feeling that repeated failure has made you intimidating to Louis."

"But how can he have sex without me?" I raised up a little and the King's hand obligingly slid back and forth between the cleft of my derriere and my clutching pussy.

"These Viennese experts are recommending what they call a 'sex surrogate.' " He took my hand and placed it atop the erection ridging his britches.

"A 'sex surrogate'? It sounds like a judge of contests in a Montmartre bordello." I laughed breathlessly and squeezed his hard and juicy scepter through the velvet.

Ahh, the King! What a randy old devil he always

was! One could depend on him absolutely to rise to the occasion—and to create an occasion to rise to if that was necessary.

"In this case 'surrogate' means 'stand-in,' " the King informed me, his erection throbbing under my hand. "Since you intimidate Louis in bed, a substitute partner will be provided. One who, hopefully, will not prove intimidating to him."

"You mean that you are going to arrange to have my husband do it with another woman?" I was so indignant that the lips of my pussy released the King's finger.

"It is for the good of the crown." The King held my hand firmly to his groin.

"The good of the crown!" I crossed my legs defiantly, trapping his hand, but allowing it not the slightest freedom of movement. "You are aiding and abetting his making love to another woman. Yet if I were to take another man, there would be the very devil to pay!"

"You are still a virgin, Marie. A royal virgin! We can't risk tampering with that." He tried to withdraw his hand from under my skirts, but I wouldn't let him.

"Who is this 'surrogate' sex partner you have picked out for my husband?" I demanded bitterly.

"A seamstress. Her name is Jeanne de Valois. You may remember that I mentioned her to you once before, Marie. She was involved in the expulsion of Prince-Bishop de Rohan to Vienna."

"Why her?" I removed my hand from the erection tenting his britches.

"She bears an absolutely striking resemblance to you, my dear. I told you that. Remember?" The King tried to take my hand in his and return it to his lap, but I wrenched it away. "The experts think that this resemblance may be helpful in easing Louis back into your bed from hers."

"It is intolerable!" I was furious. "And insulting to me personally!" I added. "My husband cavorts with another woman while I languish, a married virgin!"

"That is the way of our royal world, Marie. I didn't make the rules. But I do admit that they were made by men and do not treat women very fairly. Still, it is not my fault, so let us be friends, Marie." He pressed my hand to his velvet-sheathed erection again and tried to move his other hand between my crossed and clenched thighs.

"Oh, all right." Retitillated, I relented and uncrossed my legs. "Is she a prostitute, this de Valois?" I inquired idly.

"I told you, she is a seamstress." The King wriggled his fingers against my pussy, trying to get the feeling back into his hand.

"Many seamstresses, I am told, are also whores." The warm wetness was back and my nipples were once again risen against the inside of my bodice.

"I think the circulation has resumed." The King stroked lingeringly from my derriere to my pussy. "No." He responded to my comment. "I don't believe that she is a whore."

"If she is not a whore, then why is she doing this? Just to go to bed with a man who will one day be King of France?" My enthusiasm was mounting again now as I once again squeezed his royal scepter through his britches.

"That would certainly be reason enough." The King played with my clitty. Ahh! The old royal roué really had technique! "But there is more to it than that. You see, Jeanne de Valois realizes that her resemblance to you is of value in this matter and she is trading on it. She wants me to use my influence in a matter of some concern to her."

"And what is that, sire?" I was rubbing up and down

against the hand between my legs, bouncing slightly with the rhythm of the galloping coach.

"She wishes me to restore the de Valois family to the ranks of the nobility." His head bobbed to my bosom and he sank his teeth into the upper part of one of the breasts rising from my bodice.

"Oo-la-la!" His cock had bucked demandingly against the palm of my hand. "And is there any substance to this request?" Despite my gasping state, I found the wit to ask the question.

"*Oui*. The official records so indeed verify that she is a descendant of King Henri the Second of the House of Valois. They show that he had a son by his mistress, the Baroness de Saint-Remy, and that he legitimized this son by an official act which was both customary and legal in those days. The son married and had offspring, and the line is direct from them to Jeanne de Valois." The King sucked at my nipple, fondled my clitty, and thrust his velvet-sheathed royal scepter in and out of my loosely clenched fist.

"Then why is there a problem at all?" I inquired, wishing that he would fling up my skirts, pull down my bloomers, take out his big old randy cock and ram it all the way up my hungry quim, and the devil with the need to preserve monarchial chastity!

"The vagaries of history, my dear." The King removed one of my breasts from my gown and held the erect nipple in front of his mouth so that he might lick at it between words as he answered me. "Only a year after granting legal patrimony to his son, King Henri the Second was killed by one of his own knights in a tournament. King Henri the Third, who succeeded him, was subsequently assassinated by a monk. At this point the succession passed to King Henry the Fourth, not a Valois at all, but, like myself, a Bourbon. It was only natural that to the Bourbons any members of the Valois clan—legitimate or illegitimate—constituted a threat to the crown they now wore. Therefore, in exchange for their lives, all of the Valois at that time changed their names and renounced all of the claims that went with the name Valois."

"Were they coerced into doing this?" I wondered, feeling more and more feverish, and terribly, terribly randy.

"Of course, Marie. We are speaking of kings, not cabbages. And Bourbon kings at that. Why we Bourbons are almost as bloodthirsty as Hapsburgs, my dear." His rampaging prick moved more urgently against my hand.

"And so she wants back her family's rank?" I fisted the King feverishly.

"The Valois titles and the estates go with them," he confirmed, moaning passionately.

"And will you grant her request?" I was tugging now with both hands at the scepter writhing in his britches.

"We will see how she fares with Louis." Unexpectedly, the King stayed my hands—both of them. "I have not a change of linen, Marie. And such a stain as is imminent, Madame Du Barry would never forgive. Now I am going to take out my member, my dear. I know that you are a virgin and have never seen its like before, but do not be alarmed by its swollen and angry red appearance. Nor should you be frightened by its size."

I watched as he suited his actions to his words. In truth, he need not have bothered with cautioning me. The cock of Prince-Bishop de Rohan was half again as large and thick. Nevertheless, I was stirred by its aroused state and by its closeness to me in the confinement of the coach. "What would you have me do, sire?" My voice trembled. One of his hands was still inside my bloomers and moving against my pussy. I was perilously close to spending myself.

"Take this handkerchief, my dear." The King handed it to me. It was of lace and bore the royal monogram. "Catch the evidence in it. Now go back to what you were doing."

I did as he suggested. It was ever so much more pleasant without the velvet of his britches between my hand and his throbbing, naked cock. As I felt the shaft filling with the nectar of his lust, I bore down on his hand and buried my face between his neck and his shoulder and started to spend myself. When he realized what I was about, the King became excited and his cock jerked violently against the handkerchief and I had to struggle to hold it so that the stream it discharged would not go astray.

Finally we subsided. The King replaced his scepter inside his britches and buttoned them. I repositioned my bloomers and pulled down my skirts. Then I folded the handkerchief carefully to contain the King's contribution and started to open the window of the coach.

"Don't throw it out the window." The King stopped me.

"Why not?"

"Du Barry will see. She's a very suspicious woman. If she sees you discarding a piece of material, she will surely stop her coach to investigate what it is."

"Then what shall I do with it, sire?"

"Stuff it behind one of the cushions."

I did as he said, smiling to myself. Whatever I thought of Du Barry, she certainly had the King under her thumb. "And if your whore should learn what we've been about, sire, what then?" I could not resist teasing him. "Perhaps yet another diamond necklace?"

"That is not very funny, Marie." The King sighed. "You have no idea what I'm going through."

"I'm sorry, sire. Is it the Necklace of the Slave of Love?"

"It is. Those damnable jewelers have found a pair of girandoles, great dripping diamonds shaped like pears, and Du Barry has insisted they be made into earrings immediately without waiting for the necklace itself. Marie, I have had to add tax collectors and assign troops of soldiers to back them up just to pay for the earrings. I am seized with fear, Marie. The cost of the necklace continues to mount. There is a very real chance that it may bankrupt the country!"

I had never seen the King so troubled. He was absolutely serious. Trapped by his mistress's demands, he was really afraid that he might be forced into sacrificing France.

"Why do you do it, sire?" I asked as much out of genuine curiosity as out of sympathy. "Du Barry is but a woman. What has she got that other women have not? What can she do that they cannot do?"

"Ahh, my innocent, virginal Marie! There are things between men and women of which you do not dream. Do you remember what I told you the Valois woman was doing to de Rohan when I caught them?"

"*Oui.*"

"Well, Marie, there are some women, only a choice few, and only one who combines the talent with beauty, who have raised that practice to an art not even a King will willingly forsake."

"You mean—"

"There is only one throat like Du Barry's!"

That settled it! The King would bankrupt his realm for a woman who knew just how to mouth his scepter.

If that was so, then a queen must surely master this art. And one day I would be Queen.

I promised myself that I should not wait for that day to learn the secret of ruling kings by giving the best head in all France!

But how should I learn this technique? Who would teach me? My only attempts, with de Rohan, had been gagging, choking failures. I was reminded of this when I received another letter from Mama deploring his behavior.

"I will not have that man corrupting my nobility!" Mama thundered in a missive delivered into my hand by special courier. And then she went on to tell how he was doing just that. Some of what she wrote seemed picayune, but to Mama it signified a breakdown in tradition which was the first step on the road to perdition. Other things she related were more overtly sinful and certainly seemed to prove that her perception was sound.

"He has broken with my custom of formal dinners," she complained, a malefaction she obviously considered to be both insulting and a dangerous breach of the rules of Viennese society. "Instead of one long table with a hundred, or possibly two hundred, guests carefully seated according to rank, Prince-Bishop de Rohan has taken to giving what he calls 'dinner parties' in which perhaps no more than fifty or sixty guests are seated at small tables for four or six. These tables are then arranged in a tight circle of such shocking intimacy that it is quite possible for a landed aristocrat from the provinces to address a countess of the Court."

The meat of Mama's letter, as far as I was concerned, was in the next two paragraphs. "These 'dinner parties' frequently continue late into the night, or even the early morning. I have heard that the guests leave their tables and that there is dancing. The candelabra are dimmed and some of the couples retire to banquettes. In the shadows the most disgraceful fondlings are said to occur. It is even said that some of those involved retire to more private rooms provided by the Prince-Bishop.

"Worst of all, perhaps, are the rumors of his own behavior. His name has been linked with two ladies of my court, both married. It is also whispered that he has seduced a young maiden soon to be wed. A second maiden is said to accompany him on afternoon rides in a closed carriage. A final infamy—he is said to indulge in sodomy.

"But what am I to do, Marie? De Rohan is the official French ambassador to Vienna and King Louis XV has decreed him so. I dare not ask for his recall for fear of offending the King. The situation concerning Poland— our empire shall join with Russia and Germany to settle the fate of that troublesome land once and for all—makes it imperative that French neutrality is assured. I cannot put a strain on Gallic goodwill, and so I must continue to put up with the ambassador's outrageous behavior!"

Mama had her cross to bear, and I had mine. Hers was my former lover. Mine was my husband. And if Prince-Bishop de Rohan was not like other men, well then neither was my Dauphin.

Most husbands, for instance, might consider it diplomatic to conceal their infidelities from their wives— particularly, perhaps, if they did not quite work out as intended. Not Louis though! He had grown quite attached to me, and now he made me his confidante.

"I don't really want to sleep with this woman, this 'sex surrogate,' this Jeanne de Valois," he pouted. "But Grandpapa insists!"

"You shouldn't let him bully you, Louis. If you don't want to sleep with her, then don't."

"I'd really much rather sleep with you."

"*Merci*, Louis. It's really very nice of you to say so. And I don't just mean because I happen to be your wife."

"You see, Marie, when I sleep with you, I sleep. This de Valois woman doesn't let me sleep. If I try, she wakes me up. And you can't imagine the things she does!"

"Oh, I think perhaps I can."

"She dances!"

"Dances?" I was intrigued. Perhaps I had neglected a technique or two where Louis was concerned.

"Yes. While she disrobes. Oh, and that's another thing. She insists on disrobing in front of me."

"I believe that's meant to stimulate your libido, Louis."

"Really? Well, it bores me. Why do women wear so many layers of clothing, Marie?"

"I don't know. I've never really thought about it. Perhaps it's to fire the imaginations of men. You see, Louis, most men don't want reality, they want fantasy. I think that's what women's clothes are really all about."

"Well, I get very tired waiting for Mademoiselle de Valois to get down to the last layer and sometimes I doze off."

"And she wakes you. Well, after all, Louis, that is what she's there for."

"I know." Louis sighed. "After all, Marie, I did read that sex manual. I understand what she's trying to do. It's just that it doesn't seem to be working. And some of it, I confess, I don't even understand. Why does she use her mouth so much, for instance?"

"Her mouth?" Now I really was intrigued. "What does she do with it, Louis? Tell me exactly."

"She kisses me. On the lips. My ears. Oh, by the way, I know now what I must have done wrong with you, Marie. I think she's doing it wrong too. Sometimes when she kisses my ears they ring something fierce. It's just like getting water in them. I wonder who it was decided that was sexy?"

"I don't really know, Louis. Where else does she kiss you?" I inquired.

"Between my neck and my shoulder. And on my chest." He indicated the nipples set into his somewhat heavy and completely hairless man breasts. "And there." He pointed to the small penis beneath his fat and sagging belly.

"What else does she do there?"

"Sometimes she licks under it, where my jewels are. And sometimes she even takes it in her mouth and sucks on it."

"Do you like that, Louis?"

"It makes me feel like I want to go pee-pee."

Perhaps the King was right. Perhaps it really was a very rare art indeed. Perhaps he should have sent Du Barry to arouse Louis rather than de Valois. And yet my lover de Rohan had quite enjoyed the seamstress's mouth if I was to believe the King.

"Did you tell her the effect she was having?" I asked Louis.

"*Oui*. I really did have to pee-pee. I had to tell her. I mean, it was still in her mouth and—"

"I understand." I cut him short. "And what did she do when you told her?"

"Oh, she removed her mouth very quickly. Very quickly indeed. And then she asked me if it would excite me to do it on her. Actually, I did think that might be rather interesting, but I could never do it, Marie, and so I told her no."

"Why not, Louis? Why couldn't you do it? Why did you lie to her?"

"She looks too much like you, Marie. I could never

make pee-pee on a woman who looks that much like you. I explained that to her, but she said I was missing the point. She said that many men found golden showers—that's what she kept calling it, golden showers—quite stimulating. She said women found it stimulating too. She said that she was such a woman and tried again to get me to make pee-pee on her, but I wouldn't."

"Because she looked so much like me." I was touched. "But I wouldn't have minded if you did that, Louis." Indeed, it was exactly what I would have wished on the King's accursed sex surrogate! After all, de Rohan had betrayed me with her!

"Then she asked me if perhaps I might not like such a golden shower."

"You mean she offered to—"

"On me. *Oui*, Marie."

"She went too far! Does she not realize that one day you will be King of France?" I was indignant.

"Perhaps that is why she thought I would enjoy it, Marie. You see, as I understand it, kings pee-pee on everybody else, but they never do get pee-peed on themselves. It is something, I suspect, that every king in his heart of hearts wants to experience."

"And what did you do, Louis?" *Mon Dieu!* He already smelled always of the stables from his blacksmithing activities.

"I thanked her, but declined. Actually, I was very tempted, Marie, but—"

"Did you also decline this offer because of de Valois' resemblance to me?" I asked delicately.

"*Oui*, Marie. I mean, after all, why should I settle for a golden shower from her when it is you who are my wife?"

I stared at Louis for a long moment. This was the first enthusiasm he'd shown in our two years of marriage for any sexual activity at all. But was this really a sexual activity? I wasn't sure. I was out of my depth. I wished there was someone I could ask about it. Someone with experience. But the only one I could think of who might have that kind of experience was Du Barry, and it was my rule never to speak to her. For once I wished that I might break that rule.

"Do you really think that would excite you, Louis?" I asked doubtfully.

"*Oui*, Marie. Very much."

"Really excite you?"

"*Oui*. Who knows, Marie, it might even make my you-know-what grow hard."

"Well then—" I removed my nightie and knelt over his face. It was radiant, beaming. I did what he wanted.

The results were inconclusive. On the one hand, the deed excited me much more than I had anticipated it would. It was such a forbidden act, and yet there could be no doubt that it left Louis awash with pleasure. His little you-know-what actually did stiffen. On the other hand, alas, it became limp again just as soon as my stream had run its course.

Afterwards, I could not help wondering if Louis was right. Was this sort of subjection something all kings secretly craved? Did the King, his grandfather, crave it? Did the infamous Du Barry oblige? It would not have surprised me. Her hold on the King was such that I was sure she missed no tricks at all where sex between them was concerned. I may have spurned Du Barry, but there was no denying her cleverness.

Nor was there any denying her malice towards me. That, I am sure, is what lay behind her reading of a letter from my erstwhile lover, Prince-Bishop de Rohan, to her dinner guests one night shortly after I initiated Louis with the golden shower. The letter, sneering and insolent, poked fun at my mother, the Empress of Austria, and attacked her honor as well.

"I have just come from an audience with the Empress of Austria," he wrote, "and I found her weeping for the woes of persecuted Poland. In one hand she clutched a handkerchief to stanch her tears, in the other a sword to hack out Austria's slice of poor butchered Poland."

Austria's action in joining with Prussia and Russia to conquer Poland and subdivide it was not popular with the French. For that reason, I suppose, de Rohan's *mot* was widely circulated among the aristocrats at Versailles. But of course it was Du Barry who, by reading it aloud to her guests, started the *mot* on its way. It was her way of taking a stab at me through my mother and of keeping alive among the French the awareness that I was Austrian.

As for de Rohan, I would never forgive him. He knew well enough the situation at Versailles to realize that such a letter in the hands of Du Barry would be used as a weapon against me. He obviously didn't care. He cared for me not at all. He had simply been amusing himself by buggering a virgin who would be the future Queen of France. And now it amused him to embarrass that future Queen by arming her archenemy with words designed to spread like wildfire.

Oui, I would never forgive him. I hated him. I vowed he would never lay hands on me again. I vowed to avenge my poor Mama. *Oui!* I would have my revenge upon Prince-Bishop Louis de Rohan as soon as I was Queen of France!

That event was not as far in the future as everyone assumed. Shortly after the scandalous letter was read by Du Barry, the King fell ill with a fever. When the fever did not abate, the doctors of course bled him. When still it persisted, they bled him again. And then again. And again and again.

Finally Louis and I were summoned to his bedside. I could not recognize the white-faced and shrunken man lying there. The King was skeletal, and his eyes, which had always sparkled so with ribald humor, were dull and lifeless. His hand was bony and trembling in mine and even when I brazenly pressed it to my bosom, he had not the strength to respond. When I left his bedside, it was with the sad knowledge that there would be no more stolen moments with the King, no more randy bouncings on his lap.

The next day, May 10, 1774, at a quarter past three in the afternoon, I heard a low, deep sound like approaching thunder. It grew louder, then louder still. *Oui!* It was a terrible noise, exactly like that of thunder! And then the doors to our apartments were flung open and this thunder burst upon us, Louis and me.

The thunder was the stampeding of a crowd of Versailles courtiers running through the Hall of Mirrors. They were coming from the courtyard beneath the royal bedroom where the flame of a lighted candle in one of the windows had just been snuffed out. King Louis XV of France was dead.

"The King is dead!" they shouted. "Long live the King and Queen!"

Louis-Auguste and I embraced. He was shaking and mumbling protests that he was too young to reign. It was true, he was only nineteen, a year older than I. But his protests were in vain because he was now in fact King.

And I, Marie Antoinette of Austria, was Queen of France!

Chapter Eight

"The financial condition of the nation is appalling." My husband, King Louis XVI, immediately after his succession to the throne, realized a fact of French life which any struggling peasant or starving drayman knew all too well. "We have mass unemployment, runaway inflation, and our national treasury is depleted. With the price of a cord of wood what it is, I don't see how we can afford to heat the castle! Whatever shall I do, Marie?"

"Arrest Madame Du Barry!" It galled me that the lowborn slut's lavish expenditures might impose restrictions on the purse of the new Queen. "She is responsible! Her extravagances, particularly the Necklace of the Slave, are the cause of this recession."

The rapidity with which Louis followed this suggestion made me feel for the first time the influence I had over him and the power this gave me. I had the satisfaction of seeing Du Barry taken into custody that very evening and removed to the Abbey of Pont-aux-Dames where she remained a prisoner for many months. Her fall from eminence was complete. Never again would she exercise the slightest leverage at the royal Court. Indeed, never again would her presence be tolerated there. The dead King's whore was *finis*.

Her effect on the finances of the country, however, lingered. The spiral of higher taxes and higher prices continued after her departure. The sound of hungry bellies growling was audible even at Versailles.

It was the major problem facing the new King. Louis truly agonized over it. Then one morning he burst into my boudoir beaming. He'd had a vision; he was sure he'd seen the light at the end of the economic tunnel.

"Supply-side economics!" He pronounced the three words with the euphoria some people reserve for Father, Son, and Holy Ghost. "Marie, we're going to balance the budget with supply-side economics!"

"That's very nice, Louis." I yawned over my croissant and strawberry jam. "But tell me, just what is supply-side economics?"

"Priming the pump," he explained. "That's what they used to call it. Only they don't anymore."

"And what does 'priming the pump' mean?" I skimmed the whipped cream from the top of my Viennese coffee. A dutiful wife, I tried to be French in all things, but when it came to coffee, I would as soon have sipped from the chamber pot as drink the swill that passed for coffee in France. "And why don't they call it that anymore?" I asked as an afterthought.

"It means distributing largesse to the aristocrats to spend. When they spend it, you see, that stimulates the economy, and the benefits dribble down to the peasants and other poor people. Pretty soon everybody is better off."

"I see." I clapped my hands. "It's like when I order an expensive gown from my dressmaker and she puts all her seamstresses to work on it. I've actually created jobs and wages."

"That's it, Marie. That's it exactly."

"But why don't they call it 'priming the pump' anymore? That seems like such an apt description."

"Well, you see, Marie, they've tried it before and it didn't exactly work the way it should have. So they decided to call it supply-side economics instead."

"But what does supply-side economics mean?" I was still confused.

"Well, it doesn't actually mean anything, Marie. It doesn't actually have to, you know. It sounds so important that nobody would dare question its efficacy. After all, economists don't have to define. They simply have to identify."

"Why didn't it work when they tried it before?" I wondered.

"Some sort of a technical problem with the trickle-down effect." Louis waved it away airily. "But we've got the bugs out now. It'll work this time. All we need is a little cooperation."

"I'll cooperate, Louis," I promised him. "Really I will."

I was as good as my word, and better. I have always had a weakness for artisans, particularly *ébénistes*— furniture makers. Now I decided that they deserved to in the forefront of the beneficiaries of supply-side economics.

Since first I came to Versailles, I had admired the château known as the Petit Trianon. Of course while Louis XV was alive I had never entered it. The reason was obvious. It was the residence of his paramour, Mme. Du Barry. But now Du Barry was gone and there was no one to challenge my claim to the Petit

Trianon. I decided to turn it into a sort of play palace for myself and my friends—a kind of life-size dollhouse.

The whore's taste, as might be expected, had been execrable. I quickly set about correcting this. I called in the furniture designers Molitor and Jacob and Reisener, and together we worked out the designs which would come to be known as the Style Marie Antoinette. Together we refurbished the Petit Trianon from basement to attic. Inspired by neo-classical decor, I saw to it that all of the furnishings were dominated by my personality. Commodes and bureaus and cabinets were all long-legged and delicate. The chairs were straight-backed and the tables light and elegant. The draperies were of velvet—purple, red, gold, royal blue with contrasting pull cords ending in the most frivolous tassels. The books on the oiled mahogany shelves (I confess I had not the time to read them) were gold-embossed and bound in a most unusual blue leather.

From the very beginning my expenditures in connection with the Petit Trianon drew ominous grumblings from French people. They did not like me, of course, because I was Austrian. I had tried to endear myself to them from the first. God knows I had tried. But the French simply do not like Austrians—particularly Austrian Hapsburgs come to rule over them—and that is that. On top of this, they were simply too stupid to comprehend the finer points of supply-side economics involved in my spending hundreds of thousands of francs to refurbish the Petit Trianon in accordance with Louis' dribble-down principle. Far from appreciating this, in the slums in Paris the Petit Trianon was sneeringly referred to as "Little Vienna."

This was not the only reason for my growing unpopularity. Before I had even embarked on my interior decoration, indeed, just after I had contrived the arrest of Mme. Du Barry, I had used my influence with Louis to have Prince-Bishop Louis de Rohan removed from his post as ambassador to Vienna. I had done this at my mother's request—"Every day more indiscreet, more insolent, more unbearable!" she wrote me concerning de Rohan—and with a great deal of satisfaction as well. It felt marvelous to have the power to revenge myself on the former lover who had dared to malign my mother— the Empress of Austria!—in a letter made public by the old King's whore!

I used that power to make sure that de Rohan would not be able to return to Versailles. After Vienna, that would have been no punishment at all for him. Instead, Louis had the churchman consigned to Strasbourg with firm instructions to remain there as bishop. From what de Rohan himself had told me during one of our dalliances, that was a fate more stultifying even than the Austrian post.

The French, however, did not sympathize with the disciplining of de Rohan. The Austrians might frown on a prelate who flaunted his *épée* and cuckolded the most noble among his parishioners, but not the French. His peccadilloes made the Prince-Bishop only the more endearing to them. They bitterly resented a foreigner— the King's Austrian—designing their churchman's punishment. Thus my influence over the King was recognized and resented from the start.

I used this influence most gladly in behalf of Mme. Yolande de Polignac. *Oui*, the violet-eyed, tempestuous beauty came back into my life as unexpectedly as the nectar-shower finales of our first two meetings. One afternoon she simply appeared at Versailles with her husband under the auspices of one of my court nobles, and they were forthwith presented to me.

As she knelt before me, her lovely bosom rising above

the bodice of her gown with breathless excitement, I deliberately made no sign for her to rise. When those remarkable violet eyes looked up at me questioningly, I bestowed upon her the faintest of smiles and deliberately opened my parasol. "One never knows when precipitation may fall from the skies," I remarked. "Or from some other unexpected source," I added.

Yolande—I was already thinking of her with the utmost familiarity—blushed prettily. Her cherry lips turned up just enough to let me know that she comprehended my meaning. "I do not think you need worry today, Your Majesty," she told me demurely. "I see no chance at all of such precipitation."

"Alas." I glanced at her husband and then back at the chestnut-haired Lorelei. "You are undoubtedly correct. There is not a cloud in the sky." I reached forward and drew her to her feet with both my hands.

Our touch was electric. She felt it just as I did. I could tell, for we both caught our breath sharply and exchanged startled looks.

"Do you mind if your lady walks with me?" I addressed the question to her husband, as was customary, but it was into those fathomless violet eyes that I looked as I spoke.

"You do her great honor, Majesty."

"Amuse yourself as you will." I made sure to leave no doubt in his mind that I intended to stroll with Yolande alone. I linked arms with her, and his sweeping bow was made to our backs.

For a few moments, as we ambled in the garden, I enjoyed the warm, slightly exciting feel of her full breasts pressing against my arm as we walked. I realized that she was waiting for me to set the tone of the conversation as was proper in the company of the Queen. Finally, I spoke.

"Why do we see you so rarely?" I inquired.

"My husband and I are too poor to come to Court very often." She answered forthrightly. Despite her words, there was no hint of humility, nor of a pleading for sympathy, in her tone.

"Would you like to live at Court?"

"Very much, Majesty!"

"There is a very nice flat at the top of the marble staircase, just over my own apartments," I told her. "Do you think that might suit you and your husband."

There was a momentary look of consternation on Yolande's face.

"Your lover may visit if you are discreet," I assured her. "I do believe that the King might find a position for your husband that would neccessitate his being away a good deal. Do you think he would object to that?"

"We need money, Majesty," she reminded me frankly. "If the position pays him enough, my husband will not object."

"Then it will be done," I promised her.

I spoke to Louis that very night. He agreed to name de Polignac first equerry and to bestow upon him a title to befit the position. In keeping with his theories of supply-side economics, Louis cut the daily bread ration for the poor and settled a handsome salary on the new Comte and Comtesse.

Louis did not ask my advice in another matter. On May 6, 1775, he had the government issue a certificate restoring the titles of the de Valois family and awarding each member of that family a pension of eight hundred francs a year. The main beneficiary, naturally, was Mlle. Jeanne de Valois, the one-time seamstress whose resemblance to me was so striking.

Such was her generous reward for introducing the golden shower into the new King's life. The seamstress and quasi-whore was now legitimized. Jeanne de Valois was now a bona-fide member of the French aristocracy and persona grata at Court.

Despite the resemblance between us, I shrugged off this alteration in Mlle. de Valois' status. To me it was no more than a caprice of my husband's and surely not of a size with my own more frequent and more outrageous caprices. One thing is certain. At the time I did not foresee the far-reaching consequences of this event for myself and for France.

Indeed, I did not give it much thought at all. My mind, these days, was on other matters. I was just twenty years old and I had discovered the allure of diamonds.

"Diamonds," I confided to my new confidante, the Comtesse de Polignac, "are a queen's best friend."

I sealed this friendship with the purchase of a pair of diamond earrings which would one day be sold by the Republic of France at auction for one hundred million francs! This purchase was kept secret, but a subsequent one reached the ears of the public and created such a furor that word of it was passed along to my mother in Vienna. She wrote me that my profligacy "filled her with anguish for the future." I was quite annoyed that she had been bothered with such trifling gossip. The purchase involved bracelets worth a mere fifty-million francs.

Curiously enough, it was not my self-indulgence with jewelry which most aroused the hoi polloi, but my charities. What good is it to be Queen if one may not show generosity to one's noble friends? The first year of my reign, according to the treasury report to Louis, the "gifts and pensions" charged to the Queen's household came to 175 million francs. This included a grant to the nuns of Pique-puce for providing me with suspiciously aromatic herb salads which I could never bring myself to taste. Admittedly, other, greater amounts were bestowed upon those whose connection with me was more immediate.

Despite public insistence that such expenditures were "extravagances," Louis backed up my right to make them with his fullest authority. Even the aristocratic critics in his own government were waved away with assurances that "the Queen is doing her bit to stimulate the economy." Only once did he suggest that I take action to still their tongues.

"Somehow they've gotten hold of your dressmaker's bill, Marie—the one for the last formal ball. They're all up in arms about the expense of frivolous female frippery. But I have an idea to still their tongues. You only wear each dress on the one occasion anyway. So from now on when the occasion is over, donate the gown to the National Museum and that way it will become an asset of the nation itself, and no matter how expensive it is, you can't be accused of extravagance because your frocks will now be national treasures."

"That is really ingenious, Louis." I truly meant it. He was trying so hard to be a really kingly king. And it was quite impressive how he was growing with the job.

"Thank you, my dear. I'm rather pleased myself with the political acumen it demonstrates. I mean, here is my wife, the Queen of France, donating her ball gowns to the National Museum, setting an example, as it were, for all of the people, showing them by deed, not just word, what it means in these difficult times to bite the bullet."

"I welcome this opportunity to make a sacrifice for France, my dear." I patted his fat cheek. Louis may still have been a flop between the silken sheets, but in some ways he really was an ideal husband.

I confided this sentiment to Yolande de Polignac. She replied that I should consider myself quite fortunate. "My own husband," she told me, "is neither satisfying in bed nor generous."

"And your lover?" I inquired, teasing her. "What of the Comte de Vaudreuil?"

"Quite satisfactory in both respects, Majesty."

"Then that must be why you reward him so ardently with your mouth." I reminded Yolande of what I had seen. "Sometime you must teach me the secret of doing this without choking."

"At your pleasure, Majesty."

"My pleasure is now, Yolande. Teach me now," I told her.

We were taking tea with lemon and ice in one of the sitting rooms of the Petit Trianon, one of the chambers that was already decorated and furnished. It was a warm day, and despite the fact that there were workmen about performing tasks to finish the other rooms, we had loosened our stays and exposed our bosoms in order to fan them against the heat. Thus displayed, Yolande's breasts intrigued me. They were full and round, but seemed to curve outward in a manner quite different from my own. The areola were the faintest pink and not at all pronounced, while the nipples projecting from them were blood red and markedly long and pointy. They angled outwards from Yolande's breasts like two long fingers pointing in quite different directions.

My own breasts were more conventional in their design. They were no longer budding, but had arrived at their full ripeness now. High-mounted and round with berry tips, the cleavage between them was deeper, more intriguing and mysterious, than Yolande's. My nipples, however, were similarly stiff and red.

"We have not the masculine tool for me to teach you here, Majesty." Yolande responded to my demand.

"Then we will have to substitute for the sake of the lesson." I picked up a striped candy cane from the table and handed it to her. "We will pretend that this is the you-know-what of the Comte de Vaudreuil. Now what is the first thing that you do to it, Yolande?"

"I would roll it between my hands, Majesty."

"And how does that feel, Yolande?"

"Sticky, Majesty." She rolled the candy cane between her palms. "Very sticky." She giggled.

"Well that's probably because the Comte has such difficulty controlling himself. I've noticed that." I too giggled. "And what do you do then?"

"I hold it in my fist. Then I stick out my tongue like this." Yolande demonstrated. Her tongue was sharp and as bright red as her nipples. "And I touch the tip of his member with just the tip of my tongue. Like this." She demonstrated with the candy cane.

"Like this?" I picked up a second candy cane and emulated Yolande.

"More of a rotary motion, Majesty. You see, there's a little hole in the center of the tip, and men like it when your tongue tip circles there."

"I see. Like this." Delicately, I licked the tip of the candy cane again. "And then?"

"Well, I usually lick the shaft from the tip all the way to the base." She licked the candy cane to demonstrate.

"The underside of the shaft, or the top side, Yolande?"

"I usually go down the top side and back up the underside. The underside is more sensitive, in my experience. Also—" She paused suddenly as if afraid of going too far.

"Tell me!" I commanded. "Tell all!"

"Well, there is this little ridge of flesh just behind the

man's jewels, Majesty. It is particularly erogenous. If one touches it with the tip of one's tongue, it drives the man wild, Your Majesty! Uncontrollably wild! Particularly if your tongue strays and you put it . . ."

"Put it where, Yolande? Where?"

She leaned across to me and for a moment her warm, naked breasts pressed against mine. She whispered in my ear.

"*Mon Dieu!*" I was shocked, but also intrigued. "You mean that you actually put your tongue up—"

"It is not so untasty as you might think, Majesty. If one is excited—and by this point one is usually *très, très* aroused—then this forbidden taste may seem particularly succulent."

"When do you actually take his *épée* in your mouth?" I asked her.

"I think we have reached that point now, Majesty. However, we do not do it all at once. First we make an O with our lips and just take the tip between them. We tease this tip with our tongue, and perhaps with our teeth a bit as well. We lick it, and we nibble." She demonstrated with the candy cane.

"Like this?" I took the tip of my candy cane between my pouty Hapsburg lips.

"Gently, Highness," Yolande cautioned. Her violet eyes were suddenly grave. "You've bitten off the tip."

"I forgot. It was sweet and so I just crunched it between my teeth."

"I know just what you mean, Majesty." The gravity was gone and now Yolande rolled her violet eyes comically. "I lose more lovers that way!"

"Yolande! Be serious!"

"Very well, Majesty. I apologize." Yolande took a deep breath, her bosom rippling enticingly, and then continued. "I keep the head of his member between my lips in this fashion for a while," she told me. "I lick and nibble on it. When I feel it beginning to swell, I admit it a little more deeply into my mouth. Then, with the drawing in of the shaft I start to suck." She sucked the candy cane.

"I see." Again I imitated her.

"At the same time, one should continue licking, allowing one's tongue to wrap around the shaft, first in one direction, and then in the other. One should suck gently, not too hard, and continue licking all the time. While doing this, one should reach between the man's legs and tickle him just under the balls." She made spidery motions with her fingers as she continued to suck and lick the candy cane.

"This way?" I sucked the candy cane, licked it, moved my fingers in the air like a spider on its back.

"*Oui*. Now this will excite him, Majesty. He will probably start to move his member in and out of your mouth at this point."

I nodded, remembering that one time with the Prince-Bishop.

"It's important to fall in with the rhythm of this movement, Majesty. One should try to suck and lick in cadence."

"How military," I murmured.

"We are dealing with men, Majesty. They are by nature military."

"By which you mean aggressive." I nodded. "I know that, Yolande. And, quite frankly, it is that which most concerns me. When their thrustings into one's mouth become fierce, what then, Yolande?"

"One adapts, Your Majesty. One sucks in welcomingly, warmly."

"But one will choke!" I protested. "One will gag!"

"Not if one adapts properly, Majesty."

"I just don't see how. Show me what you mean."

"Very well, Majesty." Yolanda took a fresh, thick candy cane. She began to move it very quickly—a pistonlike movement—in and out of her mouth. Soon, although it was a good eight inches long, the candy cane was disappearing in her mouth to the hilt. Obviously a goodly portion of it was in her throat. Still, she did not choke.

"Remarkable!" I marveled. "How do you do that?"

"It is simply a matter of relaxing the muscles of one's windpipe, Majesty. One must do that. If one doesn't, when the torrent comes one really will choke most awfully."

"Let me try." I took a fresh candy cane and began moving it in and out between my lips. Yolande's breasts rose and fell quickly as she watched me. The remarkable stiff red nipples seemed to beckon to me. The sight of this aroused me and I pretended that it really was a man's *épée* in my mouth and began pumping the candy cane in and out more quickly and violently. I licked and sucked as I did this and managed to work myself into quite a state of excitement. Finally I pushed it in all the way and sucked hard with my lips as if I really was expecting a man's nectar to cascade down my throat. It didn't, of course, but I choked anyway. My breath had been cut off and I almost gagged before I managed to pull the candy cane free of my windpipe. "You see," I gasped to Yolande. "That's what happens."

"It's because you're not relaxed, Your Majesty. Perhaps some snuff," she suggested.

"I've never tried it," I confessed.

"It really will relax you, Majesty." Yolande produced a little jeweled box and opened it. White powder glittered in its satin interior. "Try some."

"I don't really know how to. . . ."

"Like this." Yolande placed a pinch between her knuckles and held her hand under her nose. Then she inhaled deeply, first with one nostril, then the other. After a moment her violet eyes sparkled and crossed slightly. "That is really great *merde!*" she exclaimed.

I followed her example. I sniffed the white powder up one nostril and then the other. After a moment visions of candy canes were dancing through my brain. How funny! They all looked like men's you-know-what's!

"Now why don't you just try another suck on that old candy cane there, Majesty," Yolande suggested.

I tried it. I shoved the candy cane into my mouth and halfway down my throat. I sucked and licked as hard as I could. I slid it in and out of my throat and sucked away. And I didn't choke. I didn't gag. Finally I took it out of my mouth and spoke. "I've had enough candy," I told Yolande. "I think I'm ready to try it on the real thing."

"His Majesty?" Yolande inquired. "Like the King?"

"I don't think so," I told her, ignoring the tickle in my nose.

"Ahh. I see, Majesty. I follow your serene drift, Serene Majesty. You require a man."

"Quite so," I told her. "That is why it is different from candy canes. The real thing usually comes attached to a man."

"Almost always," Yolande agreed. "Damn near all the time, Majesty."

"A man," I nodded seriously. "A man complete with candy cane."

"Do you have some particular man in mind, Majesty?"

"No. It doesn't matter who he is. Just as long as his candy cane is suitable to the experiment." I reached for Yolande's little jeweled box.

"Help yourself, Majesty."

"I already am," I pointed out. "I'm the Queen, and so I never wait to be offered." I sniffed the white powder and smiled warmly on Yolande. "A man," I remembered.

"With just the right candy cane." Yolande nodded.

"You will find me such a man," I told her. "That is my royal command." I got to my feet and tucked my breasts back into my bodice. "A man and a candy cane," I told her. "Report to me when you've found someone suitable—that is someone with a suitable candy cane," I amended.

"As you wish, Majesty." Yolande staggered to her feet and curtsied, her wide-spaced breasts tumbling free.

"Of course it will be as I wish." I giggled. "I'm a majesty!" I turned and left Yolande then. "Really great," I called back over my shoulder. "Really great *merde!*"

Two days later Yolande called on me in my boudoir as I was having my morning coffee. "I have located a suitable man with a suitable candy cane, Majesty," she told me, coming straight to the point.

"I trust your judgment of men, Yolande," I replied. "But how can you be sure of the candy cane?"

"He is Hungarian, Your Majesty." Yolande lowered the lid over one of her violet eyes. "Need I say more?"

Thus it was that a liaison was arranged at the Petit Trianon for myself and Yolande (I would not go without her; she was, after all, my mentor in this matter) and Count Balint Miklos Esterhazy of Franko, a direct descendant of Attila the Hun. A Hungarian army officer, Count Esterhazy was known throughout the royal courts of Europe for two things: his brutal good looks and his avarice. Although his family owned sixty townships and four hundred villages in Hungary, he had come to Versailles in search of financing for a regiment of his own and in hopes of hiring out that regiment for enough money to pay off his considerable gambling debts. Of blood royal, he was nevertheless a ne'er-do-well, and where women were concerned, he was a cad and a bounder as well. Needless to say, I found him irresistible upon our very first meeting.

He was a large man, bulky and brawny as well as tall. He was quite hairy, except for the top of his head, which had been shaved shiny-clean. His mustache and body hair were the shade and consistency of spun gold. With hands the size of bread loaves and shoulders like a prize bull, he seemed to emanate physical power. Add sapphire-green eyes set deep and sparkling like saber-points, a monocle fixed in one eye socket like the sight of a duelist's pistol, mustache tips waxed to needle sharpness, and scarlet uniform trousers so tight in his fascinatingly bulging crotch that at very first glance I feared for the strangulation of our enterprise before it even got started—add all this and it should be clear why my pussy puckered even as Yolande was presenting Count Esterhazy to me.

"Your Majesty!" His heels clicked sharply on the parquet-floored entrance to the chamber where the meeting took place. He then marched across the Persian rug as if he had a regiment at his back and bowed stiffly from the waist until his cruelly beaked nose touched the back of my extended hand. The way his long mustache tickled turned the kiss he bestowed there into an erotic prelude. "I am greatly honored."

Had I not replied, I feel sure that he would have maintained the right-angle bow beyond eternity. As it was, I released him from the locked position. "Count Esterhazy." I spoke his name softly. "I am so pleased that you could join us for tea." I indicated that he should be seated in one of the straight-backed chairs. It suited his arrogant Hungarian spine.

I confess that I had not the slightest inkling of how to

proceed. At this point in my development, despite many flirtations, I was still somewhat shy with such blatantly virile men as this Hungarian Count. I looked to Yolande for guidance. She smiled reassuringly and then turned to the Count, still smiling.

A glint of understanding lit up the green eye behind the monocle. He returned Yolande's glance and then directed his gaze towards me. Not a word had been spoken, but there was a certain subtle change in his attitude. He understood quite clearly now why he had been summoned to the Queen's secluded retreat in the Petit Trianon.

Yolande served the tea in a silence fraught with understanding. Only when we sat sipping it did she speak again. "It is *très* warm, is it not, Highness?" The draperies were open and she was seated facing the high, arched window. Her figure was bathed in sunlight, her loose chestnut hair glittering in the rays, her violet eyes sparkling with the wicked secret of our intentions, a faint patina of perspiration overlaying the tops of her breasts where they rose from her bodice.

"*Très* warm," I agreed.

"*Très* warm," the Count echoed, a hint of amusement betraying his Hungarian pronunciation of the French words.

"*Très*." Yolande's fan fluttered back and forth in front of her breasts. Then she hooked one finger in the material just over the cleavage, pulled it forward, and fanned the considerable amount of bosom she had exposed. "Are you not warm too, Highness?" she hinted.

"*Oui*, Yolande. I certainly am." I followed her example, leaning slightly forward in my stylized armchair to reveal my breasts fleetingly to the interested gaze of the Count.

"We are most informal here," Yolande explained. "I

am sure Her Highness has no objection if you wish to remove your jacket and loosen your shirt, Count Esterhazy. It is really quite private and there is no reason why any of us should suffer from the heat."

"Quite so." Casually, as if only to set an example which might put him at his ease, I unfastened the stays of my bodice.

The Count removed his uniform jacket and opened his shirt. I caught a glimpse of the muscles rippling across his chest and of the golden hairs over them. At the same time Yolande exposed her bosom and—as always—a little fillip of desire welled up inside me.

"More tea?" She offered it to me and to the Count.

We both declined. Again we were silent. A chirping of birds fell on our ears from the gardens outside the windows. Striated sunlight enriched the plum damask draperies. The aroma of fresh-cut honeysuckle arranged as a centerpiece on the tea table trickled our nostrils. The honeyed tea perked my lips sweetly.

"Some snuff, Majesty," Yolande suggested. "To soften the edges of the day."

"How nice." I accepted. "But you both must join me."

We passed the little jeweled box around, each of us tapping out a generous portion of the white powder on the back knuckles of our hands, and then inhaling it deeply. Count Esterhazy sniffed it so violently up one nostril and then the other that a deep red color spread over his neck and cheeks. Indeed, his high Magyar cheekbones became so fiery that they resembled torches.

I felt totally relaxed now. I opened my bodice to the waist and allowed my naked breasts to breathe unhampered. The berry nipples rose like flower buds opening to the morning sun.

Yolande quickly followed my example. Her pointy

alabaster breasts shimmered intriguingly behind stray strands of her loose chestnut hair. The long red nipples jutted out between the curls boldly. The Count's green eyes darted from one bosom to the other, approving both. He still sat stiffly, balancing a teacup on one knee.

Deliberately, I stared at his groin. The lump there grew, hardened, rose. The teacup started to tip.

Standing and stretching, nipples pointing like disagreeing arrows, Yolande crossed to Count Esterhazy and removed the teacup. She looked at me with her violet eyes shaded by long lashes and raised one plucked eyebrow. I nodded imperceptibly. She knelt in front of the Count and unbuckled his sword belt.

Now it was he who looked at me questioningly. I smiled reassuringly. "Yolande does my bidding," I told him. I sniffed some more of the white powder and handed it to him.

"As do I, Majesty." Once again he inhaled deeply. He lifted his thick, muscular haunches from the chair to allow Yolande to pull his britches down around his ankles.

"Like ladies' bosoms, gentlemen's equipment should also be aired on warm days," Yolande told him, licking a bit of the white powder from her lips with her sharp tongue.

It was my royal prerogative to stare, and stared I did. The genital image and reputation of Hungary was certainly secure with Count Esterhazy. He had thighs sturdy as tree trunks, and between them, rising from a wild tangle of silky golden curls, a penis that was both thick and long, pointed with bright red anger at the *trompe l'oeil* ceiling.

Yolande removed his boots and then his britches. Her

exertions left her panting and flushed. She looked at me inquiringly, as if for further orders.

"Come sit alongside me, Count Esterhazy." I moved to a white satin couch and patted the space beside me. "I want to talk to you about the garrisoning of your hussars."

He stood up and marched over to me. His lance was at full tilt, as if awaiting the command to charge. In my experience only the memory of Prince-Bishop de Rohan rivaled the sight. The sac containing Count Esterhazy's balls swung heavily, swollen with nectar, as he came to the divan.

Yolande leaned back and watched, her naked breasts still gasping. As her violet eyes focused hotly between Count Esterhazy's muscular thighs, her hand slid down her belly and pushed the tulle of her afternoon gown deep between her legs. She could not have felt her hand, but her yearning was such as to demand the pressure.

"Ahh, Hungary!" I smiled into the Count's eyes and gently patted his naked erection. It bucked towards the sunshine streaming in through the window. "Perhaps you should draw the drapes, Yolande," I suggested. "The afternoon sun is really quite strong."

"Of course, Majesty."

"The shadows are for kisses," I whispered to Esterhazy when the drapes were drawn. Delicately, I twined my long fingers around his twitching cock.

He kissed me. One of his hands squeezed a naked breast and his thumb moved rhythmically back and forth over the risen berry-nipple. His tongue stabbed hotly into my mouth and licked at the very roots of my tongue. His naked prick swelled in my grasp. I squeezed it, sucking his tongue greedily, savoring the swollen shaft of flesh, writhing under his caresses.

When the kiss was over, I glanced across at Yolande. Her violet eyes were burning. She was manipulating one of her stiff nipples with her fingers. Her skirts were raised, revealing shapely thighs in white silk stockings, and her hand was buried at the crotch of her bloomers. Those inhibitions of which snuff had not relieved her were now dispelled by watching the Count and me in each other's embrace.

In turn, Yolande's brazen fingerings freed me of my own inhibitions. My heart still pounding with the kiss, I took one of my large round breasts in my hand and bent over Count Esterhazy in such a way that the berry-nipple hovered over the little hole as the heart-shaped red tip of his straining cock. I pressed the nipple to the aperture and felt the warm, premature stickiness of a few drops of his building lust spreading over the sensitive surface. "That feels quite delicious," I told him breathlessly.

"It excites me greatly, Majesty." He slid his hand under my gown as I crouched over his stiff prick and reached above my stocking tops, between my naked thighs, groping for the dampness of my bloomers over my writhing pussy.

"No, *m'sieur*." I removed his hand. "I am the Queen of France and a virgin!"

"He is a Hungarian, Majesty," Yolande interceded. "Forgive him. He doesn't know any better."

"I forgive him. And to show I hold no malice—" I stuck out my tongue and quickly licked the tip of his prick.

It tasted—there is no other word for it!—creamy. I licked it again, and this time I reached under his balls and worked my spider fingers through the golden silky hair there. Then I furrowed the hair with my tongue and licked the balls themselves.

Without willing it, my legs were opening widely and then closing tightly. My virgin cunt was squeezing with a will of its own. I was very excited and feelings of wildness were coursing through me.

"Lick it, Majesty!" Yolande, also excited, urged me on.

"Lick it!" the Count moaned, and his hand was quite heavy on the back of my blond head.

Laughing with the thrill, I licked the shaft all the way up and all the way down. Then I scrambled to the floor, knelt between his muscular thighs, and licked and sucked his balls again. Finally, remembering Yolande's lessons, I told him to slide forward from the couch a little bit so that his virile, sculpted derriere was accessible to my mouth.

I licked the ridge of flesh behind his balls and his thighs closed around my ears. My tongue moved to the cleft between his bottom cheeks, and as it probed, his reaction became so violent that I thought I surely would suffocate in the hard flesh of his inner thighs. Nevertheless, I persisted, feeling as naughty and aroused as I ever had felt.

This feeling had as much to do with the circumstances as with my forbidden activities. Count Esterhazy was an adventurer and a scamp. I was a queen, the daughter of an empress. My mother would have been shocked and appalled by what I was doing; she would have disowned me completely for doing it with a Hungarian!

Pushing these reflections from my mind, I corkscrewed my tongue deep into Count Esterhazy's Hungarian anus. When he began shaking as with an ague, I removed it and ceased the sweet torment. I then looked up at him from under my lashes, my blue eyes hot and hungry, and took a goodly portion of the shaft of his quivering prick into my mouth.

"Suck it, Majesty!" Yolande scrambled for a closer view.

"Help me." I removed the shaft from my mouth just long enough to issue the command. "Join us."

Yolande slid between Count Esterhazy's legs and the couch. Her hand squirming between her legs, she puckered her lips upward and kissed the underside of his balls while I went back to sucking his cock. The Count reached down with one hand and reached under her skirt. In a trice his large hand had replaced Yolande's inside her bloomers and was encompassing both her pussy and her bottom. Indeed, it was so large that the Count was able to strum her clitty with his thumb at the same time that his middle finger was tickling her sensitive bunghole.

Their squirming and Yolande's moans made me randier than ever. My own bloomers were already sopping, and each time I took a hearty suck on the huge Hungarian cock stretching my mouth, a warm sticky spurt from my writhing pussy would disgrace them further. Indeed, the feel of that cock in my mouth rendered me positively savage with lust.

"I'm going to come!" Yolande breathed.

I pulled the cock from my mouth and replied ardently. "Suck my pussy!" I commanded her, my dizzying passion somehow throwing me back to the dear old days in Vienna with Helga. "Lick it, Yolande! Suck it!"

She twisted her lithe body like a pretzel. Her pink wet cunt, the chestnut bush framing it all glittery with her honey, stuck out nakedly and obscenely from under the pushed-up skirts above her pulled-down bloomers. The long nipples of her breasts pulled up against Count Esterhazy's bare bottom, one lodged between the cheeks, the other tangled in the golden nest of his balls. Her head was lost to view, under my skirts, between my legs, the teeth tearing away my silken bloomers, the tongue lapping hungrily at my wetly slapping cunt.

A fever of abandon swept over me. I blindly groped and found the jeweled box and sniffed the white powder directly from it. I felt my throat open widely, welcomingly. Count Esterhazy's cock slid easily down it and I sucked it violently from the base. He began thrusting it in and out. I sucked harder, the hot, hard shaft filling my mouth and my throat, pumping viciously.

Yolande's tongue up my quim . . . Esterhazy's hand squeezing and wrenching the orgasm inside her bloomers . . . his cock ramming down my throat, the nectar making the shaft swell and swell more . . . one of Yolande's long red nipples poking up at my chin from between his legs . . . the hungry fire tearing up from my pussy to my sucking mouth . . . and then the torrent as the lava erupted and filled my eager throat and I discovered I could swallow it after all and discovered how sweet it was to swallow it and come at the same time . . . to swallow and spend over Yolande's tongue in my quim . . . to spend as she was now spending . . . to suck all of the cream from that thrashing cock and to time each wrenching spasm of my orgasm to the hard Hungarian prick spurting its man juice down my thirsty throat. . . .

"I think I've got it," I gasped to Yolande when it was over. "I think I've got it."

That was the first time. It was not the last. The Comtesse de Polignac, Court Esterhazy, and I willed away many a pleasant afternoon at the Petit Trianon during the months which followed. I became quite expert at oral lovemaking or, as Esterhazy phrased it in his provincial Hungarian vernacular, "giving head."

Eventually, of course, it had to stop. Two events conspired to bring it to an end. They were at odds with each other and yet together they wrote *finis* to *l'affaire* Esterhazy.

The first involved my old lover, Prince-Bishop Louis de Rohan. The satyrlike prelate was most popular with the people of France; his family was well connected and second only to the Bourbons in prestige; he had tremendous influence among those who ran the government for the King. It became politically impossible for Louis to keep him exiled in Strasbourg. On March 4, 1777, the King announced de Rohan's appointment as grand almoner to the Court of Versailles.

Shortly thereafter, I wrote my mother, telling her that my opinion of de Rohan still agreed with hers. I said that "I consider him not only an unprincipled man, but even a dangerous one . . . with all his intrigues; and had the decision been left to me, he would never have had a place here at Court. Still, that of grand almoner brings him into no contact whatsoever with me—and little more, actually, with the King, whom he will see only at Mass."

Despite these assurances, I did see de Rohan now and then. Versailles was small and it was not possible that we should avoid meeting. When we did, his attitude was respectful. No one present doubted that. Only I recognized the cynically sensual sneer behind the respect.

Seeing him stirred me in ways I would rather not have been stirred. My bottom squirmed, remembering. My mouth yearned to show his cock all that it had learned. And with each such encounter, Esterhazy became less desirable.

It was the second event, however, which clinched the fact that Esterhazy had to go. The King, finally, after seven years of marriage, was taking steps to make me a wife in more than name only. After all the diets and sex surrogates and exercises and all sorts of faddish medicine, Louis had finally consented to undergo the operation which the doctors promised would render him capable of getting an erection and maintaining it during intercourse.

I had always understood his reluctance to have this surgery. There was nothing they could give him for the pain. To be cut—it required three slashes—in such a vulnerable area really did require bravery. I was touched that Louis now finally agreed to go through with it in order to relieve me of my virginity.

The least I could do to show my gratitude was to divest myself of what was becoming the much-whispered scandal of Esterhazy. Mindful of his services to me (or were they mine to him? Ahh, no matter!), I made sure that the Count's needs were met generously. All of his gambling debts were paid off and he was provided with a regiment. I even pressured the minister of war, incurring his eternal enmity to ensure that Count Esterhazy received a choice posting far from Versailles.

The end of our affair was costly. Count Esterhazy had not come cheap. Indeed, the chancellor of the exchequer lodged a formal complaint with King Louis and the minister of war was all too happy to back him up. The details reached the ears of the people, and the murmurings on the lines outside of the warehouses where bread was being sparingly rationed to the poor became more and more ominous.

The King took all of this in his stride. "Don't be disturbed by what people say about your influencing me to have the government finance your friend Esterhazy, Marie," he told me. "I'm told that the Count is a most profligate spender. What better way to perk up the economy in the village where his garrison is quartered?

Why, if what they say is true, the chap is a real supply-sider!"

Louis' attitude gratified me. It made me feel that I was right in continuing to spend money freely. Mama had drummed into me the need for keeping up royal appearances from childhood. To scrimp, after all, is not the hallmark of a first-class power.

Shortly after this conversation with Louis, the operation was performed. It took several weeks for the incisions to heal. And then, finally, after seven years of marriage, my husband and I embarked upon our wedding night.

Well, *mes amis*, all matters of sex are relative, are they not? To some men the inability to quickly raised a third or fourth erection is a disaster. To others the cutting of the mustard itself is a monumental achievement. My husband, King Louis, fell in the second category.

After his monumental achievement, Louis rolled over on his substantial belly and dozed off. I pondered what all the fuss had been about. No longer a virgin, I felt no different than I had before the event.

Alas, I found this much-heralded act a disappointment. I turned over and went to sleep myself. I was most unimpressed with what the peasants called "fucking."

But that was before I met the Swede!

Chapter Nine

The Swede's name was Axel Fersen. He was the son of a field marshal and a member of Sweden's Royal Council. Career opportunities for a professional soldier being better in France than in Scandinavia, he had followed the mercenary custom of coming to Versailles to seek his fortune.

He was pleasant without being foolish, and an air of Nordic reserve set him apart from the young dandies who formed my entourage at Court. Roughly the same age as the King and myself, he was physically quite unlike my husband. They were of a height, both tall, but Axel's blond good looks gave him a Viking stature that the King definitely lacked. "And he is very well made," Yolande confirmed, measuring his crotch with her expert violet eyes.

Yolande had noticed my interest in Axel from the first. Since the King had first dipped his inadequate wick in the well of my virginity, thereby destroying it, Yolande and I had become much closer. The confidante of my ongoing sexual disappointment, it was Yolande who steadfastly insisted that fucking actually could be fun.

I was not, however, convinced. There was more enjoyment for me in the gambling and the drinking and the general career of carousing upon which I had embarked. In particular, I was more erotically stirred—and sometimes satisfied—by the stolen kisses and embraces and licking and sucking engaged in nightly at my *intime* soirées at the Petit Trianon than I thought I could ever be by the insertion of a male organ in my royal box. I was experimenting wildly, but not with intercourse.

More than friends, Yolande and I had become lovers. It was delicious lying naked in her arms, and it was comfortable and relaxed as well. We were not jealous of each other where men were concerned and we discussed those at Court freely.

"The Swede is extremely well hung," Yolande remarked upon one of these occasions.

"This incessant crotch watching of yours must stop, Yolande," I cautioned her with mock severity. "It is surely putting a strain on your eyes."

"I've noticed no strain on the eyes, Majesty. Only a certain tension here." She took my hand and placed it between her naked thighs.

"Ahh, Yolande, you are incorrigible!" I slid down her body then with my tongue and we made love. . . .

I remembered Yolande's appraisal, however, the next time I saw Axel Fersen. At my invitation he came regularly to the Sunday afternoon card games at the château. While these were not comparable to the evening frolics at the Petit Trianon insofar as licentiousness was concerned, gambling on the Lord's day was nevertheless considered quite sinful by the moralists of Versailles. Thus it was an embarrassment to the reigning prelate on the scene, my former lover de Rohan. This of course was exactly why I insisted on the Sabbath card games.

On this particular Sunday afternoon, the gaming was sparsely attended. Yolande was dallying with her lover and altogether there were only enough of us playing to make up one table. We drank brandy as we played—Axel merely sipping—and we sniffed snuff—Axel declining. Between the two my inhibitions were somewhat lowered and I decided to find out for myself if Yolande's appraisal of the Swede was justified.

I dropped one of my hands under the table and placed it on his thigh. A golden eyebrow was raised ever so slightly, but other than that Axel's Nordic reserve prevailed and he gave no hint of my indiscretion to the others present. Amused by his control and sure as always of my queenly prerogative, I moved my hand higher on his lap under cover of the table.

It encountered his hand which blocked it from its goal. I ran my fingers lightly over his palm, all the while pretending to study my cards. Then, taking the Swede by surprise, I dug my nails into his flesh. Responding, his hand jerked away and I quickly clutched at his groin.

"You have not followed suit!" the Swede's partner complained to him.

"I'm sorry." He took back the card. "I was distracted."

"Distracted by what?" I inquired, measuring the thickness of his *épée* through his britches with my fist.

"Dreams." His voice was quite calm.

"Dreams can be made reality." I squeezed. (Yolande was right, more right than she knew; the Swede was *très—très!*—well hung!)

When the game broke up, I detained Axel after the others departed. "I understand that you are very handsome in your dress uniform of the Swedish Light Dragoons," I remarked. "I should very much like to see you in it. Why don't you put it on and join me in my private apartments?"I reached between his legs and squeezed just to be sure he should take my meaning.

There was, of course, no way that he could miss it. I received him alone, changing into a flimsy negligee over the thinnest of nightgowns. By contrast, his officer's garb was quite formal.

"*Magnifique!*" I clapped my hands at the sight of him.

The best military uniforms, I suspect, are deliberately designed to uncross the legs of ladies. Nothing makes the heart beat with more anticipation than the sight of a well-built man draped like a peacock between epaulets. Such was the effect of Axel's uniform on me.

It consisted of a white tunic worn over a royal-blue doublet. The chamois britches were so tight-fitting that I could make out the outline of his cock running down his left leg. In one hand he held the uniform bonnet, a stiff cylindrical ebony shako topped by a long, arched yellow and blue plume.

"How you must tickle the ladies with that," I murmured.

"Majesty?" His square Viking face with its cleft chin looked puzzled.

"I'll show you." I took the shako from him.

I pointed the feathery plume towards him. I leaned forward, aware of my unconfined breasts shifting under his appraising blue-eyed stare. I deliberately pushed the plume between his thighs and moved it in and out, back and forth, up and down.

Axel Fersen may have been Swedish, but he wasn't backward. He took me in his arms. His body felt young and strong as it pressed against mine. His kiss was not reserved; it was hot and insistent. "I must have you,

Majesty." One of his hands went between my legs, the other between his own.

"You are too impetuous, sir." I twirled away from him, teasing.

My response gave him pause. Then he slowly shook his head. "I think not, Majesty. I think you are in great need of a strong pike to fill your royal chalice." He undid his buttons and took out his prick.

Ahh, Yolande! If you could only see! Hail Scandinavia! How sweet to surrender to such a Viking lance.

He pressed my hand to his cock as he took me in his arms once again and kissed me. When the kiss was over, I started to sink to my knees. My negligee was in complete disarray and my berry-nipples burned as they trailed down the legs of his uniform.

"No." To my surprise Axel stopped me. "Don't suck it, Majesty. I want to put in inside you. Never have I seen a goblet so ready to be filled with cream."

"Oo-la-la! You Swedes! I only do that with my husband, the King." I danced away from him, twirled and tickled his swollen pink balls in their nest of golden silk with the plume of his shako.

Why this response? The reasons were complex and perhaps lost to the moment. Being ridden by the King was a disappointment to me every time. This had conditioned me to expect nothing but frustration and lack of fulfillment from the insertion of a man's prick in my pussy. Teasing and flirting and fingering and sucking and being touched and sucked, on the other hand, always provided me with enjoyment. I was very attracted to this gloriously hung Viking. I wanted us to pleasure each other. I did not want the evening to end in the disappointment of fucking.

The feather tickling his balls made his cock jerk

violently. "Enough flirting, Majesty." His strong hands reached for my thighs to part them.

"No-no!" I slithered away from him. "Play with my breasts," I suggested.

"That's not necessary, Majesty. Your nipples are already stiff as daggers."

"Suck them."

"While we fuck, Majesty." He grasped me and pushed me down on the couch. His hands were gentle but firm. He drew aside the folds of my negligee and raised my nightgown, baring my blond, honey-bathed pussy.

"How dare you—!" I started to protest.

"I am a Swede, Majesty. We are not good at games. But we are very good at fucking." He pushed the head of his prick slowly between the lips of my pussy. . . .

And that was the moment when the knock sounded at the door and the voice called my name: "Marie?"

Axel looked at me questioningly, the head of his cock embedded at the entrance of my slavering quim.

"The King," I groaned.

"Your husband?" Something in the way he said it told me that this was perhaps not the first time Axel found himself in such a situation.

"*Oui.*"

"Answer him." Quietly and swiftly, Axel removed his cock from my pussy and tucked it back in his pants. Considerately, he pulled down my nightie and rearranged my negligee until it looked almost decorous. "Answer him," he whispered again.

"What is it, Louis?"

"I must speak with you, Marie. May I come in?"

"Is there another way out of here?" the Swede inquired.

"*Oui.*" I showed him.

"Marie?" The King was becoming impatient.

"A moment, Louis. I have to put something on." I blew

a kiss to Axel as he departed. Then I ran a comb through my hair, donned a less revealing robe, and admitted my husband to my chambers.

"*Cherie!*" He burst into the room with his arms waving like a windmill. "Do you know what the backbone of France is?"

"We used to wonder about that in Vienna, Louis."

"The backbone of France is the family!" he announced dramatically. He looked at me expectantly like a dog waiting to be rewarded with a bit of meat for having fetched brilliantly. "The family," he repeated. "And do you know what is happening to the family in France today, Marie?"

I didn't know.

"It is crumbling! That's what! It is dissolving! Fathers have no more authority. Mothers are working in the fields instead of staying home and caring for their children. And the children are running wild, Marie. Wild! Boys run away to avoid serving in the army! That's how it is, Marie. When the family goes, the next thing to go is patriotism!"

"It could never happen in Austria," I assured him.

"And the daughters, Marie! The girls are worse than the boys! They are having sex in the backs of carts, Marie!"

"Not that!" My hand fluttered to my cheek to convey how aghast I was at the very idea.

"And do you know why they are having sex in the backs of carts, Marie?"

"For pleasure?" I guessed.

"Of course not, Marie." Louis was surprised at my answer. "We both know that sex isn't for pleasure. No, they are having sex in the back of carts because they are told too much at too early an age. While their mothers are out working and their fathers and brothers are out drinking wine, instead of doing their chores these girls are running wild and learning"—he paused dramatically—"the facts of life!"

"Not that, Louis!"

"Do you know the facts of life, Marie?"

"As a matter of fact, I don't. I've always wondered what they were."

"You don't know them because you're a decent girl brought up in a decent household by a decent family." (Somehow I suspected that this description of the Hapsburgs would not be the one which would go down in history.) "The facts of life are what is told young girls in order to lure them into sin, Marie."

"You mean that before they told the facts of life young girls didn't sin?" I inquired, confused.

"They didn't flaunt it!" he assured me.

"Oh." Perhaps it was better not to ask too many questions. In any case, it was simpler.

"I am going to institute the Family Protection Act as the law of the land," the King announced. "It is a five-point program designed to protect and maintain the sanctity of French family life. The first point will forbid—under penalty of death—any form of sex education for children under the age of twenty-one."

"But Louis—" I pointed out, "by age twenty-one most French citizens are already parents."

"Exactly, Marie! That proves my point. Heretofore they have been taught how to do it and then did it and created offspring—many of them bastards. But once the Family Protection Act is passed, they won't be taught how, and so they won't know how to do it, and so they won't do it. The act will both protect family values and cut down on the high birth rate which is already depleting our food supply."

"But are you really sure, Louis, that they only had sex because they were taught about it?"

"Of course, my dear. What's more, I can prove it. I myself never received such instruction, and so when the time came for sex—well, you remember, my dear."

"*Oui!* I certainly do!"

"The second point," Louis continued, "will outlaw contraceptives. Any person found with such a device in his or her possession will be summarily executed. And if such a person is a minor, in addition to being executed, their parents will be notified."

"That seems awfully harsh, Louis. After all, people have been using contraceptives since the ancient Egyptians. And why so much more punitive towards minors?"

"Morality begins with minors," he explained.

"Didn't you say before that overpopulation was a problem?" I reminded him. "Won't doing away with contraception make it worse?"

"Ahh, Marie. This is perhaps too complex for your simple woman's head. Nevertheless," he added magnanimously, "I will try to explain it to you. Contraception encourages people to have sex because it makes them feel safe. But often—through ingorance—they use it incorrectly and so they are not safe, and they conceive more bastards, which makes the problem of overpopulation worse."

"But if they were taught to use contraception correctly . . ."

"That is against the law, Marie! Point one of the Family Protection Act!" he reminded me.

"But why shouldn't people be able to enjoy sex without worrying about conceiving children?"

"Because that kind of sex is immoral, Marie!"

"Oh." *Déjà vu.* Louis sounded just like Mama in Vienna.

"Just as abortion is immoral. Point three punishes that by death also. If a woman sins, she must pay the price."

"And a man, Louis?"

"Well, we must be practical, Marie. After all, there is no way to force a man to have a baby."

"But men can force a woman to have a baby even if she doesn't want one," I reasoned.

"Point three is for women, Marie, but point four is for men. It balances out."

"What is point four, Louis?"

"It forbids homosexuality."

"On penalty of death?" I inquired.

"Of course." Louis beamed.

"But you said point four was for men. What about female homosexuality, Louis?"

"Female homosexuality? What is that, Marie?" He was genuinely puzzled.

I thought of Helga; I thought of Yolande. "Nothing, Louis. I was only joking. Tell me about point five."

"Point five is a program to promote the values of God, King, and Country," he told me. To implement it, I am going to institute formal daily prayer in the public schools."

"But we have no public schools in France, Louis," I reminded him.

"No matter, Marie. It's the principle that counts."

"That's what you said when you pushed through the Military Reform Act, Louis darling."

The Military Reform Act had brought Louis into great disfavor with the landowners of France who paid by far the largest portion of the country's taxes. Aristocratic landowners were exempt from these levies. Only non-nobles had to pay them. This had long caused resentment, but it was the Military Reform Act which brought this resentment to the verge of open rebellion in the provinces.

What the act did was effectively bar the sons of these non-noble families from seeking careers as officers in the French army. Before it was imposed, there were traditional opportunities for the sons of such families. The eldest inherited the family manor, the next went into the church, one joined the Order of Malta, another entered the legal profession, and the youngest almost always became an officer in the army. It was frequently the only opportunity open to younger sons.

These opportunities were cut off by terms of the act. It barred anyone not an aristocrat from holding the rank of lieutenant or higher in the army. Further, no one could rise to the rank of captain or beyond whose family had not been members of the nobility for at least four generations.

The act had no appreciable effect on peasants and other poor people. Their sons had never been free to rise from the ranks in the army. It was specifically aimed at the wealthy bourgeoisie.

Those affected by it were far from powerless in society. Many of them were very important landowners indeed and in the provinces where they resided their control was absolute. But these provinces were far from Paris, far from Versailles. King Louis—alas!—had not the imagination to perceive that they might plot to replace the king so insensitive to their stature with another. Thus were the seeds of revolution planted by the King himself, nurtured by the untitled wealthy, and finally—to both parties' horror—sown by the landless, the underprivileged, the poor. And it all began with King Louis alienating those who most thrived under the Bourbon monarchy by stiffening the military caste system so that their young sons might not be a part of it.

The slap in the face was not deliberate on Louis' part. Indeed, when he discussed it with me before the fact, it was clear that he thought the symbolism of only having aristocratic officers would be popular with the people and would help increase his own waning popularity. Louis really was concerned with this. Nothing upset him so much as when he and I were booed as the royal carriage carried us through the streets of Paris.

This was happening more and more frequently. The people did not understand supply-side economics. They were outraged by stories of my gaming losses at Versailles.

Admittedly, these losses were quite high. In one evening alone, I lost my entire monthly allowance. I sent for the chancellor of the exchequer, insisted that he make my allowance for the following month immediately available to me, and then proceed to lose not only that amount but an additional five hundred louis in credit extended to me as well.

On another occasion, I lost a wager of one hundred thousand francs involving the building of a château in the Bois de Boulogne. I bet that it could not be constructed in six weeks and it was. I laughed away my loss when the winner of the wager showed me that he had not only built the château, but also installed an entresol of pornographic frescoes and bas reliefs illustrating scenes from the works of the Marquis de Sade.

I did not take the public outrage at my gambling losses very seriously. Mama had brought me up to realize that the envy of the common people was a cross that royalty always had to bear. It was the price of superiority. It was not, after all, as if they were of the same species of Louis and myself.

It was really very simple. Louis was the sort of master whose feelings were hurt when his hounds did not wag their tails to show gratitude for the upkeep of the kennel. I, on the other hand, took it for granted that the beasts were untrustworthy and that sooner or later, if one was not vigilant, they would bite. What neither of us stopped to consider was that kennel scraps in France were becoming more and more scarce.

With increasing frequency, a populace on the verge of starvation was responding with ominous growls. Despite such portents, Louis never scolded me for the large amounts of money I spent on clothes, or jewelry, or gambled away. Nor did he interfere with the scandalous soirées at the Petit Trianon although I knew that his advisers wanted him to do so. Although the lowliest Parisians were openly snarling at court depravities, the King never interfered with our liberal sniffing of snuff or objected to the frequently naked gropings and joinings which it provoked. Only one thing upset him (I do believe that he was so naive as to think that all of the other activities stemmed from this alone), and that was my drinking.

He never spoke about this concern to me directly. He simply instructed the wine steward to retire discreetly when it appeared that I had consumed too much champagne. Louis thought that if the wine steward was unavailable that would end the drinking for the evening. Solutions were always so simple for Louis.

In truth, I was drinking too much. It was part of my feverish evenings. Everything moved faster and at the same time in a sort of comfortable blur, with the combination of snuff and champagne. My losses at chemin de fer seemed hilarious, my flirtations seemed exciting, and the identity of the limb or the face which provided the evening's orgasm seemed quite unimportant.

If my morning hangover brought with it a recognition of lack of satisfaction, it still did not stop me from repeating the pattern the next night. After the escapade in my apartments with Axel Fersen, I had looked forward to these evenings in the hope that he and I might pick up where we had left off when Louis interrupted us. When he did not appear, I was very disappointed.

I made inquiries and learned that he had signed on with an expedition bound for the Americas. He was in Le Havre, waiting to sail. I was furious with him for not even having called on me to say good-bye, but my anger subsided when I learned that he had been forced to leave Versailles most hurriedly lest he be left behind.

Of course I did not wish him to leave France for what would obviously be a very long time. This led me to have a very long and serious conversation with Louis regarding the necessity of the expedition. As a result of this conversation it was postponed indefinitely. Axel Fersen returned to Versailles, where, thanks to me, he was given the post of supernumerary officer to the Royal Deux Ponts Regiment. The night after his return and this appointment, Axel appeared at the Hall of Mirrors to join in the evening's gambling.

His presence excited me, but it also made me canny. I was Queen of France, a Hapsburg of Austria, and I would not throw myself at this Viking emigré. Deliberately, I ignored him and flirted outrageously with the other young rakehells present.

I kissed a different set of lips with every throw of the dice. With each loss I allowed an intimate caress in exchange for chips returned. I bent my bodice to probing eyes and patted thighs and clutched hands to my bosom and made laughing promises with eyes and sometimes with words.

Nor did I limit my flirting to men. I pulled Yolande to my lap and put my hand inside her gown and played with her unique breasts as she tossed the ivory cubes. I made her sit astride me, facing, and bounced her just as the old King used to bounce me. I could sense her pussy becoming more and more inflamed as it rubbed over my leg.

When I released Yolande, she slipped away from the dice game with her lover. Deliberately winking at Axel, I put my arms around a young lady-in-waiting and a pink-cheeked lieutenant of the Swiss Guards. I pulled them close together with myself in the middle and then I took his hand and placed it inside her bodice and I took her hand and placed it between his legs. "You two have won enough of my money," I announced. "Now go somewhere and make love. It really can be more fun than gambling, I am told."

The general laugh, I fear, was in response to my last three words and at the expense of my husband, the King.

I held out my goblet to be filled. Alas, the champagne was no longer flowing. The wine steward had retired for the night. We were quite out of the bubbly.

"I am the Queen and I am the great provider," I announced a bit tipsily. "I will replenish the supply."

Several young men got to their feet and offered to accompany me on this mission. I declined their offers, telling them that my destination was a royal secret and that I must go alone. "But," I whispered to Axel Fersen as I brushed past him, "I could be followed."

My heart was pounding in anticipation of his acting on this suggestion as I exited the palace and crossed the formal gardens to the road leading to the Petit Trianon. My little playhouse had a wine cellar, and I, of course, had a key to it. There was always a more than adequate stock of vintage champagne stored there. But the wine was only the excuse for my mission. The opportunity to

be alone with my strong young Swede was the real
reason.

A thrill coursed through me when a man's figure
appeared on the path. At first the moonlight was in my
eyes and I could only make out its outline. The figure
was tall and handsomely built. But I saw as I drew
closer that it was dark-haired and mature, rather than
blond and youthful. The visage was French, hawklike,
not Scandinavian. And it was draped in ecclesiastical
robes rather than the tight-fitting military fashions favored by Axel.

After a few more steps I recognized the man. I recognized him even though it had been awhile since we had
exchanged any words with each other. It was my former lover, Louis de Rohan.

Fortune had smiled on him since his return to Versailles as grand almoner. The people rightly blamed the
crown for the economic mess the country was in and
looked to the church for redemption of their wretchedness. Charismatic and popular, de Rohan came to sym-
bolize churchly opposition to the throne in the masses'
eyes.

This had given him leverage at Versailles, leverage he
was quick to turn to his own advantage, leverage that
translated into power. Soon the government was divided between the followers of the King and the followers of the cleric. Pressure was exerted to have him
appointed Cardinal of all France, a position second in
Christendom only to that of the Pope, and traditionally
quite independent of Rome. In 1778 King Louis had
succumbed to that pressure and my former lover was
indeed appointed Cardinal Rohan. Since that time
he had been consolidating his position with all of the
considerable influence he could command.

The most significant influence he could not command

was mine. I made it a point never to invite him to my soirées at the Petit Trianon or to my gambling parties. In effect, as queen I successfully excluded him from the social life of the Court.

For a man who savored court intrigues—both political and erotic—as much as Cardinal Rohan always had, such an exclusion was a bitter pill. As cardinal he kept apartments at Versailles of course, and had the freedom of the grounds, but my *intime* gatherings were private and off limits to him. Because this was understood, I was both surprised and outraged to encounter him now.

"How come you here, sir?" I greeted him coldly.

"I am taking the night air, Majesty." His blue eyes were intense. The silver tipping his straight black hair at the temples glittered in the moonlight.

"You are intruding on private festivities!"

"I apologize, Majesty. It was not intentional. I have only chosen to walk in the gardens at what would seem to be an inopportune moment. But your party is not in the gardens, Majesty. Is it?"

I sensed that he was mocking me. Had he guessed that an assignation was involved? If he became privy to such an indiscretion, he would not hesitate to use such knowledge against the King, and against me as well if it was to his interest. I must not let my scorn of him outweigh my self-interest. With this thought, I tempered my attitude.

"No," I answered him, my tone more conciliatory. "My party is not in the gardens. It is just that we have run out of champagne and I am on my way to the Petit Trianon to fetch some more."

"I will help you carry it, Majesty?" He raised a wicked eyebrow.

"I don't need any help. I can manage."

"But how, Majesty?" He spread his hands. "You are

too delicate to manage more than a magnum or two. Surely your guests require more than that. No, I insist, Majesty. Let me be of service." He took my arm.

I felt trapped. I was furious inside at the Cardinal's presence spoiling my amorous opportunity with Axel. But I also felt helpless in the face of his cunning and forcefulness.

My mind raced as we walked on towards the Petit Trianon. I was reasonably sure that Axel had followed me, but if he had, and he saw me with the Cardinal, he would probably not presume to approach us. *Merde!* Were others always to thwart our joining?

"What did you say?" My ruminations had blurred the Cardinal's words.

"I was inquiring about the diamond necklace."

The Cardinal knew that he did not have to be any more specific than that. There was only one diamond necklace. It was that one assembled by the jewelers Bohmer and Bassenge for Mme. Du Barry. Their quest for flawless gems had taken years and the necklace itself had only recently been completed. With Du Barry out of the picture, they had shown it to me and I had fallen in love with it. There was only one problem: the price.

The jewelers were asking the incredible sum of 1,600,000 livres for the necklace. Even King Louis' supply-side economics could not support such a purchase. For the first time in our marriage, Louis had refused to buy me something I wanted. His decision was final, and so I had resigned myself to doing without it.

"Nothing has changed," I told the Cardinal with a sigh. "The diamond necklace will never grace my bosom."

"It is the luster of the necklace which will suffer," he assured me smoothly.

"You haven't changed." I chuckled in spite of myself. "You still turn a wicked compliment."

"But I am completely sincere, Majesty. You and the diamond necklace were meant for each other. Beauty deserves beauty. You really should have it."

"I agree. But how?"

"You may remember, Majesty, that I once had the pleasure of teaching you something of the alternate methods of skinning felines."

"I remember." My derriere gave a little independent wiggle with the memory.

"Well, perhaps that insight applies to the diamond necklace as well."

I had no idea what the Cardinal meant. If I had, I might have shuddered rather than shrugged. And I certainly wouldn't have said what I said then: "Skin that cat for me, Eminence, and perhaps I will invite you to my soirées."

"Ahh," he replied, "with such a temptation, Majesty, it is a fait accompli!"

Had I drunk too much champagne to realize he was serious?

We had reached the Petit Trianon. I opened the door with my key, making sure to lock it behind us, and led the way to the door leading to the stairway to the wine cellar. It was dark and we paused at the head of the stairs to light two candles. We set them down atop a cask when we reached the bottom of the flight.

There were many such casks in the cellar. There was also rack after rack of vintage wine. These racks were arranged according to the type of wine and by year as well. I picked my way through them, seeking the twelve-year-old champagne. The Cardinal followed, holding a candle high over his head in order to illuminate the wood notches labeling the racks.

"Tell me something, Eminence." On impulse I decided to devil him. "Why did you not personally perform the de la Motte marriage?"

"And the consummation as well?" The Cardinal was as malicious as I, and quick to retort.

"Since the bride was Jeanne de Valois, I assumed that you had already seen to that," I told him.

"Not at all, Marie. You should remember that my attentions to the lady were strictly anal."

"It is said that on another occasion they were oral," I reminded him.

"But never coital." He chuckled. "But don't tell me you still hold that against me after all this time, Marie."

"Of course not," I lied.

"The lady's sole attraction to me was her striking likeness to you."

"Doubtless that was her attraction to Marc Antoine Nicholas de la Motte," I remarked. "Too bad that the scion of such a noble family was taken in by such damaged goods."

"Damaged perhaps, but restored by your husband the King. You'll remember he restored all of the Valois titles and estates. I'm sure that must have made the lady quite attractive to de la Motte, whose family, I have heard, is in rather dire financial straits."

"Really? Then perhaps his Valois wife will have to take to her back to restore their fortunes." I had so many reasons to loathe this woman!

"Her most attractive charms are not available when she is on her back," the Cardinal recalled.

"Really? More attractive than mine?" I could not resist the question.

"Not at all, Majesty." As if on cue, the Cardinal circled me with one arm from behind and pressed against me. His agility was such that he continued to balance the lighted candle over his head as he did this.

"Your attentions to Valois caused you to be banished to Vienna," I reminded him. "Your attentions to me might prove even more unwise and cost you even more heavily."

"Somehow, I don't think so, Majesty. For one thing we are quite alone here. For another, I cannot believe my attentions are wholly unwanted."

Men!

"Well they are," I assured him.

"Are they?" He set the candle down on a rafter over our heads. His strong hands cupped my breasts from behind. His lips were warm—strangely familiar after all this time—on the back of my neck. "Your gown is most becoming," he murmured, "but most impractical in this situation."

Despite myself, I was flattered by the compliment to my dress. With Axel in mind, I had chosen it with great care. It was a glowing beige satin with a particularly daring decolletage designed to show off the high round-ness of my breasts. It hugged my narrow waist and flared at the hips in a manner designed to hint at the plump mobility of my derriere when I moved. The movements, of course, were assumed to be undulating, and the gown was meant to both inflame and enhance the viewer's imagination without betraying the haute couture of the season.

This haute couture was the problem. Currently it dictated the empire waist and full hoops under the gathered skirts. As the Cardinal had remarked, this style was most impractical in erotic situations.

I had assumed that the problem would take care of itself with Axel. I had been quite prepared to divest myself of the hoops. The Cardinal, however, was quite another story.

"What makes you think you can just pick up where you left off after all this time?" I asked him.

"The knowledge that our pleasure was mutual." He lifted my skirt with both hands in back, exposing the scaffolding of the hoops. *"Mon Dieu!"* he exclaimed. "A pox on all fashion designers!"

"The church has met its match!" I taunted him.

"Not at all." His hands moved expertly. The gates of the hoops were opened and he stepped inside of them, separating the folds of his robes.

He did this so quickly and adeptly that I was taken by surprise. The unmistakable hardness of his *épée* pressing through my bloomers into the cleft of my derriere overwhelmed me with a sudden combination of lust and nostalgia. Momentarily, I weakened in my resolve not to surrender to him.

The Cardinal was instantly sensitive to this reaction on my part. His hands opened the ribbons at my bodice and freed my naked breasts. At the same time, his thighs and flat muscular belly and hard cock were exploring the terrain of my bottom through my bloomers.

"Don't!" I struggled weakly. "You have no right."

His answer was to turn me around and kiss me. His thrusting tongue was as demanding as his prick sliding up and down against my belly. He contrived to draw me free of the hoops and to arrange my skirts in such a way as to afford him the most free and intimate exploration of my lower body. By the time the kiss was over, his skill was such that I was garbed in nothing save my chemise and bloomers.

"You presume too much!" I tried to maintain a protest as his hand closed over the honeyed crotch of my bloomers.

"Do I?" He parted his scarlet cardinal's robe. His naked, tumescent prick was exposed. He carried my

hand to it and set it to rubbing up and down the shaft. "Do I indeed, Marie?"

"Yes. No." Hardly aware of what I was saying, I stared at his huge stiff purple cock in the candlelight as my hand squeezed and tugged at it.

He removed my chemise and pulled down my bloomers. I stood before him naked now. His intense blue eyes devoured me in the flickering light. "You have flowered into a woman, Marie." He squeezed my naked breasts and traced the areolas with his fingertips. "A real woman."

I kept stroking, kept squeezing.

"Turn around," the Cardinal said, his voice hoarse, his cock throbbing. "Assume the position!"

"No!" I protested. "I'd rather you—"

"Assume the position!" Stronger than I, he forced me to turn around and arrange myself over a barrel. Then he sprawled over me and his prick stabbed painfully between the widespread cheeks of my bottom.

"No!" I screamed. "Please! Don't! No! No!"

There was the sudden sound of feet pounding down the staircase to the wine cellar. The weight on my back was suddenly removed, the painful prick withdrawn. At the same time a flailing arm knocked the candle from the rafter and the scene was plunged into darkness.

The struggle was so close to me that there was nothing I could do but shrink back against the barrel and hope not to be struck by one of the wild blows. I protected my naked body as best I could with my hands. My eyes strained to pierce the darkness to see what was happening, but to no avail. The only information I could garner was the sound of harsh breathing and heavy blows.

Finally a particularly vicious-sounding blow was struck. It was followed by the sound of a body thudding to the

earthen floor of the wine cellar and then by footsteps running up the stairs. The door at the top of the flight slammed and then there was silence.

There was a stirring at my feet, then a groan. I groped around the floor for the candle and finally found it. "Do you have a flint?" I asked whoever was lying there.

An unseen hand took the candle and lit it. The handsome Viking features of Axel Fersen flickered into view. There was a slight lump on his forehead. Beside him was the unbroken wine bottle with which he had been struck. "Your Majesty!" he exclaimed. "Am I too late?"

It took an instant for me to realize that he was asking if I had been raped before he arrived or not. "No," I told him. "You got here just in time."

"Who was the blackguard?" He demanded. "I shall find him and kill him."

"I don't know who it was," I lied. "But please don't make any fuss. My reputation—" My honey-slicked, naked thighs clenched protectively around my vulnerable womanhood.

"Of course, Majesty. As you wish." He shrugged to his feet and stood swaying a moment, holding his injured head with one hand.

"Let me see." I made him bend his head and examined the bruise. It didn't look very serious.

"It is I who should be concerned for you, Majesty. To have been attacked by some anonymous brute—"

Obviously he had not identified the Cardinal. That was of course fortunate for the Cardinal. But it was also fortunate for me. In these difficult times, neither one of us could have survived the scandal.

There were more pressing thoughts on my mind. "I do feel a little faint," I told Axel. "And my heart is

pounding so!" I held his hand to my breast so that he might feel the pounding.

"Ahh, my poor Majesty." Axel doubtless recalled the whispered flirtation which had brought him to this cellar in the first place. "Let me comfort you." And he enfolded my naked body in his arms and stroked it in a most intimate manner indeed. "Are you cold, Majesty?" he inquired.

"Not anymore," I murmured. I made no effort to put any of my garments back on. "You are keeping me quite warm." I raised my mouth and closed my eyes and parted my lips.

Axel's kiss was avid. Ahh, youth! He was not so controlled as the Cardinal (who had not, as I recall, been controlled at all the first time we met), but his impetuosity was in itself arousing. His hands moved all over my body as our tongues clashed, and there could be no doubt that they found my naked flesh exciting. "I want you, Majesty!" He held me in a grip of iron when the kiss was over.

"But I belong to my husband the King," I told him perversely, excited at the thought of pushing him into forcing me to fuck with him.

"I thought we settled that at our last meeting." He was stripping off his clothing as we talked.

"Not quite," I reminded him. "When we were interrupted, the issue was still unresolved."

"Then let us resolve it." He exposed his red prick to the candlelight.

I danced away from him, pretending to be afraid. His chest and arm muscles rippled in the quavering light as he started after me. Now he was as naked as I, wearing only his boots. He caught me easily and pinned me against a barrel.

"You know that you want me as much as I do you,

Majesty!" His prick was hot and hard against my belly. His balls swung heavily over my pussy, tickling the silken gold curls. His chest crushed my breasts as he kissed me again, stilling my protests. When the kiss was over, he turned me around so that I was positioned over the barrel just as I had been with the Cardinal before.

"No!" This time my protest was of a different sort. "Please! No!" I wanted to tell him that I was persuaded, that I did want him to fuck me, that I didn't want to settle for being buggered. I was ready to find out if it was the same with all men as with my husband the King, but it seemed that my bottom was going to once again be the target of preference. Axel was paying no attention to my protests.

But then—wonder of wonders!—his hard prick slid down from the spread of my ass and the tip found the oily lips of my pussy. He pushed gently and they opened willingly to him. His hands kneading my breasts, playing with my nipples, his tongue in my ear, he lay over me and slowly—inch by wonderful inch!—pushed his marvelous Swedish cock into my pussy from behind. "Ahh!" I sighed, and there were tears in my eyes. "How absolutely marvelous!" And I reached behind him and squeezed his balls to show my appreciation.

The difference from Louis was unbelievable. Truly, I felt as if this was the night I was really losing my virginity. This was what my wedding night—how many years ago?—should have been like. Two young people fucking their brains out! Oo-la-la!

Axel's weight was heavy on me now as I curled over the barrel. The wood was rough against my breasts and there were splinters. I didn't care. I was concentrating on moving—actually rolling the barrel—in rhythm with his deep fucking of me.

He rotated his prick like a corkscrew. He slid it in

and out, slowly, easily, then fast and hard. The two of us rocked on the barrel, grunting and fucking, our bodies quickly growing slick with perspiration, our minds concentrated on the sensations spreading from our joined genitals.

"I'm coming!" I heard myself screaming. "Fuck me, darling! Fuck me, darling! Fuck me darling! I'm coming!" And I thrust so hard against the barrel that it rolled over the earthen floor with my orgasm.

When it was over, I realized that Axel was still inside me, still hard. Not like Louis! Not like Louis at all! Half the time Louis would spurt his meager offering inside me and turn over and go to sleep before I had even become aroused, let alone come. But Axel! Axel was still hot and hard and pumping!

He put his hands on my hips and pulled me off the barrel. He forced me to bend so that my powdered wig fell off and my long ash-blond hair grazed the floor. I gripped my ankles for support, and Axel once again mounted me from behind, this time stabbing his prick into my cunt most violently and brutally. Taken by surprise, I almost toppled, but he held me upright, his hands on my hips, and fucked me with a much different rhythm—hard and driving—than he had before.

I rocked back and forth on the balls of my feet. Before long I had hollowed out a small hole in the earthen floor where I was standing. Axel held my hips in an iron grip and pumped his hard cock in and out of me with all of the marvelous energy of his youth. My plump, round, hard-nippled, dangling breasts worked like a bellows as I gasped for air with each powerful thrust that seemed to force it from my body. *"Cheri,"* I panted. "I die! I die!" And I pushed my derriere back to meet the weapon of my fate with all my strength.

"Harder, Majesty!" His Viking laugh rang a bit insanely in my ear. "Push back harder!"

I obeyed. At the same time he thrust forward so deeply that his balls became embedded between the sopping lips of my pussy. I distinctly felt the arrogant tip of his Swedish cock penetrate the entrance of my womb.

"Again!" Tears streamed down my cheeks as I screamed. "Again! Again!" A hot surge of surrender seized possession of my pussy. "I'm going to spend again!" I wailed. "I'm spending! I'm spending!" And I pushed back with all my might and squeezed my tight cunt around his embedded prick.

Axel held me in place as shudder after shudder of my spending shook my body. The tip of his cock remained at the entrance to my womb. The length of the shaft pulsed inside my pussy. But he didn't thrust. He just held it hard and still while the honey of my spending bathed it.

When I was finally through, his prick was still inside me, still hard, still pulsing with the pressure of his unreleased nectar. *"Mon Dieu!"* I gasped, craning my head over my shoulder to look into his Nordic eyes as his groin continued to press against my quaking buttocks. "Do all Swedes wait so long to come?"

"I shall wait no longer, Majesty." Axel withdrew his cock and turned me around. I looked down at it. The stiff shaft was bright red and swollen and glistening with my juices in the candlelight.

He pulled me down to the dirt floor of the cellar and stretched out beside me. His muscular body was slick with perspiration. The blond hair of his chest and groin was shiny with it. His balls were very swollen and their pinkness seemed obscene atop his tanned thighs. His

stiff prick stuck straight up from his belly and swayed like a sapling.

"Mount me, Majesty." He showed me what he meant, positioning me so that I was kneeling over his erect prick, astraddle, my gaping cunt hovering a scant inch above the twitching tip. He put his hands on my hips and slowly lowered me.

"Ahh!" In this position, I realized, he would penetrate me even more deeply than he had before. I savored the slow englovement of his cock as my pussy closed around it inch by delicious inch. "So nice!" I stared down at his face. It was intense—almost harsh—with pleasure and lust.

Finally I came to rest on his pelvis. My pussy seemed to spread out over it, sucking in his hard prick even further. Instinctively, I reached behind me and found his balls and fondled them. He raised his head and sucked one of my long berry-nipples into his mouth. He pushed up with his bottom and moved his cock inside me with deep, circular motions. I ground my juicy cunt down in opposite circles. Slowly, deeply, we fucked.

Crouching over him as he sucked my swollen breasts, I rose high, to the very tip of his cock, and came down hard, enjoying the almost liquid, spongy feeling of my wet pussy slapping hard onto his groin. Axel in turn slammed up to meet me, his buttocks rippling, his thigh muscles hard as they slapped into my bottom. "Fuck!" he growled. "Fuck, Majesty! Fuck!"

Suddenly his hands closed over my bottom and yanked it down savagely. I felt his shaft swell impossibly inside my tight cunt. His balls were very hot against the lips of my pussy. I knew he was about to explode.

The knowledge carried me over the brink of my own third orgasm. Laughing and sobbing wildly, I clawed at his balls and let myself go. At the same moment the hot

gush of his nectar was loosed high up my quim. Thus, grinding our groins together for what seemed an ecstasy-filled eternity, we came together.

When it was over, I did not want to dismount. I wanted to savor the last feeble spurts of his softening penis. I wanted to prolong the sweet ache of my still-twisting cunt. The warm wetness of his lust was running out of me now, down the insides of my thighs, but still I did not want to end our joining. It was only when Axel's hands pushed gently upwards against my bottom that I reluctantly ended the impalement.

"That's the only thing I don't like about sex," I told him, unable to stop my hands from toying with his depleted genitals. "It has to end."

"And then begin again." Gently, he pushed my head to his lap. "Use your tongue, Majesty. Use your lips. Lick. Suck. And then we'll fuck again!"

His words excited me too much for me to mind the taste of my own honey as I obeyed. I licked and I sucked, and more quickly than I would have believed, the snake of his cock extended itself and got hard once again. Then—I was dizzy with the prospect, for each climax seemed but to leave me on a higher plane of hunger for the next—he arranged me on my back and knelt between my legs.

"Again?" I was trembling. "But shouldn't you rest a little first?"

"I'll rest between your thighs," he teased.

Axel spread my legs wide until my thigh muscles were straining painfully and then lifted them high. Fascinated, I stared down my naked perspiring body as his cock—looking larger and more murderous than before—moved up between my taut thighs towards my pussy. He stooped a little and positioned my legs on his shoulders so that they bent at the knees and hung over

his back. Then he leaned his weight on the backs of my thighs until I was bent in half. I looked down at my pink, meaty, wide-open cunt. The lascivious sight was blotted out as he mounted me.

At first I felt helpless under the violence of his pounding. His weight pinned me and it was hard to move. My pussy was stretched so wide apart, and his prick plunged in and out of it so deeply, that I felt vulnerable—a little afraid. The cheeks of my derriere were stretched apart and flattened by his weight. I felt as if all of me was exposed and dangerously so.

"I won't hurt you, Majesty." It was as if he'd read my mind. "Just relax. It will be even better than before. You'll see."

I locked my hands around the back of his neck and raised my mouth and extended my tongue. He stuck out his tongue and we dueled with the tips. The sensation made me laugh with excitement. I forgot to be afraid. Just as Axel had advised, I relaxed.

And then I was struggling, wrestling almost, to move with him. He was rocking on my naked haunches, the shaft of his cock pressing down hard on my clitty as he fucked me. His lips were curled back over his teeth as he assaulted my widespread cunt and bottom. I found the movement to match his—a sort of sliding forward and then up on my back—and suddenly it was as if somebody had struck a flame to my clitty. This time I gouged flesh from Axel's neck and shoulders as I came.

He didn't stop when my orgasm subsided. He only changed position. He took out his cock (how long could it stay hard without coming again? I wondered) and turned me on my side facing him and then reinserted it. This way my leg was high on his body, the toes under his chin. He played with my bottom, working his finger in and out of my anus as he fucked me again.

I came more quickly this time, and more quickly still the next. There seemed no limit to the orgasms he could draw from me. My pussy was sore, but I didn't care. Each time was an all-new experience. Once he played with my clitty with his fingers at the same time that he fucked me. Another time he stuck it in me and lay perfectly still while he played with my nipples until I came. And finally he came again with me backed up against a wall of the cellar with my legs locked around his waist while he fucked me standing up.

Nor was that the end of it. Axel was tireless. And so, it seemed, was I. It was only after a long, long time that we finally put our clothes back on and emerged from the cellar of the Petit Trianon. Dawn had broken by then. It was indeed a dawn of discovery in my life.

I had discovered what the peasants called "fucking." Yolande was right. Fucking can be fun!

Chapter Ten

A well-laid *fille*, *mes amis*, tends to obsess on the organ fueling her ecstasy. Many women focus this obsession on the man to whom the organ belongs. Some, however, focus on the organ itself, on comparisons between it and other such organs, on penises rather than persons, as it were. It was in this second category, I confess, that I most willingly fell.

It was not just men's pricks, however, which locked my attention. It was the act of being fucked by them which held me entranced after that night in the wine cellar. For a long time all other sexual activities palled in my mind beside the reality of fucking.

Of course I made arrangements to repeat the act with Axel Fersen many times. The thrills he provided did not lessen. But they did fire my imagination as to how other pricks might feel pumping inside my inflamed cunt.

Were all men's penises either long and thick and fiery red such as Axel's, or insignificant organs of short-lived tumescence like that of my husband, the King? Was the

choice between cocks that entered, spurted, and departed in the time it takes to boil a three-minute egg and ramrods that reamed tirelessly, performed the most titillating arabesques within one's vaginal chamber and then bathed one's orgasm with hot, overflowing cream? Could large pricks perform otherwise than Axel's? Could little ones perform tricks and deliver titillations undreamed of by the King? Were there thicker but shorter pricks than Axel's which perhaps provided a different sort of sensation? Were there longer, more slender ones which might penetrate deeper, encounter more remote nerve endings, prompt a different delirium of spending? A thin prick might make one squeeze more energetically; a short prick would inspire one to press down harder and spread one's pussy out more; a sharper tip . . . a broader, blunter tip . . . a shaft curved like a scimitar . . . a brutal, clublike shaft . . . the tickle of a bristly, hairy groin . . . the wicked thrill of lying under a hairless, adolescent pelvis . . . red, swollen balls wedged between the lips of one's quim . . . purplish balls, heavy with cream and bouncing like Spanish castanets against one's nether cheeks as one's pussy was filled from behind . . . and the potentials of different personalities dictating different movements, different pricks sliding and turning and teasing and battering and jabbing slowly and twisting quickly and . . . Ahh, the possibilities were as limitless as the numbers of men who passed through the Court of Versailles! And with that realization I vowed that the arch of my thighs should be as the tollgates of a feudal bridge between which all men must pass and pay due levy of lust.

My position, of course, dictated that these passings not be public. Indeed, as queen, it was necessary to grant them in as private an environment as possible. Having recently read Rousseau, I wanted this setting to

be as "natural" as possible without sacrificing the luxuries due royalty.

I chose the land around the Petit Trianon, a mile from the Palace of Versailles, to be the site of this environment. Here landscape gardeners created a *jardin anglaise*, a garden in the Greco-English style. No expense was spared to create a pastoral backdrop of waterfalls and footbridges and obelisks and statuary and pagodas and gazebos. A temple of love looked out on grassy swards, soft to the reclining form, and bowers strong enough to support a couple coupling and even man-built grottoes so large as to conceal the delicious wickednesses which were my personal interpretation of Rousseau's theories of getting back to nature.

When this was completed, in 1782, construction of another sort of project was begun across the lake on the other side of the Petit Trianon. This was the Hamlet, which even more than the gardens reflected my desire to live earthily à la Rousseau. The Hamlet was a miniature farm with eight cottages surrounded by fruit trees and bushes bearing a variety of berries. When finished, it was stocked with chickens and cows and goats and sheep. It was here that the ladies of the Court and I dressed up in the simple, uncomplicated garb of milkmaids and shepherdesses and played at milking cows and goats and frolicked like peasant girls with the noble bucks we had lured into donning homespun for our bucolic masquerades.

These frolics were nowhere near as innocent as I pretended they were to my husband, King Louis. Given my phallic obsession, how could they have been? My quest for learning in this area burned with a hotter flame than that of the most dedicated alchemist seeking the formula for turning dross into gold. I remember one day, perhaps the first after the Hamlet was completed,

the first of many similar days, an afternoon that was hot and sultry with air that was heavy, when we played a game, the first of many such games with many variations, a game with an erotic end dictated by its beginnings.

It started, as did so many of our summer afternoons, with snuff and champagne and the selecting of costumes. I chose a short-skirted shepherdess frock which was more Alpine and Austrian than French. It was cut square and low and frilly at the bodice. The skirt was short, showing off my long legs and revealing my plump derriere in my bloomers when I twirled about. With it I wore liederhosen and a wide straw bonnet with a bright red ribbon.

I felt free in this outfit and peculiarly physical. This prompted me to insist that the dozen guests present leave off their games of quoits and backgammon and join me in more energetic frolics. A small orchestra, hidden in the woods, played country music and we danced the intimate rural dances that were forbidden at the palace. Then we played blindman's buff on the wide lawn of the Petit Trianon. The way we played, it was a brazen game of insolent gropings and squeezings to fire the blood of those not blindfolded. Finally we played hide-and-seek.

Flushed with champagne and afternoon sunlight, I skipped through a grove of saplings to one of the miniature barns of the Hamlet. Here I danced, light-headed, through the livestock, scattering the chickens and puzzling the goats, until I came to the ladder leading up to the hayloft. I climbed the ladder and burrowed head-first into the hay to conceal myself. I would not be found here; I was sure.

I was wrong. The wine had made me careless. One of my long legs, thigh creamy white above the liederhosen, was sticking out of the hay. Nor did my short-skirted

shepherdess costume conceal my thinly bloomered bottom. Such was my state when an anonymous fellow player found me.

The first I knew of his presence was when a hand with a heavy ring on one of the fingers slid up my leg—between my thighs—and snapped the garter there. A teasing male spoke. "A shepherdess would never wear a garter on her naked thigh," he pointed out. "Not with liederhosen. And what is a shepherdess doing in a hayloft anyway? Naughty child! You must be punished!" The garter was snapped again, raising a welt on the tender flesh of my thigh. "You should be spanked!" And the open palm of the hand with the ring had come down hard on my silken bottom.

"How dare you?!"

The hay, however, muffled my indignation. Before I could revoice it, I was struck again. This time the warmth spread from my writhing bun to my clenched pussy.

I moaned at the sensation. I also decided against making any effort to prevent further chastisement. I would not reveal myself as the Queen. I would discover how it felt to be treated like a simple shepherdess ravished by an aristocrat in a hayloft. I would find out if men's pricks behaved any differently when the cunts in which they were buried laid no claim to royalty.

Towards this end, I burrowed more deeply into the hay and wiggled my derriere. Two hands pushed the hay aside, found my breasts, and squeezed them. My hardening nipples were twisted roughly, a little painfully. Then my tresses were pushed from the back of my neck and a tongue licked me there. A delicious shiver ran down my spine.

The hands moved to my protruding derriere. Fingers separated my thighs and found my bloomers sopping at

the juncture. "Not only naughty, but sinful too!" There was excitement in his voice now. "Well, we must punish you more, chastise you in keeping with your wickedness." And he pulled down my silken bloomers.

The cheeks of my bottom burned in the sudden breeze of nudity. Wisps of hay tickled my pussy and made me squirm. "Put it in me!" I pleaded into the hay, my words muffled, unheard. Would it be big like Axel's? Or petit like Louis'? Would it last long, or discharge quickly? Would its length rub my clitty, or miss it? Would its head stroke that secret spot? No matter, I knew. I was so hot that I would come the moment the cock—any kind of cock!—breached me. "Stick it in! Please, *cheri*! Now! Now!"

He could not have heard me, but there are other means of communication besides language. I felt the hot tip of his cock enter my slippery pussy and forgot to make any judgment about it at all. Before his balls were even bouncing against my ass, I was grinding hay between my teeth with the grunting violence of my coming.

"FUCK ME! FUCK ME!" I screamed silently. "And I pulled the hard cock this way and that and spent deliriously.

He was taken by surprise and lost control. He grabbed my hips and pinned me with his full weight and released a stream of hot lotion inside my twisting pussy. We came together quickly and violently. All together the whole incident lasted no longer than five minutes, and then it was over.

Perhaps embarrassed at not having delayed his response, my anonymous lover was quickly gone. I never saw his face. I never saw his cock, nor had any real sense of its dimensions. He had snapped my garters against my bare thigh flesh and fucked me to a frothing faretheewell and quickly departed.

The Phantom Cock. That's how I thought of him. Later, when I was back together with my guests, I tried to identify him and failed. Seeing me in the shepherdess costume then, he of course realized that I was the Queen and was perhaps too chagrined at his forwardness to make himself known to me. I never did find out who the Phantom Cock really was.

It was shortly after this incident that there occurred the first of the series of Paris bread riots which rocked the monarchy for years and finally toppled it. The unruly demonstration was prompted not so much by the cutting of government rations to the hungry poor as by the public's growing outrage at the national monies being expended on the ongoing saturnalias rollicking over the grounds of the Petit Trianon. It was the contrast between their own poverty and my extravagance and immorality which fired the wrath of the unwashed masses. They claimed that my licentious behavior made me unfit to be Queen and demanded that I be exiled to my native Austria. But what really brought matters to a head was the underground newspaper exposé revealing that the *jardin anglaise* had cost two hundred thousand livres to create.

What made this particularly shocking to the average Parisian was that the cost did not include the construction of the Hamlet. The total had been arrived at before the Hamlet was even started. One did not have to be too clever to realize that the Hamlet must have cost at least twice that amount. Nor was it difficult to guess how exorbitant the cost of upkeep and the ongoing extravaganzas must be. It was no wonder that an underground scandal sheet headlined its scurrilous story THE HIGH COST OF HER MAJESTY'S HAYSTACK HUMPING.

When I saw that, it crossed my mind that the Phantom Cock had a big mouth. But I was more concerned

with the accuracy of the figures regarding the cost of the *jardin anglaise*. It had to have been someone inside Versailles who exposed those figures. I had many enemies in the government. It could have been any one of them. But when I asked myself who had the most to gain by weakening the monarchy in this fashion, the answer was always the same: Cardinal de Rohan.

It was traditional in France that the church and the monarchy remained locked in a struggle for power. The struggle was usually *sub rosa* and its various aspects customarily resolved by compromise and intrigue. Rarely, however, had the church had such a popular head as Cardinal de Rohan. And rarely had France had such a blunderingly unpopular king as my husband Louis XVI. Each step down from popularity that Louis took represented a step up for my ex-lover, the Cardinal. It was certainly to his advantage to incite a hungry populace by revealing the extravagant expenditures of King Louis' sinful, Austrian-born Queen.

The Cardinal, however, was subtle, devious. At the same time that he was exposing my indiscretions to my subjects (if he was indeed the guilty one), he was also contriving to gain my favor. No, *mes amis*, I do not mean sexually. After the fiasco in the wine cellar, the Cardinal seemed to have foresworn his customary backdoor approach. Instead, since that night, during the casual encounters he arranged with me, His Eminence always managed to bring the conversation around to the diamond necklace.

How well he knew my weakness! Despite the fact that Louis' refusal to purchase it for me had been transmitted to the jewelers Bohmer and Bassenge, they continued to try to tempt me with the necklace. And how tempting it was! It consisted of 647 flawless diamonds weighing a total of 2,800 carats. Never before in the

history of the world had there been such a necklace! Never again, I was sure, would there be one like it!

Mon Dieu! how I wanted it! My whole body twitched for it the way my pussy twitched for pricks after that first night with Axel Fersen. The flesh of my bosom tingled with the idea of those priceless gems reclining there. I had been denied the necklace, and so of course I had to have it.

Cardinal de Rohan understood this perfectly. As my lover he had learned from me that a Hapsburg denied is a Hapsburg obsessed. What I could not have, I had to have. As equally as cocks to fill my quim, this applied to diamonds!

And so subtly, deviously, the Cardinal let me know that he was taking steps to circumvent the King's decision and to acquire the diamond necklace for me. I would demur by way of reply, saying that I would not flaunt my husband's decision. But the Cardinal would wink at this demurral and speak obliquely once again of the many ways of skinning felines. Hope would quicken the heaving of my breast, and my avarice for diamonds would make me tap his cheek with my fan and promise him again that he would be restored to favor at Court if he could indeed deliver on his murky promises.

It was a game, you see. Did I really believe that the Cardinal could deliver the diamond necklace to me? Did I really countenance the means he implied might be necessary to do so? Did my hunger for the necklace implicate me in the Cardinal's scheme? Was I as guilty as he and his co-conspirators of the crime in which they engaged? History would ask these questions and never satisfactorily answer them. Why not? Because, *mes amis*, I myself did not know how guilty or how innocent I was in the Affair of the Diamond Necklace.

"I have enlisted Count Cagliostro to act as a go-

between with the jewelers," the Cardinal confided to me on one occasion.

Should I have thrown up my hands in horror at the scheme then and there and refused to have anything further to do with it? Alessandro di Cagliostro (the Italian title of "Count" was very dubious) was a charlatan! He claimed to be a seer who could foretell the future, but in reality he was a trickster, an opportunist, a mountebank. Slim as a stiletto, dark as an olive, he was a slight man with intense, aquiline features, a gaze compelling as a watch swinging from a gold chain, and a laugh as intimate to the ear as honey spread to bread. Obviously a fraud, his charisma was nevertheless irresistible.

The truly amazing thing was that Cardinal de Rohan, himself the most charismatic of leaders, could not resist Cagliostro's charisma. A religious man, a high prelate of the church, the Cardinal nevertheless became a firm believer in Cagliostro's black magic. "Count Cagliostro says that a woman in white will transform my life," my erstwhile lover told me. "I believe this prognostication is somehow related to the diamond necklace."

And this from the Cardinal of France, second only to the Pope in Rome! I looked at my erstwhile lover with new eyes. Once he had seemed the epitome of masculine mastery to me. Now he seemed only a buggerer dazzled by an augurer.

At this time, Cardinal de Rohan had been bewitched by Cagliostro for some three years. I myself, however, had only recently met the compelling Italian. I was not taken in by his mysticism, nor by his magical claims, but I could not deny that I found him both amusing and oddly attractive.

"All women find me attractive, Majesty," he announced

to me upon our first meeting. "All women from scullery maids to queens."

"And why is that?" I inquired, smiling in spite of myself at his impudence.

The meeting took place at the Petit Trianon just before the start of a fête de nuit complete with geysering fountains and fireworks. I no longer recall who brought Cagliostro there and presented him to me. For all I know he sneaked in on his own and arrogantly made his own introduction. I certainly wouldn't put it past him.

"Why is that?" he repeated my question. "Because, Majesty, I am small. It is my smallness that is irresistible to all women. They empathize with it. They sympathize with it. It brings out their maternal instincts."

"Then I will surely be impervious," I told him. "My instincts are erotic, not maternal. I am interested in men, not little boys."

"Of course, Majesty." His face crumpled into mock sadness. "Why would a real woman want such a little fellow as I. Particularly a woman whose instincts are erotic. I mean, Majesty, I am really small. Everything about me is tiny. Everything, Majesty," he stressed meaningfully.

"Everything?" I could not contain my laugh. "Surely you exaggerate."

"Not at all, Majesty. My equipment is so small that I was forced to leave Italy in shame."

"But you are a magician," I reminded him. "Why do you not cast a spell and make it grow?"

"I cast a different sort of spell, Majesty. A very common spell indeed. It is called curiosity. It is this which seals my irresistibility to women. They simply must confirm my sad state for themselves."

"But now that I know your secret, I am immune to it," I assured him.

"Are you, Majesty?" His dark eyes glowed. "Are you really?"

Well, of course I wasn't. Privy to the trick or not, my curiosity was piqued. As the fête de nuit began, I was wondering if his wee-wee was really as wee as he implied. I rather doubted it. Being married to King Louis XVI, I was something of an expert on the penis petit. Surely Cagliostro's could be no smaller than my husband's.

But it was! He had told the truth!

Awhile later, as I strolled through the *jardin anglaise*, its blooms glowing in the glare from the multicolored skyrockets bursting overhead, I came on the slight Italian facing the bushes to one side of a grassy knoll brilliant with dew. I did not immediately realize that he was relieving himself in the bushes. But then he turned to me with a dazzling smile, managing a last small shake graceful as an *entrechat*, and I saw quite clearly that his equipment was still exposed. Brazen, he made no effort to cover himself.

"You see, Majesty, I did not lie." He cupped his balls and penis in the palm of his hand and held them up to the exploding sky.

"Très petit!" There was no denying it. So small indeed that I forgot to convey queenly outrage at the outrageous display.

"Perhaps a closer examination, Majesty." There was no hesitation in the impertinent offer.

Nor did I hesitate to take advantage of it. Obsessed with men's penises as I was, no specimen was too small to attract my interest. I moved up to Cagliostro and peered down at his member in the sudden flare of a skyrocket. "Why a woman would barely feel such an instrument inside her!" I exclaimed.

"The barest tickle, Majesty." He sighed a mock sigh.

I detected the sarcasm underlying his words and it

made me angry. "Of what earthly use is such a tiny tool in lovemaking?" I jeered, my unkindness quite deliberate.

"Scarce any use at all, Majesty." Again the note of sarcasm. "A slight tickle. Perhaps an ability to manipulate denied larger, more unwieldy members." It moved in the palm of his hand like a worm stretching.

"A tickle . . . an ability to manipulate . . ." I mulled it over.

"And of course great energy combined with the most ingenious innovation," he added, his tongue visibly in his cheek now.

"And just why should your wee wand have greater power and inventiveness than a large lance?" I inquired imperiously.

"Overcompensation, Majesty. When one is the littlest, one has to try harder."

"I thought that only applied when one was second, not when one was patently least."

"Lust increases as size decreases," Cagliostro assured me.

"No, it doesn't," I told him, the echoing snores of my marriage bed dictating the sureness of my response.

"It can, Majesty. Believe me, it can." Ebony eyes glowing, he reached out with his free hand and took my hand. He carried it to his other palm. He covered his naked penis with my palm. It burned against the flesh there like a red-hot ingot. His tiny balls, smaller than marbles, smaller than grapes, almost as small as raisins, squirmed over my palm like the tickling of fingers inscribing an obscene suggestion.

My nipples were suddenly hard and yearning against the bodice of my gown. "Prove it!" I blurted out hoarsely. "Prove what you have been saying!"

"Of course, Majesty." His mouth spread over mine like a damp, warm, enveloping blanket of lust. The

slender, olive fingers of both his hands dipped into my bodice and lifted out my naked breasts. His tiny cock—quite hard now—and his live balls moved over the surface of my open hand.

Truly, he must have been a master of the arts of black magic. I have no recollection of taking off my clothes, but suddenly I was completely naked there in the woods behind the Petit Trianon, naked and exposed to the rainbow bursts of the fireworks overhead. As he was as naked as I, his flesh as dark as mine was fair, as sparse over his tight muscles as mine was generous of bosom and hips and derriere.

Slight as he was, the Italian wizard was wiry and strong. He backed me up against the trunk of an orange tree, placed his hands under my buttocks, and lifted me until my legs were locked around his slender waist. In this position I clasped my hands around the back of his neck and stared into his compelling eyes as he entered me.

At first I felt very little. Cagliostro was *petit—très, très petit!* But then his tiny organ began moving inside me in a way that was new and strange and ultimately very exciting to me. "What are you doing?" I panted, my distended, burning nipples digging into the bones of his bare chest.

"Fucking, Majesty." He sucked my tongue from my mouth to still any further inquiry.

Before the kiss was over, I realized that I could feel his balls inside my cunt. The sensation made me forget that the bark of the orange tree was abrading my naked buttocks as his pelvis slammed against mine. And then I felt his small cock engage my clitoris in a fashion as controlled and teasing as the most expertly controlled of all fingers—my own.

I dug my nails into the back of his neck, drawing

blood, and pounded his vibrating bottom with my heels. My pussy made a wet, slapping sound as it moved to respond to him. Looking down my body between my naked breasts, I watched its twitching gyrations in response to the magic of his tiny cock.

And then, suddenly, the diamond-hard tip of his petit prick pressed against an area just behind my clitoris. I cannot begin to describe the sensitivity of this contact. I had never known before that this spot even existed! But somehow Cagliostro did know of its existence. His probing of it was quite deliberate—knowingly deliberate, exquisitely deliberate. Somehow he knew that it would trigger my orgasm, but instead of pulling this trigger immediately, he toyed with it, squeezed it gently as it were, tortured me so exquisitely that I lost control.

"AAAGGGHHH!" I bayed wordlessly at the exploding sky, and pushed so hard against the trunk of the tree that I bloodied the cheeks of my bottom. Tears ran down my cheeks and still I could find no words for what I was feeling. You see, *mes amis*, I was not coming yet, I was only on the brink. And I perched there—the victim of the most exquisite torture—for what seemed an eternity.

It was different from any fuck I ever knew, before or since. In every other case it was the sensation of a prick filling my quim which made me spend. (In the case of Louis, it was the absence of this sensation which so frequently made it necessary for me to pretend a passion I didn't in the slightest feel.) But with Cagliostro the contact of his cock with this mysterious, uncharted erogenous zone aroused a lust that was so self-concerned as to be almost masturbatory. Indeed, there was much of masturbation in having sex with Cagliostro. The "tickle" he had spoken of before was as different from ordinary coupling as it could be.

Suddenly, when I was sure I couldn't stand it any longer, the wily Latin thrust his long middle finger all the way up my anus and began to come inside me, spraying his thick lust over this newly identified area of arousal. Again I screamed wordlessly. And, as he spun me around, away from the orange tree, I started to spend with a tremor that possessed my entire body.

Round and round in circles we whirled, he shooting unexpectedly copious geysers from his tiny cock, I climaxing once and then immediately again. Panting, mouths opened, eyes glazed, bodies locked as if we were dancing some bizarre and savage quadrille, we turned and fucked and fucked and turned. And finally we fell to the glittering grass, our bodies slippery with perspiration and the juices of our spending, and Cagliostro's tiny cock flopped limply out of my still shuddering pussy. . . .

This then was the wily fellow Cardinal de Rohan had chosen to be go-between in the Affair of the Diamond Necklace. But so far, throughout 1783, the affair was still nothing but talk, teasing talk, surely not to be taken seriously, surely never to be considered a blueprint for action. Certainly I never took it seriously. Certainly I never dreamed events were moving from the realm of words to the sphere of action.

I knew nothing of the ongoing meetings between Cardinal de Rohan and Jeanne de Valois, the Countess de la Motte, my look-alike, the infamous woman conspirator who would one day be known to both history and literature simply as Milady. And had I known, I would not have believed that the Cardinal could have fallen so deeply under the influence of Cagliostro as to forget what he knew of the origins of this one-time palace whore and accept the Italian mountebank's assurances that she had (unbelievable!) access to the Queen.

His own access being quite limited, despite our few casual meetings, my decision barring him from Court unchanged, the Cardinal actually allowed this dark duo to convince him that Milady had become my confidante (incredible!) and was authorized by me to carry private letters from me to him.

The letters of course were forgeries contrived by Cagliostro and Milady. They were so cleverly molded that even after the entire affair was exposed, many people—from the dregs of Paris to the most illustrious members of the royal government—believed that I had indeed written them. Right up to the guillotine, my protests of innocence regarding the writing of these letters were sneered at.

And what was in these letters that was so damning? At first they consisted merely of beseechments from the Cardinal that he be reinstated at Court. Indeed, they were little different from the requests he verbalized to me upon our rare meetings. And the replies forged in my name merely perpetuated the teasing hints I had actually given that if he obtained the fabulous diamond necklace for me, he would be restored to royal favor. But then the language of the forgeries became more forceful, clearer, more direct. And finally the language added up to an unmistakable authorization from me to the Cardinal to purchase the diamond necklace from the jewelers Bohmer and Bassenge on my behalf.

The forgeries were actually committed by Cagliostro. The truly amazing resemblance to my own handwriting was a testament to his "magical" talents. On the basis of them, the Cardinal turned over large amounts of his personal fortune to Milady, believing that the money was being received by me. My gambling debts and continuing extravagances and constant shortness of cash were well known, and surely, he believed, this help

would ease him back into my good graces. So successful were Cagliostro and Milady in convincing him of this, that the Cardinal actually sold off the antique gold plate of the de Rohan estate in order to provide the funds I needed—the funds which never reached me because Milady and the mountebank pocketed them.

Oui, initially the Cardinal was a victim. But then, with the purchase of the necklace, he became a collaborator. Wittingly? Unwittingly? As with my own involvement, it is possible that the Cardinal himself could not have said.

Facts, it has been said, are the enemy of truth. So it is in the Affair of the Diamond Necklace. The Cardinal's guilt, my guilt, the degree of our innocence, our roles as conspirators or victims—none of this can be determined from the facts. And, since conscience is a vagary, only the Almighty can judge.

Nevertheless, the facts must be set down if only to make understandable their effect on history. Here they are:

The Cardinal went to various aristocrat friends of his and raised four hundred thousand francs for a down payment on the necklace. He offered this to the jewelers, but Bassenge and Bohmer refused to accept it without personal assurances from me that it was indeed the Queen who was buying it. They were, understandably, suspicious of the sudden about-face, having been convinced that the King's decision not to pauperize the treasury by buying the diamond necklace was final. They wanted me to confirm the sale in person.

Fool that he was where Cagliostro and Milady were concerned, the Cardinal was still not so foolish as to think I would ever compromise myself by a public meeting confirming a purchase which was bound to have such negative repercussions upon the poor people

of France. It was this realization which led him to compromise himself in the imposture perpetrated at the Grove of Venus.

Ahh, the Grove of Venus . . . It was truly the most romantic part of the *jardin anglaise*. Its Greek and Roman statuary, selected for its nudity and frankness of pose and uninhibited mergings, also made it the most sensual site in the gardens. Because of this, it was frequently the place where I enjoyed trysts with one or another of the succession of lovers I enjoyed. Not only did Cagliostro know this, but thanks to the spies at Court, it was known through the underground publications to the populace at large as well. Indeed, the reputation of the Grove of Venus had even reached the ears of Bassenge and Bohmer in London. Since they knew it to be the place of so many of my assignations, it seemed quite logical to them that the Queen would choose it as the place of a secret meeting where she would personally confirm to them that the Cardinal was indeed acting for her in the matter of the diamond necklace.

As remarked, however, the Cardinal well knew that I would never agree to such a meeting. And so he became a party to my look-alike Milady, née Jeanne de Valois, impersonating me for the (tryst) with the jewelers at the Grove of Venus! The meeting took place in August 1784.

Later the Cardinal would protest that he had been taken in by the impersonation himself. He would insist that he believed it was really the Queen who came to the Grove of Venus that night. He would insist that he was victimized from first to last.

I could never believe that. Once, young and naive, I had believed that he plunged his prick up the naked bottom of Jeanne De Valois thinking it was me. But I was no longer an innocent child. The Cardinal knew

both of us more intimately than any man in France—our faces and our bodies! It was simply not possible that he could have been taken in by Milady posing as me.

The jewelers however, were taken in. They really believed that the hooded woman in the grove of Venus was Marie Antoinette, Queen of France. But even this did not relieve all their qualms. I might make the down payment of four hundred thousand francs through the Cardinal, but my profligate reputation far from reassured them that they would receive the balance of the payments for the fabulous diamond necklace.

Because of these doubts, negotiations dragged on for another six months. It was during this period that the Cardinal made an oblique approach to me, inquiring if I would assure the raising of some money towards the payment of the necklace at some vague future time. This was not the price of the necklace he was asking about, but only some small token payment towards meeting that price. Typically, and quite in keeping with my devotion to Louis' theories of supply-side economics, I blithely gave assurances that the sums would be forthcoming. In substance, this was no different than the promises of payment I frequently made during losing streaks at the baccarat table. The royal treasury would take care of my gambling losses, and it would provide for this eventuality as well.

The Cardinal evidently did not take my assurances in this spirit. There was a good reason for this. They were backed up by my forged signature on a contract authorizing him to purchase the necklace. Fortified with this document, he signed notes to the jewelers which obligated him personally to meet the payments. On January 29, 1785, he signed a contract incorporating this obligation. On February 1, he accepted delivery of the diamond necklace and signed a receipt for it.

Actually, however, he never personally took possession of the jewels. They were handed over to his trusted emissary—Count Alessandro Cagliostro and his companion, Milady. The Cardinal took it for granted that Milady, whom he thought my confidante (had Cagliostro hypnotized him? I wondered when this part of the story came to light), would deliver the necklace to me.

Of course she had no intention of doing any such thing. She and Cagliostro took the diamond necklace to Amsterdam and stashed it until such time as it could be broken up and the gems individually sold. But the Cardinal assumed it was in my possession. He sat back and waited for me to demonstrate my gratitude.

He waited for more than six months. In early August of 1785, he was still waiting. It was at this time that Bohmer came to him and demanded the second payment due on the necklace. The Cardinal, failing to raise the money, assured the jeweler that I would meet the payment. And so, finally, Bohmer really did come face-to-face with me.

I had some idea of what he was talking about, but truly not very much. You see, Bohmer assumed that the diamond necklace was in my possession and it wasn't. As far as I was concerned, the whole matter was still in some vague negotiating stage, being manipulated by my cunning former lover, the Cardinal. When the jeweler informed me that possession of it had been taken in my name some six months before, I was outraged.

I went directly to my husband, the King. Louis too was outraged, but he was also elated. At last a weapon was being handed to him which could bring down the man most responsible for the shakiness of his throne— the Cardinal of the church of France!

With unconcealed glee, Louis summoned his secretary of state, Baron de Breteuil. The Baron had been an

archenemy of the Cardinal ever since he had been removed from his post as ambassador to Vienna by Louis XV in order to create a vacancy for de Rohan. Now it fell to him personally to arrest the Cardinal for crimes against the Queen of France.

The actual arrest was deliberately calculated to embarrass the Cardinal as much as possible. He was seized while officiating over High Mass in the Royal Chapel on Assumption Day, August 15, 1785, and immediately hauled off to the Bastille like the most common street criminal. Milady was arrested three days later while attempting to flee the country. Cagliostro, as might have been expected, successfully escaped.

And so the great scandal had broken. The problem was that while its web enmeshed the King's arch-rival, the Cardinal, it also caught me. Protest my innocence as I might, the rumors of my involvement persisted in spreading and gaining acceptance.

Even Axel Fersen, the Swede who had introduced me to the joys of fucking, a man who surely might have been expected to give me the benefit of the doubt, believed that I was implicated. On duty with his regiment at the time that the scandal broke, he wrote to a friend at Court as follows:

"It is said that it was only a game between the Queen and the Cardinal, that he was on friendly terms with her, that she had in fact commissioned him to purchase the necklace, that the Queen pretended not to be able to stand him in order to hide her goals, that the King knew this and reproached her with it, that this made her very ill and she pretended to be pregnant."

Louis, believing in my innocence, and wanting there to be no question of a cover-up, sent the case to the Parliament of Paris for trial on September 19, 1785. Immediately there were mass protests in the streets of

Paris. Demands that the Cardinal be released from the Bastille were widespread. There was no precedent for a prince of the church being tried by civil authorities in France and many claimed it was illegal. The Cardinal, more cunning now that he was no longer under Cagliostro's spell, took to wearing his ceremonial purple robes whenever he could. He realized that his best hope lay in the impression that the unpopular crown was persecuting the church.

Despite his status as the accused, the Cardinal still had great influence. He brought this to bear on the politicians of Parliament charged with trying him. As a result, they dragged their feet in setting date for the trial and allowed public sentiment favoring the Cardinal and opposed to the crown to build. As time passed the prelate was regarded more and more as a religious martyr by the people while I was assigned the role of his Jezebel persecutor.

Finally, on May 30, 1786, the prisoners were brought before Parliament and a hearing was held. The next day, May 31, judgment was rendered. The Cardinal was acquitted! Furthermore, the verdict was phrased so ambiguously as to deliberately imply that I had compromised myself with my involvement in the Affair of the Diamond Necklace!

Dear, sweet, much-cuckolded Louis brought the full weight of his power as king to bear in my defense. He said publicly that "it was all a scheme to put money into his [the Cardinal's] pocket, but . . . he found himself cheated instead of being the cheat." He exiled de Rohan to a remote abbey of the church and stripped him of all of his titles and offices.

Politically, this was a mistake on Louis' part. When the Cardinal was acquited, the streets of Paris had rung with cries of "*Vive le Cardinal! Vive le Parlement!*" Traf-

fic had been blocked by the joyful dancing of his supporters. Now, when the public heard how Louis was punishing de Rohan despite the verdict, resentment was such that the first murmured threats to depose the monarchy were heard.

I myself was appalled at the Parliament's action. The day after they rendered their judgment, I wrote in despair to Yolande de Polignac: "Come and weep with me, come and console your friend. The judgment that has just been pronounced is an atrocious insult. I am bathed in tears of grief and despair. . . . Come to me, my dear heart."

In this dark hour it was the softness and peace of a loving woman's bosom which I craved. For once this seemed preferable to the assaults of pricks and to the cruelties I associated with their male owners. But of course this feeling quickly passed.

Perspective returned to me when I reflected upon the judgment pronounced by the Parliament on Milady. They found her guilty of all charges and sentenced her to be flogged, branded with the fleur-de-lis like any common criminal, and imprisoned for life in the Salpêtrière, most horrible of all French prisons. There was solace for me in Milady's fate, but even so, I was appalled at accounts of the carrying-out of the sentence.

The branding was performed in public. She was dragged to the scaffold wild-eyed, spitting, and screaming. The red-hot iron was intended to imprint the scarlet fleur-de-lis on her shoulder. She struggled so energetically, however, that her full ivory-white breasts (so like my own) were completely exposed. When the onlookers cheered this lascivious, hard-panting sight, Milady redoubled her struggles. As a result, the branding iron was applied to her naked breast instead of her shoulder. By all accounts she then howled like a ban-

shee and bit the executioner so hard that her teeth went through his coat and tore a wound in his flesh.

Her behavior seemed to fascinate the nobles who attended my soirées at the Petit Trianon. The Marquis de Sade was enjoying a fashionable revival that season and the whipping and branding of Milady was viewed as inspirational after a certain amount of snuff had been sniffed and wine had been drunk. It was certainly a more palatable topic to these nobles, myself included, than Louis' most recent closing of the granaries to the poor and the predictions of bread riots by his political foes.

"That lovely body," Yolande remarked. "How must it have looked stripped to the waist and writhing under the whip?"

"How do you know her body is lovely?" I inquired, a sudden jealousy penetrating the shimmering haze created by the white powder I had been sniffing.

"How could it be other, Majesty? As like to your own beauty as Milady's is?"

"And how do you know that?" I opened my bodice to the warm summer air of the Hamlet.

"Have you forgotten, Majesty? There was a night when you and I and Milady, just the three of us—"

I had indeed forgotten. Nor did I choose to be reminded. I had been very, very drunk and suddenly seized with the desire to have sex with my double, to watch her having an orgasm at the same time that she supplied one to me. And so I had dispatched Yolande to fetch her and the three of us, very drunk, had made love all through the night. The next morning I had been appalled at having consorted with the one-time palace whore. I had refused to see her and had instructed Yolande to send her on her way. Subsequently I had blotted the incident out of my mind.

"You are mistaken," I told Yolande coldly now. "The event of which you speak never occurred."

"Of course, Majesty." Yolande knew me well enough not to insist. "I am mistaken. It was a dream. I frequently confuse my dreams with reality. Particularly dreams of an erotic nature."

Her last remark was overheard by a young dandy strolling past. His name was Pierre and he was the middle son of a prominent land baron. In keeping with the informality of the Hamlet he had taken off his jacket and opened his ruffled shirt. His chest with its sprinkling of curly blond hair was most comely and at the juncture of the legs of his fawn-colored britches there was a truly intriguing mound.

"Dreams of an erotic nature?" With a good-natured if slightly foppish grin, Pierre echoed Yolande's last remark. "How naughty. You should be punished for that. Don't you agree, Majesty?"

"I don't know if I agree or not." Aware of Pierre's eyes on my semiexposed breasts, my breathing quickened. "That depends on what kind of punishment you mean."

"Perhaps the kind bestowed on the infamous Milady." Pierre was too young to realize that his gibe might be in poor taste.

"Would you have me branded then?" Yolande clasped her hands to her bosom in an exaggerated fashion, as if pleading for mercy. "Save me from this fiend, Majesty!"

"Not branded." Pierre's eyes danced from my bosom to Yolande's and back. "Only flogged perhaps, lightly flogged."

"Majesty!" Yolande ran to me and curtsied deeply, exposing the long, pointy nipples of her breasts.

"Do not fear, child." I quaffed deeply from my goblet of champagne. "It is not you who shall be whipped. It

is this impertinent rogue here." And I pointed a dramatic, imperious finger at Pierre.

"Let me administer the punishment, Majesty." A new voice, male.

I turned to face the speaker. He was a count a few years older than Pierre. His name was Armand and he was one of the more enthusiastic disciples of the infamous Marquis de Sade at Court. Confirming this was the crop he held lightly in one hand now as he joined us.

"You are too eager, Armand," I told him. "I think it will be better for your soul if you too are chastised rather than the instrument of discipline."

"But then who will administer the punishment, Majesty?"

"I will. And Yolande will help." I directed the two men to take off their shirts and stretch their hands over their heads. As the other guests gathered to watch, we tied their wrists to tree branches over their heads, using their ruffled silk shirts as the tethers.

Anticipation welled up in me as I studied the muscles of their arms and back rippling in the moonlight. I had a sudden inspiration. "Men's nipples are as sensitive as women's," I told Yolande, remembering. You play with the nipples of these two bold fellows while I teach them some respect."

Obediently, Yolande went up to Pierre and parted the gold hairs on his chest and tickled his nipples with her fingertips until they were quite erect. Then she turned her attention to Armand. She bent her head and stuck out her long, pink, pointy tongue. She licked first one of his nipples and then the other. By the time she was through, not only were they standing up, his straining cock was tenting the crotch of his britches as well.

Inspired by this, I raised Armand's crop and brought

it down over his shoulders. The stroke was not heavy enough to do any real damage, but it did inflict a certain amount of pain. Quickly, I delivered a similar lashing to Pierre. His golden flesh, more sensitive, shuddered visibly under the punishment.

"Pain should be mixed with pleasure," I recalled, turning to Yolande. "I well know that you are expert at giving pleasure, my dear. Do not withhold it from these poor gentlemen now."

Yolande understood immediately what I meant. She moved to Pierre and stroked his thighs through his britches as I brought the lash down over his shoulders again. Then she rubbed her bosom against Armand's bare chest while I whipped him.

Soon both men were writhing with a combination of erotic arousal and pain. Also, the scene was having an effect on the onlookers. Kisses were being exchanged, caresses were openly indulged in, stays were loosened, bodices invaded. The beginning stirrings of yet another Petit Trianon orgy were in evidence.

I was not immune to the general heat. Whipping two such excellent masculine specimens as Pierre and Armand was firing my royal blood as well. When I saw Yolande take her extraordinary breasts out of her bodice and rub the tips of the distended nipples over the naked flesh of both men, I felt the warm honey gathering inside my pussy.

"They are bad boys and it is their bottoms that should be birched," I decided hoarsely. I tossed aside the crop, found a suitable branch and peeled it. "Take down their britches," I instructed Yolande.

She obeyed with obvious enthusiasm. Both had plump red bottoms and she could not keep her hands from fondling them when they were bared. Then she sank to her knees in front of them and shook her unique,

outwardly angled breasts so that the long, swollen nipples dueled with the tips of each of the exposed cocks.

Pierre and Armand's *épées* both became impressively long and hard as I proceeded to apply the birch to their squirming nether cheeks. My own breasts were bared now and they swung wildly as I exulted in the appearance of welts on both men's behinds. Soon these stripes were as red as my own yearning berry-nipples.

I was close behind them now with my improvised birch rod, panting heavily and watching the interaction with Yolande as I whipped them. She was on her knees in front of them, licking first one hard prick and then the other and playing with herself. Her hands were moving violently under her dress and her tongue and lips were glistening with the lust she brought to each long, delicious suck of each of the men's long, delicious candy canes.

My own lust built as I whipped harder and harder. Finally I could contain myself no longer. I flung the birch aside and joined Yolande in front of the two quivering organs. I sucked Pierre's hard prick deep into my mouth and sighed with satisfaction.

Yolande continued sucking and licking Armand's shaft. After a while, however, we looked at each other with complete understanding and switched. I licked Armand's hairier balls and she nibbled on the rosy young tip of Pierre's aristocratic mace. Then we switched back, and then back again.

Finally Yolande released Pierre's prick from between her lips and rolled back on the ground. She flung up her skirts and plunged both her hands inside her bloomers. Sobbing at the moon, almost baying, she thrashed over the grassy sward in the throes of a powerful orgasm.

Watching her, I was overcome with my own lust. I grabbed both pricks—Pierre's and Armand's—and

crammed them into my mouth. I clasped their bleeding buttocks with my hands and dug my long, sharp nails into the swollen flesh. Breasts bouncing violently with my gasping passion, I carefully sucked both cocks down my throat and squeezed my thighs together.

Yolande, dear girl, her own violent spending temporarily over, saw my predicament. Surfeited with cocks, I had not enough limbs to reach my pussy with a frigging finger. Quickly, she crawled under my skirts, pulled down my bloomers, and fastened her moist, hot lips to my honeyed cunt.

Feeling this, I all but bit down on the two hot, hard shafts filling my mouth. I managed to control myself, however, and sucked ecstatically on them as Yolande lapped my frenzied quim. She was going to make me spend quickly. I knew that. I was only holding back until I felt the cream filling each prick reach the exploding point.

And then they did explode. And so did I. Swallowing fiercely as Pierre and Armand bathed each other's mouth-embedded pricks with the overflow of their lust, I came over Yolande's face and gloried in the duality of dongs dousing my throat with delicious nectar.

It was precisely at this inopportune moment that the messenger from my husband King Louis arrived. "His Majesty wishes me to inform you," he announced, "that the poor people of Paris are storming the food warehouses. They are hungry and there is no bread for them. They demand bread, and still there is none. The King is distraught. He does not know what to tell them."

It was then that I uttered the statement so misheard by history. Ejecting the two still-spurting phalluses from my lips, I launched the misconception that led me to the steps of the guillotine, the misconception which, I am sure, will outlive me by many, many centuries. It is

useless, I fear, but I must make the attempt to straighten out the record. When hearing of the people's demands for bread, I never—never!—said, "Let them eat cake!"

You see, *mes amis*, my mouth was too recently filled with penises, my throat too clogged with male nectar for me to be properly understood. I said nothing about my starving subjects eating cake at all. What I said was . . .

"Let them eat cock!"

Chapter Eleven

The starving poor were not alone in their dissatisfaction with the monarchy. Outrage at the treatment of Cardinal de Rohan forged a cabal of high-ranking churchmen and top government magistrates in opposition of the crown. Within a year the King's enemies had engineered the escape of the infamous Milady from the Salpetrière and her flight to sanctuary in London.

Opposition became more and more open over the next two years, and by 1789, when Milady published the first volume of her memoirs under the by-line of Comtesse de la Motte, the French public was ripe to receive them with complete credulity. From my viewpoint, of course, "vicious" and "scurrilous" were the mildest adjectives suitable to describe the memoirs. Milady's brand still burned in her breast and she obviously considered me to blame for the disgrace of the fleur-de-lis.

Milady wrote that she was completely innocent in the Affair of the Diamond Necklace. She had not stolen it and only confessed to the crime in order to shield

her Queen. Loyalty to me, she claimed, was her only crime.

And why such staunch loyalty? Because, wrote Milady, she and I were lesbian lovers. (Ahh, *mes amis*, if there is one universal truth that follows women down through the ages it is that our one-night stands always come back to haunt us!) She left no doubt as to her own reluctance regarding woman love and implied strongly that I had used my royal status to force her into the relationship. She also claimed that upon my arrival in Strasbourg from Vienna in 1770 I became the mistress of Prince-Bishop—now Cardinal—de Rohan.

Thousands and thousands of copies of the book were sold. Scenes of unwashed illiterates gathering in small groups to hear Milady's vile prose recited by "readers" became common in villages all over France. And nowhere was the book's reception so enthusiastic as among the hungry poor of Paris.

The King became truly alarmed. The monarchy was demonstrably weakened by Milady's calumnies. At his request, the government supplied funds to bribe Milady to recant her revelations and forgo publication of any further memoirs.

Typically, Milady accepted the bribe and then, safe in London, reneged. She published another, even more revolting volume aimed at embarrassing me. She revealed the bribe and the result was that the crown was compromised to an even greater extent.

Milady's revelations spawned a flood of brochures, booklets, pamphlets, leaflets, and caricatures vilifying me. These were now hawked openly in the streets of Paris. Fraudulent "unexpurgated" love letters from the Cardinal to me and me to the Cardinal were circulated. (Curiously, these did not lessen his popularity with the populace. It was taken for granted that a man—even the

most eminent churchman in France—might indulge his libido, but a woman who did so, Queen of France though she might be, must be a slut, a witch, a Jezebel!) Exposés with titles such as *The Nymphomania of Marie Antoinette, Fureurs Uterines,* and *A List of All the Persons with Whom the Queen Has Had Debauched Relations* received the widest acceptance.

There was some truth in these publications. Much of it, however, was either pure fabrication or imaginative description built upon the merest tidbit of fact. Had I done everything erotic they claimed, I would not have had time to go to the bathroom and would certainly have been too sore to do so.

All of this added fuel to a fire already well stoked by the disgraceful state of the country's finances. To the people, this faltering economy meant the growl of hungry bellies. Well informed by Milady of how profligately I had spent on my libidinous pleasures, they blamed the condition of the economy on me. To the extent that I had followed the King's theories of supply-side economics, I suppose there was more than a little justification in this attitude.

Probably too late, Louis became alarmed at the growing unrest caused by the shambles in which the economy had plunged the nation. Alienating those who had believed in his economic programs, he opted for practical politics and tried to conciliate the forces aligned against him. In this spirit, on May 5, 1789, he called into session the Estates-General. This quasi-democratic assembly which had not met in 175 years was composed of representatives from all strata of French society. A Hapsburg who believed in the absolute power of kings and queens to reign over their subjects, I considered this action a mistake.

Immediately the democratic elements of the Estates-

General demanded a constitution along the lines of the nonsense perpetrated by the American colonists against that hopeless bourgeoise milksop King George III of England. Gradually, clerical and noble members of the assembly endorsed these demands. Aghast, the King reversed himself and announced on June 23 that the Estates-General was dissolved.

Count de Mirabeau, the assembly's spokesman, defied the order, replying to the King's messenger with these words: "Go tell your master that we are here by the will of the people and nothing but bayonets shall drive us out."

"What shall I do?" Louis wailed to me when he received this impudent answer.

"Do?" I had difficulty hiding my contempt. No Hapsburg would ever have found it necessary to ask the question. "Hang the lot of them! What else?"

Louis didn't follow my advice literally, but he did act in the spirit of it. He ordered the army to march on Paris. Troops surrounded the city and then invaded it to institute martial law.

On July 8 a group of deputies from the Estates-General, led by de Mirabeau, drew up a resolution demanding that the King withdraw his troops. Again Louis vacillated. Only my wifely strength shored up his resolve. The soldiers remained.

But not for long! On July 12 a mob stormed into the Place Louis Quinze and assaulted the troops with clubs and rocks and knives and broken bottles and with their bare, hairy hands as well. The soldiers were forced to flee. The Financial Exchange was threatened and the bankers had to close it. Street fighting continued intermittently for the next two days.

Then, on Tuesday, July 14, 1789, a day that shall surely live in infamy for anyone with a drop of royal

blood, a ragtag rabble of men, women, and even children stormed the barricades of the Bastille, the fortress-prison where so many of the monarchy's enemies were incarcerated, routed the guardians of this supposedly impregnable symbol of Bourbon absolutism, and freed all those held in its dank dungeons. The governor of the Bastille was found and beaten to death by the bare fists of the citizenry. A cleaver was produced and his head was severed from his body. Impaled on a pike and raised high, the bloody head was paraded through the streets of Paris. When night fell, the gory spectacle continued by torchlight.

It was difficult for Louis and me to believe that the Bastille had actually fallen. We reacted to the news quite differently. The very night that I heard it, I set about burning all of the records having to do with royal finances. I also packed all of my jewelry into a small trunk which could be easily transported at a moment's notice.

Louis acted in what I privately considered to be a more cowardly fashion. He went personally to Paris and humbled himself to the leaders of the constitutional forces. When he returned, there was a red, white, and blue cockade sticking up from the ribbon of his tricorne.

Seeing this symbol of revolution in his hatband, I pulled away from him. "I thought I had married a Bourbon king," I told him coldly. "I did not know I had married a commoner!"

"I did what I had to do in order for us to survive, Marie." There was a great weariness in his voice.

The King's attempts at appeasing the revolutionaries, however, were not too successful. Even as we huddled behind the walls of Versailles, rumors were sweeping France that I had asked my brother, now the Emperor of Austria, to come to the defense of the French

monarchy. It was widely believed that Austrian troops were already in France and marching towards Paris. The only answer to this incursion as far as the great majority of French people were concerned was the head of the Queen.

It was not this, however, which finally roused Louis from his apathy of appeasement. It was another movement—perhaps the most revolutionary of all—which sprang from the first rebel manifesto, "The Declaration of the Rights of Man." It dazed even the male revolutionaries. It was a demand for equal liberties for women!

"Are they mad?" Louis was genuinely shocked. "It is one thing to question the Divine Right of a Bourbon king, but to doubt that God created man superior to woman is heresy!"

"Mmm." I was noncommittal. I was a queen, but then I was also a woman, *n'est-ce pas?*

"God has decreed this biologically!" Louis pounded his fist.

"Has he, *cheri?*"

"Of course He has. Men are stronger than women."

"The men in the shops aren't stronger than the women in the fields," I pointed out mildly.

"Don't quibble, Marie!" He took my arm and twisted it, not too hard, just hard enough to drive home the lesson. "Men are stronger. And they are by nature more intelligent."

"Ahh, then." I struggled. "This is a demonstration of your intelligence, is it, Louis?"

"*Oui.*" He twisted my arm a bit harder. When I winced, he spoke again. "Men have greater stamina too. They withstand pain more courageously." His point made, he released my arm.

"You have never borne a child. Louis." I stroked the soreness he'd left behind.

"Only men are fit to govern!" He ignored my remark and folded his arms above his protruding belly.

"Only royalty is fit to govern!" I corrected him haughtily. "Only kings and—you will remember—queens! There have been many queens, many empresses, many tsarinas who have ruled, Louis. The Blood Royal is not thinned by gender!"

"Peasants may be ruled by queens! Not kings!"

I reflected that many a king had been ruled by his Queen, and that Louis more times than not might be considered in this company. I did not say this aloud, however. Instead, I asked my husband the King a question. "Would you rather be ruled by peasants then, Louis?"

"So long as they were men!"

Oui! The masculine intelligence certainly is superior! And such a sure instinct for survival too!

"How will you deal with these women's demands?" I inquired.

"With cunning," he assured me. "With masculine cunning, Marie."

"How fortunate that France is in such capable male hands."

"I will ignore your sarcasm, Marie. No doubt it is the result of your Austrian upbringing. Nevertheless, I will be cunning. I will carefully select three ladies and appoint them to high government posts in order to silence these ridiculous demands for female equality."

"Which three ladies? Which three posts?" I wondered.

"Baroness Duvivier. Comtesse le Mornay. Duchesse Rambeau."

Baroness Duvivier owned large estates in the provinces and was infamous for damming up the water supply to irrigate her farms, thereby causing the publicly owned lands around her to fall into drought.

Comtesse le Mornay was an outspoken advocate of the death penalty for anyone—including children—caught stealing a loaf of bread and had most recently written a manifesto stating that if the American colonies could profit through slavery, then France might well be able to solve her economic problems by reinstituting it. Duchesse Rambeau was a proponent of launching an invasion force into either Africa or South America on the theory that the booty it brought back would restore prosperity to the nation.

"And the positions you have in mind for them?" I inquired.

"The first shall head the new Environmental Protection Department the constitutionalists demand. The second will be France's new chief magistrate. And the third lady will be our roving goodwill ambassador to all those little countries who are always screaming about European imperialism."

"But Baroness Duvivier has already alienated small farmers and conservationists with statements like 'The business of agriculture is business' and 'The environment be damned,' Louis."

"*Oui.*" Louis beamed. "I know."

"And Comtesse le Mornay is on the record as favoring a code of justice with a double standard, strict for commoners, lax for aristocrats. She would make castration mandatory for adulterous peasants while at the same time doing away with any penalty for rape perpetrated by aristocrats."

"Those are indeed her views."

"The citizenry in six widely separated nonwhite countries have already burned Duchesse Rambeau in effigy because of her blatantly racist statements."

"So they have." Louis' equanimity was not disturbed.

"The reform elements you are trying to conciliate will be furious at these appointments," I pointed out.

"*Oui*. But they will not dare say anything. My appointees are women. If the so-called reformers object, they will be accused of being sexist and chauvinist."

"But Louis," I protested. "That's so cynical!"

"It was you who taught me, Marie, that cynicism is the first requirement of ruling over others. 'The Divine Right of Kings' is the ultimate cynicism,' you said. And you also said that if the rabble ever succeed in replacing the Bourbons and the Hapsburgs, the first quality of democratically elected rulers if they are to survive would have to be cynicism."

"How wise I am." I sighed, suddenly quite weary. "And how well you learn the Hapsburg lessons I pass on to you. And how hopeless is the lot of women."

"Then let them be content with their lot." Louis shrugged. "Let them stay home with their children; let them stay out of politics." He yawned. "Let them tend to their knitting." Louis turned over and went to sleep.

"They *are* tending to their knitting!" I warned into the deaf ear of his snores. "They tell of a common woman of Paris, one Madame Defarge, who does nothing but knit all the time. They say she knits names for the guillotine; they say she knits your name and mine, my dear; they say she knits revolution, this Madame Defarge."

But King Louis only kept on snoring, secure in his positive dreams that nature had shortchanged women of that aggressive quality which might tilt the crown from his head—and mine! He did not dream—nor, truthfully, did I—that it would be a women's army which would sweep us from our thrones. Nor did either of us guess just how close at hand that event was.

The immediate event which preceded it was a ban-

quet at Versailles to welcome back the Flanders Regiment to guard the palace. The regiment had been recalled because it was one of the few in the French army whose loyalty to the King was absolute. The banquet was meant to demonstrate our royal appreciation for that loyalty to the two hundred officers of the regiment who attended.

I suppose too much wine was drunk—most certainly by me. It made me forget the precariousness of our situation. For a few dizzy hours it seemed to me that I was back at the Court that used to be, the Court where frivolity and flirtatiousness and snuff and champagne and kisses and gropings behind curtains and tapestries were nightly pursuits. My apprehension dwindled and my libido swelled, and this relaxation, this permissiveness, quickly spread to the guests.

A young lieutenant of the regiment filled my slipper with champagne and quaffed it to loud applause. I kissed him by way of appreciation for his chivalry and when our lips tarried there was a second round of clapping, and other officers began following our example with other ladies of the Court. A few husbands grumbled and some of the men went out to the gardens to prove themselves at sword tip, but these duels barely constituted an interruption to the growing licentiousness of the proceedings. The King, ever tactful when it came to my erotic meanderings, retired early, and after that the candelabra were dimmed and the scene degenerated into one of hungry, writhing bodies.

By this time I was quite drunk. I remember pulling down one side of the bodice of Yolande's gown and sucking her nipple while a group of officers cheered us on. I remember an Alsatian captain with long, tickling handlebar mustaches lifting my gown from behind and lowering my bloomers just enough to bestow a series of

bites on my squirming bottom, bites interspersed with deep, insolent, probing kisses. I remember an anonymous and erect cock bobbing in front of my pursed, moist lips. I remember being spread-eagled on a rug of white fur, borne down by five—perhaps six—hard-ons, lying there in dizzy ecstasy with pricks in my hands, my mouth, my bottom, my quim, bringing them off and groping and clutching for other hard shafts to replace them whilst a circle of voyeuristic onlookers, both male and female, cried *"Vive la Reine!"* and "Long live the Queen!" . . . And I remember the most God-awful hangover the next morning! . . .

I did not recognize this terrible hangover as the omen it was. I did not guess that the banquet—and the orgy into which it turned—would be the last such affair I would ever attend at Versailles. I did not know how it was being viewed in the streets of Paris.

It was widely believed by the common people that the recall of the Flanders Regiment was not merely to protect the royal household at Versailles, but rather to put down the movement to enforce the Declaration of the Rights of Man. This suspicion was stirred up by accounts of the banquet-orgy welcoming the officers. Plebeian morality was once again offended by my free Austrian spirit. The ultimate provocation occurred on the day after the Versailles celebration when the warehouses of Paris ran out of flour and there was no bread in the shops for the people to buy. Immediately the inflammatory and inaccurate quote "Let them eat cake!" was resurrected and the rumor was spread that the reason for the shortage was that the Queen was hoarding flour at the palace for future orgy-banquets. (Well of course we did store flour for the needs of the royal Court, but it was hardly enough to feed the starving populace of

Paris. And we were royalty, their King and Queen—
Noblesse oblige!—how could they have forgotten that?)

The situation came to a head on Monday, October 5,
1789. Early that morning church bells drew crowds of
women to the Place de Greve. Most of these women
were poor and hungry. Some among them, however,
wore the powdered wigs of the aristocracy. They were
the distaff side of that element which had joined with
the clergy in the cause of Cardinal de Rohan, and later
tried to force certain reforms upon the King. Among
the others present were prostitutes and petty criminals,
and a few men dressed in women's clothes. But the
great majority, it must be admitted, were wretched
lower-class working women turned militant by the hunger of their children.

No one person was more the symbol of their oppres-
sion than I. Perhaps this was so because I too was a
woman, and one who offended their decency as well as
their self-interest. Or perhaps it was because I was an
Austrian and the deterioration of their circumstances
paralleled my tenure as their Queen. In any case, their
mounting wrath found verbal release with me as the
target.

"The Queen must die!" they chanted.

"Open her belly!" A knife was wielded.

"Reach inside her bleeding breast to the elbow!" A
clutching hand turned into an angry fist.

"Tear out her heart!"

"Her guts!"

"Her entrails!"

The growing crowd began to arm itself. A few muskets appeared. They were lost in the mass of broomstick
clubs, sickles, pitchforks and kitchen knives. Four cannon appeared. Flanked by ten women drummers dressed

in the rags of their poverty, they formed the vanguard of furious, shouting women.

In front of the cannon, in front of the drummers, in front of the hoard of fiery women, a figure appeared. It was recognized—first by one voice, then by many, then by all. A cheer went up. "Lead us! Lead us! Lead us!" There was no other woman in all France who so personified the hatred of Frenchwomen for their decadent Austrian Queen. The woman was my look-alike, my nemesis, the Comtesse de la Motte, née Jeanne de Valois—Milady!

She had sneaked back into France from England to lead this mob of women bent on murdering me. She raised a hand and received respectful silence. She turned it into a fist and shouted into the silence. "Death to the Queen! On to Versailles!"

"On to Versailles!" Her cry was echoed and became a roar. "Down with the King! Death to the Queen!"

Thus began the march of six thousand women on the palace. A torrent of rain enhanced their misery and their wretchedness when, a few hours later, they confronted the National Guardsmen waiting behind the low stone parapets surrounding the château. They were wet to the skin, the nipples of their breasts visible through their soaked clothing, and spattered with mud. But their faces were shining with a determination and a rage that transcended their condition and focused the destiny of France.

At first it was a standoff. The disciplined ranks and cocked muskets of the uniformed soldiers gave momentary pause to the women. But then voices were raised among them. They rallied around Milady and there were cries demanding punishment for the "Austrian bitch" and "the bastard baker"—the rabble's epithet for the King—and the resolve of the crowd of women became a real threat once again.

The commander of the troops came to our apartments and asked the King for permission to fire a volley into the crowd in order to disperse them.

"Fire on women!" Louis jeered. "You must be joking!"

"The mood of these women makes them dangerous, sire!"

"They are women!" Louis was contemptuous. "There is nothing to fear."

Within the hour he had cause to change that opinion. The women charged the troops and wrested the weapons from their hands. Many of the soldiers were shot with their own muskets. Two were killed as the women poured into the courtyard and up a staircase of the palace.

The King was in his apartments and I was alone in mine. My door was bolted and on the other side, guarding it, were eight members of my personal Swiss Guard.

The mob of women didn't hesitate. They fell on the guardsmen with their kitchen knives and slaughtered them to a man. Swiss blood soaked into the priceless Persian carpets outside my door. Cries of "Death to the Austrian whore!" reached my terrified ears. No ire of man can twist the nerve ends with fear like the higher-pitched, merciless wrath of women.

I slipped out of my boudoir through the servants' entrance and fled barefoot in my nightgown to the King's apartments. When I got there, I found that he was in the "protective custody" of the well-known republican, the Marquis de Lafayette. The Marquis would not put his troops at the service of the palace, but neither would he use them to help the women capture us. Playing his cards quite close to his chest, it was clear that the Marquis was both eager to depose us and loath to throw in his lot with the most radical element of the burgeoning revolution.

The windows of the King's sitting room opened onto an outside balcony. Hundreds—perhaps thousands—of angry women had congregated there and now they were chanting. "Give us the Queen! Give us the Queen! Death to the Austrian! Give us the Queen! *Morte à la Reine*!"

Suddenly my terror abated. I remembered who I was. I was Marie Antoinette, daughter of the Caesars, Princess Royal of the House of Hapsburg, Queen of France! If the rabble were going to kill me, I would not be their quivering, tearful, pleading victim! I would show them what it meant to be a queen!

Chin high, shoulders back, features composed, I threw one of Louis' ermine-trimmed robes over my shoulders and stepped out on the balcony. Deliberately, I did not cover my breasts. Let their outrage at my shamelessness have brazen focus; I was their Queen and not account- able to their petit-bourgeois morality! With my full bosom thrusting arrogantly against the flimsy nightgown, I looked down at the mob of fierce women with all the arrogance I could muster. I spied Milady immediately, but gave no sign of recognition. I stood without moving for what seemed an eternity.

"Shoot the bitch!" Led by Milady, they howled up at me. "Cut off her head! Cut off her breasts! Impale her!"

At first the cries were like the roar of an avalanche. But as I simply stood there, meeting their rage with serenity, the women began to quiet down and the shouts became more scattered. Then they were reduced to a mutter, then a hum, and then only an occasional epithet, or demand for my life. Finally, Milady faded away into the mass of the mob and there was complete silence.

I let the silence continue for a long moment and then I curtsied deeply to the crowd, turned around, and

reentered the King's apartment. Behind me there was a mighty roar, a roar of a different sort. *"Vive la Reine! Vive la Reine!"*

I thought it was over. I thought we had prevailed. So did the King. So did Lafayette. But we were mistaken.

Once I was no longer visible, the wrath of the women, reinspired by Milady, slowly began to build again. At first their demands were directed at Lafayette. They wanted him to escort the royal family to Paris and turn us over to the leaders of the Revolution. But as Lafayette vacillated, they once again began their chants of "The Queen! The Queen! Off with her head! The Queen! The Queen! Off with her head!"

"I will die at the King's feet!" I blurted out my decision aloud.

"No, *madame.*" The Marquis de Lafayette took my hand in his and led me back out onto the balcony. I was sure that we would be greeted with a lethal shower of sticks and stones. The air was thick with menace, even more so than before. Milady gazed up at us with an expression that said she was sure her revenge was at hand. Lafayette held up a hand to silence the mob. To my surprise, they did indeed respond to the gesture with silence. But the silence was so thick with hatred that it seemed more threatening than the demands for my head which preceded it.

With a cavalier flourish, Lafayette raised my hand, bent his head and kissed it. Then he made a short speech to the people. He told them that I had been foolish and headstrong and misguided, but that I was now going to turn over a new leaf. He said that I would henceforth love my French subjects, that I would "be united with them just as Jesus Christ is with His church." (This last was a clever effort to imply that I would cease

prodding the crown to persecute the popular Cardinal de Rohan.) The crowd cheered and Lafayette kissed my hand again and led me back inside. The last thing I saw was Milady's face, the features a reflection of my own, but not the expression. The expression said she had just witnessed the branding of a fleur-de-lis on my proud Hapsburg soul!

The Marquis probably saved my life. I was not, however, grateful for the gesture. He had treated me like a naughty child and humiliated me before the rabble. I never forgave him.

His action seemed to help Lafayette arrive at a decision regarding the King and myself. Having defused the angry and radical women, he now decided to lay a claim on their support by acceding to their demands. At the head of his troops, he escorted the King and me to Paris where our fate would be decided by the leaders of the Revolution.

I looked back through the coach window as Lafayette's soldiers led us off. Versailles was glittering with last night's raindrops in the early dawn. There was a rainbow forming, a multicolored arch stretching over its towers. The naked Greek statuary danced naughtily over the shining wet green grass. I sighed. I suspected, rightly, that this was the last time I would ever see my beloved Versailles.

The King's voice interrupted my reverie. "Women!" he said, dazed. "Who would have thought that women could . . ." The sentence trailed off in disbelief.

"Behave like men and take what they want by violence?" I phrased the concept for him. "Not ladylike." I laughed ruefully. "But then these were no ladies, Louis!"

"I don't understand," The King muttered.

"I'm sure you don't, my dear." I smiled to myself and

spoke the next words under my breath. "Men never do."

We were taken to the Tuileries, a rather rundown château in the heart of Paris. It had not been lived in by the royal family in more than sixty years. Nevertheless, we settled in here under the "protective custody" of successive troops of revolutionary guards. We never dreamed that our tenancy would last for two long years.

During those two years our situation grew more and more desperate. Quite early, I realized that there was no hope in France for our situation. Only our fellow European monarchs would have sympathy and concern for our predicament.

A letter smuggled to me from Axel Fersen in Brussels gave me hope for a course of action that might activate royal concern elsewhere. My erstwhile lover had fled to Belgium because his affair with me had become common gossip and the people's new government had put a price on his Swedish head for sullying the honor of France in concert with the despised Austrian Queen. Now, in his letter, he begged to be allowed to arrange a plan to rescue me from France. A bit grudgingly, he suggested that perhaps the King too should flee his native country.

I wrote him back immediately, and after that a series of letters passed back and forth between us. Mine were penned with the help of invisible ink and lemon juice and smuggled out of the Tuileries and across the border to Brussels. Our correspondence discussed two main aims. The first was to rally foreign support behind the throne of France. The second was to arrange to get myself and the King safely across the border to Belgium.

Finally Axel Fersen himself came back to France to arrange the escape. He set up the route and arranged for sympathizers to expedite our journey at the various

places where we would have to stop for food and rest and to change horses. Our destination was the Belgium border just beyond Varennes. On the other side of it we would be met by the Royal German Regiment, mercenaries under the command of a French general loyal to the Crown.

We set out on June 20, 1791. Louis and I left the Tuileries separately. He was disguised as a valet and had no difficulty making his way to the coach that Axel had waiting. I disguised myself as a governess, and as I was leaving the palace I was challenged by a sentry who didn't recognize me. It was half an hour before he deserted his post in pursuit of one of the scullery maids and I was able to sneak away and join Axel and the King.

That half-hour delay was to prove fatal. Axel had timed the escape very carefully and now his timetable was off. The result was that those sympathetic to us were not always where they were supposed to be when we arrived. One result of this was that the King was recognized when we reached Chaintrix some time after noon of the next day. The man who recognized him was a monarchist and generous. He insisted on feting us with a banquet-type meal—an offer which Louis characteristically couldn't resist. Subsequently the man also proved to have a big mouth. When our pursuers arrived, he didn't hesitate to put them on our trail.

Then the King was recognized again at Pont-Sommevesle, this time by a revolutionary. The identification was made from a gold *louis d'or*, the coin bearing Louis' likeness. The man who recognized him rode ahead to alert the local revolutionary militia in the area. At the same time the troops pursuing us from Paris were narrowing the distance.

Matters came to a head when we reached Varennes.

The bridge across the river there had been blockaded by local revolutionaries. We couldn't cross it to reach the Royal German Regiment waiting there. Neither could they cross it to come to our aid as the local militia blocked our way and the troops from Paris converged on us from the rear.

There was nothing to do but surrender. The commander of the Royal Germans watched helplessly from across the river as the King and I were roughly pushed back into our coach and started on our journey back to Paris. (In the confusion and excitement, Axel Fersen slipped away to freedom.) The escape was a failure, and hope a fleeting memory.

Our returning coach was met at the outskirts of Paris by a howling mob. The royal vehicle was pelted with dung until the stench was overwhelming. Once again the rage seemed primarily directed at me and the roar of "Austrian bitch! Slut! Whore!" was so vicious as to make my eardrums ache.

Somehow the arresting troops got us through the crowds and back to the Tuileries. This time our residence was quite different from before. There was no pretext that we were anything other than the prisoners of a government too busy to decide just how to dispose of us.

Shortly after our return to the Tuileries, news reached us that Milady had left France and gone back to London. She was starting work on another volume of her scurrilous memoirs. The prospect of such a work, however, was viewed disapprovingly by those in control of the French government at this point in time. They were concerned that the image of La Belle France had suffered all the damage at the pen of the Comtesse de la Motte that it could sustain. It was rumored that—just as we, the monarchy, had done—the current republican

government was trying to make an arrangement with her not to publish anymore.

Two months later word reached the Tuileries of Milady's death in London on August 23, 1791. Despite my hatred of her, I was shocked at the news. She was only thirty-five years old, the same age as I was. And we looked so much alike!

From the very first the accounts of Milady's death seemed mysterious, suspicious, even questionable. There was not just one version of the circumstances, but three. The first said her demise was caused by an accident, the second blamed suicide, and the third—murder!

The accident ostensibly occurred in the apartment of a friend, in the dark. Milady had become dizzy and disoriented, a side effect of a respiratory ailment from which she was suffering. Groping for the door to the lavatory, she had walked instead into the low sill of an opened window. She had plunged three stories with disastrous results.

The suicide, it was said, was the result of debtors hounding her. Milady was indeed very deeply in debt, and one night bailiffs representing her creditors came to arrest her. She evaded them by a back door and ran to the next building where she sought sanctuary in a third-floor apartment of a friend. The bailiffs followed her there and pounded on the door, demanding that she give herself up. When they started battering in the door, Milady lowered herself out the window, hanging on to the sill by her fingertips. "If you do not go away," she threatened, "I will let go and fall to my death." They did not go away, and she fulfilled her threat, not dying immediately, but suffering mortal injuries.

The murder purportedly occurred because she fell in with evil companions in London. It was preceded by a wild night of liquor and drugs and orgiastic group sex.

Milady evidently had sex with everybody at the party, male and female, and successfully engorged all of her orifices not once but quite a few times. Then some new orgiasts arrived, a gang of brutes from the gutters of Soho. They seized upon Milady and demanded she grant them her erotic favors to the utmost. She pleaded exhaustion. When she tried to put her clothes back on, they picked her up by her arms and legs and tossed her naked out of the third-floor window. Barely alive when found later on the sidewalk, Milady's injuries included a shattered torso, a double break of the hipbone, a left arm reduced to shards, and an eye hanging out of its socket. In this pitiable state she lingered on until her death in the hospital.

There were many in Paris, however, who believed none of these three versions. They insisted that Milady wasn't dead at all. They claimed such stories were fabrications by enemies who had driven her underground. She would one day reemerge, they said, to lead the next phase of the Revolution in France. Still, she remained dead to me until that night two years in the future when I peered out of the window of the Little Pharmacy death cell and identified the woman being buggered by the Englishman in the prison courtyard as Milady.

Presently, I had other things on my mind than the death of Milady. Our situation, mine and Louis', was deteriorating daily. One by one Louis' powers were taken from him and conferred upon the assembly elected by the people. Demands that the monarchy be officially declared illegal and that we be executed were growing.

I was again smuggling out letters to the crowned heads of Europe. My aim was to convince them that the overthrow of the French monarchy put all of their thrones in danger. If the rabble could depose the monarchy in France and take over the country, then surely the rabble

of every other European country would be inspired to emulate them. To abort the Revolution in France, by arms if necessary, should simply be a matter of protecting their own self-interest.

My efforts were most successful, as might be expected, in my native Austria. As a Hapsburg, I had been married off to a Bourbon in order to cement relations between Austria and France. Any attack on my throne was quite naturally also viewed as an assault upon the alliance between our two countries. The French Revolution was a direct provocation to my brother, the Emperor of Austria.

He was concerned not just with my interests, but with his own as well. He wanted me set back firmly on the throne and the rebellion quashed. Towards this end, he embarked on an extensive correspondence requesting armed backing from the rulers of Spain, Prussia, Russia, Sweden, and even the divided kingdoms of Italy.

This correspondence was intercepted by agents of the French revolutionary government. There was a furor in the assembly and it quickly spread to the streets of Paris. The patriotism of the people was aroused. Austria—hated, despised Austria, homeland of that whore, the Queen!—was trying to take their revolution away from them. They demanded that war be declared.

And so, on April 20, 1792, France did indeed declare war on Austria. Immediately, accusations were made against me as an Austrian spy. At first wild, they were later narrowed down, documented, and brought before the assembly. Here they were debated and redebated while the days turned into weeks and the weeks into first one month, and then another, and then a third.

Finally the people's impatience with this official indecision came to a head. Late in the afternoon of August 9,

a mob gathered outside the Tuileries. It was composed of men as well as women and its mood was ugly. Viewing it from a high window, I saw that it was only a matter of time until its rage broke and they stormed the château.

There was nothing between us—King Louis and I—and them save our beloved Swiss Guard. It was the one armed group we had been allowed to retain in our captivity after Varennes. Reluctantly, our captors had been forced to grant that no other military force in France could be trusted not to disobey orders and slaughter us. Only the mercenary Swiss Guard, loyal to us because we paid them, could be trusted with our protection.

The moment was at hand and I went to the Swiss Guard now. They were in a downstairs hall, busy making cartridges for the imminent confrontation. They were surprised when I appeared and leaped to their feet, standing at attention.

I regarded them bravely. Then I picked up one of the bullets and deliberately held it to my mouth. I bit down on it so hard as to leave a dent in the casing. A cheer went up from the guardsmen. "*Vive la Reine! Vive la Reine!*" It was still ringing in my ears as I swept from the hall and up the staircase. "*Vive la Reine!*"

Afternoon turned into evening and the crowd grew. So too did its surliness. By midnight there could be no doubt as to their ferocity. Their torches turned the scene outside from night to day. It was obvious that they were only waiting for daylight to make their move.

At five-thirty that morning, August 10, 1792, pistol in hand, I went to the King's apartment. I handed him the weapon. "You must stand at the head of the Swiss Guard and order them to fire into that mob of vermin!" I told him. "You must yourself fire the first shot!"

Louis blanched. "I cannot do that, Marie."

"You are afraid!" I accused him.

His silence confirmed it.

I took the pistol back from him, turned on my heel, and myself went downstairs to where the Swiss Guard was manning the barricades of the Tuileries. They were facing a mob made up primarily of Parisians. But in the forefront of the mob was a contingent of dockworkers recently arrived from Marseilles. These brutes had blood in their eye and had spent the night getting liquored up for the action daybreak would bring.

Now daybreak was here. I went up to the commander of the guard. "Disperse the rabble," I told him.

"Do you wish me to fire into the crowd, Majesty?"

"How else shall they be dispersed?"

"As you wish, Majesty." He saluted, turned to his men, and gave the order.

The volley was deafening. It was followed by screams and chaos as those at the front of the demonstration attempted to flee and were prevented from doing so by the pressure of those behind them. There was blood everywhere.

But the very predicament of the demonstrators in being unable to escape the musket fire worked against the Swiss Guard. Unable to flee, the rabble reformed their ranks and charged the guardsmen. I was back in the château now, and I observed the scene from an upstairs window.

The Swiss Guard had no chance. They were only eight hundred strong and there were thousands attacking them. The battle lasted through the morning, and when it was over, not one of the eight hundred were left alive. To a man they had been slaughtered—some with bare hands—by those they had infuriated beyond common humanity with their opening volley of shots. In the

morning sunlight the fountains of the Tuileries ran red with their Swiss blood. Never in history had mercenaries so suicidally earned their pay.

By the time the mob reached the King's apartments where I was waiting with Louis, their blood lust had spent itself. We were spat upon, but hotheads were prevented from doing us violence by cooler ones. These latter citizens turned us over to the authorities and we were subsequently incarcerated in the Temple Prison to await trial for all the crimes of our rule.

I was overwhelmed by the simple fact that a queen of France who had been brought up in Viennese castles to reign from French palaces should be held in a common jail cell. My mind recognized the reality of the situation, but my emotions refused to accept it. For the first time my Hapsburg strength deserted me and I broke down and cried in front of Louis.

"There there, Marie." He tried to comfort me.

"It's so awful!" I sobbed.

"The slaughter." He nodded understandably. "All those fine young men in their lovely red uniforms dead." He sighed. "Yes, Marie. It is awful."

"That isn't what I mean."

"Why did you have to order them to fire into the crowd?" He hadn't been listening to what I said.

"Because you wouldn't!" My response was bitter. "You're a coward, Louis!"

"If there were more cowards, there would be less dead men."

"You're not a real man, Louis!"

"Have some more quiche, Marie." He passed me the platter of food which even in prison was always at hand for the King. "It's foolish for us to quarrel. Our situation is such that we really do have only each other. Our

time may be short. We should be friends. We should solace each other."

I looked at him speculatively. Unlike my later prison situation in the Little Pharmacy of the Conciergerie, our jailers had granted us complete privacy here. There was a peephole in the stoutly bolted door, of course, but other than that, we were as alone as in the privacy of our royal boudoir at Versailles. I felt wretched and I knew from experience that there was only one thing that would relieve my wretchedness: making love. And despite the insult I had just directed at Louis, he was a man. Perhaps not much of a man, but—a man!

"All right, Louis." I softened my tone and the intent of the arch look I gave him was unmistakable. "Let's solace each other."

He sprawled in his chair, his heavy legs in their fawn-colored britches flung wide apart, and looked at me. His eyes gleamed in the flickering candlelight. There was a small, but unmistakable lump at his crotch. "Take off your clothes, Marie!" he ordered me in a husky voice. "Undress slowly."

Fear spawned by revolution had succeeded where all my wiles had failed. It had made King Louis XVI of France randy!

"Like this?" I untied the ribbons at my bodice slowly.

"*Oui.*" The single syllable was hoarse. His eyes never left my body. A moment later he spoke again. "Lift one of your breasts free now," he commanded. "Cup it in your hand."

"Is this what you want?" I held it out to him like a white and panting dove.

He nodded. His fingertips moved down from his waistcoat to drum his substantial belly. "Lift it higher. Push up as high as you can."

"So?"

"*Oui*. Now bend your head . . . that's it . . . now your tongue, *cheri*. Stick it out."

"Shall I lick my breast?"

"*Oui! Oui!*" The lump in his britches was throbbing visibly now.

I stretched my tongue and touched it to the tip of my nipple. "That feels good!"

"Can you get it in your mouth?"

"I think so," I panted.

"That's it! Suck it! Suck it! I want to watch it swell up and get long and hard from your sucking!"

I sucked it for a long, thrilling time until my neck began to feel very stiff indeed, and then I stopped. "This is making me feel very hot," I pleaded. "Aren't you going to make love to me, Louis?"

"In good time, Marie. In good time." There was a feverish perspiration on his brow in the candlelight. "But first we will watch each other. And you will do as I say."

It was as forceful as Louis had ever been in our sex life together. The change added to my excitement. "What do you want me to do now?" I asked him.

"Release your stays altogether so that both of your delicious breasts are swinging free. Then play with both the nipples at the same time with your fingers."

"And what will you be doing?"

"This." He rubbed his stubby fingers over the outline of the small, thick erection running up his belly under his britches.

I licked my lips. My nipples were hot coals between my fingertips. "I want to see it," I moaned. "Show it to me."

"In good time. First sit down and remove your shoes and stockings."

I did as he said, staring at the cock throbbing under his tight pants all the time.

"Now take off your gown and hoops. . . . Good. Now your petticoats."

Finally I stood before him only in my chemise, bare to the waist. My naked breasts strained for breath. I was all sticky-wet between my legs. I didn't feel like a queen; I felt like a female animal in heat. "Take it out," I begged. "Please! Please!"

Slowly, his eyes fastened on my face, Louis unbuttoned his tight fawn trousers. He stood and lowered them. His naked small-sausage erection twanged against his substantial, rotund belly. His small balls, swollen and pink, the skin stretched tight over them, swung enticingly in the glow from the taper's flame.

I started for Louis, my hands held out greedily, my mouth already forming into a lascivious O.

He held up a hand to stop me. "No," he said. "Sit down. There." He pointed to a chair opposite the one in which he'd been sitting. "Now pull up your chemise. Slowly . . . Slowly . . . Ahh, Marie, your thighs are lovely!" His fingers danced ticklingly under his balls. "See how they tremble! Lovely! Lovely!" He took his small, naked erection in his hand and pulled it perpendicular to his fleshy belly. "Now tuck your chemise in above your waist. That's it! That's it!" He ran his fist loosely up and down the short shaft. "Now pull down your bloomers. . . . No! Not all the way! Just to the knees. Now hold your knees wide apart so that the flimsy garment is stretched there!" He fell to his own knees on the rug in front of me now, still tugging at his hard-on.

I could feel the hot reflection from the candle flame in my eyes as I stared at Louis' cock. I wanted to feel it in

my mouth, in my yearning pussy. I wanted to taste it. I wanted to fuck it.

That, however, was not what the King had in mind. He was peering between my legs, studying every detail, every evidence of passion revealed by my exposed pussy. He was poring over the sopping ash-blond bush, the swollen, purple lips, the meaty, pink inside. With more than a little perversity, he forced his cock this way and that as he pulled on it and gave me further instructions.

"Put your fingertips on the lips and hold them open wide so I can see all the way up," he told me. "Ahh! Your clitty is like a tiny little hard red prick. Touch it now. Good! Good! How does that feel, Marie?"

"Randy! Very randy! If I keep touching it this way, I will surely spend."

"Do it! Spend! Come! And then you shall spend again!"

I strummed my clitty, bouncing a little, swaying this way and that, holding my cunt open with my other hand so that he might see, excited at how bawdy it must look to him, all raw and exposed and framed by the tight-stretched bloomers down around my knees.

"Bounce higher!" Louis jerked at his small, pink prick violently and his little balls were a red blur of motion. "I want to see your ass move when you start to come."

The crude word as much as anything else did it. I bounced higher and thrust my bottom up and out over the edge of the armchair. An uncontrollable giggle of sheer pent-up hysteria started somewhere deep in my pussy and bubbled from my lips. Hand on my clitty, eyes on the King's tiny, naked cock, I spent in a delirium of mirth.

"Don't stop!" That's what I realized he was saying when I was once again capable of hearing. "Keep frigging yourself! Frig yourself deep, Marie! And hold it

open so I can see!" He pulled me over to our small, narrow prison bed and flung himself down there on his back. He pulled me over him so that I was straddling him in a kneeling position with my fingers holding my cunt wide open and suspended just over his eyes. Staring up into it, he began jerking off with both hands, squeezing his balls with one and stroking his short shaft with the other.

Louis' belly jiggled wildly as he did this. Somehow that made the whole thing seem more obscene, more forbidden, more arousing. I had come once, and now, holding my cunt wide open over his staring eyes, I strummed my clitty and came a second time. As I did so, I made an automatic attempt to lower my climaxing pussy to his cock. But Louis quickly took one hand from his groin and prevented me from doing so. He was determined to observe the inside of my spending pussy in the act of orgasm again. This time he had a somewhat better view.

"Don't you want to fuck me?" I panted when it was over, for Louis was still jerking at himself.

"No!" he gasped.

"Would you like me to suck your—"

"No!"

"Then what would you like me to do, *cheri*?"

"Hold your cunt wide and play with yourself some more."

"Louis!" I protested. "I'll make myself sore."

"Just one more time, Marie."

"Very well." I curled my fingers and drew my cunt wide apart again. I craned my head over my shoulders and watched his hands strumming his small, hard, cream-filled prick. I stuck one long finger all the way up my pussy and then pulled it out. I repeated the maneuver, pumping. My naked breasts were shiny with perspira-

tion now. My stiff nipples were sore from straining. My thigh muscles ached, and my bottom was weary of writhing. Nevertheless, as I held my pussy wide and pumped the one finger in and out of it, I once again became aroused. I was on the brink of yet another orgasm when Louis broke into my concentration.

"Marie." He had a hard time getting the words out. "I must ask you something."

"What?" I gasped, tottering on the edge of this new ecstasy. "What is it?"

"When you come again . . . Well, while you're spending . . . Could you? Would you—?"

"What is it Louis?" My voice skittered up the scale. My finger plunged deep into my quim. The inner flesh of my pussy closed around it. "Say it!"

"While you're coming, could you pee on me?"

"I don't think so, Louis," I bleated. "I don't think that's possible."

"Oh." He was disappointed. The hand on his cock subsided.

"When . . . I'm . . . through . . ." Somehow, in the middle of spending, I managed to get the words out.

"Oh, good, Marie. Thank you!"

I ground down over his mouth before he could stop me and finished my orgasm there. Then, almost without stopping, I reached behind me and found his prick. I stroked it as I rose up again so that he might see what was happening inside my pussy.

"Now, Marie?" Louis was beside himself.

"Now Louis!" I squeezed his prick. As it started to spurt, His Majesty King Louis XVI of France screamed these words:

"Après moi le deluge!"

And I released my golden shower over his face

just as the prison clock struck midnight, heralding September 21, 1792, the day the National Convention issued the first official proclamation of the French Republic!

Chapter Twelve

A funny thing happened on my way to the guillotine. Fantasy collided with real life and ghosts from my past materialized to thumb their noses at my future. Although resigned to losing my head, this was confusing to me to say the very least.

Still, this happening and the events leading up to it were at least a change. The past year had been duller for me than any other period of my life. There is nothing so tedious as prison life, *mes amis*. There had been only three interruptions of any consequence to this boring routine.

The first was the execution of poor Louis on January 21, 1793. That of course was noteworthy. He was, after all, King of France, the first Bourbon to lose his head to Madame Guillotine.

Subsequently I had been moved from the Temple Prison to my Little Pharmacy cell in the Conciergerie. Although this placed me back within the familiar confines of the Tuileries, it also forced upon me a solitary confinement duller than any routine I had previously

known. My only amusements were watching the other prisoners through the boarded-up window in my cell and teasing my guards hidden behind their screen. As I have related, I made the very most that I possibly could of these diversions.

Nevertheless, the tedium prevailed until I was brought to trial before the Revolutionary Tribunal. This third interruption of my prison routine lasted two days, and then I was sentenced to die on the guillotine the following morning. Now dawn was breaking, the following morning was here, and soon there would be a fourth and final break with regularity.

As I watched the sun struggling to break through the thick clouds on this early morning of October 16, 1793, my mind proved incapable of any longer losing itself in my erotic past. Daylight brought the future—a prospect both brief and bleak—and there was no avoiding it. My next assignation—soon! too soon!—would bring me to the embrace of the executioner.

I pictured him, this man of the people who would be the instrument of my fate. He would be large, burly, hairy. He would have a chest like a wine cask and limbs like tree trunks. His aroma would be that of a virile peasant, a mixture of strong tobacco and horses, harsh new-made wine and charcoal-cooked boar poached from some former master's game preserve, ever-present lust and the perspiration of stoop labor. His face would be shaped like an anvil and his features would be heavy, coarse, in keeping with his full, black, knotted beard. His eyes would be dark, fierce, deep set, perhaps a bit bloodshot. If I was very, very lucky, there might be just a glint of kindness buried in their depths.

He would be standing atop the scaffold as I climbed from the tumbril. His arms would be folded and he might be staring down at me. His homespun britches

would be stretched tight across his crotch. Anticipation could have given him a noticeable erection. After all, it is not every day that an executioner presides over the beheading of a renowned Hapsburg beauty who is also the flaxen-haired Queen of France. He would have heard all the lewd details of my depraved career and now, seeing me in the voluptuous flesh, he might lick his lips with a thick, red, thirsting tongue.

"OFF WITH HER HEAD! OFF WITH HER HEAD!" The women would be the most impatient to see the blood spurt from my severed neck. "OFF WITH HER HEAD!" Those whom toil had beaten into hags and crones at an early age would be the most eager. "OFF WITH HER HEAD!" The prostitutes and female petty thieves would take up the chant, the spittle flying from their lips in a spray of cheap wine. "OFF WITH HER HEAD!" The men of the gutters would chime in, groins aching to violate their beauteous Austrian Queen, and settling even now, as they had been forced to settle all their lives, for second best—the violence of decapitation, instead of sex. "OFF WITH HER HEAD!"

I would mount the ladder steps to the chopping block. The click-click of the women's knitting needles would provide a beat to my progress. The gurgle of wine jugs would serve as counterpoint. As I reached the top a hush would descend over the Place de la Revolution—a sudden awe perhaps at their revolution having brought their Queen to such a state as this.

Then the executioner would unfold his massive arms and reach out a hand to help me over the threshold of the scaffold. I would mount the platform and confront the crowd defiantly. Doubtless I would be panting with fear and the half-moons of my breasts would be rising and falling to spill over my bodice. The executioner

would gaze down at this fleshy display and perhaps find in the sight some confirmation of the rewards of his vocation.

"Be gentle, *m'sieur*." I would look into his eyes pleadingly, the sort of look a virgin might bestow upon her first lover. "Gentle."

"Have no fear, citizeness!" His hand would hold mine firmly and a powerful current would pass between us, a current that would be strangely erotic given the circumstances. "I have taken the greatest care to hone the blade until it is razor-sharp. You will feel nothing!"

Despite this reassurance, I would doubtless shudder.

"Be so good as to kneel, *madame*." His hands would press down gently on my soft, bare shoulders.

I would feel the calluses on the executioner's palms, the strength of his fingers. Lifting my skirts a little, showing a bit of ankle, a bit of calf to draw a sigh of erotic appetite from those watching, I would sink to my knees.

"Allow me to position you, *madame*." He would move around behind me. His thick legs and brawny bottom would block off the view of the crowd as he bent over me.

I would feel his hands on my hips as if to move me. Then, quickly, I would feel them under my skirts, moving over my bottom, caressing it through the silk of my bloomers. A workmanlike finger would move between my legs and draw forth the honey of my terror.

"There is no insult, *madame*." His voice would be strangely soft in my ear, persuasive. I might even be able to convince myself that it was loving. "It is only to make it easier, to end with pleasure that will blot out any pain that might be felt."

"I understand." My heart would be beating wildly

with fear, but there would be a fire in my pussy as well. "I give my permission."

"Thank you, Majesty." The "Majesty" would of course be whispered so that only I might hear it. To pay me such homage aloud would risk putting his own head on the chopping block.

He would position my head in the notch meant for it. He would close the stocks around my wrists, and while bending over me to do this, push aside my bloomers and insert two very large fingers in my tight, wet pussy. Quickly, he would frig me to a remarkably high pitch of sexual excitement.

"Ahh!" I would force myself to refrain from reacting aloud. The watching crowd would have no idea of how my thigh muscles were clenching and unclenching, of how my nipples were hardening. They would think the tongue peeping from my lips a sign of fear, not lust. "Oo-ooh!" Visions of all the different tumescent organs which had stabbed into my twisting hungry pussy, my squirming bottom, my hollow-cheeked, wide-stretched mouth, in the deep, passion-slicked cleavage between my breasts would pass lingeringly through my mind. *"Oui-ee!"* A hungry quim has no conscience, *mes amis*, not even on the guillotine!

The executioner would move in front of me now, blocking off my view of the crowd and their ability to see my face. He would open a long scroll, one curled end of which would fall to the platform. He would begin to read the long litany of the "High Crimes of Citizeness Marie Antoinette Against the People of France." And as his deep, harsh, slightly guttural voice began, I would spy that which belied the cruel judgment.

My eyes, as my neck rested in the notch of the chopping block provided for it, would be on a level with the crotch of the executioner's coarse homespun britches.

I would see that he had unbuttoned them and drawn the flaps aside. I would see the forest of tightly curled black pubic hair growing wild over his naked groin. I would glimpse the heavy, wrinkled, obscene sac containing his balls as it swayed between his massive thighs. I would catch sight of the muscles of his inner thighs tensed with anticipation. (Of what? The fall of the blade? The severing of my head from my body? Or of some less violent, more erotic fulfillment?)

Finally, in the shadowy recesses of the executioner's britches, I would perceive his truncheon of a male organ, not grown to its full capacity yet but only semitumescent. It would lay back there like a snake made lazy by having just glutted itself on the fattest of mice. It would be alarmingly thick, this peasant prick, and it would curl out over his thigh almost to the knee.

I would purse my lips and focus on it. As if the hole in its brutal, wedge-shaped crest were indeed an eye. It would return my gaze and respond. It would slowly uncurl, wriggle, stretch. The tip would swell out from the purplish foreskin. The eye would open wider. A faint, gleaming lubricity would spread over the angry, bright red tip.

". . . engaging in a conspiracy with her brother, the Emperor of Austria, to overthrow by force of arms the duly constituted government of the people of France and . . ."

"DEATH TO THE AUSTRIAN! OFF WITH HER HEAD!" As if engaged in a responsive reading, the mob might punctuate each of the damning charges.

High over my neck the sharp, angled blade of the guillotine would be poised and waiting.

I would stick out my tongue and touch the tip to the quivering tip of the executioner's truncheon. He could shift on his feet without missing a syllable of the judg-

ment against me and keep right on reading as the head of his prick entered between my lips. I would sip delicately, savoring the strong peasant bouquet, dimming the wrath of the mob in my ears, blotting out my apprehension of that moment when the blade must fall.

". . . further conspiring that a foreign army, the army of a country with which France is at war, might cross our borders and enlist royalist traitors into its ranks so that . . ."

Fastening my lips over the foreskin, I would push it back so that my mouth might encompass the naked ruby tip. The splintery wood of the stock would be rough and abrasive against the naked top halves of my panting breasts. Perhaps the bodice of my gown would have slipped and my swollen, aching, naked berry-nipples might be pressed painfully into the wood. Surreptitiously, not wanting to give the crowd further cause to jeer and mock me for my lechery, I would be rubbing my naked thighs together and squeezing the moist lips of my pussy so that my sopping bloomers would be swallowed up to provide friction for my aroused and secretly thrusting clitty. Closing my eyes, I would lick the cock tip in my mouth and suck at its titillatingly spongy surface.

". . . engaging in immoral debauches of so debased a nature, debauches involving not only men other than her husband, the King, but also women of the royal court, many of them themselves married, and servants, and sundry beasts and . . ."

Fishes? I might wonder as I sucked his cock. Was I accused of having had sexual relations with fishes too?

"KILL THE WHORE! CHOP OFF HER HEAD!" The reverberation of their voices would set the blade over me to vibrating.

Desperately, I would suck the thick peasant shaft into

my mouth. My Hapsburg cheekbones would become prominent as my cheeks hollowed out with the entwining of my tongue around it. My nipples would quiver and my cunt would clench as I savored how hot and hard it felt against my licking tongue and the sucking, inner surfaces of my cheeks.

Soon the truncheon would begin to pulse under this variety of oral caresses. My breasts, hidden from view by my kneeling position at the stock, would bounce violently against the punishing wood. My bottom would be on fire under my petticoat. My inner thighs would be a honey-drenched disgrace. And my empty cunt would be pumping as if fucking some giant and beastly prick found in unexpurgated Greek legend.

I would be so randy by now that I would cease being concerned with the circumspection dictated by the public nature of the occasion. I would stretch my neck (long, swanlike, patrician, the fairest of fodder for Madame Guillotine) and dip my face into the opened depths of the executioner's britches. I would feel his thick cock slither down my throat and his heavy, hairy balls bounce against my rounded chin. More fiercely now, I would lick and suck and nibble at the shaft and base of the still-expanding cock.

". . . and for sins against common decency, against Holy Mother Church and the Cardinal who is its most eminent dignitary in France, offenses against the citizenry of France and the nation itself, sins and crimes and offenses perpetrated against the Almighty Himself, the judgment of the People's Tribunal is that Citizeness Marie Antoinette shall suffer death by . . ."

"OFF WITH HER HEAD!" the crowd would chant, working up to a frenzy as the moment approached. "NOW! NOW! OFF WITH HER HEAD!" And the cackle of Mme. Defarge would screech above the roar,

and her knitting needles would go click-click in anticipation of the whoosh of the falling blade.

I would suck hard now, so hard. My body, my mind, my very being would center on the shaft thrusting in and out of the entrance to my throat. I would feel the cream gathering along the length of the shaft until it seemed as if the skin must burst before discharging it.

The secret fire between my legs would be raging now. My breasts would be wet with the perspiration of lust, heavy and gasping. My anus would clench as it used to in those bygone days when it engloved the impaling ecclesiatical prick of my lover Cardinal de Rohan. My pussy would tighten as if filled with the corkscrewing prick of Axel Fersen. My licking, sucking mouth would remember the taste of Yolande and Count Esterhazy. And then it would forget them and exult with the thick, long peasant cock filling it to the throat.

". . . sentence to be rendered publicly at the Place de la Revolution by the People's Executioner on the morning of . . ." He would be reading the last of the scroll.

"DO IT! DO IT!" The hysteria would become uncontrollable. "DROP THE BLADE! OFF WITH HER HEAD!"

Seized with terror and lust, I would start to come then. My nipples would assail the stock like nails being hammered in by my swinging breasts. My bottom would jerk this way and that in the throes of orgasm. My mouth and throat would engulf the executioner's prick as it exploded in a geyser of thick nectar which I might have choked on except—

Except that the dread blade would fall and I would lose my head whilst giving head!

Such was my fantasy as I performed my ablutions that last morning in the Little Pharmacy and waited

for the special guard to escort me to the Place de la Revolution and the arms of Madame Guillotine. I clung to it even though I realized that the reality when it came would be very different. And then the reality arrived.

There was a rhythmic tramping of feet outside the door to my cell. It was followed by a loud pounding at the thick door and then the scraping sound of the bolt being pushed back by the two guards behind the screen. They moved the screen back against the wall and then stood at attention and saluted as four members of the citizens' militia and their corporal marched into the Little Pharmacy.

"We are here to take custody of the prisoner, Citizeness Marie Antoinette." The corporal handed a piece of paper to the taller of my two guards. "We are to escort her to the Place de la Revolution where the executioner awaits."

"It is our pleasure to deliver the wanton whore and traitor to France into your hands." My guards saluted.

Rising to meet my fate, I turned to the corporal. "I am ready," I told him simply.

"Citizeness." He motioned me to the center point of the four guards who would escort me to the waiting tumbril.

As I assumed this position, one of the militiamen behind me spoke. "The morning air is quite chill, citizeness. You would be wise to take your cloak." His accent was strange; perhaps he was from the provinces.

"It is forbidden to talk to the prisoner," the corporal told him.

I went to the small wardrobe closet I had been provided and took my only cloak, a long, gray one from it. I arranged it around my shoulders and drew the drawstring loosely at the neck. Raising the cowl, I tucked my long, ash-blond curls into it. (I had been forbidden to

wear my powdered wig, a symbol of the hated aristocracy, on this final journey.)

The cowl also shaded and half hid my features as we emerged from the Conciergerie into the sunlight. I had not been marched through the courtyard, but rather through an interior passage that led directly to the street outside. Here the tumbril waited.

Two more militiamen guarded it. Three women in soiled, aristocratic finery were seated on the only bench of the flatbed wagon. One of them, recognizing me, arose to offer me her place.

"Sit down!" One of the guards roughly pushed the butt of his musket into her belly. "There's no more royalty. Here it's first come first seated. The Austrian whore is last, so she'll stand!"

Pushing me ahead, the corporal and the four guards clamored onto the tumbril. I was unprepared in the confusion for the sudden whisper in my ear. "When we reach the Rue Devoe, insist you must relieve yourself." That strange accent again!

An instant later I caught a clear glimpse of the face of the whisperer for the first time. It was the English scribe I had first observed taking notes at my trial before the Revolutionary Tribunal the previous day. He did not look quite so slight, so scholarly, in the homespun he was wearing. Balancing this was the missing arrogance of his long, naked, elegantly English prick battering Milady's cunt through the wrought-iron fence the night before.

My heart beat faster as the tumbril began to move, jostling us roughly as it bounced over the cobblestoned streets. Hope! I had resigned myself to bloody death, and now—however slim—there was hope. That accented voice had whispered hope!

Holding the cowl around my face against the wind, I

peered with hidden eyes for the Rue Devoe. Finally I saw the intersection marking it. "We must stop!" I spoke imperiously, suspecting that these peasant guards might respond to such a tone from habit. "I must have a chamber and a pot."

"A chamber and a pot, is it?" One of them hooted. "The Austrian slut thinks she's back at Versailles! Well, you're just one of the common folk now, Your Bitchiness! A wall and a rain gutter like the rest of us is all you'll get."

"All right then. But quickly please. It is urgent."

"I'm not authorized to stop for anything." Revolution or not, obedience came first with the corporal. "Besides, aristocrats always get the runs on the way to the guillotine."

"I can control my need no longer!" I insisted.

"Best stop and let her do it, Corporal," the disguised Englishman advised. "We've three more trips to make with the tumbril today and we don't want her stinking it all up. Not to mention how it'll spoil the party for all the citizens waiting at the Place de la Revolution," he added. "Nothing casts a pall over a queen's beheading like the stench of *merde*. Pull the tumbril up over there by that alley. I'll take her and get it over with."

Persuaded, the corporal had the tumbril halted. "You four all go with her and stand guard," he ordered my original escort.

"I can handle it alone," The Englishman offered. "The alley's a dead end; she can't get out. It will be faster."

"No." The corporal was adamant. "I'm not taking any chances with our star attraction. All four of you go."

Grumbling, the other three fell in behind us as we proceeded to the alley. The Englishman had been right.

The alley was a dead end. When he halted in its mouth, there were only the dark, concealing shadows of a crumbling stone building beyond us.

They had brought me to a halt in a shaft of sunlight. Now they spread out, cutting off any exit from the alley. I turned to face them and found myself looking directly into the Englishman's eyes. There was despair written there. Whatever his plan was, it could not be accomplished with the other three watching.

"I can't do it with all of you staring at me!" I protested.

"Then back in the tumbril!" The sloppiest of the guards obviously had no patience with my royal sensibilities.

"Hold on!" the Englishman protested. "If she goes back and does it there, an hour from now Her Royal Prudishness will be dead, but you and me will be riding around with the mess and the stench all day."

"So what do you suggest, citizen?"

"You three turn your back and I'll watch her do her stuff." He addressed me. "One pair of eyes is the best compromise you can get, Your Delicacy. That or the tumbril. What do you say?"

"All right," I replied. "But please be quick."

"I'm not taking the responsibility!" the sloppy one announced firmly.

"The responsibility is mine," the Englishman told him. "All mine. Now let's get it over with."

As soon as the other three had turned their backs, the Englishman gestured urgently to me to move into the shadows. I took three steps backwards and a strong arm clasped me around the waist. At the same time a long-fingered hand closed over my mouth to keep me from exclaiming aloud.

I watched as three figures emerged from the murky area to my right. Two of them seemed to be half

carrying, half dragging the third. I recognized the two as Yolande de Polignac and Axel Fersen.

The third person, obviously a woman, was wearing a gray cloak identical to mine. The cowl was pulled as far over her face as it could be. A few tendrils of ash-blond hair similar to my own trailed from the cowl.

Then, as Yolande and Axel arranged the woman's form in the pool of sunlight where I'd been standing, the cape fell away from her loose bodice for an instant and I saw the bare upper half of one of her breasts. The brand of the fleur-de-lis stood out ugly and purple! The cowl tumbled briefly from around her face. She was, of course, Jeanne de Valois, the Comtesse de la Motte, Milady, my nemesis, my look-alike, my salvation!

Quickly the cowl was pulled around her features again. The prostrate form was arranged so that the face was towards us, away from the backs of the militiamen. The shameful brand was concealed. Silently, Yolande and Axel faded back into the concealing shadows.

"The Queen has fainted!" As soon as they were gone, the disguised Englishman called out the news.

"*Merde!*" The sloppiest of the guards wheeled around. "Damn Austrians! No guts! They either get the runs, or they pass out! Anything to stall on the way to the guillotine! Now I suppose we'll have to carry the bitch up to the scaffold."

"I'll carry her," the Englishman offered good-naturedly. "After all, it was my idea we stop and let her unload."

"True. So you get the hernia, citizen."

The Englishman picked up the obviously unconscious Milady in his arms and carried her to the tumbril. He was careful to keep her features hidden in the crook of his arm. And when they reached the tumbril, he deposited her facedown.

My rescuer still held a hand over my mouth as I

watched the tumbril roll away. Nevertheless, I was filled with exultation. I had escaped! I would live!

"Don't speak!" The hand was removed from my mouth. "Wait!"

I waited. A moment later a closed coach rolled up to the alley. It stopped in approximately the same spot where the tumbril had stood. In a trice, I was propelled from behind and into the interior of the coach. My rescuer climbed in after me and quickly shut the door.

Looking for Yolande and Axel to follow us, I pushed aside the window curtain. In the light it provided, I saw the face of my companion. It was Cardinal de Rohan!

I gasped. Even though I had seen him in the court-yard with the Englishman the evening before, his presence under these circumstances surprised me. Why should the Cardinal, darling of the revolutionary rabble and archenemy of the crown, risk his life to save me from the guillotine?

Before I could find the words to phrase the question, he had reached across me and redrawn the window curtain, plunging the coach back into dimness. Slowly, it began to move over the cobblestones. "What about Yolande?" I wondered aloud. "What about Axel?"

"They'll join us later," the Cardinal informed me. "Right now they're going to your beheading to make sure everything goes off smoothly."

I shuddered at the graphic image conjured up by his inadvertent pun. "How has this happened?" Now the questions tumbled from my lips. "Why have you—?"

"All in good time. Let us just ride silently now. We're not out of danger yet."

As the coach proceeded at a slow pace, my eyes accustomed themselves to the dimness. I perceived that the Cardinal was dressed in homespun like a commoner. I had not seen him in a very long time, but my image of

my erstwhile lover was always of him clad in the splendor of his purple, ermine-trimmed ecclesiastical robes. Yet his arrogant, mature good looks seemed even more on display in the drab, coarse material which now encased his flesh.

He was tall and slender as ever, but the wideness of his shoulders and the athletic tapering of his chest to his narrow hips and long but sturdy legs were more in evidence in this peasant garb than they had ever been in church finery. There was a surprisingly unaristocratic bulge of muscles at forearm and thigh that stretches tight the cloth over them. He looked more the hunter of his reputation, more the virile outdoorsman than he had ever looked before.

By contrast, his visage was still noble and handsome. The cleft chin, the Grecian nose, the high cheekbones had lost none of their strength, none of their arrogance. There was perhaps a touch more gray at the temples, but other than that his straight, silky hair was as jet black as ever. And there was that old, familiar glint of irony in his deep-set blue eyes. It was just one more proof that the Cardinal's charisma prevailed.

The streets outside grew quieter as the coach proceeded at its unhurried pace. We had been moving against the last-minute flow of the citizenry to the Place de la Revolution to witness my execution. Now we had passed all but a few stragglers, and there were stretches where we were the only thing moving on wheels or on foot.

Abruptly, our progress halted. A panel in the roof of the coach slid open. The face of the driver appeared. Like the Cardinal, Yolande, and Axel, he was an old libidinous acquaintance. Like them, he was dressed like a denizen of the Paris streets. Peering down at me was that incorrigible gambler, military mercenary, and mem-

ber (along with Yolande) of my first ménage à trois at the Petit Trianon, the Hungarian Count Esterhazy.

I started to speak his name, but his finger went quickly to his lips, silencing me. At the same time, he winked to acknowledge our familiarity. The words he spoke, however, were directed to the Cardinal.

"There are two sentinels at the city gates," Count Esterhazy reported.

"As arranged." The Cardinal nodded. He passed a small cloth bag a-jingle with gold coins up to the Hungarian. "We should not be bothered," he assured him.

The roof panel was closed and we resumed our journey. About five minutes later we again halted. There were muffled voices outside and some laughter with a jeering note. Then, once again, we were on our way. The wheels were no longer bouncing over city cobblestones. Shortly, with the smoothness of the road, we picked up speed. The team of horses pulling the coach was soon proceeding at a fast trot. And then they broke into a gallop and we were fairly hurtling along.

"Paris is behind us now." The Cardinal heaved a sigh of relief. "Only the open road between us and the border."

"Where are we going?" I inquired.

"To my estates at Ettenheim in Baden."

"Germany?"

"*Oui*. Just across the Rhine from Strasbourg."

"Where it all began." The words sprang unbidden to my lips.

"I suppose that's true in a way." The familiarly cynical smile curled the Cardinal's lip. "You had questions before," he reminded me.

"I have them still."

"The answers may be complicated."

"They would have to be." I smiled thinly. "Only complexity can account for my survival."

"Your first question?" The coach was hurtling along now and the Cardinal and I were both clinging to the side straps in front of the windows to keep from being thrown from our seats.

"Jeanne de Valois? Milady? She was reported to have died in London."

"The reports were exaggerated." The Cardinal shrugged. "She will of course die in your place on the guillotine. Her resemblance to you, I fear, has sealed her fate."

"But how—?"

"Drugged. A sleeping potion in her wine. Hopefully the effects will not wear off until after her beheading."

"I didn't think she had willingly agreed to change places with me," I reflected ironically. "But what was she doing in the courtyard of the Conciergerie last night? She was having sex with that Englishman who posed as one of the guards today. How did she get in there? And how did she manage to get out?"

"I arranged the visit for her," the Cardinal told me. "I have many admirers in the new republican government. One has charge of the guards at the Conciergerie. His good offices, plus a small bribe, greased the way for Milady to get in and out of the prison."

"But towards what end?" I wondered. "Why would she want to—?"

"You, Madame. You are the reason she contrived to get into the Conciergerie. The red-hot iron that branded her with the fleur-de-lis also branded her with a hatred of you that was just as deep, just as lasting, just as eternally imprinted on her soul as the mark of shame was on her flesh. She burned with a desire for vengeance on the Queen responsible for her punishment. Foreseeing that the Revolutionary Tribunal would sen-

tence you to die on the guillotine, that vengeance was now at hand and Milady was determined to savor it. She wanted to see you in your final degradation, jailed like a common criminal, without hope, awaiting public execution. She wanted to view your terror at first hand."

"She told you all this?"

"*Oui.* She had to. You see, I was the only one who might have the influence to make her wish come true. She came to see me to ask me to get her into the Conciergerie."

"But how did she dare?" I wondered as I was tossed from side to side on the seat of the rocketing coach. "After all, she had done you great damage in the Affair of the Diamond Necklace. You went to jail because of her!"

"Not just because of her," the Cardinal reminded me pointedly.

"True." I sighed. So much blood under the bridge.

"But to be honest with you, Majesty, I don't think it even occurred to her that I might refuse to cooperate because of past crimes she had committed against me. You see, Milady was in no way the woman that you doubtless remember. Too much champagne, too much snuff, too many debauches—the sting was out of her."

"It wasn't out of her the last time I saw her." I remembered Milady's fury as she incited the women's march on Versailles.

"Perhaps not. But it isn't just energy to which I refer. Drugs and wine wreaked havoc with her memory as well. Truly, I don't believe she recalled that she had ever done me harm. In her befuddled brain, I was a former lover who, if discreetly reminded of past embraces, would surely not refuse her a favor. And so she came to me asking to be smuggled in and out of the Conciergerie so that she might see your terror just before the end."

"But she was having sex with that Englishman in the courtyard just as if she was herself one of the condemned," I recalled.

"I said her mind was fuddled. But there was nothing wrong with her libido, which has always been strong. Milady's pussy has always been a target of opportunity. Like your own, Majesty," he could not resist adding.

I ignored the insult. "Who is that Englishman, anyway?"

"A writer. A novelist. A friend. You'll meet him later."

"And so you got Milady in and out of the Conciergerie," I mused. "And did she see me? Was her despicable wish gratified?"

"I'm not sure." The Cardinal shrugged. "What's important is that she thought it was gratified."

"What do you mean?"

"I made sure that while she was in the prison she would have a plentiful supply of wine and snuff. I'm not sure what she actually saw, and what she imagined. An opportunity was provided for her to observe you in the passageway when you returned from the tribunal. She thinks that she saw you wailing and beating your breast and crying for mercy. She described the scene quite vividly just before she passed out from the drugs we gave her in order to effect the substitution for you."

"Oh, yes," I told the Cardinal. "That was most certainly me."

We both smiled.

"How did you involve Yolande and Axel and Count Esterhazy in this scenario?" I asked.

"It wasn't hard. They are friends of yours. Milady actually went to the Countess de Polignac first. It was she who brought her to me. And it was she who sug-

gested that the Swede and the Hungarian would not hesitate to aid in your escape."

I was touched. "And I thought it was just sex." I brushed away a tear.

"What are friends for?" The Cardinal smiled.

"Sex." I smiled back. "What else?"

"Occasionally something else, it would appear."

"And you?" I asked. "Is that why you've involved yourself? Are you my friend."

"It would seem so."

"How strange. I always thought of you as an enemy. Indeed, the entire nation has taken it for granted that you and I are enemies."

"I have been an enemy of the crown, Marie." He addressed me by name, just as in bygone days when I was a child and not yet Queen. "But I never considered myself an enemy of yours."

"Yet you sided with Du Barry against my mother and me," I remembered.

"And tried to make up for it every way I knew how. But you wouldn't let me."

"When we were lovers, you were unfaithful to me."

"That didn't make me your enemy, Marie. Only your unfaithful lover. Indeed, not even that. You may remember that after an entire summer of assignations with me you were still a virgin."

"Why am I arguing with you?" I wondered aloud. "Of course you are my friend. If you weren't, I wouldn't be here. I would be mounting the steps to the guillotine."

"Quite right. But even if I were not your friend, my dear Marie, I should have had to rescue you."

"Because you're a churchman and a humanitarian?" My dimples flashed with this characterization of the lusty Cardinal.

"Because we have never made love as a woman and

man should." He took my hands in his. "And I could not let you die without that. It would be too cruel to both of us."

"*Oui*." Responding to the tug of his hands, I moved to the seat beside him. "Too cruel." I raised my lips to be kissed. "When first I arrived in France," I remarked when the kiss was over, "I heard ribald stories about your behavior in traveling coaches. A choirboy who was not a choirboy at all, but rather a passionate married lady, was involved, I believe. In any case, by all accounts, yours was the definitive behavior for lovemaking in coaches. I do hope the passage of time has not dulled this talent."

"It most certainly has not!" The Cardinal kissed me again. His hand opened the drawspring of my cape. His long, elegant fingers dipped into the bodice of my gown. In a trice the ribbons were loosed and my breasts bounded free. His handsome, chiseled face moved over them. His hands raised my gown. They caressed my thighs. They separated them and moved up to the juncture of my bloomers.

"Indeed it has not," I panted. I squirmed as one of his hands now found mine and carried it to his crotch. His prick was hard and pulsing in his britches. With trembling fingers, I opened the buttons and took it out. It was as long and aristocratic as always.

I bent and kissed it. I licked it quickly. I stood, lurching with the coach, and removed my gown and petticoats. I pulled down my bloomers. My cunt was wet and puckered and ready.

The Cardinal pulled me to his lap and sat me down facing him. My quim slid over his upstanding cock like a glove finger. He took one of my naked breasts in his mouth. He grasped the writhing cheeks of my bottom

and his fingers played inside my anus. His bottom heaved upwards and he started fucking me.

The hurtling, rattling coach established the rhythm. It was erratic, and all the more exciting because it was so. The Cardinal's prick moved in and out of me in a series of unexpected and thrilling ways. Areas of my hot, honeyed cunt that had never been touched by a prick before were touched now.

A fire built quickly in the hot oven of my lust. *"Oui!"* I moaned. "Why did we wait so long? *Oui! Oui!* . . . Do it that way! . . . No! That way! . . . Ooh! Where did you—? How could you—? Do that again! . . . Not, not that! That! . . . Oh! But that was nice too!" I reached under us and found his balls and squeezed them as his thighs continued to slap against my fiery bottom and his prick described all of those unexpected probes. I extended a middle finger and played in his bottom just as he was playing in mine. His cock jerked and quivered unexpectedly and I felt the angry tip at the entrance to my womb.

"Fuck me!" I panted. "Do it, darling! Fill me! Give it to me! Give it to me! Give it to me!"

The Cardinal rose up in the careening coach. His cock and balls buried themselves in my clutching cunt. A shudder went through his body and a powerful, hot geyser of man cream filled me.

"Mon Dieu!" I screamed. *"MON DIEU!"* And I pushed down and spread my wet cunt over the Cardinal's groin and—the tears rolling down my cheeks—I started to come with him.

It lasted a long, powerful time. The Cardinal's prick kept on spurting and spurting. My cunt kept wrestling the ambrosia from the hard shaft. His cream ran out of me, soiling his britches, soiling the seat, but still he kept firing it.

"More! More!" I sobbed. And, miraculously, there was more. It had been a long time since I had been fucked so well. And I had never been fucked quite like this before.

Finally it ended. Exhausted, I curled up against the Cardinal's chest and went to sleep.

I slept for a very long time. When I awoke, I dressed as best I could. A little later we stopped at an inn to eat. We didn't linger. Although it was still night, we resumed our journey. That was the pattern of our travels.

We followed it for three days. We made love. We slept. We stopped for food. We made love. And finally we crossed the Rhine and arrived at the safety of the Cardinal's estates at Ettenheim in Baden, Germany.

A day or so later we were joined there by Yolande de Polignac and Axel Fersen and the English scribe. They were exultant with the news from Paris. They described the torchlight parade which had been forming behind them as they left the city. The streets, it seemed, had echoed with the chants of the citizenry: "THE QUEEN IS DEAD! LONG LIVE THE REPUBLIC! THE HEAD OF THE AUSTRIAN HAS ROLLED! *VIVE LA FRANCE!* MARIE ANTOINETTE ROASTS IN HELL! VIRTUE HAS TRIUMPHED! MARIE ANTOINETTE IS DEAD!"

"Your place in history is assured." A faithful monarchist, Yolande was delighted.

"And you did not even have to lose your head to gain it, Majesty," Axel added.

"This calls for a celebration," our host, the Cardinal decided.

A celebration, of course, meant champagne. And snuff. And kisses. And embraces. And . . .

Whenever I have heard that popular revolutionary term "the masses," it has conjured up a vision for me of

a group of obscenely entwined proletarian bodies. If there is truth to that vision, however, it is not really a truth of lower-class flesh, *mes amis*. Only true aristocrats have leisure to cultivate the lack of inhibition necessary to stage such a scene. Only a queen and a cardinal, a comtesse and noblemen from Sweden and Hungary have the savoir faire to merge their bodies and twist them into pretzels of cohabitating flesh while the royal Courts of Europe crumble into anachronism around them. But then how better to stave off the end than with impulsive new beginnings of lust?

Some such reflections passed through my mind and quickly departed in the heat of the moment as Yolande's pointy-tipped naked breast found its way to my lips while her own mouth engulfed the hard Hungarian *épée* of Count Esterhazy. I forgot them entirely as Axel Fersen tossed up my skirts and pulled down my bloomers and raised my legs to his shoulders and plunged his stout Swedish cock into my willing pussy. They were replaced in my mind by the nostalgic vision of Cardinal de Rohan mounting Yolande from behind and piercing her to the quick between the widespread, writhing cheeks of her ass.

"It is as if the Revolution had never happened," I panted, locking my ankles behind Axel's neck and springing up with my cushiony behind to meet each new thrust of his thick shaft. "Here we all are just like we were."

"The aristocracy will always prevail!" Count Esterhazy pulled his prick out of Yolande's mouth. Her lips popped softly as he removed it. He presented the glistening cock to me. I stuck out my tongue and licked it up and down one side.

"And the Princes of the church!" The Cardinal reached

under me and tickled my behind as he continued to bugger Yolande.

"We are truly the elite." Yolande arched her neck and sucked my nipple.

The five of us contrived to move closer and closer together. Soon we had merged into one mass of writhing, sucking, licking, buggering, fucking flesh. I grew dizzy with our combined heat and could no longer keep track of who was doing what to whom—let alone which of my loyal subjects was doing exactly what to me.

There were two cocks in my mouth and one in my behind, and a long, hard nipple shoved far enough up my cunt to duel with my clitoris. . . . Hands held my breasts close together while a hard prick pumped in the perspiration-slicked valley between them and its velvety head tickled me just under the chin; there was another prick in each of my hands and a tongue licking from my ass to my pussy and back. . . . I was on my hands and knees with a prick buried in my slavering pussy and fucking me dog style while I licked a sopping pussy joined with another fucking cock while the third cock was standing to one side and firing a stream of thick, translucent white nectar over all of us. . . . I was coming now, a prick geysering deep inside my pussy, another one reaming my clutching anus, a third corkscrewing at the entrance to my throat and a climaxing pussy rubbing hard against my breasts. . . . And still it didn't stop, for now the other pussy was being brutally pounded by a newly engorged cock while a second cock was stiffening for a second time in my mouth and a third cock was swelling in my right hand and a fourth cock . . .

A fourth cock?

The Cardinal, the Hungarian, the Swede . . . One,

two, three . . . I counted again. . . . One, two, three, four . . . No mistake. There were four cocks!

It was the English scribe. He had helped rescue me. It was only natural that he should join our little party, except—

Except that he was not a blueblood! He was not an aristocrat! He was not a noble!

So much for theories as to the erotic rights of the elite. His shiny English prick was a fresh delight in the palm of my hand and I was not about to relinquish it. Thus it was that in the end I surrendered to the demand of the common folk for equality—at any rate, erotic equality. *Oui*, in the end I fucked this commoner without a thought of crown or throne.

It was just after that delicious event that limitations of the flesh decreed a pause in our group activities. We lay over each other in a panting, exhausted mass. For a long time no one spoke and no one moved. And then the English scribe broke the spell. He started to wriggle out from under the surrounding naked flesh.

"Where are you going?" Yolande inquired lazily.

"My pen and parchment. I want to make some notes on the execution while the event is still fresh in my mind."

The English! The common folk! A European aristocrat would never have been so gauche in the wake of such erotic ecstasies!

When he returned with his writing utensils, we all observed him curiously. He sat down at a small table, rested his arms on his elbows and his chin on the palms of his hands. He was obviously deep in thought.

"What are you pondering?" The Cardinal inquired.

"The death of Queen Marie Antoinette," he replied. "I am trying to conjure up the words to paint that vision of royal dignity mounting the scaffold."

"Dignity!" Yolande hooted. "She was so out of it she couldn't navigate the steps. They dragged her up by her hair with one hand pushing her ass from below."

"That noble visage looking out over the hostile crowd. . . ."

"She was drugged, " Axel reminded him. "Her eyes were crossing. She couldn't look out over anything."

"Her demeanor and poise so queenly that in these final moments she gained the crowd's respect."

"They pelted her with dung and rotten tomatoes. By the time she knelt to the guillotine, she was smeared with filth."

"Head high, she sinks to her knees."

"She tripped over the executioner's foot and fell. He cursed her," Yolande remembered.

"She speaks. 'I ask pardon. I did not do it on purpose.' Thus her apology to the France she loves."

"She muttered an apology to the executioner for stepping on his foot. She was afraid that as she knelt he would kick her to get even."

"The Queen—the unwitting imposter, but surely now, if ever, a queen—lifts her eyes to heaven and speaks: 'It is a far, far better thing that I do, than I have ever done. . . .' "

"What she said just before the blade fell and her bloody head landed in the basket," Yolande corrected, "was this: 'Like it's a far-gone cooler trip that I'm on than I have ever tripped. . . .' "

Ahh, literature! Despite the witnesses, it was the stubborn English scribe who engraved for future generations Milady's last words as the blade fell:

"It is a far, far better rest that I go to than I have ever known."

Ahh, literature! Ahh, history!